I0612330

# DAWNMAID

Suzanne Francis is a captivating author. Her writing
pulls you from the realm of reality and places you
into the world of imagination so smoothly that
you may not know you have arrived there.
Dianna Doles Petry, Sage Fire Reviews

Ms. Francis paints her setting with specific, colorful
details that completely drew me into the land of Yrth
and its ongoing civil war. I recommend it highly.
Dandelion, Long and Short Romance Reviews

Suzanne Francis, author of the "Song of the Arkafina"
Series, is one of the best small press authors. Suzanne
delivers an exceptional, unforgettable story every
time. Her worlds are filled with colorful details and
captivating characters that kept me turning the pages.
Pat Bertram, author of *A Spark of Heavenly Fire* and
*More Deaths Than One*, from Second Wind Publishing

Also by Suzanne Francis

*Heart of Hythea*
*Ketha's Daughter*
*Beyond the Gyre*

# DAWNMAID

Suzanne Francis

*Published by*
Bladud Books

This book is lovingly dedicated to one of
the nicest people I know...
my sister Elizabeth.

First published in 2008 by Mushroom eBooks

This Edition published June 2009 by Bladud Books,
*an imprint of* Mushroom Publishing, Bath, BA1 4EB
United Kingdom
www.bladudbooks.com

ISBN 978-1-84319-815-4

Printed and bound by Lightning Source

# Contents

# Prologue

There is only darkness in this part of the Cosmos. A warm, seething broth of darkness, alive with unseen potential. Sparks and quarks fly, as time spirals inwards, trapping itself within a maze of unpredictability.

Within this inchoateness something is waiting to be born.

It collects energy, painstakingly nudging azimity into form. Slowly, patterns appear—tenuous repetitions that almost always fly apart again. But the ones that are strong remain, gathering identity and cohesion, layer upon layer.

It grows.

The embryo has no will, except for the will to become.

# 1

## Wanmoon + Ruber + Prox

He searches the endless Darkness for a sign. Ben'aryn carries a shard of memory, of another time, when he flew unfettered between the stars. Now the light he holds in his heart is all that keeps him going.

~~~~~~~~~~~

Gwenn used a stick to poke the back end of the shaggy, dark brown yak, trying to move the sulky beast forward. Gunnar, cursing, pulled the halter attached to the front.

He threw down the rope in disgust. "It is no good, Faircrow, we are never going to get this useless creature up the pass. We might as well stop now and head back before it gets too dark."

A voice, dimly echoing from the rock faces around them, weirdly selected only one of his words to repeat.

"*Stop, stop, stop...*"

Gunnar sat down on a rock and stared unhappily at the stubborn beast of burden. The animal looked placidly back at him.

The yak carried a mysteriously shrouded bundle, and a pannier hanging off each broad flank. Gwenn moved forward to check the contents of these two panniers now. A well-swaddled, two-month-old infant rode contentedly in each, and she carefully tucked in both blankets before she answered.

"We have to go on, Gunnar. The last village is miles back, and the boys need a warm place to sleep tonight. I don't like the looks of that cloud bank building to the east. It could start snowing at any time. That is the last thing we need."

She shaded her blue eyes with her hand, and looked ahead up the rutted, winding track that led to a high pass between two mountains. The village of Khalama lay somewhere on the other side and they had to reach it by nightfall. The sun would soon be dropping behind the shoulder of the rocky prominence before them, and then the temperature would sink like a stone.

She aimed a kick at the yak's flank, and the animal gave a protesting groan, but did not move further. A snowflake drifted lazily downwards, and landed on Gunnar's outstretched hand. Gwenn looked at him worriedly. So far he had been stoically uncomplaining throughout this very long journey; they had traveled from the windswept shores of Yr, up the wide Bresla River through the heart of Ruboralis, and then along a series of ever-narrowing water courses until they reached the foothills of the T'Shang Mountains. Now he looked worn out, exhausted by days of high altitude trekking and the constant struggle to find food and shelter in this strange land.

He shook his disheveled blond head mournfully. Again he urged, "We should go back. This fool's errand has gone on long enough."

Gwenn stared at the bulky object wrapped in white linen, slung across the back of the yak—the body of Arkady Svalbarad. "I said I would bring him back to T'Shang. I promised. We have to keep going."

Gunnar stood and grasped her shoulders, then shook her roughly. "We cannot! Would you risk the lives of your children? He would not want you to do that, Gwenn."

More snowflakes fell, sticking to the yak's back. One of the babies woke and began to whimper. Gwenn gave a cry of frustration and grasped the yak's halter. She threw all her considerable strength into dragging the animal, but only succeeded in getting it to move forward a few feet.

She cried, "Move, damn you! I won't give up now. I won't!"

Now it was her voice that rang in their ears. "*Damn you, damn you, damn...*"

Gunnar stepped forward and calmly started untying the ropes that held the shrouded body on the yak's back. She stared at him, bewildered, and then asked, "What are you doing?"

"I am leaving him. We aren't going to make it to Khalama by nightfall. Jakob and Arvid can't survive a snowstorm. Now are you going to help me, or shall I go back alone?"

"*Alone, alone, alone...*" the echo added mockingly

He turned his back on her after a few seconds and went on untying the ropes. Gwenn stood still, paralyzed by indecision. Once again she was going to have to choose between the two of them—Kadya and Gunnar.

Just then the sound of bells in the distance brought her blond head up sharply. "Listen, Gunnar, someone is coming! Maybe they can help us." She looked hopefully at him, and he sighed.

"We don't speak the language in this country, remember? How are we going to make ourselves understood?"

But seeing the despair in her blue eyes, he took his hand away from the yak and waited for the distant figure to approach from the top of the pass. An old man, swinging a walking stick festooned with bells, made his way quickly down the slope. He wore a long robe of some bright yellow material, wrapped over one arm, and tied with a thick piece of silken cord. Long braids of iron gray hair, decorated with yarn and turquoise, poked out either side of his outlandish peaked cap. When he drew up before them he grinned madly, his almond-shaped eyes almost disappearing into a thousand wrinkles, and bowed low.

"Hello, hello, hello..." the old man said laughingly, and his voice faded away exactly like an echo.

Then, catching hold of the yak's bridle, he gave it the gentlest of tugs, and the beast set off at a steady pace up the path the way he had come. Gwenn and Gunnar looked at each other a moment, nonplussed, then had to hurry to catch up to the old man. Though his head did not even reach Gunnar's shoulder, he set a blistering pace.

Breathlessly, Gwenn asked him, "Khalama? We go Khalama?"

He grinned again and nodded, and she could only hope he at least understood their destination. The path grew steeper but he did not slow down, nor did he allow the yak to tarry as the snow fell even more thickly. Gunnar forced himself to concentrate solely on getting enough of the thin air into his lungs so as not to pass out. Still, after a moment, gray spots swam in his vision and he staggered to one side of the path. Gwenn, less affected by the altitude, caught his arm and dragged him forward.

"The top is just ahead, I can see it. Soon we will be headed down again, and it will get easier."

Gunnar allowed her to pull him upwards, too tired to let this affront to his masculinity bother him much. Only his love for her kept him going now, as it had the last few weeks of their journey through this strange land of mountains and ice. On his boat, the *Fire Drake*, he had felt more or less happy, even as the rivers of

Ruboralis carried him further and further away from his beloved ocean. Any stretch of navigable water meant freedom and high adventure to Gunnar, for he had once been a Fynära raider, the most feared denizen of the frozen northern seas.

Inevitably, the day had come when the shallow hulled vessel scraped the bottom of a narrow channel, and he had to abandon his cherished boat. That was a very hard moment for Gunnar, who had captained the *Fire Drake* for seven years, and been part of her crew for three before that. Gunnar knew the local population would strip and break her apart if he left her behind, so over Gwenn's strenuous objection he had set the boat alight and watched unhappily as the dragon figurehead went up in red flame. Then he had turned away, so that his wife would not see him weep.

Gwenn could see a large cairn of loose stones ahead, surrounded by many colorful strings of flags, printed with curious pictures and symbols. They finally reached the top of the pass, and the old man paused briefly to toss a stone into the pile. Then he pointed down into a misty valley stretching away below them.

"Khalama," he said, and broke into a fit a giggles that thoroughly discomfited Gwenn and Gunnar.

Yet they had no choice but to continue at his side as he set off down the track again, even faster than before. Soon the air warmed and thickened, and Gunnar found he could breathe again without effort. The temperature in the valley became so mild they had to remove layers of clothing as they went downwards. The old man, who wore only a thin cotton robe, seemed untroubled by the changing conditions. Now as they reached the terraced fields above the village, Gwenn saw men and women at work harvesting barley. She shivered, remembering the lateness of the season, and wondered whether they could possibly return through the mountains with winter approaching.

*If not, what can we do? Stay here in this strange land?*

Gwenn shook her head at this. Neither she nor Gunnar could speak T'Shanga. Nevertheless, after a few moments earnest reflection, she decided not to worry about it. They had money enough to buy food and shelter for the winter. A month ago, Eydis, Gunnar's grandmother, had given them a goodly store of gold pieces, saying smilingly that she had no need of them. A few hours later she was dead, in a terrible fire that almost claimed Jakob and Arvid as well.

The village of Khalama fanned out in front of them, as the old man hurried down towards the muddy main street. The precipitation had turned to rain in this more hospitable valley, and Gwenn marveled at the lush greenery she saw all around her. Huge forests of rhododendrons clung to the sloping hills above the village, inexplicably in full bloom, though spring was long past. Tiny gardens grew beside each little hut, with melons and cabbage competing for space on the carefully furrowed ground. Several villagers called out cheery greetings to the old man as he passed, still leading their now utterly obedient yak. Gwenn felt sure she heard someone shout the name "Dawa." Could this inexhaustible old man be Kadya's old teacher, Dawa Tinley?

They stopped before a two-story square structure with a steeply pitched roof. The old man smiled and gestured for them to enter through a red door decorated with brightly painted symbols. Gwenn stood by as Dawa, if that indeed was the old man's name, managed to untie the ropes holding Arkady's inert form to the yak. Gunnar looked on in disbelief as he hefted the body across his shoulder and sent the yak packing with a slap on the rump. The old man appeared to handle Arkady's considerable weight with ease.

They went inside. Gwenn and Gunnar each carried a basket containing one of the twins, Jakob and Arvid. The front room looked bright and warm, despite the rain that fell outside the window. A fire blazed in an open square hearth that filled the centre of the room. A stone chimney carried the smoke up through the ceiling and warmed the upstairs as well.

After laying Arkady's shrouded body down on a blanket by the fire, the old man turned towards them saying, "Welcome to my humble home. You must think of it as your own."

He spoke Dalvolk perfectly. Gunnar stammered, "Thank you, but we do not know your name, kind sir."

The old man laughed uproariously. "I am sure you do. Dawa Tinley am I. Did you not come to find me?" He busied himself with a cast iron kettle on the fire and soon had hot water for tea.

Gwenn looked at him with interest. "How did you know we were coming? And that we needed help?"

He smiled and patted the side of his head. "The birds told me. They keep watch for Dawa, so that he knows who comes and goes through the pass. I sent them to look for you many days ago, once my friend said you were on your way." He laughed. "Such very big people are easy to find." Gwenn stood just over six feet, and Gunnar closer to six and a half. Both had to bend quite low to enter the house.

"Your friend," said Gunnar, thoroughly baffled. "How did *they* know?"

Dawa looked surprised at this. "Hana is my friend. Why would she not know? It was because of her last instruction to Griffon that you came here, was it not?"

Now Gwenn looked baffled. "Who is Griffon?" She bent down to retrieve Jakob from his basket, and he snorted sleepily. Absently, she sat down by the fire, and put the baby to her breast.

"Arkady," Dawa pointed to the body on the blanket and smiled. "He used to be my pupil and a very good one he was too. I gave him that nickname, for the way he consumed the teachings, just like a griffon vulture attacks a dead yak."

Gunnar sighed at this, and turned away.

Arvid stirred in his basket and Gunnar went to pick him up. Dawa beat him to it, and cradled the baby carefully in his arms. He looked down on the tiny face and smiled. "Your boy Arvid is a fine-looking fellow. Like his brother Jakob."

Gunnar's eyes went wide at this casual statement. Not only did Dawa know the names of the twins, but he had been able to tell them apart, something that Gunnar did not always feel confident doing. Dawa met his eyes and said seriously, "You love them. That is very good. All sons need the love of a father." Gunnar nodded firmly, wondering to himself if the old man before him could read his mind. He did love his sons, more than anything.

Dawa laughed. "No, no. It shows on your face." But his words did not reassure Gunnar. Then the old man said softly, with his eyes on Arkady. "I loved that one as a son too." Gwenn stood and brought Jakob over to Dawa, and exchanged him for Arvid, who wailed hungrily.

As Gwenn made her way back to the fireplace, she asked, "Why did Kadya need to come back here, Dawa? He begged me not to let them bury his body at Starruthe. Is he truly dead?"

Dawa nodded and Gwenn's face fell. He said solemnly, "Griffon wanders now in the Vastness and it is beyond my power to call him back to the living world."

Gwenn said sadly, "I thought, perhaps, you know... His heart stopped beating quite a while ago, weeks actually, but his body still looks... fresh. Are you sure?" She looked hopefully at him, and Dawa smiled and stroked Jakob's cheek.

"If Griffon practiced Firemma,* as he was taught, then there may be a way. But it would be dark and dangerous for the one who undertakes it. Hana gives only a very few fortunate ones the ability to cross the heavenly plane between the living world and the Vastness. Fewer still are allowed to return." Dawa looked over at Gunnar, but he said nothing else.

Eagerly Gwenn said, "I will go to the Vastness and bring Kadya back. I am not afraid."

It came from his mouth before he could bite it back. "You cannot! I won't let you."

She stared back across the room at him and shrugged. "What would you have me do, Strong Arm? I must help Kadya if I can, after what he did for me." Gwenn looked down at Jakob, now sleeping with his mouth still firmly attached to her nipple.

Gunnar asked quietly, "Even if it meant that your children would lose their mother?" He would not beg her to stay for his sake, not in front of Dawa. The flash of anger made him feel suddenly very weary, and Gunnar stood and stretched. He did not wait for Gwenn to reply, because he knew her answer already. "Is there a place for us to sleep in your house?" He looked expectantly at Dawa, who nodded.

"Come upstairs. I will show you the sleeping quarters. You have had a long and wearisome journey, and there is no need to go any further this night or for many days and nights to come." He turned to leave the room through a curtained doorway leading to the stairs.

Gunnar put Arvid back in his basket and said to Gwenn, "I am going to lie down for a while. Are you coming?"

She answered quickly. "Not yet. I want to talk to Dawa some more. I must find out everything I can about this journey to the Vastness before I undertake it." Gunnar sighed deeply but did not argue further with her. Instead he walked over to study an intricate silk hanging on the wall, of a beautiful green-skinned woman. Dawa joined him.

* A teaching that keeps the body and spirit together for a time after death.

"My friend," he said softly. "She understands. When the time comes to choose, she will help you." Gunnar had no idea what he meant, and did not feel like asking. He followed as Arkady's teacher took the steep, uneven steps quickly, two at a time. He led Gunnar along a narrow hallway to a small side room. Romping red beasts colorfully decorated the door curtain. "They keep bad dreams at bay," said Dawa, smiling. "Will you like to bathe before your rest?"

Gunnar nodded and fervently hoped that there would be hot water. Weeks of traveling had left him heavily bearded and filthy. He allowed himself to be led into an alcove off the bedroom. Dawa bustled in and out with steaming buckets of water, and soon the deep, blue-tiled bath was full to the brim. Gunnar undressed and settled back contentedly, only wishing Gwenn would come and join him. After soaping his skin thoroughly, he took his knife and scraped the reddish-blond bristles from his face and neck. Dawa took his clothes away and promised to have them washed by the morning. He provided a soft woolen robe for Gunnar to wear in the meantime, along with some slippers with curiously pointed toes.

Surprisingly, Gwenn appeared just a few moments later, and sighing, joined Gunnar in the tub. He looked at her with concern. She seemed very upset about something, but when he questioned her she only shrugged. After a long soak and a wash they left the bath together and dressed in identical loose-fitting robes of sky blue, which tied at the waist with silky knotted cords. In the bedroom Dawa had left a tray with two bowls of barley soup. Gwenn sat on the bed and started to eat, but still did not speak. Gunnar sat beside her and ate his own portion, wondering what Dawa had said to upset her so.

Later, as they lay together in the double bed waiting for sleep, she said unhappily, "I cannot go to the Vastness. Dawa says I do not have the ability to cross the heavenly plane. Then he told me that he doesn't know how to cross it either. He says there might be someone who can, but we cannot ask him if he is willing. It is so unfair, Gunnar." She began to cry quietly, and Gunnar, never able to remain annoyed with her for long, put his arms around her comfortingly.

He stared up at the low ceiling, and the ornately carved, dark beams. More than anything he wished that Gwenn could somehow let her old lover rest, and give her heart solely to him. He asked more because he knew she expected it, rather than from any real desire to know, whether Dawa knew the name of this person who had the ability to cross the heavenly plane. He felt Gwenn's nod in the darkness.

She said vehemently, "But he will not tell me who it is! Dawa says that they must come to their own decision."

Gunnar could think of nothing to say to this, but an uncomfortable feeling pricked at the back of his mind that *he* might know who Dawa meant. But that thought died as Gwenn left his arms and turned away from him, facing the wall. He stroked her back tentatively, hoping she would respond. Gunnar had been patiently waiting for many days for a chance to make love to her, but the frantic journey across the steppes of Ruboralis had given them few opportunities. Now, as the babies slept quietly in their baskets, and he and Gwenn shared this warm and comfortable bed, he wanted her very much.

But she merely shook his touch away and said, "Not tonight. I have too much on my mind. It wouldn't be any good for either of us."

He withdrew his hand, sighing, and rolled over. Gunnar knew it would be of no use to argue. Though the room was very quiet and dark, he thought his need would make it difficult for him to get to sleep. Nevertheless, he found himself dreaming almost right away. A beautiful green-skinned woman stood before him, smiling tenderly. She said, "The time has come for you to find yourself. Will you undertake the journey?"

Gunnar shook his head, saying, "I don't understand. What journey?"

Hana laughed merrily, like the sound of many small bells. "To the Vastness, of course. To bring back Griffon. He is my Seed Bearer and I need him here in the living world. And you have work to do of your own."

He stammered, "Me? How can I go there? I am but an ordinary man, Hana. Surely Gwenn should be the one to go. She knows much more about Goddesses and the uncanny."

"You are the grandson of the Numen. She is more powerful than any Goddess. Have you not always known this in your heart?" He thought about this, and then nodded. Gunnar had lived with his grandmother Eydis until age twelve. To his young eyes, she had been a witch—benevolent and wise—practicing her gentle magics among the people of the village. Only in the last weeks of her life did Gunnar begin to glimpse the real depth of his grandmother's power.

"I cannot cross the heavenly plane. I don't know how." He tried to make his voice firm but it sounded doubtful, even to his own ears.

Hana laughed again. "Why don't you try it then? Prove me wrong, Cousin of Fyn."

He started to ask her how to make the journey, but to his chagrin he realized that the answer was there in his mind, and had been all the long—a small step forwards and to the left would carry him across the heavenly plane. Grinning at her sheepishly, he tried, and found himself in the profound silence of the Vastness. Another step to the right brought him back again. Hana still waited at the foot of the bed, watching Gwenn as she slept. Gunnar stood beside her and asked quietly, "Why do you need him?" He pointed to Gwenn. "It has something to do with her, does it not?"

Hana nodded. "Griffon must join with her so that the Dawnmaid may be born. She will be the savior of my people, and the Guardian of the West."

He stared at her in amazement. "Holy Lutyond, woman! Are you proposing that I risk myself to rescue that sniveling Southerner so he can father a child with the woman I love? You must be completely mad."

She nodded sadly. "I know it is a lot to ask of you. But you must understand. Gwenn gives her heart to you both, but when the time comes for her to decide, she *will* choose you. Until then, can you not share her for a time with your brother Griffon? The future of the whole Yrth may depend on it."

Gunnar growled, "He is *not* my brother. I tried to kill him once. Did you know that? I might do it again. I don't like him, and he certainly doesn't like me."

But Hana seemed to know the story already. "Ketha convinced you to, did she not? I don't believe you would kill him now. You owe him much, for he died to give Gwenn life again."

He sighed. "I know that well enough, so don't remind me. How can I ever make it up to him?" Gunnar meant this rhetorically, but Hana answered anyway.

"By showing him the way back to the living world," she suggested gently.

Gunnar looked at her gloomily. "I don't know if I can..."

"Think on it this night. You need not make your decision right away. Tomorrow the way may seem clearer as the sun lights the minds eye. Farewell, my Northman." The green-skinned woman faded into the darkness and Gunnar started, wondering if he had actually been asleep at all. Turning on his side, he watched Gwenn's chest rise and fall, her blond hair glowing softly in the moonlight.

Gunnar tucked a stray lock of hair away from her face, thinking back to the day he first met her. Sif of the golden hair, she had called herself, and Gunnar had believed her to be a Goddess. She looked too beautiful to be mortal—then or now. He loved her deeply and he could not imagine, even for a moment, sharing her with another man. But that is what Hana asked of him.

She stirred and rolled over to face him with half-open eyes, and her gaze was unfocussed and sleepy. "Gunnar? Did the babies disturb you?"

He shook his head and smiled. "A dream woke me. Jakob and Arvid are still sleeping soundly. It won't be time for their feeding for a little while yet." Suddenly, his need for her became desperate and in order that she might fulfill this need he spoke without thinking further. "Gwenn," he whispered in the darkness. "I know the name of the person Dawa was talking about. The one who can cross the heavenly plane."

She raised her head sharply, saying, "Who? Who is it? You must tell me."

He blinked hard several times in the darkness, but she could not see the tears in his eyes. There was no going back now, though her eager response pierced like the keenest of knives. "I am the one. Hana came to me just now. She told me so." He waited, holding his breath, wondering if she would believe him.

At first she seemed not to. "You? Gunnar, don't be absurd. You are just a mortal man."

A few seconds later she snapped her fingers and said, "Wait a moment! Of course—it does make sense. Because of Eydis. She has given you the power." Then she lay back abruptly on the pillow. "But you won't go, will you? Not for Kadya's sake. You hate him."

"Not for his sake, no." Gunnar replied softly. "But for you, I would do anything, you know that. I swore as much to you on the beach, the first day we met, when you spared my life. So you have only to ask me, and I shall go, willingly."

Her blue eyes filled with tears. "You would do that? For me?"

"Yes," he said, solemnly. "For you."

She gave a small cry, and threw her arms about him, pulling him close. Her kisses were grateful, at first, and then more ardent as her fingers struggled to untie the knot in the soft robe he still wore. Laughing softly, Gunnar pulled it off over his head, and then pulled hers off too, with her help. It was not long before she drew him closer still, and he entered the heat of her body with his own. Part of his mind remained somehow detached from this intimacy. It wondered coldly if this lovemaking was worth the price—the dangerous journey to the Vastness to bring back his rival. But as Gwenn cried out in her passion, and sank her nails into the dragon tattoo on his back, the incessant pulse of his own gathering climax drowned out that voice completely. When it ended, and the weeks of frustration drained away, just before sleep he thought, tiredly, that whatever trials he must face, it would be worth it, for her sake.

The next morning dawned bright and clear. After breakfast, Dawa and Gwenn looked on anxiously as Gunnar readied himself for the journey. He wore his own clothes, miraculously washed, dried and mended overnight by their host, and carried a long knife. Dawa instructed him, saying, "Griffon's spirit will linger somewhere close to this house, for it is still attached to his body by the narrowest of threads. I do not know how much longer the thread will hold, so you will have to make haste. You must pull him back across the heavenly plane with you, close to the place his earthly form rests by the fireplace."

Gunnar went to stand before Gwenn, who passed the babies up to him one at a time. He stared for many moments at his sons, without speaking, and Gwenn knew then he did not believe he would return from the Vastness alive. After she placed Jakob and Arvid in their baskets she put her arms around him and whispered, "Go gentle, my love. Our boys need their father to teach them to sail. I am useless with an oar, remember?" Her attempt to lighten the situation did not make him smile

He raised his eyes to meet hers and asked quietly, "And you? Do

13

you need me, Gwenn? Or would you rather that cursed Southerner returned alone?" She hesitated only briefly, but it communicated more to Gunnar than anything she might have said afterwards. He abruptly stepped away and a little to the side. Gwenn stared sadly at the blank space remaining, cursing her indecision, and wishing that he would come back to her so she could tell him she loved him. Jakob and Arvid both began to cry, as the first flakes of snow drifted down outside the windows.

# 2

## Methuit Sequent

He is lost. Ben'aryn has wandered too long, and too far in that all-encompassing darkness. His mind has no more thoughts of self and substance. He drifts, dreamily, like an unmoored sailboat on a flat, black sea.

Then they come, and pull him back from the brink of dissolution.

~~~~~~~~~~

When Huw Adaryi first spied the familiar green caravans he raced forward with a cry of joy. His people, the Firaithi, were camped by the Sharm River, close to the ford that marked the boundary between Mardon and Secuny. Huw had been searching for them for many weeks, with his companion, the former Queen of Beaumarais, Katrione du Chesne Benet. She rode behind him, on their horse, Ajax. Katkin hung back as he approached the circle of caravans, nervously wondering how well Huw's Kindred would receive her.

A woman, shabbily dressed, was the first to notice the approaching figures. As Huw shouted a stream of Firai, she hurried forward, drying her hands on her apron. Katkin watched as the two embraced warmly. Suddenly the caravans emptied and three dozen people, mostly women and children, surrounded Huw. A tall man stepped forward, with his arms extended, crying, "Huw! The moon gives you greeting. By the Un-Named One, you come back to us! I believed you had perished on the ship of those cursed slavers. How did you escape, my brother?"

Huw smiled broadly. "And I thought you might be dead as well, Padarn. We have many stories to tell, it seems. May we share your fire?"

"We? Who is your companion, Huw?" Padarn peered over at Katkin, who had dismounted from Ajax, but still hung back, waiting for Huw to introduce her.

Huw walked to stand beside Katkin. "You know her already. This is Katrione Benet, of the Kindred of Anandi." Padarn stared at the petite woman before him. She had long, wavy chestnut hair and striking green eyes. Her left arm ended just below the elbow, but she wore a cunning wooden prosthesis, shaped like a hand, with jointed fingers that could be locked into any position by sliding a switch on the back of the wrist.

"The ex-Queen of Beaumarais? Can it be true she belongs to one of our Kindreds?" Padarn still used the Firai tongue, thinking that Katkin wouldn't understand him. "She is a dangerous friend, Huw. Her son, King Tristan, has placed a high price on her head. You would be well-advised to send her on her way alone. But you, of course, will share our fire and reclaim your rightful place as our Tane,* now that your father has crossed through *Tsmar'enth*.†"

Katkin could speak Firai well, but she thought that it might not be wise to let these secretive people know she understood their language, so she merely said in Maraison, "What does he say, Huw? He doesn't look very happy to see us."

Huw spoke softly to Padarn in Firai. "Have a care, my brother, for I love this woman, and I would not send her away, even if the price was all the gold in Yr. If she cannot share the fire of our Kindred, then I will not stay either."

Padarn looked very distressed at this. Suddenly, one of the women screamed, pointing at Katkin, "That is her! The mother of the one they call the Faircrow. I have seen her picture nailed up on nearly every tree. The one-armed traitor of Beaumarais. She helped that murdering *Gruagá*‡ bitch escape." Katkin knew she could not

---

* Leader

† The Moon-Gate, or passage into the beyond. Death.

‡ White devil.

15

explain her actions without giving away her knowledge of Firai, so she remained silent and stared at the ground.

Now Huw stepped in front of Katkin and drew his short curved blade. Padarn raised his hand for silence, and the group of Firaithi fell back. He spoke quietly. "Huw Adaryi, do you intend to protect this enemy of the Kindreds?"

Huw nodded grimly.

Padarn sighed. "Then you leave me no choice. I must banish you from the Kindred of Chandrathi. We mourn your passing, Huw. You must leave now, or I cannot be responsible for the actions of the rest of my brothers and sisters. Go at once and never return." Under his breath, he whispered to Huw, "Camp on the other side of that belt of trees. I will come and speak with you, after the moon rises."

Huw and Katkin retreated into the shelter of the willows by the Sharm River ford. Huw, depressed by his unexpected banishment, set up camp in silence. Later, as Katkin stirred a pot of vegetable soup over the fire, he pulled a wooden flute from his pack and played a mournful air. She listened until the last note had died away, and then said, "That song is so beautiful. I wish I could still make music. I had an old vielle that my father taught me to play, but the Guard destroyed it when they burned down our house. Jacq said he would make me another, with a special crank I could use with my artificial hand. But he was always so busy with blacksmithing that he never did." She sighed regretfully. "It is too late now."

"Then *I* will build you one. When we find somewhere to live." He added disappointedly, "I counted on our being able to shelter with my Kindred over the winter. Soon the weather will grow too cold for us to sleep out of doors. Perhaps we should head further South—into Spanja or perhaps to Shadion. It is always warm there, and they will not be looking for you."

"We should just split up." Katkin said glumly. "Then you could go back to your Kindred, Huw. You should not have been banished for my sake."

A curious low whistle from within the trees interrupted Huw's response. Huw cupped his hands over his mouth and echoed the sound several times, and then Padarn stepped into the ring of firelight. He squatted and accepted a bowl of soup while apologizing, in Maraison, for the Kindred's quick judgment against Katkin. "If it were up to me, I would allow you to stay. Your dealings with our Kindred were always fair and respectful. But many who lost loved ones the day your daughter's men attacked cannot forgive your actions in helping her escape. They will never allow you to join our Kindred."

Huw asked, "Why is it you now risk their wrath to speak with us? I have been exiled."

Padarn answered quietly, "Because Gwenn Faircrow allowed my wife and daughters to go free, rather than selling them as slaves to the Haba. For that I owe her a boon. So I came to warn you of something." His voice filled Katkin with foreboding, and she shivered. Huw wrapped a blanket over her shoulders and she hugged it gratefully.

"Of what would you warn us, my brother? We met no danger in our travels from the coast of Danica." In fact their passage had been exceptionally quiet, and Katkin had remarked more than once about the lack of people and traffic on the back roads they traveled.

The tall Firaithi ran his hands through his graying hair. His voice dropped to a whisper. "We who follow asparitus* observe things the settled peoples do not. The travels of men and horses, the rape of the land—the Kindreds know of these things well before others learn of them. Now we see troops massing on the borders of Secuny and Spanja, secretly gathering arms and ammunition. Also food and supplies for many men—a mighty army."

Katkin looked at him fearfully. "Who... Who leads this army?"

Padarn sighed. "Your son, King Tristan of Beaumarais. We believe he intends to conquer all of Yr, one country at a time, with this new army he is raising. He calls them the Black Guard." Katkin gave a cry and put her hand over her mouth, then turned away in anguish. Huw looked at her before beginning to speak rapidly in a low voice to Padarn. He spoke in Firai, thinking she would not understand.

"Then the Firaithi will soon be in even greater danger, my brother. That Gruagá spawn will begin hunting down all the Kindreds ere long. He will not want us roaming free, exchanging information on his movements. We will be a threat to any plan of conquest he has undertaken." He spat into the fire, and it hissed angrily. "Curse him to Revenna and beyond. Why can the Gruagán† not leave us

---

* The Firaithi life way—use little, return much.

† Lit. *Gruad* – Devil, *gá* – White. The Kindred's uncomplimentary name for the non-Firaithi residents of Yr. Borne of resentment at their persecution by the settled peoples.

alone?" Katkin turned back and gave Huw an unhappy look, but he did not see.

Padarn nodded. "I fear you speak the truth. The Chandrathi plan to keep moving south, mostly by night, and try to attract as little attention as possible. We will cross the border at the highest pass, where there will be few guards posted. Eventually, I hope we will be able to reach Bryn Mirain˙, and then continue even further south—into Shadion. It will not be easy. Food is growing ever scarcer. King Tristan has many men abroad. They have threatened some of the farmers in our Catena† already."

Huw said firmly in Maraison, "Katkin, Padarn says we must head south at once."

Padarn said, "Hold on, Huw. If you intend to travel with her, then you must avoid the borders, at least for now. We have seen drawings of the former queen's face posted in every guardhouse between here and Spanja. They are looking hard for her. You will never make it through Beaumarais."

"What other choice do we have? We cannot stay here and freeze."

Katkin said again, "Let me go on alone. You will be in less danger with your own people."

He took her by the shoulders and shook her. "No! Do not suggest such a thing. I won't leave you and that is final."

Padarn said quietly, "I have an idea that might be of some use to you. You know Brunner's place?"

Huw nodded and explained to Katkin, "Jakob Brunner is a farmer. He is one of the few people we can trust unimpeachably, because he is married to a Firaithi woman, of the Kindred of Gitasha. He has a farm about twenty leagues north of here, as the crow flies, in the bottom of a deep valley."

Padarn continued, "We passed through there a week ago, and Brunner gave us a lot of news along with the bags of lentils and grain he had saved for us. His hired man had just gotten married and left his employ, and he begged Stephan, one of our older boys, to stay and work for him during the winter. There are very few men left in our Kindred, so Stephan refused."

---

* The secret summer camping grounds of the Firaithi Kindreds.

† The Firaithi depend on a select group of farmers for trade, called the chain or Catena.

Katkin gave him an unhappy look, because she knew the reason for this—Gwenn's raiders had slaughtered most of the men, with the exception of Huw and Padarn, when they attacked the Kindred on the coast of Secuny.

"Old Brunner needs someone, Huw. He has a lot of stock, and after the first snow falls his valley is nigh impossible to get into. Why not go to him and spend the winter quietly? You will be as safe there as anywhere else, and more snug. In the spring you can journey on, and perhaps find the Kindred of Anandi. They will also try for Bryn Mirain."

Huw nodded enthusiastically. "I know Jakob well. He is a good man, and a good friend to the Kindreds. I will do as you suggest. Which route do you think we should take?"

Katkin listened intently as the two men slipped once more into Firai, discussing goat tracks, overhanging rock shelters, and a secret mountain pass. She felt slightly irritated Huw had not bothered to consult her before announcing they would be heading for Brunner's. Then she shrugged, thinking they had little choice but to follow Padarn's suggestion anyway.

Huw clasped Padarn's hand gratefully. "Thank you for your help, my brother. I hope that we may meet again in happier times. *Tsmare an fyr arterre*." Katkin quietly added her own thanks.

Padarn said, "Many more will pass through Tsmar'enth before then, Huw, I feel it in my bones. I think I may not see you again in this life. Farewell, my brother and sister. May the Un-Named One protect you both." He turned and melted back into the darkness. Katkin stared for a long moment into the woods, but she could see no sign of his passing. As she raised her eyes, a shooting star lit the sky in a brief blaze of light, and she smiled.

"Look! Up in the heavens. Did you see it?"

He nodded. "The Un-Named One also sends us her blessing. If you are not too tired, I would like to journey a little farther tonight. We should try to do as much travel under the cover of darkness as we can. The four Wayfarers will light our way."

"The Wayfarers? What are they, Huw?"

"Our people have studied the skies for many generations. We have seen the travels of the stars and the moon as they somberly tread the black velvet curtain of night. But there are four heavenly

---

* May the moon light your way home.

bodies whose blazing light could be said to dance across the skies—Unda, Herd, Zephur and Ruber. They are the Wayfarers. You have seen their signs on the Triske stones."[*]

She nodded, remembering the worn ruby-red stones that her grandmother, Neirin Mare, had shown her once, long ago, in the kitchen of Acorn cottage.

Huw continued. "They are special to the Firaithi, for they travel, just as we do."

Katkin looked worried as she pressed a steaming cup full of soup into his hands. "Speaking of traveling, how on Yrth are we to cross twenty leagues of open country without being seen? If there are as many of these Black Guardsmen around as Padarn seemed to think, then we will be in danger every minute. And where will we find shelter?" She shivered in the chill evening as the wind stirred the flames, sending many shining sparks spiraling into the night air.

"There are many secret paths that will carry us safely to Brunner's Valley. The Firaithi Kindreds have been traversing this country for over a thousand years on the Greater and Lesser Ambits. We have many caches of food and supplies along our routes that we can use in case of difficulties. Remember, this is not the first time the Gruagán have subjected us to persecution. He sighed. "Nor will it be the last, I expect."

"What do you mean, Huw? How can you know that?"

"I don't know how I know. I just do." He sat down by the fire and sipped at his soup. Katkin handed him a hunk of hard black rye bread, and then ate her own meal in pensive silence. After a time she asked Huw, "What is Bryn Mirain? Padarn said my people would try to go there."

"The Firaithi peoples have no homeland, but they do have Bryn Mirain. It is a hidden valley, deep in the Altas Mountains, between Beaumarais and Spanja. Our Kindreds have been gathering there for many hundreds of years. Every other summer we go to exchange news and meet with friends and relations. Many celebrations and weddings take place then." Huw's voice dropped to a whisper, and he seemed suddenly distressed, as though her question had reminded him of some unhappy memory.

---

[*] Octahedral stones used for divination. For more information see Appendices I and II.

Later, as Katkin packed up their few belongings and loaded them onto the patient Ajax, Huw kicked dirt over the fire to extinguish it. They were careful to leave no sign of their camp site behind, in case anyone should stumble upon it. The moon rode high in the sky, and she helpfully lit their way as they passed back along the silent road. Katkin took this to be a sign that Lalluna, the moon Goddess, also approved of their decision to shelter at Brunner's farm.

A rough track went off to their left, winding up the valley and over a low saddle, and Huw directed Ajax that way. Dark pines clothed the steep face of the hills on either side. In the darkness the valley looked lonely and forbidding. He said, "We must keep to this track for several hours, until we find a patteran.* It may be difficult to see at night. There will be a dry camping spot hidden a few hundred yards away, sheltered by an overhanging rock."

Katkin spoke to his retreating back. "A patteran? What is that?"

"A sign left by another Kindred. Sometimes a small pile of stones, or a few twigs woven together. But I will know it when I see it," he said cheerfully, and turned around to smile at her.

Katkin smiled too, feeling a little ashamed of her earlier irritation. Huw had chosen to undertake this risky journey with her rather than remain with his own Kindred, and had done so without a word of blame or complaint. She was very grateful for his company on that cold and dark evening, so she said softly, "Thank you, Huw."

He seemed to know her thoughts without asking. "You don't have to thank me. I would rather stay here with you, my queen." They walked together in companionable silence, until the moon set and the darkness became thick around them. Huw slowed his pace a little, afraid he would miss the patteran, but he dared not stop altogether. An icy drizzle began to fall, and soon soaked through their woolen cloaks, chilling them both to the bone.

Katkin shivered and tried to keep her fingers from freezing by tucking her hand in her opposite armpit. Her stump ached miserably. She judged it to be well after midnight, and both she and Ajax stumbled from tiredness. Just as she was sure she could not take another step, she saw a small heap of white stones shining brightly in the deep shadow to the right of the path. She thought

---

* A distinctive arrangement of stones or twigs, used by the Firaithi to indicate a secret route off the side of the main path.

surely this was the patteran Huw had referred to, but to her surprise, he walked right by it. Katkin forced her leaden legs forward and stopped him, then pointed out the stones.

He squatted down before the patteran and then laughed sheepishly. "I shall speak less proudly of my journeys through Yr, henceforth. I made a mistake we teach even the youngest *lathie*\* to avoid. Thinking of a dry bed and a hot drink before you find the camp is a good way to get lost in the dark. I am glad your eyes and mind are sharper than mine this foul night." But he gave her a curious glance all the same, for the heap of stones she indicated had been all but invisible to him in the darkness.

The worsening weather soon tested Katkin's naturally cheerful disposition to the limit. The leaden drizzle that began on their first night march persisted, until it even soaked through their waxed canvas travel bags. Their woolen clothing kept them from freezing, but travel became thoroughly uncomfortable. On the fourth day of their journey, as they traversed a line of high hills, she begged Huw to stop for a few hours so they could build a fire and dry out their sodden garments.

He said patiently, "We cannot stop here. It would be far too dangerous. The Gruagán use these hills for hunting and a fire would draw them to us. I wouldn't have even come this way if we did not need to make all haste possible. We must keep going until we reach the saddle over there. You can make it that far, can you not?" He pointed to a dip between two distant hills. Katkin's heart sank. It looked another ten miles away at least. She put her head down miserably and walked past without answering him.

Huw looked at her in concern. He knew this journey was difficult for her. She hadn't been brought up to follow Asparitus, as he had, and her long imprisonment in the Citadel had left her physically weakened. He wondered what he might do to lift her flagging spirits. Suddenly he smiled and walked forward to catch her hand. "I will tell you a tale to ease the pain of the miles we have yet to cross. A story that my Patre used to tell me when I was a lathie, and ill-tempered, as you are now." She looked up at him, and smiled tiredly, but there were tears in her eyes. Huw squeezed her hand encouragingly.

"This story takes place in..." He paused and scratched his head.

\* Child

"I don't know the word for it in your language. The Firai word is *aza'thuwlas*."

She mentally translated the word as beyond-futures-past. Katkin, thinking this made no sense, asked him, "Is that a place—like a different country?"

Huw shook his head. "It is a time—but not a time that has been or will be on this turn of the Gyre. So, in a way, it is a different country. Certainly the men and animals were very different then."

He caught Katkin's interest, despite her fatigue. She asked, "How do you know about the rising Gyre?" He shot up an eyebrow and gave her a sideways glance.

"I might ask you the same thing. The Gyre forms the backbone of the knowledge and understanding passed down to the Kindreds by the Elders of the Firaithi. The endless passage of time winds around the Gyre and everything that is, or ever will be, can be found there. Perhaps your mother or grandmother told you something of it when you were a child."

Katkin did not dispute this, although it was untrue. Tomas de Vigny had told her of the Gyre only a few weeks ago, the night he made love to her at her old home, Acorn. The same night he told her he had become one of the Amaranthine. She wondered now if there could be some connection between them and the Firaithi, but she dared not question Huw on that. He might ask too many questions of his own.

Huw continued his tale. "So in the time of aza'thuwlas, there lived a graceful bird of prey—a great-hearted warrior bird with shining feathers of silver, and talons as sharp as broken crystal. His jet black beak could tear through the sinews of the mightiest of deer, and he hunted the forests of Vangesu for them, summer and winter. With his keen eyes, no prey could escape him, and he ruled the skies year in and year out. Ben'aryn the Swift was his name, the king of all birds, and he had but one love."

Huw paused, remembering his own father's telling of this tale for the first time. He had been a lathie of six or seven years, trotting along beside his Patre, with his hand in his, hunger and fatigue forgotten as he was transported into the panoply of fables concerning his people—the unbroken chain of memory stretching both forwards and backwards along the Gyre.

---

\* The Gyrestone Nowhen also refers to this time.

Now, just as he had all those years ago, Katkin, her eyes shining, asked impatiently, "What did he love?"

Huw smiled. "He loved flying. It was his greatest joy. Ben'aryn spent his days among the clouds. In the balmy days of summer, they looked just like the fleecy sheep he sometimes chased for sport among the green pastures of Vangesu. The rising waves of heat from the Yrth reminded him of the gyre, for he could stretch out his mighty wings and soar ever higher, until the air became as rarefied as a distant moment in time. Then, at last, when the stars appeared in the sky, though it was still day, and the curvature of the Yrth spread out below him like a shining arc of fire and ice, he would fold his wings and plummet back down to the ground, shrieking with abandoned delight. It was for these moments he hunted deer in the forests of Vangesu and drank the waters of Lake Lisane. Nothing else mattered to him."

Katkin listened, entranced, and forgot her aching legs. A mile passed and two, as Huw described Ben'aryn's mighty eyrie on Mount Nindras, so high the freezing fogs of winter lived there all year round. With his far-seeing eyes he watched the forests and plains below, always searching for prey, so he might stay strong. His eyrie was far from the habitations of other birds, but Ben'aryn did not want company. For as Huw said, "He cared only for the feeling of the wind in his feathers, and he told himself it felt better than any lover's touch.

"One winter day, when the clouds were dark and threatening snow, Ben'aryn perched high on the cliff side and watched the plains beneath. He felt hunger, for of late, game had been scarce and his last meal had been several days ago, when he chased down and caught a young mountain goat. A movement on the ground below caught his eye, so he spread his great silver wings and spiraled downwards. As he was preparing himself for his killing flight, with wings well back and talons extended, intending to break the unlucky creature's spine, a song echoed in the rushing winds around him.

"At first he thought it just the sound of the east wind, but when he questioned her, she replied, 'Nay, my song doesn't pierce the soul, Ben'aryn. Beware.'

"He drew closer to the creature, and the music grew louder, and he asked the west wind if she sang the song. The west wind shook her head, saying, 'My song will never make your heart bleed, Ben'aryn. Beware.'

"Now he drew within striking distance and beheld the creature closely."

Huw paused and retrieved the water bottle from one of the bags slung across Ajax's saddle. He drank deeply, wiped the mouth and passed the bottle to Katkin, who took a sip, and demanded, "Go on with the story. What happened next?"

The clouds broke up and watery sunshine filtered through to warm the late afternoon air as they began to walk again. On the path leading to the pass, Huw said, "What Ben'aryn saw surprised him so much he folded his wings and had to shear off from his attack. He came to rest on the ground not far away. This creature was like none he had ever seen before. She might have been a doe, for her skin was as sleek and delicate, but she had no fur except for a long reddish pelt growing from her head. Even more strange, she walked on two legs, instead of four, and as she walked she sang the beautiful song which had drifted up amongst the winds. She stopped singing when she saw him land beside the path, and looked a little fearful, for Ben'aryn was the mightiest of birds, and even on the ground he was an imposing figure. But the girl-child did not run away.

"Ben'aryn looked at her for a long time before he spoke. Her face was the only thing he had ever seen that made him feel as though he might want to stay close to the Yrth for a time. He asked her, 'What are you?'

"'I am lost and hungry,' she replied, for she was a young child, and did not truly understand the speech of birds. Then her eyes, the color of Lake Lisane on a sunny day, filled with tears, and she wept, with her hands over her face.

"Ben'aryn, who had been hungry himself until he heard her singing, now said, 'Wait here, and I will bring you something to eat.' He flew off, shrieking, and soon found a fat, fleecy sheep. For the most part, he left sheep alone, for they were slow, stupid animals, and beneath his dignity. But now he was in a hurry. He caught a young one easily and flew back with it in his talons, then dropped it at the girl's feet. 'There,' he said. 'Eat.'

"To his dismay, she began to cry all the harder saying, 'How can I eat a whole sheep? I cannot cut it without a knife.' Then he looked at her hands and saw she had no talons or even claws, just useless flat nails. So he attacked the carcass with his strong beak, and soon shredded enough flesh to make a fine meal for her. But her tears did not stop flowing.

"'Now what is wrong?' he asked her, impatiently.

"She stared at the bloody hunks of flesh on the ground before her and turned away in disgust. 'It must be cooked, with fire. I won't eat it raw, I would rather starve!' Ben'aryn looked at her in confusion.

"'Fire is the red flower that eats the trees after a lightning storm?'

"The girl nodded and said plaintively, 'Please fetch me some. I am so cold and hungry.'

"'Will you sing for me again if I do?'

"She nodded happily, and Ben'aryn said, 'Gather some sticks and dry wood. I will return as soon as I may.' Then he took off again, with a great rush of wings, and flew away. He journeyed far, and at great speed, but not for the joy of it. For he knew a smoking mountain lay to the west, and when he reached it, he grasped a fallen tree in his talons and swept right down into the crater at the top. The heat and the fumes almost overcame him, but he was able to dip the top in the liquid fire that seeped from the mountain. It burst into flame, and he carried it back to the girl. When she sang her song for him again it filled his heart with joy."

The path they traveled began climbing in earnest, as the sun sank below the level of the high hills. A cold blue shadow covered the forest but the saddle above was still bathed in golden light from the setting sun. Huw stopped his tale for a few minutes, needing his breath for the climb. Finally, they reached a level place, where the track turned before beginning another ascent. An icy rill pooled across it, before gathering speed and splashing down a stony gully. Someone had constructed a wooden bench just to the side.

"Our people," said Huw in answer to Katkin's question, and agreed they might rest for fifteen minutes.

Katkin sank down on to the seat gratefully, as Huw rummaged in his pack for a parchment twist of dried apples and cob nuts. As they sat together, sharing the food equably, she asked, "Did Ben'aryn and the girl become friends?"

"We are almost at the top now. You don't need to hear the rest, do you?" He smiled at her fondly as she growled back in mock anger.

"Very well, I shall finish the story. Though I should warn you now, like many tales of our people, the ending is not altogether a happy one." He sighed, and watched the westering sun sink a little lower. Ajax strayed free, cropping the short green turf.

"The girl, whose name was Elleranne, stayed long in the forest of Vangesu, and Ben'aryn helped her build a hut. He would have preferred for her to live in his eyrie, but she could not fly, so he abandoned his high lonely place on the cliff, and settled close to her, roosting in a tree like a common fowl. No more did he care for the soaring freedom of flight. Now he protected the girl from danger, and caught her things to eat when she hungered. In return she sang for him, and sometimes stroked the soft feathers between his mighty wings, and these things gave him more joy than flying. Springs and summers passed, and the girl grew into a young woman. Ben'aryn thought her very beautiful. Now, when she touched his downy feathers, it woke in him a different sort of need, like nothing he had ever experienced, and he tried with his wing tips to touch her in return. But always she sighed, and turned away. One summer day, when he came home from hunting, he found her weeping and it troubled him greatly.

"For many nights, Ben'aryn sat in his tree, wide awake in the darkness. He tasted fear for the first time—fear she would leave him and seek her own kind—and it was as bitter as ashes on his tongue. So he rose up silently, and flew deep into the mountains, to the cave of a sorcerer, named Nys. Ben'aryn said, 'I wish to become human. What must I do?'

"The sorcerer, a thoroughly evil man, said, 'Give me your soul and I will grant your wish, but I must warn you, it will be very painful.' Ben'aryn, because of his love and need for the girl, agreed. The sorcerer tied Ben'aryn down to the ground and began plucking out his beautiful silver feathers one by one. It was agonizing, but Ben'aryn did not cry out. Then the evil sorcerer took boiling wax and poured it all over the bird's raw, naked flesh. Ben'aryn screamed and screamed as the wicked fingers of Nys molded and shaped his form into a twisted parody of a human body.

"When the wax cooled and cracked open, Ben'aryn stepped forth, and caught sight of himself in the looking glass hanging on the cave wall. He shrank back in horror at the hideous hunchbacked creature staring back at him from the mirror. 'I am ugly!' he cried to the sorcerer. 'She will not love me like this.' He shuddered and began to weep, for his body was wracked with pain.

"Nys rubbed his hands together wickedly, saying, 'I never promised you would be handsome, Ben'aryn. Only human. But in return for half your remaining life, I will cast a spell to make you look pleasing to her eye.' Ben'aryn once again agreed.

"Ben'aryn had to walk back to the girl's hut, and it was a long and painful journey, for although on the outside he looked fair and broad-shouldered, inside he was still a crippled hunchback. When the girl saw him, of course she did not know it was her protector Ben'aryn. But the stranger's handsome face and kind eyes soon won her heart."

Katkin said, very quietly, "Ben'aryn should have stayed as he was. She would have loved him that way too. It wouldn't have made any difference to her, whether he was handsome or not, only that he was kind."

Huw looked at her, a bit startled by her words, then stood and stretched. "Are you ready for the final climb? Once we cross the saddle there is a snug and dry cave on the far side, where we may shelter this night. Tomorrow we will reach Brunner's valley." He bent and refilled the water bottle from the stream, then returned it to the saddlebag.

They started climbing again, and Huw led Ajax by her halter up the hillside. The sky above them shaded to pink, orange and deepest fiery reds. The stars shone forth, like ice-pale jewels on a mantle of blue velvet, as Huw finished his tale. "Ben'aryn and Elleranne left the forest of Vangesu together, and settled by the shores of Lake Lisane. Sometimes Ben'aryn gazed over the waters and thought on how he used to soar above them, and he felt sadness. But then Elleranne would come and kiss him tenderly, and Ben'aryn rejoiced again for he knew the things he had given up were insignificant next to her love. And yet, as he aged, the pain he carried inside him troubled him more and more, until he grew short-tempered and jealous of his wife's beauty and happiness. He did not want to feel this way, but he could not help himself. On the day the sorcerer came to him and said his agreement must now be fulfilled, Ben'aryn felt relieved, knowing his anguish would at last come to an end. He wanted only to see Elleranne once more, so he could tell her he loved her."

Walking well behind him, Katkin covered her mouth with her hand. Huw did not see her.

"He begged the sorcerer to break the spell, so his beloved could finally see him as he truly was. Perhaps he just wanted to prove to himself that she could have loved him, even if he had not been fair. Nys cruelly refused and laughed at his fancy. When Elleranne came home at last, Ben'aryn lay dying and could only tell her the truth—that he loved flying, but he loved her more. Always he loved her more."

Huw reached the top of the saddle and began to descend. It might have been five minutes before he thought to look back at Katkin, to see why she had not spoken. Later, he told himself it must have been utter exhaustion that made her weep so very bitterly at the end of his tale of Ben'aryn and Elleranne.

# 3

## Dardisea Nowhen

Ben'aryn doesn't know who they are—or even what they are. He cannot see their faces. But they speak reassuringly, even though their language is not his. Hands draw him onwards—back to the fringe, where the distant stars turn the darkness to burnt umber.

When he sees them for the first time, he is very afraid.

~~~~~~~~~~~

The King of Beaumarais, Tristan Dinrhydan, could not sleep. He tossed restlessly in his bed, in a cold sweat. The whispering had begun again—a voice, low and mellifluous, echoing in his mind. It had come to him for the first time right after his father's callous betrayal on the parade field—the day his sister Gwenn had attacked the City with her Fynäran raiders. The voice had been sympathetic then—and helpful. It had given him the idea of forcing the invading horde into the moat and then blasting a hole in the lake wall. The plan had worked spectacularly well, and the grateful Deputies had given Tristan all the credit for saving the City. Later, he was given other suggestions, including locking up his treacherous mother in solitary confinement for the rest of her life. Then there had been the creation of the Black Guard, and the stealthy accumulation of resources for the invasion of Yr. Always the Voice desired for him to consolidate his power, or increase it. After a time, Tristan did not even question whether this was right or wrong, he just did as the Voice said.

Now it told him to rise from his bed and make his way to a cell deep in the lowest level of the Citadel. Tristan sighed, and scratched his aching head. Nowadays, the Voice often brought him pain if he did not do as it "suggested" right away. It had ceased to be kind and sympathetic some time ago. He knew he must do as it asked, so he put on his robe and left his bedroom, adroitly avoiding his contingent of guardsmen. It took him many minutes to reach the lowest levels of the Citadel, where dank cells housed the longest-term prisoners. Everything was quiet now, except for the pitiful moaning from some of the more recently tortured captives. Such sounds did not bother Tristan, who regarded torture as just one of many useful weapons he needed to keep his fractious subjects in line.

He stopped outside a cell that he had recently taken for his own, for use as a laboratory. It had once housed his mother, the traitorous Queen Arkafina, who had somehow escaped from solitary confinement, though her door had still been locked. Several of her gaolers had found themselves unhappily on the wrong side of a prison cell door after this breach, and although most died in agony during prolonged bouts of torture, not one had genuinely admitted to aiding her. Her whereabouts remained a mystery.

The cell had been vacant since her escape, and Tristan kept it locked. No one but himself possessed a key. Or so he believed, until he saw the faint light coming from under the door. Suddenly the temperature seemed to plummet, and yet he felt uncomfortably sweaty. He unlocked the door with a trembling hand and pushed it open.

The rusty hinges screamed as the Voice said, "Welcome."

It sat on the sleeping bench—a cataclysm in black—with wings that shimmered in the darkness, as though they somehow reflected the lack of light. The skin on its body was white, as white as the sightless eyes of some slimy groping creature from the depths of the abyss. Tristan stared blindly ahead, in shock and terror. This apparition thoroughly repelled him, but as he turned to run it stopped him with a languid wave of its clawed hand. The pain in his head ratcheted up to the unbearable and Tristan fell to his knees.

He said chokingly, "Make it stop. Please. I will do whatever you wish."

The Voice laughed mockingly. "Yes, you will. Little Tristan, always so obedient..." His headache stopped abruptly, and Tristan surreptitiously wiped his eyes with his shirt. He dared not speak. It softly questioned, "What is the meaning of all this?" and gesticulated at the racks of ground glassware and stoppered bottles of chemical essences that filled the cell.

"I... I am studying the chymerical arts, to learn the powers of transmutation." He paused and licked his lips nervously. "What is your name, O Great One? Are you... Are you my father come back to haunt me?"

The black wings stirred and a noxious reek filled Tristan's nostrils, making him want to retch. Dead men, left long in the sun after a battle, must smell something like it, thought Tristan to himself.

"My name? You must have guessed it already, little Tristan. Perhaps I *was* once your father—I have little memory of my earlier lives. No matter. Now I have been reborn as the Prime God. Rejoice, for you and your people have been chosen to see my true form on Yrth."

Tristan could not help feeling flattered, although the dark apparition still filled him with terror. The God leaned forward conspiratorially. "I will tell you something secret—I have another name, a name I will share with you, though none other of your kind knows it." The creature fanned its leathery wings once again. "You may call me... Maggrai."

Tristan nodded slowly and rose from his knees. "Very well, Lord Maggrai. How shall I serve you?"

Maggrai smiled. His fangs were stained yellow, like the ivory keys of an old spinet, and very moist looking. He said sharply, "I do not require your toadying. It is I who will serve you. Do you wish for power? Is that why you dabble at this chymerical nonsense?" He waved a claw and Tristan took a sudden step backwards, expecting the pain in his head to begin again. Now Maggrai laughed, and the sound was like the screeching of a great bird of prey. "You fear me.

That is good, Tristan. As long as you do, you and I will get along very well. Very well indeed."

He smiled again and patted the bench beside him, but there was menace in the gesture and implacable mastery. "Now come. Be seated and answer my questions."

Tristan forced his trembling legs forward, and tried to breathe shallowly so the stench wouldn't make him vomit. He sat on the bench, but as far away from Maggrai as he could.

His voice would not, at first, obey him. It cracked miserably, and he had to start again. "I found an ancient book, among the papers of the former King, Benedict. It told of secret experiments, of ways to increase life span, and turn lead to gold. I want..." Tristan stopped speaking and cut his eyes sideways to look at Maggrai. The God nodded at him to continue. "I want to live forever, and become the most feared ruler on Yrth. I have suffered, and now they will suffer. I must make them pay for what they did to me."

Maggrai nodded. "A worthy goal. I shall very much enjoy helping you reach it. But first, those you wish to punish, your mother and half-sister, must be found. Am I right?"

Tristan nodded, in awe of Maggrai's understanding. Never to anyone had he divulged the hatred he nursed for his surviving family, but the God knew of it. He had a sudden uncomfortable feeling that his entire mind might be laid bare before this dark force, like some vivisected animal, under the harsh glare of a laboratory gaslight. He swallowed and said, "I have my men out looking, but they have not yet located the traitors, Maggrai. But they cannot hide forever."

"Do not worry; I will assist you even in this, little Tristan. Let me assure you, your sister is exactly where I want her at the moment. She has something I need, and soon I will take it from her. Then you may have her, to do with as you wish." Maggrai muttered, "My father's little pet, Katrione, has been more difficult to locate since her escape. She is hiding somewhere with the Autochthones. But once you round them up..." He turned to look at Tristan and his black eyes glittered with malice. "We will begin by improving your laboratory. You have the rudiments of something here, but you require more power to bring about the results you want. Most chymike is rubbish, of course, but there are one or two interactions that can be very useful indeed. I will bring you the power source you need, and then I may wish to perform a few little experiments of my own."

Tristan nodded, unbelieving. Was this powerful God actually going to help him live forever? "What must I do until your return, Maggrai? Shall I continue with my research into immortality?"

Maggrai snarled and a sudden, sharp pain made Tristan's head spin. "Fool! I just told you that was nonsense, did I not? Right now we need more space for our experiments. Much more space, and secure rooms in which to keep my... specimens. You are the king of this pathetic country—requisition the use of some buildings! Perhaps your mother's old home. Yes, the Infirmarie will do nicely. See that it is done, and then I will return to you." He waved a hand and the pain stopped again, as suddenly as it had begun. A black door opened in the far wall of the cell. Maggrai stepped through it without any further comment, and was gone. Tristan sat for a very long time in the pitch dark cell, wondering fearfully who and what he had just allied himself with.

The next day, Tristan addressed the Chamber of Deputies, telling them that the Infirmarie, the jewel of the City of Isle St. Valery, would be immediately emptied of patients and its great gates closed forever.

"The Infirmarie is a haven for harlots and idolaters—the nest of that worm, Lalluna. She is no longer the guiding spirit of St. Valery, for her ways are both corrupt and sinful. We now recognize the Prime God and no other as the Protector and Savior of our fair city." He stared belligerently over the podium, and the cowed Deputies did not protest.

They were, by now, accustomed to such dictatorial maneuverings from their boy king. When he was just fifteen years old, Tristan had been made King of Beaumarais by the Prime Minister, Philip Tremayne. He was well aware that it was his youth and seeming malleability that had won him the post. Now six months had passed since Tristan's father Jacq Benet had murdered the Prime Minister in a fit of rage and given his son complete control over the country. In that time the Chamber of Deputies had called for another election several times, but always Tristan managed to put them off with a promise of more freedoms once the "present crisis" had passed. He never divulged the nature of this crisis, and the Deputies, still reeling over the sham trial and life imprisonment of the former

Queen, Katrione Arkafina, did not like to question their new king too closely, lest any of them suffer the same fate. Since Maggrai had come to him, in the guise of the Voice in his mind, Tristan had moved to seize more and more power from the Deputies. Now that he had actually seen the God, and had been assured of his assistance, Tristan felt he needed the Chamber no longer.

"It is my pleasure that you now disperse," he said imperiously. "The Chamber of Deputies is formally dissolved as of this moment. Return to your homes and await my orders."

There were shouts of outrage at this suggestion, but Tristan had his own Black Guard stationed throughout the chamber. After the fourth Deputy was led away, bloodied and in chains, the rest left quietly enough. Tristan lounged in his throne, above the empty chamber where his mother had once ruled in peace and prosperity, and rejoiced.

After an hour or so, a uniformed man approached the throne, and bent down on one knee. He then removed his peaked cap and held it over his chest, holding this position for some minutes before Tristan deigned to acknowledge his presence. Finally, the boy yawned cavernously and said, "Well, General Abelard. What news have you to report? Have the Black Guard managed to ferret out any more traitorous farmers indulging in trade with those stinking darkies? Speak, Uncle!"

Yannick Abelard grimaced at this familiarity, but said nothing as he climbed stiffly to his feet again. Tristan was the son of his ex-best friend, the Dinrhydan. Yannick and Jacq Benet had fallen out, before Jacq's death, on the subject of his wife, Katrione, whom Yannick believed to be a witch. When Jacq had abandoned Tristan during the invasion of the Fynära, leaving the boy to manage the defenses of the City alone, Yannick had been at his right hand during the ensuing battle. The grateful Tristan had made him a General in his fledgling army shortly after the victory, even though Yannick had been married to the Queen's sister Willow for years. But Yannick was a fervent believer in the Prime God, and in the purity of Beaumarais. His prejudices were a perfect match to Tristan's rabid hatred of the former Queen, and her people, the Firaithi.

"Our men are presently combing Secuny, your Majesty. We have executed another four farmers who were rumored to be members of the Firaithi Catena, and reallocated their farms, as you ordered.

Prince Dmitri and the Ruling Council did not, at first, wish to assist us with our inquiries, but after I threatened to blockade their ports on the Ariane River, they saw the wisdom of our position."

Tristan laughed childishly and clapped his hands. "Well done, Uncle! No point in wasting valuable resources on an invasion—not yet anyway. How go the negotiations with Mardon?"

Yannick shifted uncomfortably. "Well, as you are no doubt aware, my King, the Mardonne are a stiff-necked people. They hate the Firaithi as much as anyone, but they will not give their permission for our Guard to hunt within their borders."

Tristan's expression darkened. "They do not recognize our suzerainty?"

"No, Sire. They still consider themselves a fully independent state." Yannick stepped back a pace as Tristan stood and then paced back and forth upon the dais.

Tristan pounded his fist into his opposite hand. "This will not do, General! Have you spoken to Proxime Pallus personally?"

Yannick stuttered, "N... No, Your Majesty. I understood that the negotiations were to be carried out by the diplomatic corps. They..."

"Silence, simpering fool!" Tristan tried to make his voice sound thunderous, but it cracked embarrassingly in the middle of this tirade. He continued, stabbing his finger into Yannick's chest. "I gave the order that the Mardonne were to be subdued by whatever means necessary. If they refuse to recognize our sovereign right to pursue the darkies through their miserable country then we will make them bow. Do you understand?" Yannick nodded nervously and gave the kneeling salute again. Tristan waved him off with a haughty gesture, and sighed to his retreating back. The business of managing the country was *so* boring...

A moment later he brightened as a Page hurried into the room, and knelt with an obsequious flourish of his pillow-like cap. The Page's uniforms, replete with brightly colored silk hose, had been designed by the fledgling monarch, based on pictures he had seen in one of his history texts. They belonged to an earlier age, and everyone besides Tristan found them thoroughly ridiculous. But no one dared tell him so.

"A visitor has just arrived and wishes an audience with Your Highness. She says her name is Roseberry and she comes bearing a message from the Infirmarie. Shall I say His Majesty is indisposed?"

Tristan's eyes flashed as he snarled, "For Cousin Roseberry? Certainly not! Send her in at once, jackass. Never again presume to know the will of your King or I will see to it personally that the rack reminds you of your error."

The Page blanched and backed out of the room, still on his knees. A moment later, Roseberry strode towards the throne, wearing the simple vesture of her position as a Unity Juvenie.* She, quite pointedly, did not perform the kneeling salute. Tristan cleared his throat impatiently but she remained standing, and obstinately made eye-contact with her monarch before he addressed her.

Behavior of this kind from any other of his subjects would have brought the King to a froth, but now he just blinked at Roseberry mildly, and asked, "Well, Cousin. To what do I owe the honor of this visit?"

Roseberry twisted the ends of her fichu nervously, allowing Tristan a glimpse of her ample cleavage. He unashamedly ogled her breasts, and she sniffed in derision. "You know perfectly well why I am here, Tristan. How could you be thinking of shutting the Infirmarie? What about the patients? They need our care."

Tristan did not even get angry now, when his cousin stubbornly refused to use his title. The first time he had rebuked her for this she had told him haughtily that she was three years older than he, and not in the habit of fawning to spotty-faced boys. He had had no good answer to this, then or now, as his complexion remained traitorous and she would always be three years his senior. So again he cleared his throat and whined, "You must call me 'Majesty', Berry. That *is* my proper title, you know."

She only laughed. "I will when you act like one. Now what on Yrth are you doing closing the Infirmarie?" Tristan stood and approached her, and she held her ground. "If you don't care about the patients, then what about me? I will lose my Juvenead,† and the Maitress already told me I am in line to replace her one day. It isn't fair!" She stared up at him unhappily. Though Tristan was not tall, he still stood a head higher than Roseberry, who had inherited her

---

* Younger sister of the Unity, not yet twenty-one years old.

† Apprenticeship

mother's diminutive stature. Her hair was long and very dark, and her wide set hazel eyes bore a hint of some exotic ancestry in their almond shape. Tristan thought she was very beautiful.

He kept his voice low. "I am sorry. It is just that I need the Infirmarie facilities right now, for a far more important undertaking."

Roseberry gave him a skeptical glance. "More important than the well-being of your subjects?"

He nodded earnestly. "Yes, Berry. And once I am finished with this duty then I will allow the Infirmarie to reopen again, I give you my word." This was, of course, a lie, but Tristan delivered it with wide-eyed mock sincerity. In fact, he had no intention of ever allowing the Infirmarie to open its gates to the sick and injured, not as long as Lalluna, his mother's patron Goddess, remained the focal point of worship there.

Roseberry still did not seem convinced. "But what shall I tell Maitress Rebecca? She sent me here to plead with you, in the name of Lalluna."

Tristan said sharply, "Speak not the name of that pagan witch in here, Berry, or I shall cease to be so understanding. The Prime God is the protector of St. Valery and Beaumarais now."

She looked momentarily taken aback. "But Tristan, where will I go if you close the Infirmarie? I don't want to go back to Belladore and be a burden to my mother."

He smiled at her hopefully. "Then you must stay here at the Citadel, as our guest. Your father would be pleased to have you so close, I am sure. He was here just a few moments before you came to see me." Then, hoping to please her, he added, "General Abelard is my most trusted Commander, you know."

Roseberry seemed indifferent. She had had little contact with her father since she had entered the Unity against his wishes. "I suppose I don't have a lot of choice but to accept your offer. But once the Infirmarie reopens, I will want to go straight back to my Juvenead, Tristan."

He nodded encouragingly. "Of course, Berry. Of that I have no doubt. But right now I will command one of my pages to ready a suite of rooms for you. Do you need one servant or two to help you move your things from the Juvenie hostel?"

She giggled at this. "I don't need any, silly boy. I am used to taking care of myself. Life at the Infirmarie has no luxuries like the ones you enjoy here. We work hard and live very simply."

Tristan said softly, "Perhaps, after you get settled, you might come and talk to me sometimes—tell me of your life at the Infirmarie or anything else you want to talk about. I should like that very much."

Roseberry replied breezily, "Oh, I don't know about that. You are so very stiff and solemn these days. All this 'Your Highness' nonsense and that ridiculous kneeling bow you introduced. It gets very tedious, Tristan. I don't think I can be bothered, frankly."

The king's lip curled in anger, but he bit back his response. He could *make* her come, of course. It would be as simple as giving an order to the Guard. But Tristan wanted, more than anything, for Roseberry to find his company pleasing, so he said reassuringly, "You need not worry with all that. Are we not close relations, after all? I will grant you permission to address me as Tristan henceforth and excuse you from venerative gestures. All right? Please, Berry, say you will."

Roseberry shrugged. "Why not? I won't have anything else to do until you reopen the Infirmarie. I hope you don't intend to keep me away from my duties for too long, Tris."

After he had reassured her once more of his intention to allow the Infirmarie to resume business as soon as possible, she turned away and left the room, without so much as a curtsey. Tristan had to remind himself that she was well worth the insolence she displayed. The young king, although surrounded by sycophants of every order and description, was profoundly lonely. Roseberry was the only person who seemed willing to risk his wrath in order to be true to herself. Tristan made a private note to investigate, as soon as possible, the legality of marriage among first cousins in Beaumarais. Then he smiled, thinking that if the law went against his wishes it could always be repealed. There was no Chamber of Deputies to thwart him any longer. Tristan sat back down on his throne, very pleased with himself and his day's work. He had been thinking for some time about his cousin Roseberry and found his desire for her only increased with every impertinence. The acquisition of her undivided company had been an unexpected bonus from acceding to Maggrai's wishes. Tristan convinced himself that the Prime God had planned it all the long.

# 4

## Pindaen Prox

They show him their treasures—crystalline leaves, their shapes pleasingly familiar. When the leaves sing he is comforted, and so, it seems, are they. For twenty heartbeats there is silence. Then they bring him the thing he has been searching for.

She has a mind, but it is shallow; unformed. Her guardians cluster round her, offering their protection until the moment she must depart. Ben'aryn takes her hand. He knows the time has come for her to leave the Darkness behind. The Gyre is calling.

~~~~~~~~~

Gwenn blew on a spoonful of thin gruel before she brought it to Arkady's lips. He sat in bed, propped up with pillows, in one of Dawa's upstairs bedrooms. His hazel eyes, though half-open, stared blankly, and Gwenn knew he could not see her. Nor did he ever speak, though she had tried many times to question him. Dawa assured her Kadya's spirit had come back to his body, but to Gwenn he still seemed lifeless. Yes, he could swallow the food, and take sips of water from a cup, but he had to be washed and dressed like an infant and toileted like one as well.

When she sent Gunnar to the Vastness to recover Arkady's spirit, Gwenn had hoped Kadya would be well and whole when he returned to the living world. After Gunnar left her on that snowy morning, she had gone back into the house with Dawa. They had carried Arkady's body between them and laid it out on the low dining table. As she carefully unwound the linen shroud, Gwenn remembered thinking that her former lover looked thoroughly and irrevocably dead—his skin was the color and texture of yellowed parchment. Dawa then lit the body with four candles, one on each side of the table. He and Gwenn kept watch in shifts, all day and night.

On the fourth night after Gunnar's departure, Dawa had been

on duty when Arkady's body first started jerking spasmodically. Dawa called out, "Gwenn! Gwenn! Come quickly. Griffon has returned"

She came pelting eagerly down the stairs from the bedroom. But after a few minutes of spasmodic twitching, Arkady did nothing else. Dawa listened to his heart, checked his lungs, and pronounced himself satisfied that Gunnar had succeeded in bringing the Griffon back to the living world. After watching Arkady for a few moments, Gwenn gave a guilty start. She had not looked for her husband to make sure he had also returned safely.

"Gunnar!" she called. "Where are you?" She ran out of the door and through the freezing night.

After a moment, Dawa, looking grave, stopped her with the words, "He is not here, Gwenn. Only Griffon's spirit has crossed over."

Gwenn's eyes filled with tears. "But he must come back. His boys need him."

Dawa shook his head. "I explained to you both that the way was dark and dangerous. You wished him to attempt the journey, and he chose to go for your sake."

"But, Dawa, I never thought... I sent him away, without so much as an 'I love you.' Now he is dead." She had begun to cry in earnest, and Dawa patted her sympathetically.

"Remember the Numen has great power, and Gunnar is her grandson. He may yet return to you, in a way unseen by the wise. In the meantime, we will care for Kadya. He may sleep for many months before his body will be well enough to bear him in the living world."

Gwenn continued to feed the gruel to her former lover, and wiped his long salt and pepper beard, between bites, with a napkin. The thin mixture was made especially by Dawa each day, and contained barley fortified with liver strengthening herbs like ginger and turmeric. It seemed to be working, for in the three months since his return Arkady's cheeks gradually turned from yellow to pale cream, and then back to a healthy shade of pink. But his catatonia did not show a concomitant improvement, and Dawa had to remind Gwenn each day on the importance of patience.

She finished the gruel, and then offered the cup of water. Arkady took several sips, and as she took it from his lips, he said, in a cracked voice, "More." Gwenn gave a startled cry and dropped the cup, soaking his shirt and the covers. He looked up at her, blinking, and then murmured slowly, "Why did you do that, Gwenn? Now I am all wet."

She called for Dawa, and then sat on the bed and took his hand. Her own hands were shaking. "You have not spoken for three months, Kadya. It just surprised me, that is all. How do you feel?"

He smiled at her and said softly, "Alive. I feel alive. And, well... wonderful."

Dawa burst through the door, carrying a baby in each arm. When he saw Arkady's alert expression he gave a whoop of joy. "Welcome back, Griffon. It is very good to see you awake and aware."

Arkady stared in shock at the babies, who had grown a great deal larger since the night he healed Gwenn's legs at Feringhall, on the island of Starruthe. He shook his head. "I feel as though I have been asleep a night and a day since I left the living world. Has it truly been three months?"

"It has. Your body was very ill and needed a great deal of rest and healing. You may be weak for many months more, Griffon. But Gwenn and I will help you recover your strength."

Gwenn, who sat silently by Arkady's side during this exchange, now asked, "What happened in the Vastness? Why did Gunnar not return with you?"

Before he could answer Dawa said, "Whisht, child. We will hear the story in due time, when Griffon is stronger. Not now."

Gwenn argued, "But Dawa, I need to know..." He silenced her with a fierce look, and then handed the babies to her.

"I think they need their wrappings seen to, little Mother. Now go and leave Griffon to rest." She left the room, muttering, and Dawa smiled at Arkady. "Such a strong spirit, that one. She reminds me of you, when you first came to Khalama. Do you remember?"

Arkady lay back on the pillows and closed his eyes. His mind felt dense and sluggish. Gwenn's tactless question disturbed him a great deal. To distract his thoughts, he said tiredly to Dawa, "Will you tell me the story of my first visit here, Teacher? My head feels like Lake Gyatsin on a windy day."

Dawa settled himself in a chair near the bed. He spoke now in T'Shanga, his native tongue, a language Arkady knew well. His former student, the Griffon, could speak many languages, for he had studied at the University of St. Ekaterina in Ruboralis. Dawa began the story. "Do you recall the winter's day you first saw a silk painting of the Goddess Hana in the marketplace?"

Arkady gazed thoughtfully into space. "Yes. I wanted to find out everything I could about her, so I went to the basement of the University library. There was an old, dusty volume there—on Hana and the Kingdom of T'Shang. It said the borders had been closed to outsiders for many years."

Dawa smiled. "You decided to try and find T'Shang, even though your grandparents forbade you to make the trip. They did not want you to cross the wide lands of Ruboralis on such a fool's errand. But you set out in the spring, after spending all your savings on an excellent horse. What was her name, again?"

Arkady's eyes closed as he considered this. "Borlass," he said slowly. "Her name was Borlass."

Dawa clapped his hands. "Well done! Yes, her name was Borlass."

Arkady kept his eyes closed, and pressed his lips together, just a little.

His teacher continued. "It took you all summer and autumn to travel across Ruboralis, and by the time you reached the mountains the passes were already closed for the winter. So you made friends with a group of nomadic yak herders, and lived with them in their skin tents. Of course it was difficult at first to communicate with them, for they spoke T'Shanga, but you learnt the language quickly. In the spring you moved on, and came over the pass into Khalama. I met you on the main street that day, and you looked as lean and hungry as a fox in a hen house." Dawa chuckled to himself, recalling Arkady's appetite after he had invited the travel-weary young man to dinner.

"We had not many strangers through Khalama in those days, so I felt honored by our felicitous meeting. I invited you to stay with me here, in my house, and you agreed, on one condition. I had to give you the teachings, and in return you agreed to work for me in my garden."

Arkady laughed ruefully. "I did not know you were going to make me work for four months before you would teach me anything! I almost got fed up and left many times."

Dawa smiled, his face dissolving into wrinkles. "The gardening was important! You learnt patience and discipline. Otherwise you would not have taken to the teachings like a Griffon later on. Then I taught you to sit and follow the meditation bell, and we practiced all the next winter. You were a very good student, and as the next spring blossomed I sent you on your way again to find a pupil of your own."

He peered at Arkady. "Does that help clear some of the mud away?"

Arkady nodded. "But there is still a great deal I cannot remember. What did Gwenn ask me? She seemed to think it was important."

Dawa smiled reassuringly. "Do not let it trouble you. Your memories of your time in the Vastness will be the last to return, but return they will. Until then, Gwenn must learn patience, as you did." He smiled again. "I will put her to work in the garden."

Many more days passed until Arkady could stand and move about slowly. Dawa still had to carry him down the stairs and out into the garden, where Gwenn worked, with Jakob and Arvid next to her in their baskets. Arkady, well wrapped in a patterned blanket, sat with her as she weeded the beans and melons in the weak sunshine. They mostly talked of inconsequential things, and Gwenn was careful not to ask him any question that might upset him. He still remembered little of his past, and she recalled for him their time together in Secuny. When Gwenn led the Fynära, with Gunnar at her right hand, Arkady had been her thrall. It all seemed very long ago to Gwenn, but Arkady listened to her tales with rapt interest.

"You say I could make fire with my hands? How did I do that?" he asked her.

She shrugged. "I don't know. You never told me. Only that Hana gave you the fire because you were her Seed Bearer." Gwenn blushed and dropped her eyes, remembering, too late, the details of the Firaithi prophecy that linked them together very intimately.

"Gwenn," he said softly. "Look at me." She slowly raised her head and found him staring at her with an odd intensity. "I know there is much I do not remember of my past life. But one thing I have not forgotten... I love you. Now we can be together, do you see? Nothing stands between us." His voice grew stronger. "We have to be. The prophecy says you and I must make a child. I did not see how it could happen, until now." He reached down to stroke her blond hair, and she took his hand and held it.

Gwenn felt nothing but confusion. Such words from Arkady would have filled her with joy, not long ago, but now—"

"Kadya, there *is* something standing between us. My husband, Gunnar Strong Arm."

Arkady made an impatient noise. "He is gone, Gwenn. It has been four months. He is not coming back. You must realize that."

She said quietly, "I cannot accept it. Until I know what happened in the Vastness, I will continue to believe he is alive." Gwenn stood and brushed the dirt from her knees. Arkady rose as well and moved towards her falteringly. She reached out, intending to steady him, and then found herself in his embrace. He kissed her warmly, and despite her confusion she could not help responding.

"My beautiful crow girl," he whispered. "Let me share your bed this night. I want you so much and I know you want me too."

Gwenn fought with her desire. "Not until I know where Gunnar is." Just then Arvid stirred, and she said stiffly, "Please excuse me. I have to go inside and feed the babies." She picked up the baskets and walked away, leaving him standing alone amongst the runner bean poles. Arkady sighed, wondering how much longer he could get away with pretending he could not remember what had happened to Gunnar in the Vastness.

Gwenn carried both babies inside and sat down on the padded bench, then bent to retrieve Jakob from his basket. The boys were both growing larger by the day. They ate solid food as well as taking breast milk now. Gwenn stroked Jakob's reddish blond hair as he rooted for her nipple, thinking sadly how proud Gunnar would have been of his strong grip and the two little white teeth that were just poking through his gums. Both boys already had his bright blue eyes and cleft chin. Gwenn sighed deeply. How could her sons grow up to be brave and bold men of the North without knowing their father? She reached up to brush a tear away, and then felt a hand on her shoulder. Dawa stood next to her, though she hadn't heard him come in.

"Oh, Dawa, I wish I knew what to do. Kadya says I should just forget him, but how can I?"

"Sometimes, when the road is dark, the smallest flame lights the way." He smiled at her and she looked very confused.

"What does that mean?"

Dawa laughed. "That is something you must decide for yourself, little Mother. Now I am going to the village to buy some eggs. Do you want to come with me? Griffon can watch the babies for awhile. It will do him good to share in some of the responsibilities around here." Gwenn looked unconvinced at this, but reluctantly agreed to leave Arkady in charge of the two boys.

Once Gwenn left, with many a doubting backwards glance, Arkady spread out a blanket and settled himself on the floor with the twins. They crawled about, and tried hard to pull themselves up on the corners of chairs and tables. He studied them for a few moments in silence, thinking happily to himself that Jakob and Arvid would soon be his children too, after Gwenn got over her grief and agreed to marry him.

The twins also watched him solemnly. He made a funny face at them and they both broke into grins. Sensing his willingness to play, they crawled up on him, pulling at his beard, and giggling happily. He made them laugh with peek-a-boo games and silly songs. After a time they grew sleepy and curled up side by side on the blanket. Arkady watched them, as their eyes blinked slowly and two thumbs found their way into tiny mouths.

He said softly, "Well boys, perhaps I should tell you a tale to send you off to sleep. We will call it the story of the brave Northman who saved the ungrateful Southerner. It starts like this...

"Once upon a time there lived a Northman, named Gunnar Strong Stench. He was your daddy; did you know that, little Jakob and Arvid? A brave and bold individual, especially when it came to beating up starving thralls. One day he decided to visit a very dark place to try and rescue an enemy of his. I know that *sounds* heroic, but he only did it because someone very special asked him to. So he searched and searched, and finally he found the man he was looking for. Now this man did not like the Northman very much. He thought he was dirty and smelly and very stupid. So he told him that, and the Northman got angry. He told the Southerner that he was an ungrateful beast of burden, and that he should just leave him there to rot in the Vastness. And so..."

Arkady dropped his voice to a whisper, for he saw that Jakob and Arvid were both sleeping soundly. But Dawa's voice came from behind him, saying dryly, "Don't stop, Griffon. Gwenn and I were enjoying your story too. We both want to know how it ends." He walked in the open door, carrying a string bag full of eggs in one hand.

Gwenn followed, saying reproachfully, "You said you did not know what happened in the Vastness. How long has it been since your memory returned?"

"A couple of weeks. I just did not want to tell you what happened. Actually, I still don't."

Dawa cleared his throat and said diplomatically, "I will just go and make us some lunch. You two carry on without me." He breezily disappeared into the cooking shed, leaving Arkady and Gwenn alone. In a moment they heard his voice through the curtain, loudly chanting a mantra prayer.

Gwenn glared at Arkady and then hissed angrily, "Why don't you want to tell me what happened? Have you done something you are ashamed of?"

Arkady would not look at her as he slowly got to his feet. "I just wanted everything to be all right between us," he said, in a voice he judged loud enough to be heard in the kitchen. "We belong together, Gwenn. The prophecy made that clear. If I had not acted so stupid and jealous, that day in the dunes, you never would have gone running to that rat bag Northman. Why can't you just forget him?"

Despite the fact that Gwenn's sword keth'fell had been securely wrapped in silk and stowed away under her bed for weeks and weeks, she still groped for it in her anger. Arkady recognized her action and stepped back a pace. Gwenn, trying not to be overheard, said in a low voice. "Don't you dare call him that! He rescued you from the Vastness. You wouldn't be here now, if not for him."

"Have you forgotten that he almost murdered me in Celeste? Face it. He is a common thug, just like all the other Fynära scum. How can you blame me for hating him? You don't know how much Huw and I suffered on the Moon Drake."

Gwenn spoke in loyal defense. "He is different now. After the battle for St. Valery, he gave up being a raider forever. Gunnar is a good man. I love him. Do you understand?" She said each word with emphasis. "I... Love... Him."

Arkady looked at her with narrowed eyes. "And me? What does that leave for me?"

She shook her head. "First tell me what happened in the Vastness." Gwenn crossed the living room and sat down on the padded bench. She patted the seat beside her. "Tell me the whole story."

He sat down and crossed his arms, saying sullenly, "I spent a long time wandering in the Vastness alone. It is lonely there, and so silent. Everywhere I could see these white, legless creatures. Not one of them would talk to me. When I saw another human in the distance it filled me with joy. You can imagine my disappointment when I found out who it was—my old enemy and chief tormentor, Gunnar Strong Stench. At first, I naturally assumed he was dead, so after congratulating him, I asked him what happened and were you all right. I was very polite."

Gwenn said, under her breath, "Is that so?"

"Yes, truly, Gwenn. Then he said he had come looking for me because you and Hana asked him to." He peered at her. "Why did you not come yourself? I thought that if anyone had the ability to cross the heavenly plane it would be you, because of Ketha."

"Gunnar's grandmother is the Goddess known as the Numen. She possesses extraordinary magic. Dawa said Gunnar was the only one of us with the power to cross over." She sighed. "He said it would be dangerous, but I did not listen. I wish now that I had."

Arkady snorted. "Death must have pretty low standards. He will let any old rubbish in the Vastness." After Gwenn growled at him to continue with the story he said, "Gunnar said I needed to go back to my body and he would take me back across with him. So, after a bit of discussion, I agreed to go."

"What sort of discussion?" Gwenn wanted to know.

Arkady spread his hands wide. "Use your imagination. I am sure you can figure it out. We are not exactly the best of friends. After a little while, Death appeared. He did not speak, but he made it clear that only one of us would be allowed to leave the Vastness. You know about Death always having to keep a soul?" Gwenn nodded disconsolately and he continued, "I said that I should be the one to go, because of the two of us, you obviously prefer me, and anyway there was the prophecy to consider. I told him I had to give you my seed to create the Dawnmaid."

Gwenn said, in a shocked voice, "Kadya!"

"I know you will find this hard to believe, but Gunnar actually agreed with me for once. He said he would not be able to bear the sight of the two of us together, so it was probably best if he stayed behind. Then he turned around and walked away. Death pointed out a door and I could see Dawa's living room through the opening. I went through and found myself in my body."

She whispered, "Did Gunnar say where he was going?"

Arkady replied, "He said he was going back to Celeste because he wanted to be near the ocean and the place he first learned to like taking a bath. It did not make a whole lot of sense to me."

Gwenn's lower lip began to tremble, and Arkady put his arm around her. "You can see now why I did not want to tell you. I figured if you knew he sacrificed himself for me then you would feel badly for him. But he wanted to stay, Gwenn, truly he did. He knows that you and I belong together."

She stared at him and then said forcefully, "Get this straight in your head, Kadya; I cannot just pretend that Gunnar has ceased to exist. You have no right to ask that of me." Gwenn ran her fingers through her hair in frustration. "The truth is I love both of you. I wanted you to come back. That is why I brought you here to Dawa. But I never thought I would lose Gunnar because of it." She put her hand over her mouth to smother a sob.

Arkady said heartlessly, "I am sorry, but I just don't see how you could love us both. We are very different men. You are going to have to make a choice, and since he is gone, well…"

Gwenn threw off his arm, and walked away, just as Dawa came into the room bearing a tray of food and a cast iron tea pot. She brushed past him, saying, "I am going for a walk. Something made me lose my appetite."

The sky threatened rain, and the air felt as heavy and dull as her heart. As she made her way along the muddy road leading towards the village, threading her way through the puddles, she thought about Gunnar, and wondered where he was on his solitary, silent journey through Death's kingdom.

*When he reaches the ocean, will he cast himself down on the shore and weep for me?*

Spying a roadside shrine, Gwenn stopped and stared for many moments at Hana's face. Her expression spoke only of kindness and compassion. Why would she send Gunnar to such a dark place if she knew he would not be able to return? Gwenn sent a silent prayer to the Goddess for understanding, and then picked a handful of wild flowers to leave as an offering. Wiping her tears away with the back of her hand, she continued down the road towards the village, not paying attention to where her feet led her.

In the town center, the market stalls were starting to close up. Gwenn stopped to admire some carved animals painted in bright colors, thinking they would make excellent playthings for Jakob and Arvid. She pointed to the blocks and asked, in careful T'Shanga, "How much?"

The woman behind the table blinked in amazement. Though Gwenn had become a familiar sight in Khalama, this stallholder was new to the market, and had never seen a yellow-haired girl before. But she would not be so discourteous as to ask where this blond giantess might have come from. She merely inquired, "Do you like them? My husband carves them out of the wood we gather from the forest."

Gwenn nodded enthusiastically. "They are very nice. I think my baby sons would like to play with them. The colors are beautiful—like jewels."

"Thank you," said the woman. "My other husband paints them. He mixes the colors himself out of plant dyes so that they are safe for babies to play with."

Gwenn had been studying T'Shanga very diligently since arriving in the country four months ago, and had acquired a fair amount of fluency. But she thought she could not have understood the stallholder's words correctly, so she asked cautiously, "Did you say your other husband?"

The woman smiled and nodded. "Yes, dear. I have two husbands to help me. How many do you have?"

Gwenn looked so sad at this question the woman patted her hand sympathetically. "Don't worry. Even if you already have children, a pretty girl like you will soon find a man or two to marry."

"Do all the women here have more than one husband at the same time? Where I come from it is illegal," Gwenn said in surprise.

She shrugged. "Some do, some don't. But why would it be against the law? In T'Shang women inherit the property in the family, so they need husbands to help them keep the farms running." She smiled and shook her head, obviously bemused by Gwenn's questions. "I think it is easier to live with two. Less work and more play for me."

Though she realized she might be prying, Gwenn could not help but ask, "But don't they get jealous and fight with each other over you?"

The woman looked at her seriously. "No, why should they do that? They both love me and they know I love them. We all get along fine."

Gwenn paid for the carvings and thanked the woman for her kindness. She walked back to Dawa's house very slowly, thinking about small flames, and how they might make a big difference.

# 5

## Wanmoon + Zephur + Quondam

*She speaks, for the first time.* You have beautiful wings. Are you an Angel?

*He smiles at this. Ben'aryn is anything but. He has interfered before, against the spoken wishes of the leader of his kind. And now he has dared the Deres' wrath in bringing the Dawn. But the creatures who rescued him are servants of the trees, and perhaps they will intercede for him, once again.*

~~~~~~~~~~~~~

Huw looked at Katkin with concern. "Will you be all right here by yourself for awhile? I want to take Ajax and scout the lay of the land ahead. This farm may be a safe haven for us, as Padarn believes, but I would take no chances with you, my Queen. When I have spoken with Brunner, and know his mind, I will return." He shaded his eyes with his hand and looked down the valley, curving away out of sight. The farm and outbuildings lay further up the road, well-hidden from view. There was no way to approach them except by the main path.

She smiled bravely at him. "Of course, Huw. I will take shelter in the trees over there, and keep very still until you return. I won't come out until I hear the secret whistle you used with Padarn."

Clasping his hand suddenly, quite hard, she said, "You will come back, won't you? If you think anything is amiss, don't stay and fight. Promise me you won't." Huw could plainly hear the dread she tried to hide in her voice, so he pulled her into an embrace and stroked her hair. She buried her head on his shoulder.

"Don't be afraid, Queen of my heart," he said softly. "I won't leave you alone." Katkin raised her head to look at him, and her mouth was close to his. He wanted very much to kiss her—had wanted to ever since they began their travels together—so he waited, breathlessly, to see if she would bring her lips to his. But she did not. Katkin pulled away from his embrace, and turned towards the forest, and did not look back. Huw sighed and watched her until she became a shadow amongst the other shadows in the trees. Then he mounted Ajax and rode slowly down the rutted track to the farm.

Katkin sat down beneath a large holly tree, and pulled the branches close around her so she could not be seen from the path. She thought about Jacq's last words to her, as he lay dying on the floor of Acorn, *"I gave up my wings for you, Katkin. I loved flight— the freedom of it was my greatest joy, but I loved you more. Always, I loved you more..."*

She had never understood what he meant—still did not—but the eerie congruence with Huw's tale was too odd to ignore. She wondered about her dead husband, what he had been, or would be again. She had no doubt he was of the race of Gods, but was he the son of Shiqaba, as Tomas alleged? Or was he something far more powerful? Katkin sighed and shook her head. She wished she could speak with Dai, the winged God who had once saved her life. Somehow she felt sure he had the answers she sought.

Though the late afternoon sun still shone down wanly, it provided little heat. The chill afternoon winds finally forced her to her feet, and she paced back and forth between the trees. As she did, Katkin talked to Lalluna about her traveling companion, Huw Adaryi. "I know he loves me and I want to return his love, but something always makes me hesitate. He is a good man, and he has been very patiently waiting for me to make up my mind. We have been friends for a long time, but what do I actually know about him?"

The Goddess could not answer her, for she was too weak, but Katkin always felt a reassuring flutter in her chest when she reflected on the Amaranthine she continued to serve faithfully.

Once, as Lalluna's vessel, she had been able to fly on gossamer wings and heal the hurts and wounds of others. Now Lalluna's power in the living world was all but gone, a victim of the waning belief of her people. But the Goddess still gave her what small boons she could—including especially sensitive hearing. That is why Katkin heard the voices long before she saw two figures making their way warily down the track from the farm.

By their talk she could tell they were male, and spoke the language of the Secunians. One whispered, "That little darky had a woman's things in his saddlebag, and she's probably waiting around here somewhere for him to come back." He sniggered. "Even if he wouldn't admit it after we put flame on his black hide." Katkin's heart constricted. Huw must have been captured and perhaps tortured as well. It seemed Brunner had not been at all welcoming.

The other said, "Bert will keep him occupied until we get back with her. I told him to make sure the darky don't die until we return. It will be more fun to make him watch what we do to his woman." He laughed crudely, and Katkin's fist clenched.

She stood very still, until she could see the two men clearly. Then she slowly reached for an arrow from the quiver she wore strapped across her back, and nocked it in the string of her bow. Jacq had made the bow for her long ago and taught her to fire with deadly accuracy. She knew killing the first man would be easy. The second would present more of a problem, because he might run from her, but Katkin quickly came up with a plan.

After a few seconds an arrow whizzed through the air and struck the larger of the two men in the eye socket. He screamed in agony and crashed down to the ground, and the second man quickly dropped beside him, cursing.

Katkin ran from the trees, calling wildly for Huw. "Where are you, my love? Someone is shooting arrows and I heard a scream. Huw, please, come back to me..."

She aimed her steps to take her close to the fallen man, and as she went past, the second man leapt up, and tried to lay hands on her. With a deft movement she withdrew a long pearl-handled dagger from within her cloak, and opened the man's chest with a single upward thrust. With a surprised gurgle he joined his dead companion in the bloody grass. Katkin watched coldly as he writhed for a moment, and then lay still.

She rifled through the men's pockets, and cursed when she found Huw's curved knife. Both were roughly dressed, in filthy sacking breeches and ripped tunics. Katkin wondered if they might be vagabonds. She prayed that whoever Bert was, he had followed his comrade's instruction to keep his prisoner alive.

Katkin made her way stealthily along the side of the track, keeping to the long grass as much as she could. As it curved away to the left, she climbed a hill and looked down on the farmyard from above. The main house was small, perhaps three or four rooms, with a stone chimney. A lean-to shed with a tin tiled roof probably housed the kitchen. A big barn lay across the yard, and several smaller sheds. Nothing seemed out of place. Katkin sat back on her heels, considering her next move.

Suddenly the silence shattered as a huge bull mastiff dog found her scent, and approached her, growling, with hackles raised. She reached out to him with her hand and whispered soft words. The dog quieted instantly, and licked her face. Katkin silently thanked Lalluna for another of her gifts—the ability to send her thoughts and desires into the minds of animals. She looked up sharply as a door opened in the main house.

A man stepped out into the yard calling, "Jari, Mick—are you there? Did you find that darky's bitch?"

The answer came hurtling towards him as the mastiff attacked its former owner, and ripped out his throat. Katkin moved forward stealthily, for she could not be sure the dead man had no other companions. The dog wagged its tail happily as she patted its head.

Katkin whispered, "Good boy. Are there any other people in the house? Will you show me where they are?"

Catching hold of the dog's studded collar, she followed him into the kitchen, which had been thoroughly ransacked. Obviously the men had been after something besides food, because they had carelessly dumped bins of flour and dried beans on the floor. The dog stopped to sniff idly at a pile of oatmeal, and Katkin urged him forward. He led her along a narrow passage, and she moved silently behind, straining to catch any noise. She heard nothing at first—then a faint, rasping wheeze came from one of the bedrooms to the left. The door stood ajar, and Katkin paused outside for a few seconds. So far, she had been able to keep terror at bay with determined action, but now, in the darkened hall, fear clawed at her chest with fingernails of ice. But, after taking a deep breath, she stepped through the open door.

A man, bound and gagged, sat in a chair in the center of the room, lit by both a shaft of light from the curtained window and a candle, still burning on the table. She wondered irrelevantly why they had needed a candle when it was still daylight outside. Katkin stifled a sob with her hand as she saw how savagely Huw had been beaten, and rushed forward, no longer concerned whether or not Bert might have other accomplices.

*Please Lalluna, let him be all right,* she prayed silently, and cut the ropes that bound his unconscious form upright in the chair.

He slumped forward and she lowered him gently to the floor, and then opened the curtains a little further with a trembling hand to survey the extent of his injuries. They had smashed his face to a pulp. Both arms hung at oddly twisted angles. It seemed Bert had not listened to his partner's adjuration to keep the prisoner alive, for Huw was nearly dead already. Katkin knew there was nothing she could do to help him—he had long since passed beyond whatever limited medical treatment she could have offered. So after covering him with a blanket from the bed, she sat beside him and took his hand. The blistered skin flaked away under her fingers, and she realized his captors had used the candle flame not for light, but to try and persuade Huw to tell them her whereabouts. She cried quietly, thinking of a time, long ago, when, with Lalluna's help, she might have healed his wounds.

Then a voice, faintly echoing in her mind. Only one word, "Try..."

Katkin did not stop to question this Voice, or what it might mean. Nor did she consider the inevitable consequence of her attempt to heal him—she would feel each wound as if it were her own. Such thoughts might have made her hesitate, and if she did so, Huw would be lost. Katkin had lost her husband Jacq, and Gwenn's father, Tomas de Vigny. She would not lose the Firaithi man who lay before her now. Closing her eyes, she placed her hand over his heart, and let the healing power flow through her fingers. Katkin screamed as the first of many blows struck her face.

Huw stirred and woke, wondering if he had been dreaming. He lay on his back in almost complete darkness. Perhaps he was dead?

That would explain why he felt no pain, just a curiously heavy sensation on his chest. But it was not at all how he expected death to feel, because he could distinctly perceive his own heartbeat. Experimentally, Huw raised his arm and flexed his hand. A heavy object trapped his other arm, and he used his free hand to explore. Something lay on his arm and chest—or rather someone—with long, curly hair, bound in a ponytail.

*Katkin...*

With a cry, Huw struggled to sit up, and clutched Katkin's still form to his chest. He could not fathom how she came to be with him in his death. Then his hands searched in the darkness and found her pulse. She lived—and that meant, somehow, he did too. A faint glow appeared as the moon emerged from behind a cloud and now Huw could see the indistinct outline of a heavily curtained window.

After carefully lowering Katkin to the floor, he stood and crossed the floor, then threw the curtains open wide, allowing moonlight to flood the room. He saw the chair he had been bound in, and the blood soaked rag they had stuffed in his mouth. There, too, was the candle they had used on him, now burned down to a tiny flame in a puddle of grease. Another stood close by in a brass holder, and Huw lit it with a taper. On the floor at his feet, Katkin moaned and tried to sit up.

Huw quickly knelt beside her, saying, "It is all right, I am here."

"Huw? Are you well?" Katkin whispered. "I have not lost you, have I?"

He pulled her close. "No, Queen of my heart. You have not lost me, though I know not how I have been found."

Katkin's arms tightened around him. Huw could not stop himself from kissing her. This time she did not pull away. But after a moment, he tore his lips from hers, knowing that until they searched the house, he could not be sure she would be safe.

They took the remaining candle and explored the house together. Katkin returned Huw's curved blade, and kept her own dagger at the ready. Huw thought there had only been three men, but he could not be absolutely sure. After a thorough search turned up no one else, they retired into the kitchen for a cup of tea.

"How did you come to be captured like that, Huw?" she asked him.

"I knocked on the door, looking for Jakob. A stranger answered it and said Jakob Brunner no longer owned this farm. I did not think it possible that Jakob could have sold up and moved on so quickly, so I asked many questions. Before long the first man called his friends and the three of them jumped me. I did not stand a chance."

He sighed deeply when she related the story of his rescue. "You should not have risked yourself for me, Katkin. I wanted to protect you. That is why I did not tell them where you were."

Katkin smiled and shrugged. "I had to save you. You promised to make me a new vielle, remember?"

Her lighthearted comment did not move him to smile in return. He said, seriously, "Those Gruagán beat me up very badly, and twisted my arms until they broke. Now I am uninjured. I don't understand how it happened. Did you heal me?"

Katkin did not want to tell Huw about Lalluna's presence inside her. Though she trusted him, she could not be sure how he would react. So she nodded her head briefly, but gave no explanation. "You don't want to tell me more? Then at least answer me this—did it cause you pain?"

She nodded again, and lowered her eyes so that he would not see the tears that welled up.

Huw gave a cry, and rose from his chair in agitation. He walked over to the fireplace and stared at the cold, blackened ashes. "It must have been terrible, beyond terrible. You should have let me die."

Katkin came to stand beside him and put her arm around his waist. "I did not want to lose you." She took a deep breath. Now that she *had* almost lost him, the confusion that troubled her in the forest abruptly cleared. "I care too much for you. How could I let you die?"

Now it was his turn to smile. He said gently, "There must be easier ways to get a new vielle, Queen of my heart."

Katkin laughed softly and brushed his lips with her own. "No doubt you are right, Huw."

Huw sighed and rubbed the back of his neck, then absently started to braid his long, black hair. "My friends the Brunners had a daughter of four years old, last time I passed this way, and Elsa was pregnant with another child, which would have been born this past spring. I wonder what happened to them. Those Gruagán would say nothing of where Jakob and his family went."

"Perhaps they have gone to stay with some relatives?" Katkin suggested.

Huw shook his head. "Brunner has no relations or even any friends. He deliberately isolated himself here in this valley, because of Elsa. He was a stubborn old man, who would not heed the law of any government he did not agree with. Trading with us always put him in danger, and well he knew it. I can only hope the Un-Named One will protect them wherever they are."

"What are we going to do now? I guess it will be all right if we sleep here tonight, but we cannot stay all winter as we planned to, not if Brunner and his family are gone." She sighed. "I suppose we will have to leave tomorrow. I am not looking forward to making that trip again." Tears sprang to her eyes.

He shook her gently. "It must be very late. We should go to bed. The pillow speaks its own counsel. Things may look different in the morning."

Katkin suddenly felt very tired. "You are right. We should not be making any decisions tonight. I feel as though my face will crack open if I yawn any wider." She told the dog to stay in the kitchen and he obligingly sank down onto his haunches. After making sure he had food and water, she left him on guard.

Huw took her hand and led her back down the hall to the bedroom wing. They passed by the room in which he had been tortured and neither wanted to enter. The next room down the hall held a double bed, covered by a handmade quilted coverlet. Katkin looked at it from the doorway and thought briefly about the farmer, Jakob Brunner and his wife. They slept the long winter nights together in this bed. She wondered if their spirits still lingered in this room, and whether they would care if a stranger slept in their bed—or two strangers. Katkin impulsively asked, "Do you want to share this bed with me, Huw?"

He touched her cheek with his hand. "Yes I do, very much. But not tonight. You have been through hell for me, and you need to rest. I can wait a little longer, queen of my heart."

Katkin hugged Huw gratefully, and said, "Good night, then. Sleep well."

Huw continued down the hall to a room obviously belonging to the Brunner children. Wooden toys and dolls lay scattered about on the floor. He picked up a stuffed rabbit, and looked at it with longing. Then he sighed regretfully, and rubbed his eyes. After undressing, he crawled into the narrow bed, pulled the covers up high to ward off the draft from the windows, and blew out the candle.

When an hour had passed in his fruitless quest for sleep he sat up and lit the candle again. Memories tormented him, of the merciless interrogation at the hands of his captors this night and other, even more grievous tortures by the Fynära. Huw was thirty-six years old, just a year younger than Katkin. He had been spontaneously healed twice, once by her and once by his blood-brother Arkady Svalbarad. Such miracles made him question his very existence and he sent a fervent prayer to the Un-Named One for understanding. Suddenly fatigue overtook him, and he lay back on his pillow with a sigh, regretting whatever chivalrous impulse had led him to turn down Katkin's offer to share her bed. Then he slept, and when he slept—he dreamed.

Eira, his dead sister, came to him. She spoke, her voice low and urgent. "You must protect the one who bears Shiqaba's feather. Keep her safe until the Dawnmaid comes. Remember, Huw, the dark ones are not the true enemy." In the dream, Huw tried to question Eira, as she slowly faded from his view. Her last words were delivered by a wavering shadow. "I can say no more. Do not forget my words, my brother."

A fearful cry woke him, and he sat up, heart hammering. Huw left his bed, and quietly retrieved his knife from under the pillow. He prayed that Katkin's scream had been the product of a night terror, but if there were flesh and blood intruders about then he did not intend to give them any warning of his coming. Huw moved down the hallway like a shadow in the darkness—as silently as a breath of wind. Katkin's door was closed, but the flicker of candlelight could be seen from underneath. Huw took a deep breath, tightened his grip on the knife and threw open the door. Katkin looked at him with wide, shocked eyes. "Huw? What on Yrth are you doing?"

He blushed deeply, leaving a crimson stain across his dark skin. "I heard a cry and I thought perhaps there were more of them." Huw lowered the hand that held the knife, and wished desperately he had paused long enough to slip into his breeches. But Katkin only laughed, unconcerned by his nakedness.

"I am sorry. A dream woke me and then I singed my fingers trying to light the candle. I did not mean to frighten you." Then she raised the covers on one side of the bed and smiled. "I think we will both sleep rather better if we are together. Don't you?" Huw nodded sheepishly, and joined her under the quilt.

The next morning, they both slept very late. Sunlight streamed through the open curtains as Huw woke. Katkin lay beside him, still sleeping soundly. He studied her face, and his thoughts drifted back to the first time they met—at the horse fair in her home country, Beaumarais. The Firaithi paused their restless wanderings once in every odd-numbered year to stay in Beaumarais a month. Firaithi horses were considered amongst the best in Yr, rivaling the steeds of the broad steppes of Ruboralis. Katkin had come, with her contingent of guardsman, to buy herself a new pony. Then she had been Queen Katrione, beloved by all the people of Beaumarais and famous throughout Yr for courageously healing the heart of Hythea, the mountain overlooking the City. Though that victory had cost her an arm, her grace and beauty remained untouched.

Huw spoke Maraison well, so his father, the Tane of the Chandrathi Kindred, had given him the task of helping the Queen select a suitable beast. He, as mistrustful as any of his people, had expected a cold and condescending Gruagán ruler, but she surprised him by being both funny and warmhearted. They spent the better part of three days together and Huw tortured himself with the idea that she had deliberately dragged out the selection process in order to spend more time with him, waiting until the day the Firaithi were leaving to make her choice—and then laughingly choosing the very first animal he had shown her. Despite the fact she was happily married and completely out of his reach, Huw had quickly fallen hard for her.

His father, Grigor, spoke sharp words to him, saying coldly, "Stay away from her, fool. No Queen of the Gruagán could ever care for a man of the Firaithi."

Still it was with deep regret that Huw bade good-bye to the purple hills of Beaumarais that year. On a different and much less felicitous visit, he met her husband, Jacq Benet—better known as the Dinrhydan, the finest swordsman in all Beaumarais. Jacq had pretended, at first, to be friendly, but he quickly became abusive when Katkin left the Citadel alone to innocently say farewell to Huw at the Firaithi camp.

Now Jacq Benet was dead, and Queen Katrione deposed. The woman who slept at his side was only Katkin, of the Kindred of Anandi, but Huw loved her no less for that. Quietly, he lay beside her, watching the covers softly rise and fall with the movement of her breath, and thinking of the previous night. After he had extinguished the candle and joined her in the double bed, he gallantly suggested, once again, they both try and get some rest. Katkin had immediately and unashamedly begged him to make love to her. He did so, more than once, and only as the cockerels in the yard crowed with the dawn did they finally drift off to sleep, still entwined in each others arms. Huw sighed, thinking how perfectly her body matched his, and wanting her again, right then.

Katkin stirred and stretched. She rolled to face him, and brought her mouth to his for a long kiss, leaving little doubt that her desire also perfectly matched his. He pulled away and regarded her seriously. "Queen of my heart, there is something I must tell you. I should have spoken last night, but my need for you overtook me, and I could think of nothing else for a time."

She rested her head on her hand and looked at him curiously. "What is it, Huw?"

"Last night you honored me beyond any expectation. I shared your bed, and your sweet passion. Such has been my heart's desire since the day we met. I would take you again this morning, and every morning, but I must face the truth. You would eventually bear my child, and before that happens I must make you my wife." He sighed and looked at her with his eyes full of tears. "I cannot do that."

"Why can you not?"

"Because I am already married."

Katkin sat up suddenly, shocked that he would keep such a thing secret from her.

He said miserably, "I know I should have told you before."

She did not bother to disguise her anger. "Tell me now. Where is she—your wife? Are there children too?"

He nodded, more and more unhappy. "She came from the Anandi, as your mother did. Her father was the son of the Tane,

Ifan Mare. I met her at Bryn Mirain and we were married the summer Cara turned eighteen and I, nineteen. She came to live with the Chandrathi, and bore me a baby girl."

Katkin said bitterly, "I met your wife once. Cara is my cousin, Huw."

Huw looked startled at this. "How could you..."

"She came to Acorn with my grandmother, Neirin. I thought her very beautiful and very bad-mannered. Did you love her?"

He nodded. "Yes, Katkin, I loved her, and I loved my daughter. Please understand, I don't tell you this to hurt you, but that you should know the truth."

Katkin looked away from him, so he would not see the tears in her eyes. "Go on with your story. If I am hurt it is my own business, I suppose."

"After two years, she left me and took our baby daughter with her. I don't know where she is now, or whether she is alive or dead. For a long time I believed I was dead as well. It was only when I met you that I remembered how to be alive again." He covered his face with his hand and started to cry in earnest. "Please don't hate me."

Her anger cooled and she reached over to stroke his back. "Why did she leave? Do you know?"

He nodded. "Oh yes, I know very well. The tale begins properly before I was born. A man came one day to the Chandrathi. He had dark skin, as we do, but he was not from one of our Kindreds, though he spoke Firai well. They took him in, for he was gravely wounded. A Gruagá girl traveled with him, but she was shy and fey, and left soon after. After many years had passed he announced that he intended to travel back to his land in the west and he wanted us to go with him, saying it was our home as well. I did not believe this to be true, because of the prophecy of the Dawnmaid. But though I begged her not to, my wife wanted to go, along with some of the others."

He paused and looked down at his hands, which were clutching the faded counterpane that covered Jakob and Elsa's bed. Self-consciously, he unclenched his fingers and spent a moment smoothing out the wrinkles he had created in the fabric. After some time had passed in silence this way, Katkin asked, "So what did you do then, Huw?"

"I grew angry and locked her in our caravan, thinking once

Shiqaba and the others had gone she would settle down and be happy with me again. The next day, as I was out hunting near the Sharm River ford, she stole away and took our baby with her. I trailed them easily at first, for Shiqaba was tall, and wore an unusual talisman." Huw, intent on his story, did not notice the startled look Katkin gave him. "They left Scarfinda on an ocean-going vessel, and from there I could not follow." He added dully, "As I said, I don't know where she is now."

Katkin did not speak right away. She was remembering a conversation she had had not long ago with Tomas, about Jacq. Tomas had said that Jacq was the *son* of Shiqaba. Katkin's voice sounded curiously intense as she asked, "Tell me again—what was the man's name, the one who left with your wife?"

Huw stared at her, a little surprised by her question. "Shiqaba. It means feather."

Katkin's hand groped in her nightgown and pulled forth a carved crystal feather strung on a leather thong. "Did the talisman he wore look like this?"

Huw stared at the object dangling between her fingers, profoundly shocked. "That was his! Where did you get it?"

She sighed, almost unwilling to believe her own words. "It belonged to Jacq. And before that—to his father. Perhaps the girl with Shiqaba was Jacq's mother, Elisabeth." Katkin shook her head in confusion. "I asked her once who Jacq's father was and she told me Francois Benet. He was a blacksmith at my parent's estate. But I could tell even then that she was lying."

Huw looked unhappy. "My sister Eira came to me in a dream last night with a message for the one who bears the feather talisman."

Katkin said, "Tell me."

"She said, 'The dark ones are not the enemy,' and she told me to keep you safe." Sighing, he said, "None of it makes any sense to me. Do you understand it?"

"Perhaps she means the Angellus. It is strange she would say that, for Dai once told me the same thing."

He gave her a fearful look and asked, "Who are you truly? Something more than just a simple woman of the Anandios—am I right, Katkin?"

Katkin knew she had no choice now but to tell Huw the truth about Lalluna.

When she finished he said reverently, "So you are allied with the Amaranthine? No wonder you could heal me." Then he groaned and slid away from her to the very edge of the bed. "I have sullied your purity with my wanton desires. I will never be forgiven."

She sighed and moved over towards him, saying dryly, "I think my wanton desires had something to do with it as well, Huw. I am still a flesh and blood woman, despite what you might think, and I care about you very much."

He looked hopefully at her. "Do you mean it? You are not angry with me about Cara?"

She shook her head, but her next words were not reassuring. "What difference does it make whether we are cleaved by a piece of paper? Who can say where we might be in a year's time, anyway?"

Huw stared at her, more than a little discomfited by her words. "But... but what about children, Katkin? It would not be right to raise a child with such uncertainty."

"I have a great deal of medical training, Huw. I know of many herbal preparations that will prevent pregnancy. There is no danger of that happening."

He did not argue with her further, though Katkin could see the hurt and disappointment in his eyes. But she knew it would be wrong to mislead him into thinking she wanted more children, when she did not.

In the afternoon the sky looked heavy and dull, and the falling temperatures presaged snow. As Katkin sorted through the supplies in the kitchen to see what foodstuffs they might be able to take for their journey, Huw walked out to the barn to see to Ajax. He found the body of his captor, Bert, lying stiff and cold on the dusty ground, and half-carried, half-dragged him off behind the row of untidy sheds that clustered around the yard. Although he did not wish to honor this particular dead man with a burial, it was only prudent to conceal as much evidence of their stay as possible. He dumped the man unceremoniously on the stony earth and went inside to find a shovel. A brown and white cow lowed mournfully at him, and he took a moment to fill up her manger with hay, noting with some surprise that it seemed someone had milked her quite recently.

After unsaddling Ajax, Huw found to his dismay that the squatters had thoroughly ransacked all their travel supplies. He gathered up what clothing and cooking gear he could find, and folded it neatly in a pile on the work bench. After hunting a few moments he located a heap of tools against the far wall of the barn. Huw selected a sturdy-looking shovel and went back outside to dig a shallow grave.

Katkin joined him outside after a few minutes. "Let me help you, Huw. It is too cold to work outside for long."

Huw was glad enough of the break. The soil was heavy with clay and stones, and though the day was growing colder he had worked up a good sweat. He sipped the cup of tea Katkin provided as she dug further down into the dirt. With her artificial hand she worked very slowly, but doggedly continued until she had almost finished the grave. Huw respected Katkin too much to intervene, knowing he might hurt her pride, but after a time he suggested gently she might go in the house and find some old sheets in which to wrap the body, since she would know much better than he where such things would be kept.

She threw down the shovel with a relieved sigh and held up her hand. Huw helped her scramble out of the hole, and then watched her walk back to the main house, with her head held high. Remembering with a smile that she used to be a queen of the Gruagán, he turned back to the business of digging. By the time Katkin returned with the sheets, Huw had completed the shallow grave and was now collecting rocks to pile on top. They tied the body roughly in the sheet, and Huw used his booted foot to roll the bundle into the hole. He quickly threw the piled earth back on top and artfully arranged the rocks so it looked as though the ground had not been recently disturbed.

The sight of the grave reminded Katkin of something. "What about the men I killed yesterday, Huw? We should not leave them on the track to the farm. Someone will be bound to see their bodies eventually."

Huw used his shirt tail to wipe the sweat from his face. "We must hide the bodies on our way back out the valley, I suppose."

Flakes of snow drifted lazily down. Katkin bent to retrieve the shovel and walked back to the barn. Huw trailed behind her, unhappily aware that the failing weather might make further travel very difficult indeed.

"What should we do about this cow? If we leave her locked up in here she will starve to death." Katkin walked over to the beast and stroked her distractedly.

Huw sighed. "After we have something to eat I will slaughter her. I do not want to, but it is the only kind thing to do. Winters in this valley are very hard. We could not leave her outside to fend for herself. That would be more cruel than a quick death. Then we had better make our way south. I don't see what else we can do." He looked at Katkin sorrowfully. "I brought you all this way for nothing. I wish..."

But Katkin was not listening to him. She threw up her hand in a slashing motion and Huw fell silent, wondering what she could hear. When she crept towards the back of the barn, he drew his curved dagger and followed behind her, now thoroughly alarmed. The wall seemed solid, yet Katkin seemed to think something lay behind it, for she placed her ear to the boards.

"It is probably just rats," he said, and again she furiously signaled him to be quiet.

After dropping down on her knees, she could just see the disturbed pattern of dust on the floor. A trap door, so cunningly fitted the joins were barely visible, lay hidden in the darkness. She pointed it out to Huw and he inhaled sharply. Quickly, he fetched a lantern from the workbench and lit it. He turned to face Katkin.

"I am going down first. No arguments."

Katkin stepped in front of him. She whispered, "There is a baby whimpering down there. And another child telling it to be quiet. That is what I heard a moment ago. If you go down there with your knife drawn you will frighten them to death. Let me go."

Huw took his knife and wedged it between the boards, then slowly raised the light wooden panel. A set of rough stone steps descended into pitch darkness. He could hear the sound of the baby now, very faintly, and he wondered how Katkin could possibly have heard it before. She took the lantern, and started down the stairs, then whispered back to him, "What tongue did Brunner and his wife speak to each other?"

"Firai. He spoke Firai like one of us." Huw was very surprised to hear Katkin's voice softly murmuring in Firai a moment later, as she comforted Jakob and Elsa Brunner's two terrified children. A moment later Katkin called for him, urgently, to come down. She knelt by Elsa Brunner's prostrate form on a straw pallet. In response to Huw's questioning glance Katkin shook her head slightly, but said nothing in front of the children.

He picked up Elsa and carried her into the parlor of the house. Katkin examined her after telling Huw to take the children into the kitchen and wait for her there. Elsa had evidently suffered a serious head wound, and Katkin did not think she would regain consciousness. But after a moment the woman began to mumble, and Huw quickly came through from the kitchen and knelt beside her.

"Elsa... Elsa, it is Huw Adaryi. Can you hear me?"

Her eyes opened into agonized slits as her head slowly turned towards him. "Huw? Of the Chandrathi? Are Poppy and Gwillam with you?"

"Yes, they are all right. What happened, can you tell me?"

She moaned. "Black Guardsmen came to the farm, a week ago. Jakob made me hide with the children. They looked for our bolt hole, but they did not find it. Then they took Jakob away and hanged him in the village square. He did not even get a chance to defend himself before the Magistrate."

Huw asked in disbelief, "Are you sure? Perhaps he is just imprisoned somewhere."

She shook her head, almost imperceptibly, and closed her eyes again. "No, Huw, I am sure. I could hear them talking as they searched. They are after all the farmers in the Catena. Anyone found to be trading with our people receives a death sentence now, by order of the King of Beaumarais. Then their farms are reallocated—that is the word they used. Curse that *Gruagá* Tristan Dinrhydan. He isn't even our ruler, but the Council fear him enough to follow his wishes."

Huw asked, "What happened after Jakob was taken?"

Elsa opened her eyes. "I wondered why the Black Guard did not just burn the place down, but a few days later some other men arrived. I soon discovered that they were the new "owners" of our farm. The children and I were running out of food by then, and they caught me as I tried to steal more from the kitchen at night. One of them hit me over the head with a cudgel and held me down, while the rest took turns with me. You know..." Elsa did not want to describe her rape at the hands of the three men, in case Poppy could hear.

Huw answered in a voice choked with fury. "We understand, my sister. What happened then?"

Her words grew faint. "They ransacked the kitchen looking for gold. But instead they found the rhubarb wine that Jakob had laid down a few years back. They all got very drunk. I was able to slip away back to the bolt hole, but I kept passing out. Thank the Un-Named One that you have come. Now I can sleep in peace..." Her voice trailed away. When Katkin checked her a moment later she had stopped breathing. Huw stood and walked over to the door, his hands clenched in helpless fists of rage.

A few moments later, as Katkin warmed some milk for the baby on the fire, the little girl shyly answered Huw's questions. After volunteering her name was Poppy, and that she was five years old, she paused to take another mouthful of porridge. Her long black hair had been braided in the style of the Firaithi, with ribbons and colored yarn. She wore a calico dress, made from a flour sack, and a starched, light blue apron. Katkin thought she looked remarkably tidy for a child who had been forced to fend for herself and care for a baby for four days with no help.

"How many days did you stay in the hiding place? Did you have anything to eat?" he asked her.

She peered up at him, her brown eyes solemn. "My Ma took Gwillam and me down there, when the black men were coming. We had lots of dried meat and oat biscuits, and some jugs of milk for Gwillam. She said we had to be real quiet while the bad men hunted for us. After a while we ran out of food so Ma went to get us some more. She was gone so long I was afraid she was not ever going to come back. When she did she acted all funny. First she cried a lot, and then she went to sleep. I tried to wake her up, when Gwillam needed his wrappings changed, but she wouldn't. So I had to change him myself, lots of times. Then when the milk was all gone, I sneaked up and milked old Bessie for Gwillam, so he wouldn't get hungry and cry. Where is my Ma? Did you wake her up?"

Huw looked helplessly at Katkin, who was cradling Gwillam in her arm and feeding him warmed milk from a cup. Katkin passed the baby to Huw, and knelt before the little girl. She said gently, "Your mother has passed through Tsmar'enth, Poppy. I am sorry. She was already badly injured when she came back down to the hiding place. You could not have done anything to help her." The little girl's eyes filled with tears, and her lower lip trembled.

"And my Patre? Has he gone too?" Poppy wept in earnest as

Katkin nodded unhappily. She wrapped her arm around the little girl and held her, then looked up at Huw's face without speaking. The question in her eyes was plain and he inclined his head slightly in response. What else could they do?

Katkin held the girl at arm's length and said firmly, "You and Gwillam will be all right, Poppy. Huw and I are going to take care of you. Just like your Ma and Patre did. Now you must be a big girl, and dry your tears. Your mother would want you to be brave."

To her surprise the girl did as she was told, though she continued to hiccup sobs for a few moments afterwards. She wiped her eyes on her apron, and said, "What is your name, pretty lady? What happened to your hand? It is very funny looking." Huw smiled and shook his head as he passed the baby back to Katkin, wondering how on earth they would manage with two children to take care of. Travel would be much more difficult, for Poppy and Gwillam would have to ride Ajax, meaning she could carry less baggage. Nor could the children sleep out in the open the way he and Katkin had. He sent a silent prayer to the Un-Named One, asking for her help, then sat down next to Poppy and ate his food, while trying to answer her rapid-fire questions.

A fierce gust of wind sent the shutters rattling violently, and Katkin stared out the window in alarm. "Huw, look at the snow..." It was falling thick and fast, and had blanketed the yard several inches deep since they had come inside to make dinner.

Poppy said, "Better get the rope, Patre, before it is too hard to find the barn. Once the snow begins to fall like this it might not stop for days. My other Patre kept it in the cupboard by the door. I will show you." She caught Huw's hand in her own and dragged him to the wooden dresser. Coiled neatly in the bottom was a long length of rope, and Huw guessed she meant him to tie it from the front entrance of the house to the barn door. That way he could always find his way, even in the most blinding of storms.

He thanked the girl and headed out the door, trailing the rope. After tying the rope securely to both doors, he made sure both Bessie and Ajax were well-fed and watered. By the time he had fought his way back to the house against the howling winds and swirling snow, Huw knew unequivocally they would not leave Brunner's valley that day.

# 6

## Waxmoon + Unda + Prox

Why did you take me away from the Darkness? I was happy there.

*He sighs.* I had no choice. You are needed to right a great wrong on Yrth.

*She knows that this is true, for her Guardians told her long ago, when she first formed out of the stuff of Darkness.* Will you come with me, Angel?

*He cannot. Ben'aryn pushes her into the Vortice and listens to her terrified screams as she falls. Then he disappears again, confident that the trees will send her on her way.*

*There will be other tasks, but for now he has only to pray—and to wait.*

〜〜〜〜〜〜〜〜

That night, Gwenn already lay awake, waiting, when Arkady slipped silently into her room. After her conversation with the stallholder in the marketplace, she was hoping she might have another chance to talk to him. But once she returned, jubilantly bearing the carved wooden toys for Jakob and Arvid, Dawa had kept both of them busy for the rest of the evening with cleaning out the storeroom under the eaves of the house. Arkady, tired from this unaccustomed labor, had been sent to bed early by his teacher. Was it her imagination, or did it seem Dawa watched them both carefully, to make sure they had no chance for private conversation?

Arkady knelt by the bed and put his lips to her ear. He whispered, "Gwenn, wake up. Don't be frightened. I must talk with you."

She turned her head, eyes wide open. "I was not sleeping, Kadya. Get under the covers. It is too cold to stay outside the bed." Gwenn raised her blankets and Arkady huddled underneath, but made no move to touch her. She continued in an undertone, "I have wanted to talk to you too, ever since I came back from the market."

"Gwenn," Arkady begged her. "Let me say what I have to say first..."

She ignored this interruption and continued blithely on, determined that he understand immediately about her change of heart. "I learned something important at the market. Something that helps me see a way through our difficulties." She slid across the sheet and closed the distance between them, then gave him a lingering kiss on the lips. Arkady stared at her, dumbfounded, as she murmured, "I know why you came here tonight. You don't have to say anything more. Make love to me, Kadya..."

He stammered, "Gwenn, please... I came to tell you..." But her hands were already tugging at the fastenings of his robe and Arkady found he could no longer think very clearly about what it was he had come to tell her. Instead, he concentrated on throwing off his clothing and helping her to do the same. For the first time since his return from the Vastness, he felt truly alive and he clung to that feeling as her hands and tongue searched his body, and found all the places she knew gave him pleasure. Her touch and her mouth grew ever more demanding, and as she drew him into her, he forgot all about his errand and concentrated solely on fulfilling her desire.

After a time, when they lay close together, and Arkady was stroking the small of her back with his fingertips, Gwenn whispered, "Did I guess right about what you wanted to say to me?"

Arkady grinned in the darkness, thinking she had no idea how very wrong she was. "First tell me what made you change your mind. This afternoon you seemed pretty angry, Gwenn."

She stroked his hair, shining like a bar of silver in the moonlight from the crack in the curtains. "I heard someone at the market today saying that most of the women here have two husbands. Don't you see? When Gunnar returns we can all be together as a family."

He snorted in disbelief. "What?! You think he would agree to such a scheme? There is no way the two of us could share you. We would end up killing each other, you must see that?" He chuckled softly at the insane idea that he and Gunnar could live together under the same roof.

"He would, if I asked him to. Gunnar would do anything for me, Kadya. But would you?"

He abruptly stopped laughing. "Oh no, don't put this in my lap. What difference does it make anyway? He is not here." His arms tightened around her as he said softly, "There is only you and I, Gwenn. Can you not be happy with that, my beautiful crow girl?"

"Yes," she agreed. "Of course, I can be happy with that, for now. But when he returns, Kadya..." Arkady grimaced in the darkness, but she did not see.

The house was very quiet. Only the occasional snuffling sounds of the babies stirring in their baskets broke the stillness, as Gwenn stretched and sighed. Abruptly, she waved a hand before her face.

Arkady, who had very nearly dropped off, was suddenly wide-awake again. "What are you doing, Gwenn?"

"It is very strange, but sometimes I think I see a faint light hovering around, close to the head of the bed. I wonder if it is some kind of insect, like a firefly, but with a red light in its tail." Gwenn sat up and pointed. "Look! There it is again."

Arkady saw the light right away, but disagreed softly. "You must be imagining things, Gwenn. There is no light in here. Sometimes our eyes play tricks on us in the darkness, don't they? Now lay down before you catch your death."

She continued to stare up into the darkness, and Arkady knew he must quickly find a way to distract her. Fortunately, such a distraction was close at hand. He slipped his foot out from under the covers and nudged the basket holding Jakob. The baby snorted and then began to cry.

"Gwenn," Arkady whispered. "I think one of the babies is awake."

She groaned in the darkness, then rose and picked up Jakob. After putting him in the middle of the bed between her and Arkady, she gave the baby her breast. Arkady lay beside her and stroked her hair, silently thanking Hana that Gwenn had seduced him before he had time to deliver his message. He sighed and closed his eyes, and fell asleep wondering how on Yrth he would manage to tell her the truth, now that he knew Dawa was eavesdropping on her as well.

Gwenn took longer to find sleep. She held Jakob close and thought again of his father, Gunnar Strong Arm. Was Arkady right in thinking that her plan to take both men as her husbands was doomed to failure? Although she had professed absolute faith in Gunnar's willingness to agree with whatever she asked of him, in truth she had no idea if he would go along with such an outlandish idea. He had been raised as a Fynäran man on the island of Starruthe, where women were considered, by tradition, mere chattels. True, Gunnar had embraced many new things of late, such as bathing, but would he be willing to share her with a man he had once, in a jealous rage, tried to kill? Gwenn had no answer for that, but of one thing she was dead sure. Wherever Gunnar was, she still loved him and still longed for his return. Nothing Arkady said to her would change those feelings. She yawned, placed a kiss on Jakob's soft forehead and slept deeply.

Now she wandered in a soundless world, where the sky loomed low, flat and white above her head. She knew somehow at once that she was dreaming, but this awareness did not disturb her passage. On either side of her, as far as she could see, white creatures sat on the ground in gentle repose, their double wings beating softly in rhythm, though not a breath of wind stirred the drifts of leaves that lay around their scaly bodies. Each creature held a person in its arms—a person who slept peacefully and eternally.

Gwenn strolled between the rows of creatures, seeking a familiar face. The atmosphere changed, at first only subtly, as a new energy manifested itself all around her. The iridescent wings beat more quickly, and each creature in turn looked up as she passed. Though they had no faces, she could feel an emotion rising and resonating within them, like the plucked string of an instrument.

One after the other, they whispered, "Myriadne. She brings Myriadne..."

In the morning Dawa said cheerfully, "I hope you both slept well. Today I am going on a journey, over to Benahar village. I want to take Griffon to visit my old teacher, Nochen Sang. Will you be all right while we are gone, Gwenn?"

Gwenn was about to agree with him, saying, "Of course..." when Arkady's foot swiftly moved under the table and kicked her in the ankle. She paused only briefly before finishing, "...not. I can't stay here on my own. What if something happened to me? There would be no one here to see to Jakob and Arvid. Can you not go alone, Dawa?"

Dawa looked briefly annoyed and covered it up with his thousand-wrinkle smile. "I *can* go alone, but I would rather not. Are you sure you cannot manage without Griffon for just a few days? I will ask one of the other villagers to look in on you now and again."

Arkady's foot delivered another invisible nudge and Gwenn shook her head quite firmly.

"No. I need Kadya here. We have a lot of planning to do for our wedding." Dawa's eyebrows shot up at this, and his startled expression neatly matched Arkady's, who sat back in his chair abruptly, but did not speak.

Gwenn grasped Arkady's hand and held it firmly as Dawa muttered, "A wedding is it? Well, now. This is news of a different sort. Of course he must stay if there are celebrations to plan." He smiled again, and this one looked quite genuine. "Very well, I shall go on my own. But you must make sure that Kadya does not leave the confines of the house while I am away, Gwenn. He is not strong enough to walk in the forest yet. Do you understand?" He gave her a peculiarly intense look, and she nodded in baffled agreement.

After breakfast, Dawa bustled about packing his bag and within an hour he was gone, after repeating his admonition to Gwenn not to let Arkady leave the house. Arkady watched him walk down the muddy main road with mingled hope and fear. Was the old man so sure of himself that he would leave them alone for several days? Arkady decided he would have to risk it. Turning back to Gwenn he said, "I am going to lie down, but I will watch Jakob and Arvid if you want to go out for awhile. It looks like a nice morning for a walk in the forest. The rhododendrons are still flowering up there."

Gwenn gazed out the window, at the darkly clothed sides of the mountains. The sun peeped out between the clouds that chased one another across the sky. She did want to get some exercise, so she said, uncertainly, "Are you sure, Kadya? If you want to nap then the babies will be nothing but trouble."

He answered softly, "Oh, yes, I am sure. They will be no trouble at all."

So she pulled on her colorful cotton jacket, block printed with the images of many whimsical animals, and then grabbed a walking stick from the stand by the door. "Which way are you going?" Arkady asked casually, and Gwenn stopped in the doorway, still fastening the carved bone toggles on her coat.

"Up the path behind the house—the steep one that leads to the rocky outlook. There is a nice view from the top. Do you know it, Kadya?" Arkady did, and he sighed inwardly.

After Gwenn smiled and waved goodbye, he went to wrap the boys in their warmest clothes. Then he went back into his bedroom and lay down with his eyes sleepily half-closed, until he saw the very faint red light in his room stop blinking. Working quickly, he made the rough outline of a body under his covers with a rolled up blanket, and added another pillow for the head. Then he grabbed the babies and hurried out the back door, to follow Gwenn up the mountain.

Gwenn climbed, admiring the overhanging rhododendron trees on either side of the path. A cool breeze stirred the branches, showering the ground with petals of cerise and white. The sun peeping through the gaps in the trees was warm and bright. As the way grew steep, she stopped to drink some cold tea. She studied the unusual container, recalling a strange discussion she had had with Dawa.

A few days ago, she had come upon him unexpectedly, as he had been about to put a bottle back into a cupboard. When he saw her approach, he quickly slammed the door. Gwenn peered suspiciously at him, thinking that in all her months in Khalama, she had never once seen the inside of that cupboard.

Dawa was frowning, about to turn away from her, so Gwenn asked him about the bottle in his hand.

"It is made of a very useful material. Notice how strong it is? You will find you cannot break it, even if you try very hard."

"Where did you get it, Dawa? It is almost clear, like glass, but very light. I have never seen anything like it before." But he had only given her that maddening smile and a shake of his head.

Afterwards, he had strolled casually away, leaving it out on the kitchen bench. Gwenn had surreptitiously taken it, intending to show it to Arkady, but after all the excitement yesterday she had forgotten about it. Now she tucked it back into her bag and continued on her way, the bells on the walking stick providing a musical accompaniment to her walk through the ancient forests of Khalama valley.

Gwenn strode up the mountain tirelessly, her breathing still even and slow. Up ahead, she knew, the path narrowed and became rough, before ending in a rocky promontory that overlooked the village. She did not slow her pace, intending to reach the top and make her way back down quickly so that the twins might not be too much of a burden for Arkady. As she walked she wondered why he had not wanted to go to Benahar with Dawa. He had given no good answer to that question when she asked him, saying only he did not feel up to the trip. She was somewhat surprised by this admission. Certainly, last night when he was making love to her, he had seemed in very good health, but perhaps his weakness came and went?

The top was in sight now, and Gwenn put on a burst of speed. Once she reached the overlook she paused again, and threw her pack down on the rough stone bench. A pile of rocks lay to the side of the path, and she tossed a small stone onto it before sitting down with a sigh. The village spread out below her, the main street a darkened muddy slash between the square stone houses. Pocket-handkerchief gardens and larger fields covered the valley, and now, in the late spring, the green jewel tones of the new vegetation shone in the sun. Gwenn idly considered how much longer she would stay here in Khalama, if Gunnar did not return. Though Dawa had been very kind, she did not want to go on living in his house forever. Perhaps, after she and Kadya were married they would go back to Yr and find a place to live—someplace where the people had never heard of the Fynära raiders and Gwenn Faircrow. She sighed, wondering sadly if such a place truly existed.

Gwenn had another swallow of tea then stood and stretched. She decided she would take the roundabout way home—a little used goat track that meandered back to the village, rather than the main path. After one more lingering gaze over the valley of Khalama, she headed back down the mountain.

When Arkady reached the stony overhang he was close to collapse. The trip would have been hard enough alone, but lugging the heavy baskets containing Jakob and Arvid had made it triply exhausting. Now as he flopped down on the stone bench, despair overtook him. He assumed that since he did not meet Gwenn coming back down again, she must still be at the top, resting and admiring the view. But she was nowhere in sight. The babies were stirring, and as Arkady bent to tuck the blanket back around Arvid, he caught sight of a curiously-shaped bottle on the ground. He picked it up, and studied it carefully. Had Gwenn dropped this? Arkady's eyes narrowed as he stuffed the bottle into Jakob's basket. He did not want to think it possible that his lover and Dawa were, in fact, allies, but her possession of this strange artifact from the future seemed an inconvenient and incontrovertible truth.

Arkady stood, and forced his trembling legs to carry him back down the way he had come, just as Gwenn emerged from the forest to his right. The sound of the bells on her walking stick brought him to a quick halt, and he ducked out of sight behind a large rhododendron.

Gwenn strode hurriedly back to the bench and squatted down by the rough stone base. "Where is it? I know I left it here..."

Arkady's heart sank utterly as he looked once more at the bottle half-hidden under the blanket. After a moment she stood abruptly and looked around, now holding a brightly colored woolen bootee in her hand. Arkady saw, at the same moment, that Jakob's little nearly-square foot was bare. He cursed under his breath as Gwenn walked slowly towards the rhododendron forest, her expression now one of wary confusion.

Seeing that she was bound to discover his hiding place, Arkady stepped out from behind the shadow of the rhododendron tree and stood in the pathway, holding the baskets containing the twins. She drew up short as she caught sight of him and asked breathlessly, "What are you doing here, Kadya? Are the babies all right?"

Arkady nodded distractedly, as she bent down to reunite Jakob's foot with the missing bootee. She spied the drink bottle before he could think to tuck it beneath the blanket. Gwenn smiled up at Arkady, saying, "Thank goodness, you found it."

"What is this, Gwenn?" He gazed at her intently, waiting to see what explanation she might give.

"Dawa's funny bottle. I thought I must have dropped it somewhere along the track back there. He might be angry that I took it without his permission, and I wanted to put it back before he found out. Have you ever seen anything like it, Kadya?"

Her wide blue eyes stared into his without even the slightest hint of guile. He sighed his relief and went to sit again on the bench. She joined him there and as she gave her breast to Arvid, she asked, "Why did you follow me?"

Arkady looked over at her and thought, as he always did, how intoxicatingly beautiful she was—especially now as she bent her head over Arvid and held the baby close as he suckled. Her spun gold hair fell in waves and ringlets around her neck and shoulders, and the perfume of it filled Arkady with desire. Must he now tell her the truth about Gunnar? He pushed such selfish thoughts resolutely into the back of his mind as she waited for his answer. Finally he said, "I had to talk to you privately."

She interrupted. "You did not need to come all the way up here. Surely this morning after Dawa left would have been a better time? You are hardly well enough to climb the track, Kadya. Dawa told me not to let you leave the house. He is your teacher and you should listen to him."

"Listen to me," Arkady said. "That creature who left this morning for Benahar is *not* my old teacher. What is more, he has hidden spying devices all over the house. I could not risk his overhearing what I have to say to you."

Gwenn stared at him with wide, shocked eyes. "Spying devices?" She looked suddenly alarmed and clutched Arvid closer to her chest. "Is Dawa...? I mean, is this creature dangerous?"

Arkady nodded. "Yes, he is dangerous. Very much so. The red light you saw last night is the thing he uses to see and hear everything we do, Gwenn. But there is much more I must tell you as well. Gunnar is..." The sound of bells and distant singing drifted down from above them. Arkady stopped speaking and listened intently. His expression changed to one of terror. "He is on his way here! I have to get back before he finds out I left the house. Stall him as long as you can." Before she could think to question him, Arkady had gone, running stiffly and unsteadily down the track to the village. Gwenn thought she might call out to him, and then thought better of it as the creature known as Dawa drew up beside her, smiling his thousand wrinkle smile.

He said softly, "Well, little mother, it is a surprise to see you so far from home and with the young ones too! It must have been a difficult climb carrying both baskets *and* a walking stick." His sharp eyes seemed to slice through her and Gwenn felt suddenly menaced.

"Kadya wanted to nap, so I brought the boys on a walk with me," she said defensively, and did not look at Dawa. "I thought you were to be gone several days," she added with undisguised sharpness.

Dawa gave no explanation of his sudden appearance. "Indeed,

Griffon does need much rest," he agreed. "But I understood you wished to discuss your wedding?"

"Oh, that," she added carelessly. "We have already decided what we want to do." In an effort to distract him from further questions she launched into a long description of the fictional wedding she said they had discussed. Dawa listened politely and seemed in no hurry to continue down the hill. Gwenn rambled on until she hoped she had given Arkady enough time to get home. Then she said, "We should be getting back, Dawa. I told Kadya I wouldn't be more than a few hours on my walk."

He quickly stood and grasped the basket holding Jakob. Dawa started off down the mountain path, chanting lustily. Gwenn watched his retreating back. Could it be true that this man, no... *creature*, Arkady had called him—this creature could be dangerous? It did not seem possible, but Gwenn had seen the terrified look in Arkady's eyes as he talked about this thing that had somehow taken over the body of his old teacher. And what did he mean to say about Gunnar? She pondered this as she walked back down the track behind Dawa and wondered too when she might get another chance to talk to Kadya alone. She could not help thinking that Dawa's appearance at the stone bench had not been at all coincidental. The track to Benahar came nowhere near the place she and Arkady had had their hurried conversation.

After some assiduous spying, Gwenn ascertained that Dawa disappeared for an hour or two every day. But wherever he went, it did not seem to involve leaving the house. Gwenn watched the doors and windows carefully, and found reasons to visit all the rooms in the square stone structure. Now she searched for hidden exits or alcoves, using the excuse that the springtime wedding she planned required much cleaning out of corners and crawl spaces. Often she asked Arkady to help her, but when they were alone together and she tried to whisper questions to him, he only shook his head in warning. She might have taken some comfort in the fact that he now came to her bed every night to make love to her. But this passionate yearning for her frightened Gwenn far more than his cautionary words might have. She drew from this attention the understanding that each whispered tenderness and fervent embrace might be his last with her.

Dawa bustled cheerfully around the place, oblivious to Gwenn's poking and prying. Once the house was as clean as she could realistically make it without arousing suspicion, she could think of no other method for gathering information. She now suspected that the answer to the riddle of Dawa's disappearances must have something to do with the mysterious cupboard in the kitchen.

One night, as Gwenn lay in bed, sleepless with worry, Jakob stirred in his basket and began to cry. Shortly afterwards he woke Arvid, who appended his wails to his brother's. Arkady grunted and turned over, saying sleepily, "Shall I pick them up?"

Gwenn's milk production had slowed as the boys had started on solid food, and she knew both were hungry now. She whispered, "I will get the bowl of gruel I left down in the kitchen, Kadya. That will keep them content until morning." She slipped out of bed and into her woolen robe as Arkady gathered up both boys and snuggled with them under the covers.

The moon had already risen and set that night so Gwenn padded quietly down the stairs in almost complete darkness. A tiny noise made her pause in the hallway, just beyond the kitchen, and peer through the arched portal. Her night vision was extraordinarily sharp, perhaps due to the long presence of the Goddess Keth Dirane inside her body. What she saw made her stop breathing for a long moment. Certainly Dawa must not have expected anyone to be about in such darkness, for he had left the door to the perennially-locked cupboard slightly ajar. Gwenn approached it slowly and silently, half expecting Dawa to appear and slam the door before she could see inside. Once she reached the cupboard, she swung the door outwards, then gave a little gasp of surprise and fear. Revealed beyond was a swirling dark haze of some grayish-white substance, like many faint stars packed tightly together. That it was not of this world Gwenn had not a shadow of doubt. As she stood uncertainly before the doorway, frozen in fearful indecision, a shove propelled her violently forward into the mist. She fell, screaming, into a bottomless void.

# 7

## Dunmoon + Zephur + Prox

*Hana and Fyn are together, before Geya's mirror.*

*The tall, blond Amaranthine sighs.* Lut and I have pursued many Angellus, but always we come too late to prevent their devastation. I left him on the sixteenth pellicle, to watch over the remaining Uri'el. The Angellus have already destroyed the rest of the astaren* there.

~~~~~~~~~~

Huw Adaryi sat in Jakob Brunner's tiny parlor, staring into the blaze in the fireplace and thinking about the events of the last day. Bleak despair lurked just on the edge of his consciousness—he could feel it treading on soft paws, following him everywhere he went. Despair at Elsa and Jakob's horrible deaths at the hands of the Gruagá, and despair at his and Katkin's situation. Soon, he feared, he would have to give way to it, but now he must try to be strong, for as long as he could, for her sake. And for the sake of the two children they now had to take care of, together. He looked up as Katkin sank down next to him on the sofa, and took his hand. Huw studied her face by the firelight, thinking how tired she looked. For a moment, while he was still able, he put aside his own sorrow and asked quietly, "Are they asleep?"

She nodded. "Gwillam was a little bit restless until Poppy found his stuffed rabbit for him. Then he went to sleep as soon as I laid him in his cot. I told Poppy a couple of stories after that and she dropped right off. She is being very brave. I have never met a child like her." She looked at Huw and her eyes filled with tears. "Every time I think about the two of them, down there in that *hole,* for four days with their dying mother... Oh Huw, what would have happened if we hadn't come in time?"

He squeezed her hand. "We did come in time—by the grace of the Un-Named One. But now we must decide what we are going to do."

---

* The spirit bodies of the dead.

"I thought you said we were leaving. What if those Black Guards-men come back?"

"Can you hear the wind howling outside? There is a foot of snow on the ground already, and more is falling. The quicksilver is still dropping and I think we are in for a serious blizzard. But we may not be able to leave the valley, even if the weather improves."

"Why not?"

"The track will become impassable with drifts of snow until the spring thaw. We won't be able to get Ajax through, especially with Poppy and Gwillam. But perhaps that is for the best, Katkin. For it means that no one can get to us, either. We could spend the winter here, as we planned—only now we'll have the children with us as well. It is what we *must* do, Queen of my heart."

Katkin sighed and stared into the dying fire, wondering now if she had done the right thing in coming to Brunner's valley with Huw. Although she did care for him, the sudden addition of two very young children had given their relationship a permanence she was not at all sure she wanted. Katkin thought of her husband, Jacq, now dead, and her former lover Tomas, gone back to the Vastness. Huw was a very different man from either of them—though he let Katkin have her say, he would make all the decisions now, and expect her to obey blindly. That was the way of the Firaithi. What would their life be like, trapped in this lonely valley for the whole winter, with no one but each other for company? *Trapped*...

Katkin rose suddenly, walked to the window and threw back the curtain. The snow swirled just outside, and she could see nothing beyond it. In her heart she cried to Lalluna for counsel, and it came back to her with certainty. Poppy and Gwillam had come into her life unasked and, though she was loath to admit it, unwanted—but there was no doubt they needed her now. As Huw came to stand beside her, and placed his arm around her waist, she slowly nod-ded her head. Did she really have a choice?

"You ate flesh when you were on the island with Arkady!" Katkin glared angrily at Huw, but she kept her voice low, in case Poppy, who slept in the room next door to them, should still be awake. She continued, "I will do the hunting anyway. It is nothing to do with you."

He sighed and rolled to face her. "It has everything to do with

81

me. It is too dangerous for you to hunt alone, and we cannot all go together. How could Gwillam and Poppy manage in the freezing conditions outside?" His voice was firm. "If there is any hunting to be done, then I must do it, and I will not, unless we are starving, as Arkady and I were on the island. Otherwise, I go against the wishes of the Un-Named One, who shares her bounty equally with all living creatures. We have plenty of beans and dried stuff to last the winter, you know that. Asparitus demands that we not take any more than we ourselves need."

Katkin sat up in bed, and pulled the quilt up under her chin. Though this was a long running dispute between the two, ever since they had arrived at Brunner's valley several weeks ago, Katkin had avoided telling Huw the real reason she wanted to hunt. Now she had no alternative. She took a deep breath. "Asparitus be damned! I promised *them* I would, in return for their vigilance. They are watching the valley for us, against intruders."

Huw looked alarmed. "What? With whom have you been speaking? I thought no people had passed through this valley since the first snows fell."

Katkin studied the faded flowers on the wall hangings, just visible in the semi-darkness of the bedroom, lit only by the dying fire in the hearth. "Not people," she said gravely. "Eagles."

Huw stared at her in astonishment and wondered if their long confinement indoors had made her feverish. He spoke gently. "Tell me this story of the eagles, Queen of my heart."

Katkin smiled in the darkness, knowing by the condescending tone in his voice that he did not believe her. "Do you remember the first break in the weather? I went outside to dig in the garden, to see if poor Elsa had left any carrots or potatoes or other root vegetables in the ground. The ground was hard, almost frozen, and it took me quite a while. You were inside mending the flour bin that those murderers had broken." Huw nodded, remembering the day. Katkin had been outside for more than an hour in the bitter cold and had returned flushed and triumphant, with a few wrinkled but sweet carrots and potatoes, saying there were many more outside, buried in layers of straw and sand.

"I heard the rushing sound of wings, and I ducked down as a huge bird swooped low over my head and landed on the ground not two feet away. He just stayed there, staring at me, and sometimes preening his feathers." Katkin shrugged. "Sometimes Lalluna gives me the power to communicate to animals, so I tried to talk to him. Somehow though, this time it felt different." Her voice trailed off uncertainly.

"What do you mean?" Huw asked her.

"I don't know. I just don't think Lalluna had anything to do with this eagle. I think it came from somewhere else."

"Why do you say that?"

"Because I have never heard an animal's voice respond to me. Usually, they just do something if I ask them. Like Varg, when he killed Bert. But this eagle *talked*, out loud, after I spoke to it."

Huw shook his head. "I think you must have imagined it. Eagles do not speak the language of humans, my queen."

Katkin said firmly, "I know what I heard."

"Then what did you hear? Tell me."

"I said to the eagle, 'Why have you come, my brother? How can I help you?' or something like that—I don't remember exactly now. He walked forwards a couple of paces and I felt a little afraid because he was a big bird. I raised the shovel in my hand, though I would have been loath to use it on such a magnificent creature. Then he spoke. I swear it. He said, 'I came when you called me. You said you have need of sharp eyes to watch this valley. We have many. But you must give us something in return—at every full moon place a freshly killed carcass by the fallen oak tree in the forest.' Then he said that he would warn us if anyone was coming up the path or down the valley from the other end."

"But why? Eagles have no interest in the affairs of men. He said you called him. Did you?"

"No, I did not call him. Not as far as I know, anyway." She faced him and her eyes were stern. "Now you see why I have to go. It was my agreement with the eagle, so I must be the one to honor it. The full moon is tomorrow night. Only one carcass, and then I will return. The Un-Named One will understand."

"But how do you know they are keeping their end of the agreement, to watch the valley for us?"

"I have seen them outside, wheeling in the sky over the trees. So have you. You pointed them out to me only last week."

Huw nodded, unwillingly. She was right—he had seen many eagles, and wondered on it. Katkin lay down again by his side and turned towards him. He softly stroked her cheek, but his words were unequivocal. "You must not go. I forbid it. How would Poppy, Gwillam and I manage if anything happened to you? We will have to do without the vigilance of the eagles."

Katkin disagreed sharply. "Don't be silly. I will be all right. I have Lalluna to protect me. And..."

Huw waited for her to continue. "And...?"

Katkin faked a yawn. "Nothing. Are you sure you won't change your mind? I still think we need the extra protection."

"No. You must do as I say, my Queen. It is for the best."

She turned away from him without speaking further, and quickly pretended to drop off. After an hour, as soon he slept in earnest, Katkin rose quietly, found her clothes and left the room. Once she reached the kitchen she lit a candle and retrieved the supplies she had already put aside for her journey. The dog who had once belonged to Bert whined and she patted his head.

She sent a thought to him, "*Shush, Varg. You can come with me, but right now you must be very quiet. If Huw wakes up there will be hell to pay.*"

The dog stood, expectantly wagging his tail. Katkin guessed she might be gone for two days, and she packed enough twice-baked bread and clay pots of lentil spread to last her, as well as some honeycomb wrapped in a cheesecloth. After leaving Huw a brief note, she stole outside to the barn, found some old horse blankets, and rolled them up to use as bedding. Varg padded silently behind her. It was bitterly cold outside, but halemoon rode high and with the snow on the ground it seemed almost as light as day. Katkin briefly considered taking Ajax, but decided against it, thinking Huw might have more need of the horse than she.

Although she knew he would be very angry with her, she felt no guilt as she crossed the yard on foot and traversed the fields that led towards the silent woodlands clinging to the steep sides of Brunner's valley. She had no choice but to honor her part of the agreement, for the eagles had kept theirs. But Katkin knew there was more to this trip than her desire to keep a covenant with their sentinels. She had once ruled over an entire country, and the thought that she might now let one man rule *her* brought a grim smile to her face. The sooner Huw learned that she did not intend to become a meek Firaithi wife, who obeyed without question, the better.

In the first few weeks of their stay at Brunner's they had argued frequently, about anything and everything. Huw would wear her down until he got his way, always obstinately sure of the rightness of his position. Katkin could be just as stubborn, to be sure, but most of the time she gave in, especially if Poppy was in the room with them. After the traumatic loss of her parents, Katkin wanted the little girl to have no other worries. She took in everything around her with her big brown eyes, and often noticed subtle changes in the weather or the mood of the household with far more perception than Katkin would have thought possible.

Now as Katkin climbed breathlessly up the steep path that led to the thickly forested head of the valley, she thought of Poppy. As an orphan herself, Katkin knew first hand what pain she must be feeling, yet the girl remained steadfastly cheerful and obliging, always ready to lend a hand with Gwillam or the household chores. The other day she had astonished Katkin by producing a perfectly serviceable batch of oatcakes, "for Patre Huw."

When questioned, she replied, "He is getting skinny, Katkin. Patre does not eat enough, so I made him his favorite."

Katkin had looked at her, nonplussed, and then studied Huw herself when he came in to breakfast. There was no doubt the girl was right—the sharp planes of his face looked almost as chiseled as they did in the days when he first came off the island with Arkady. Katkin wondered why she had not noticed the dark smudges under his eyes before now, and resolved she must do a better job of watching over him in the future.

At this thought, the first prickling of guilt about her forbidden hunting trip hovered over her, but she ruthlessly cast it aside with the resolution that she would make it up to Huw somehow when she returned.

The sun was rising now, and illuminated the icy forest with rosy streams of light, creating a crystalline wonderland. Varg ran away from her side, barking madly, and flushed a covey of quail.

"Varg! Leave it," she shouted.

She thought she might find deer hiding deeper in the forest, so she continued to walk for several hours, following faint trails. Occasionally she stopped to blaze marks in the trunks of the birch trees along the way, so she might find her way back again, if Varg could not. When Katkin judged the sun to be at its apex for the day, though it was still low in the sky, she stopped and made herself a midday meal. Varg she sent off to hunt for his own provender, knowing he would not be interested in her vegetarian fare. After a few minutes he happily returned with a dead rabbit flopping about in his massive jaws, and Katkin watched a little enviously as he devoured it. She missed eating flesh, sometimes, but that was another point on which Huw was intractable.

It was too cold to sit still for long, so after a long draft from her drinking skin, Katkin stood and prepared to make her way deeper into the forest. Varg stood too, and unexpectedly growled, from deep in the back of his throat. Katkin's heart began to pound as she grasped the dog's collar, feeling the fur on the back of his neck as it rose and stiffened. She peered into the surrounding trees, but could see nothing out of the ordinary.

"Easy, boy," she said softly. But Varg did not relax his tense stance, and continued to growl at intervals, as Katkin slowly retrieved the knife from her pack.

Together they walked forward, past the cluster of rocks that she had made her picnic place, and towards a dense grove a little off to their left. Suddenly, with a crash that echoed in the stillness around her, something landed in the middle of the thicket, and began thrashing around, obviously in distress. Varg exploded into furious barks and strained at his collar. Katkin could not hold him. He dived into the undergrowth, still barking, and though she immediately called him back with a mental command, he did not obey. But a few seconds later he gave a startled yelp and fled, with his tail down between his legs, and came to rest behind Katkin, trembling violently. Katkin turned to flee, thinking she wanted no part of any animal that could frighten Varg like that.

A single desperate word stopped her: "Wait..."

Katkin dropped the knife and put her hand over mouth to smother a cry.

The voice was unmistakably Jacq's.

Slowly, so carefully, she turned back around. Varg whined as the figure struggled in the thicket, his feathered wings hopelessly caught in the thorny bushes. After a moment, Katkin walked forward and said, uncertainly, "Dai... Let me help you."

She tried to disentangle the feathers as gently as she could, but after moment he snarled, "Hurry, I haven't much time left."

Gripping the wing in his hand he tore it free with a cry of pain, and collapsed forward on to the forest floor.

In a second she was by his side, forgetting her fears. "Are you unwell? How can I aid you?" His teeth were chattering, so she brought her blankets and covered him warmly, then waited for him to speak to her.

Dai said, "You cannot help me. Where is your husband? I must speak with he who is called Benet. I have to warn him..."

Katkin looked at him in confusion. "Jacq is dead, Dai. He has been gone nearly eight months. Keth Dirane killed him and stole his anafireon."

His face was a study in anguish. "No... Then I am too late to stop it." Dai closed his eyes and wept, and Katkin, feeling thoroughly distressed, took his hand in her own. His skin felt feverish, though he still continued to shiver madly with the cold.

She said, "I will make a fire. We need to get you warm, somehow. Just wait here while I get my tinder box."

He looked about to object, but then he said resignedly, "Go ahead, if it will make you feel better. I may as well die warm."

She chided him softly as she hurried back for her pack, "Don't say that. I am going to help you."

He did not speak as Katkin gathered enough tinder and kindling to get a good blaze started. Once the fire had gathered strength, she added dry branches from the middle of the thicket, and set some clean snow to melt in a tin cup for tea. As she knelt once more by his side, Katkin stared down at Dai's gray face, so like Jacq's on the day he died. The pain at the loss of her husband cut through her keenly, as though it were happening once more. Abruptly she stood and fetched the tea, and pressed the warm cup into his trembling hands, then held his head as he took a sip. A few seconds later he retched uncontrollably, and the tea melted the snow as it ran in rivulets into the stony soil and disappeared.

Slowly she lowered his head back to the blankets and asked, "What is this illness that afflicts you? Do you know?"

"Poison. You cannot do anything for me. I told you, I am going to die."

Katkin sat back in shock. "Who poisoned you? Why would they do such a thing?"

He smiled wearily. "I did. I needed to die, so I could be reborn."

She looked at him as though he were raving. "I don't understand. Why did you want to be reborn?" Dai did not answer. A further bout of vomiting took him, and Katkin helped him sit up so he could empty his stomach once more. This time the contents left a bright reddish stain in the snow, and Katkin cried out in alarm. "Is there any antidote? Anything I can do?" Then she spoke beseechingly to the goddess, "Help me! Don't let him die, Lalluna. He is your brother Amaranthine, is he not?"

But Lalluna stayed cold and still inside her.

With a groan of agony he laid back down on his side, and she tucked the blanket around his magnificent gray wings. Dai said slowly, "Stay with me, dearest, until the end. I will try to explain to you why I did what I did." His red-rimmed eyes met hers, and the irises still glowed like the captured moon. She rested beside him, and took his hand once more in hers.

Though she very much wanted to cry, she did not. "I will stay by your side, I swear it. Tell *me* of the thing you came to warn Jacq about. Perhaps I can do something."

He shook his head. "It cannot be helped now. I came back too late." He sighed. "I always told the others that treating with your kind was wrong and would lead to trouble, but in the end it was I who brought ruin to human and Amaranthine alike. It has not happened yet, but it will. Nothing can stop it. Nothing..." He sobbed quietly as Katkin stroked his forehead.

"Begin at the beginning. Please, Dai. Don't leave me until I understand," she pleaded.

With effort, he sat up again, and Katkin helped him prop his back against a tree. Quiet agony filled his voice to overflowing. "I watched this world for many lives of your kind. The others were at home here, but I had no home, Katkin, only the spaces between the stars, in their infinite loveliness. I grew lonely, and I wanted companionship, but my brethren thought of me as a traitor. Then I saw... something that made me wish to come to your world, so I decided to be reborn as a human. I wanted to experience life fully, knowing that I could die at any time. Do you understand?"

"What did you see?" she whispered, though in the back of her mind she knew the answer already.

He reached a palsied hand to brush the hair from her face and softly she kissed each fingertip. "Oh, my love... You must know by now. I saw you, Katkin. So I made up a mixture that carried my essence, and I came to Yrth. I could see enough of the future to know where I must be born in order to meet you in this life. I found a suitable human woman and gave her my essence so that I might be incarnated through her. Then I poisoned this body, so it would die."

"You impregnated Jacq's mother, Elisabeth Benet? But what about Shiqaba? Tomas said..."

"The woman, Elisabeth, was with Shiqaba, but I placed my essence in her body as she slept. I did not want the others to know what I was doing."

Katkin looked askance at him. "You had relations with her without her knowledge? That is rape, Dai. Are such things not considered immoral in the future?"

He tried to explain in words she would understand, but his increasing infirmity fogged his mind. Though her gaze was uncomprehending, he plowed ahead. "I did not need to have intercourse with her in order to make her pregnant. I attached my essence to carrier virinos and placed a tiny lozenge filled with them under her tongue. From there the virinos infected her blood cells and then found their way to an unfertilized egg in her ovary."

The science was well beyond Katkin's time, but still she understood the fundamental nature of his actions all too well. She said firmly, "I still believe what you did to Elisabeth was dishonorable."

He sighed. "Perhaps you are right. Perhaps I should have known by what happened after, because everything must have gone terribly wrong." His voice sounded very bleak, and Katkin shivered, though the fire still burned brightly.

"Nothing went wrong. You were born, as Jacq Benet. We met as children and fell in love. But even then I knew Jacq was different from other people, Dai. He could cross into the Vastness, for one thing. And as he grew older he started remembering things—memories that must have been yours—of strange worlds and ecstatic flight. He thought he was going mad."

"We learned how to save our memories, so that when our bodies grew old, we could make a new one and pass into it with our minds intact. That is why the Amaranthine seem immortal to your kind. But my encoding must have been faulty, if Jacq did not know the truth of who he was."

Katkin said softly, "I think he did, at the end of his life. Just at the end. But what did you do, once you took the poison?"

He shifted his position slightly, and grimaced with pain. "I decided to go to a favorite place of mine, called Rythis, where there are many trees. I wanted to die somewhere beautiful."

Katkin nodded. "Yes, I remember when you took me there. The trees..."

Dai lifted his head sharply. "I took you? To Rythis? That is not possible, my love."

Katkin said stubbornly, "You did. The day I fell from the window. You saved my life, Dai. Do you not remember?"

He became very agitated at this. "There is a paradox? A paradox in the Gyre? I have failed, and yet..." A second later he gave a cry of agony and clutched his chest. Katkin caught him as he slumped over sideways, and arranged herself so his head could lie in her lap. Though his voice grew very weak, he doggedly continued with his tale. "The poison must have worked too quickly. Somehow I became disoriented on my journey to Rythis and I found myself in the future—the very distant future, many turns of the gyre from now. Further than any living Amaranthine can see. The Yrth was in ruins, and all her people enslaved to a cruel tyrant, named Maggrai. I wandered like a ghost through burned-out cities, watching helplessly as children in scarecrow rags died of hunger and neglect. I called out to my brothers and sisters for help, but in return I heard only the silence of the hollows between the stars. I knew then that Maggrai had destroyed all the other Amaranthine as well. With my little remaining strength I tried to find this despot, and finally I caught sight of him, in a high tower on an island by the sea."

He stopped speaking and took several shallow, rasping breaths. Katkin sat by his side, and felt very afraid. Now he could only whisper. "I saw my own face, twisted with hatred, on a body with ugly jet-black wings. Then I knew the truth. Maggrai was my child, created somehow in my life here on Yrth. I fled at once and tried to get back to a time when I could warn myself not to have children, but as you can see, I failed. I failed utterly."

Katkin shook her head in horror. "It was Keth Dirane. That demon made you lie with her, on the day you died, and then she stole your anafireon. She must have borne the child of whom you speak, Dai."

Dai could barely breathe. He caught Katkin's hand and held it to his lips. Then he muttered, "Tell me... of some happy reminiscence. Something you and I did together in my life on this world, so I can carry it in my heart, to the place Death takes me. Please, love..."

Katkin was crying, but she managed to quiet her sobs. She stared off into the distance, thinking of her life with Jacq. Of so many bittersweet memories, which one would she recall for Dai, now? After a moment, she smiled through her tears. "Once, after we had been married a few years, and I had become Queen Arkafina of Beaumarais, we went on an excursion through the countryside to an inn called the Seven Coachmen. In the morning, we rose early, with the sun, and stole away from the official delegation, and my bodyguards. You had a bottle of wine and some breakfast hidden away in your pack and we walked together down a country lane, holding hands, until we reached a huge field of sunflowers."

"Sunflowers," Dai repeated in a whisper. "They are so beautiful."

"In the middle of the field there was a perfect circle of green grass, completely hidden from view by the tall stems of the sunflowers. It looked otherworldly—as if some magician had created it especially for us. So we threw off our clothes and lay down, and the grass was soft and warm against my back as you made love to me. I can remember, even now, looking up at the sunflowers framed against the perfect blue of the sky as I felt the power of your body and your spirit moving in mine." She wiped his cheek tenderly as a tear seeped from his eye, and then placed her fingers to her lips and tasted the bitterness. "You were so strong, Jacq, and yet so gentle. I loved you more than anything." Her voice broke into sobs. "I still love you. Please don't leave me. Please..."

Katkin stopped pleading as she felt Dai shudder and then lie perfectly still. The knowledge she had lost him again tore through her like a quickening fire, and she buried her face in the downy feathers of his wing. She cried for a long time as Varg whined at her side. Only when the afternoon grew bitter cold and still did she force herself to rise. Katkin knew she could go no further that day, so she set about gathering more wood, and then built the fire up again. She stared down at Dai's stiffening corpse, wondering what she should do, since she had no tools with which to dig a grave. In the end she decided she had no choice but to cremate him, though the thought of seeing his magnificent wings burn away filled her with unbearable anguish.

After piling his body high with dry wood, Katkin watched as the bonfire ignited. She had no doubt that Huw would be able to see the smoke, and she wondered if he would use it to track her to this place. After a moment she decided she did not care. Huw and the Brunner children seemed part of a different world—one that at this instant had nothing to do with her and the winged being whose lifeless body burned before her.

"Farewell, my love," she whispered brokenly. "May you find peace in the silence between the stars." The flames shot high as the wing feathers caught.

She turned away, not wishing to see the skin shrivel and split on his burning flesh. The smell nauseated her, and she walked many paces from the fire in an effort to be free of it, and sat down by the rocks where she had eaten her lunch. Though it was long past dinner, Katkin had no appetite, and only drank a little water as she waited for the fire surrounding Dai to burn itself out. Night had fallen before the last red coals faded into glowing ash, and she made her way back to the fire, to wrap herself up in her blankets. For many hours she lay awake, replaying her conversation with Dai, trying to gather some meaning from his dire words about the future of Yrth. It all sounded so bleak, so final—except for the paradox in the gyre, whatever that was. Dai had seemed surprised about that, and to that little shard of hope she decided she must irrevocably cling.

Katkin woke, stiff and cold, just as the sun rose the next morning. She jumped up and flapped her arms, trying to warm herself, as Varg playfully bounded around her. The remains of last night's fire still smoldered slightly. Katkin steeled herself to examine Dai's pyre, knowing she must leave no trace of him behind. To her dismay, she could clearly see many bones, charred and blackened, but perfectly recognizable among the ashes. Cursing, Katkin hauled rocks and stones from the surrounding ground and threw them on top to form a cairn. It took her most of an hour to cover the evidence completely. As she rested, sweating and tired, by the bole of a tree, she saw a herd of deer passing in the distance.

"Down, boy!"

The sharp command to Varg sent him on to his haunches, and she hurried over to her pack to retrieve her bow. She tried, with the force of Lalluna, to get the deer to slow their pace, so she might get a clear shot, but instead they looked up in alarm, and bolted away through the trees to safety. Katkin wondered grimly if the Goddess had withdrawn all her boons, for the presence of Lalluna still seemed frozen and silent within her.

After a hasty breakfast of bread and honeycomb, Katkin and Varg struck off deeper into the forest, following the trail of the herd. After two hours she caught up with them, and this time she crept very close on the downwind side. After selecting a smallish male, probably one of last year's fawns, she took careful aim with her bow. The arrow struck him cleanly and pierced his chest cavity. He collapsed on to his knees and then on his side, legs thrashing wildly, as the others scattered in terror. Katkin strode forward and drew her knife across the deer's throat. Removing some rope from her pack, she tied the legs together and prepared to drag the carcass back the way she had come, towards the valley, and the fallen oak. Suddenly Varg growled again, and threw himself before her, as a large dun-colored bear lumbered out of the bushes.

Katkin screamed and dropped the rope. Varg attacked as the bear reared up on to its hind legs, and the beast knocked him aside with a sweep of its huge paw. The dog howled in pain and then lay very still. Katkin turned, running blindly, and prayed the bear would stop to feast on the deer carcass rather than pursue her. But almost right away, she heard its heavy footfalls crashing through the undergrowth. She searched in vain for a tree she could swarm up. Just ahead, she could see a dense thicket, and she plowed straight into it, hoping the bear could not follow. Abruptly she felt herself scrabbling for purchase as the ground fell away steeply on the other side, to a hidden drop of about fifteen feet. Katkin fell, shrieking with terror. The bear stood at the top of the bluff, watching her motionless form where it lay on the rocks below, and then shambled away again.

# 8

## Sisciot Prox

*Why do they do this? To tear apart the bodies of the fallen like that... It is horrible.*

*We may never know, Hana. No one can speak to them. Our only hope is to destroy them and their Master.*

*But how?*

*We have an arrangement, Lut and I. But he is not too happy about it.*

*Hana nods her head in agreement. Lutyond is not happy about anything in this turn of the Gyre. I tried to talk to him, but he will not listen. He clings to his humanity like a snail clings to its shell. Hana smiles ruefully. Maybe you can convince him otherwise.*

*Fyn only laughs at this.*

~~~~~~~~~~~~~~

When Gwenn regained consciousness it was to the smell of mouldering damp and the drone of conversation. Someone, whose high piping voice sounded very familiar, was saying, "Hail to you, O Prime God. From the depths of the unknown you have brought my enemy back to me. Now vengeance shall be mine!"

Another voice, darker and more sinister by far, answered in a growl, "Did I not promise you I would? Do you have so little faith in me, Tristan?"

The first voice squeaked, "No, Lord Maggrai. Of... Of course I do. Have faith in you, I mean." Then he whined, "Please don't punish me again."

Gwenn lay in the corner, bound with chains. Although she was now fully awake, she did not move or speak. Her eyes strained in the dim light to catch sight of her brother and the creature she had known as Dawa Tinley. Eventually, she knew they would come and check on her, and in the meantime the longer she could eavesdrop on her brother and Maggrai, the more information she might be able to learn. Silently, she took stock of her situation. The Dawa/

Maggrai creature had somehow managed to transport her to the Citadel. She had no doubt of her location—Gwenn had thoroughly explored her mother's fortress as a child, and knew the lower levels well.

Now Maggrai was saying, "Punish you? I only do what is right and just for my servants. Torment from me is a privilege, do not doubt it. Now down on your knees, like the wriggling worm you are, and be thankful my chastisement is gentle. I could tear the very anafireon from your beating heart, and watch as your quivering body slowly decays to putrefaction without it." Tristan screamed and clutched his head.

"I am sorry, Master. Don't kill me..." Gwenn made a face in the darkness as her brother begged and babbled incoherently.

"But you would not die, little Tristan. I could keep you in agonizing torment forever. Remember that, always." Abruptly Tristan's screams stopped. Maggrai said, "Go and see if your sister has awoken. The shock of the passage through the Mebbain should have worn off by now."

Tristan, in a very small voice, asked, "What are you going to do?"

"To her? Nothing very much," Maggrai said dismissively. "But she is carrying something I want. I am going to take it from her, and then destroy it utterly. You may do whatever you wish with her when I am finished."

"Really?" repeated Tristan happily. "Whatever I want?"

Maggrai stifled a yawn. "So long as it doesn't prevent her death, yes. Now do as I ask, or..."

Tristan scuttled towards the corner. "Yes, My Lord. I hear and obey."

Gwenn kept her eyes closed. She could feel her half-brother's fetid breath on her cheek as he bent close in the darkened corner of the dungeon cell. "She is still sleeping, Maggrai."

"Let us try an experiment, shall we, worm, to test your grasp of the situation?" Maggrai crossed to the table and removed the glass shade from the candle lantern. "Hold up her foot."

Tristan nervously grasped Gwenn's ankle and held it steady. Although he knew the guards had chained her very firmly to the wall he could not help feeling afraid—Gwenn had thrashed him on many occasions when they lived together at the Citadel. But his fear turned to exultant triumph as he watched Maggrai hold the naked flame of the candle against his sister's heel. After a few seconds he felt her leg stiffen and then jerk wildly as she let out a strangled scream.

"Ah yes," said Maggrai softly. "I thought that might be the case. You have been awake for some time, I believe, my dear." He moved the candle away from Gwenn's foot. Tristan stared in fascination at the blistered, blackened flesh on her heel and licked his lips.

"Who are you?" Gwenn answered him angrily as she jerked her foot from Tristan's grasp. "What do you want with me, Hell bat?" She struggled against her chains until she managed to stand, and then glared at Maggrai, eye to eye.

Maggrai turned to Tristan, smiling unctuously. "Do you hear that? Your sister doesn't cower before me, as you do, Tristan. I almost wish I had picked her to assist me instead of a slime-sucking toad like you."

Tristan ground his teeth together angrily, but said nothing. Maggrai was not the first person to compare him to Gwenn and find him lacking.

Maggrai turned his attention back to Gwenn. "I do not want *you*. But there is a small matter I must attend to that concerns you. You are with child, I believe."

"What?" Gwenn interrupted. "I most certainly am not. Let me go."

"Yes, you are, I assure you. Your liaison with the one known as the Seed Bearer has been most fruitful, fortunately. The timing is perfect."

"How do you know I am pregnant?" she asked.

Maggrai smiled evilly. "The embryo possesses a strong anafireon that has created ripples up and down the Gyre, so it was easy for me to find the source. Her name is Myriadne. Once, in a time long distant from now, she and I were enemies. So I have come back to engineer the moment of her genesis, and make sure she will never trouble me in the future.

"How? How can you do that, Master?" Tristan interrupted brightly, eager to show off his special relationship with the Prime God to his sister.

"Silence, worm!" he thundered, and Tristan abruptly clutched his temples once again. Maggrai turned his attention back to Gwenn.

"I have here a little innovation of mine, called an anametronicus. As you can perhaps guess, it discloses the location and strength of anafireon. My servants find it very useful, as they wander the Vastness, searching for corsfyre to harvest." He held up a palm-sized blue globe, which glowed faintly in his clawed hand.

"Corsfyre?" Gwenn repeated, not because she wanted to know anything more, but rather to distract Maggrai. At least if he were talking he wouldn't be doing anything painful to her.

"Do you know of it?" he asked her. When she shook her head he patiently explained. "There is an organ in the human body that some call the *epiphysis cerebri.*ˢ It lies deep in the brain, behind the eyes. For many thousands of years many of your kind worshipped it as the seat of the soul—the third eye of mystical vision—though they did not fully understand its true nature. In later, supposedly more enlightened, times it was thought to be an insignificant gland for the production of small quantities of hormones." He made a dismissive gesture. "Hormones! Hah! The scientists who studied this organ never guessed the truth—the epiphysis is the receptacle for the anafireon, the greatest power source in the universe!"

Gwenn gave him a carefully contrived quizzical look. "But how can you possibly harvest this energy? My mother told me that anafireon is everlastingly guarded by the Uri'el."

He gave her a wicked smile, and she recoiled from the sight of his curving yellow fangs. "It can easily be taken from the Uri'el. They do not defend it." He abruptly grew more businesslike. "But now, my pet, enough of this idle chit chat." After barking an order to Tristan to unchain his sister, Maggrai sauntered back to the center of the room and waited expectantly.

Tristan said in a trembling voice, "Unchain her? But... But what if she tries to escape?"

Maggrai laughed so foully that Gwenn would have covered her ears if she could have moved her hands. Tristan did. "She will not flee. Now that she is conscious I can control her brain as easily as I control yours, worm. When I tell her to walk to the centre of the room she will obey my command. Watch and see."

Tristan moved close to unlock the chains and Gwenn, speaking in a just audible whisper said, "Don't be a slave to that monster, Tris. I will help you escape from him if you let me go." He gave her

* The Pineal Gland

a startled look, and quickly shook his head. As he unlatched the last of the chains he stepped back into the light, and Gwenn saw the look of abject misery on his face. He quickly turned away from both her and Maggrai, and went to stand in the corner.

"Now," Maggrai commanded. "Come closer to me, my sweet."

Gwenn had once been able to countermand the orders of the Goddess Keth Dirane by repeating a special phrase that Arkady had taught her—*Ana Hana shawm tok duna.** Now, as she concentrated hard on these words she felt an inexorable pressure growing in her solar plexus, until she felt she could hardly breathe. But she did not move.

Maggrai, with an annoyed rustle of his leathery wings, shifted back towards her. The pressure increased until Gwenn was gasping for air. "Impressive. But your resistance is futile. I will have the child." She screamed as her head exploded with pain, and she found she could no longer concentrate on the mantra. As soon as she stopped the repetition in her mind she felt her unwilling feet sliding heavily across the floor towards Maggrai. Though she fought this progress with every ounce of her strength, she was no match for the power that controlled her now.

When, at last, she stood before him, he smiled malevolently. "That is better. Now pay attention." Holding up the blue sphere, he passed it in front of her eyes. The anametronicus began to pulse a brighter blue, and emitted a high-pitched whine. "There is your anafireon, my dear." Now Maggrai lowered the sphere, slowly, until it was level with Gwenn's pelvis. As he did so, the pulsations quickened and the hue changed from blue, to green, to yellow and then orange in rapid succession. She looked on as the globe continued to flicker, until it took on a light pink shade. The sound, meanwhile, had continued to rise in pitch until it almost passed the threshold of hearing. Gwenn felt the silent vibrations pulsating in her abdomen and she shivered involuntarily.

*A child... Kadya's daughter and mine. The Dawnmaid.*

Maggrai, meanwhile, tutted in disappointment. "What a pity you blundered on my little passageway! I had planned to leave you in Khalama for several more weeks yet. The child's anafireon is still too diffuse to pinpoint accurately. I cannot destroy her now."

---

* In the language of the people of T'Shang this means "Hana lights my way up to the heavens."

He stroked Gwenn's cheek softly, and she felt her skin crawl. "I am afraid you will have to stay here at the Citadel, as my guest." His fingers slipped moistly down to her throat, and then tightened. "Of course, you will try to escape. I would not expect less of one so courageous."

Gwenn swallowed against the inexorable pressure on her windpipe. "And if I do?"

He smiled. "Then your children and your lover will die. As slowly and painfully as I can contrive it. Do not forget that I have them safely tucked away in Khalama. That fool, Arkady, still believes I am his old teacher, Dawa Tinley. When I return later to tell him you have run away and cannot be traced, he will not question me."

Gwenn dropped her eyes, not wishing to give Maggrai any clue to the information that she and Arkady had already discussed on the mountainside. She said softly, "I give you my word I will not try to escape. Please don't hurt my children." But inside she sent a desperate plea to Hana: "Let them be gone when he returns. Arkady must save Jakob and Arvid..."

"You spend all your time at the Infirmarie these days, Tristan!" Roseberry complained. "How are we supposed to plan a wedding if we never talk to each other?"

They sat on the Tower battlement, sharing an upholstered settle that the pages had dragged outside for them. The sun shone brightly, casting crenellated shadows on the paving below their feet. Tristan patted her hand lovingly. "I am sorry, Berry, but I have a lot of important work to oversee at the moment. The Infirmarie has to be completely gutted and refitted for the new purpose for which I intend it. There must be laboratories, and holding rooms, and..."

He paused, thinking perhaps he had said enough. Lord Maggrai might be angry with him if he gave too much away. But, in truth, there *was* a lot to do. The first ragged bands of Firaithi prisoners were already arriving, escorted by legions of Black Guardsmen. Many more were expected. And down in the Citadel dungeon...

Gwenn was still there. She had kept her word for the last few weeks, and had not tried to escape, though they had, at first, been required to force her to eat. The Master had seen to that. He had said it was important for Gwenn to remain healthy, so that the child would grow strongly inside her. He checked her abdomen every day with the anametronicus. Each day it turned a little darker pink, shading into magenta.

"When it is the color of blood," said Maggrai, "then it will be time to perform the operation."

After a couple of inspections the first week, Tristan had left the guards to their work. He found the sight of his brutally chained sister's obvious suffering far less satisfying than he would have thought possible.

"Tristan!" Roseberry shoved him so hard he almost fell off the settle. "You have not been listening to a word I am saying! I just asked you if we should use the Cathedral or the great hall at the Citadel for the wedding ceremony?"

"Whatever you like, my dear," Tristan murmured and went back to his private contemplation. He remembered that a few days ago he had asked Maggrai what he planned to do when the budding embryo inside Gwenn was ready.

"We will transport your sister to the special room I have constructed in the Infirmarie," he had answered. Tristan knew this room well. It was not actually in the living world at all—but in the Vastness. There were Uri'el scattered about, and though they gave Tristan the creeping horrors, Maggrai blithely ignored them as he went about his business. This room contained something that looked very much like a surgeon's table, with a set of birthing stirrups and many strong leather restraints.

His Master spent a great deal of time there, fiddling with a tank in the corner, adjusting the...

But, no, he would not think about that.

Roseberry's voice brought a welcome end to these deliberations. "So, I was thinking white roses, in huge red vases, with lots of greenery."

Tristan nodded uncertainly, and then wondered what he had just agreed to. Roseberry droned on about their forthcoming wedding and he found his thoughts inexorably drawn back to the room in the Vastness. Maggrai had said that after they had tied Gwenn down to the table he would quickly cut out her womb with a scalpel. The thought of this had made Tristan feel ill, but he bravely asked, "Why do you need to tie her down, Lord? You have already proven that you are able to control her."

"Because the pain may make her pass out and then I could keep her still no longer. Anyway, her agonized screams will be so much more... entertaining, don't you think, little Tristan?" Tristan had nodded his head enthusiastically in agreement, but he wondered secretly if he might arrange to be absent from the whole proceeding. Maggrai continued. "Then I will proceed with the destruction of the child's anafireon. It will produce a great deal of energy—quite enough to flatten the Infirmarie and most of Mount Hythea as well. So, the release must be carefully contained. Once I have the child separated from her mother then I will place her in the special chamber I have built. I will focus the Anafiremad globe upon her anafireon, and then, well—Myriadne will be no more." He rubbed his hands together appreciatively, and the clicking of his claws against one another brought Tristan almost to tears.

Tristan had wondered, unwisely as it turned out, why his Master had not just executed his sister Gwenn when she first arrived in the Citadel dungeon. Would that not have the same effect? A splitting headache had been his reward as Maggrai growled, "No, of course not, you idiot! Just to kill her mother in this life would not be enough! The child would be reborn, again and again. I cannot hunt her down in each of her lifetimes. Therefore I must finish her—now! The Anafiremad will destroy her anafireon utterly, so she can never again return to haunt me in the future." Here, Maggrai's eyes had looked almost fearful.

After his headache subsided, Tristan had asked softly, "Then will your time here be at an end, Lord? Will you return in triumph to your distant Kingdom?"

Maggrai had smiled and stroked Tristan's back with his curving yellow claws. This always made Tristan want to run away or wet his pants, but his legs invariably would not obey him, even if, sometimes, his bladder did. "Nay, little Tristan, for I have much else that concerns me. The cure for a certain... disease, for one thing. And I do not have nearly enough corsfyre collected to make the jump back to the outer pellicula. So I will be here with you for quite some time yet. Does that not please you?" Tristan had unwillingly agreed.

"Why are you nodding? I just said I did not want Jessamine as my matron of honor." Roseberry shook him, and Tristan realized he had been lost in thought yet again.

Standing briskly, he said, "Must run now, Berry. I have to check on a prisoner in the dungeons." He hurriedly left the battlements. As his private guard fell into step behind him, he headed down the endless ramps and staircases to the lowest level of the Citadel, where his sister was imprisoned.

After dismissing the Guard, he called Gwenn's name softly and she slowly turned her head. Blond hair, now almost gray with oil and dirt, hung lankly around her face. Her skin looked as ashen as the moon on a dark night.

"What do you want, Little Shrimp?" she said weakly. "Come to gloat, have you?" She gave him a sickly grin. "Go ahead. I am in no position to stop you."

Tristan watched silently as his sister got up and shuffled across the floor towards him. Her chains clanked and scraped on the filthy stone floor. Prison issue clothing, no more than rags, clung to her emaciated frame. Tristan thought, irrelevantly, that Maggrai must not have had much success in forcing her to eat. He became aware of a moment of swelling pride—at his sister managing to defy the most powerful being he could ever imagine.

Gwenn reached the bars of her cell and asked, "Why don't you come inside, Tris? You have no need to fear me. I can't hurt you, not now." He stood for a moment, uncertain, and then she said, "There is something I would like you to see. Please?" She looked and sounded utterly broken. Tristan found he could not refuse her.

He signaled to the gaoler, who brought forward a huge ring of brass keys. "Open it," Tristan ordered, and waited. Gwenn clanked back over to the bench and sat down heavily. Once inside, Tristan did not approach his sister, but rather stayed close to the iron-barred door that the gaoler had closed and locked behind him. He asked, after she did not speak, "What did you want to show me?" She patted the bench beside her.

"Come and sit here. You cannot see it from the door." He hesitated momentarily, thinking surely this must be some ploy on her part—some trick...

*She will make a grab for me, hold me hostage, force the gaoler to open the door—and then make her daring escape, with me in tow. We will both be free—free from Maggrai forever!*

Such was his belief in the strength and determination of his sister.

He went and sat down at her side, hoping all the while.

She did nothing, except stare blankly at the thickly mildewed stone wall opposite the bench.

When a minute had passed in silence he said in dismay, "Come on, Gwenn. Are you not going to do something? Take me prisoner? Storm the door?"

"I cannot, Tris. I just don't have the strength any more." She sighed. "I just wanted you to read what is written on the wall over there. See? Scratched into the rock? I found the carving a few days ago but I had to scrape away a lot of black mold to read all of it."

Tristan got up and knelt by the stones, trying to fight back his disappointed tears. After a moment, he swore in frustration and called for a light. Gwenn's eyes were obviously more used to the dimness of the cell.

The gaoler brought in a lantern, and hastily left again after an irritated command from his King. Tristan held the light close to the wall, and squinted. There *were* words there—and he could just read them.

*Bee of gud cher, whoe'er fynds humself heer.*
*If curage you lac, then neds must fynd it on the rac.*
*With spirt un braken, yor comrads name unspokn.*
*Frend Deth wil singe depe and yu shalt hav slepe.*
*Slepe o brav warior, slepe.*

"Do you see, Tristan?" Gwenn called softly to him. "Do you see who wrote those words?"

Tristan did see—after he had angrily dashed the tears from his eyes. Underneath the scrawled words, the name was barely visible in the crumbling stone—Jacq Benet, Dinrhydan. His almost illiterate father had etched the poem on the wall when he had been imprisoned in the Citadel for spying.

He whirled to face his sister. "Why did you show me this, Gwenn? Just to remind me that he always loved you best?"

She slowly shook her head. "He was your father, Tris, not mine. And he was locked in this cell, a prisoner of *my* father, Tomas de Vigny. But don't you understand? Even though he faced torture and death, Papa still took the time to scratch those words on the wall to hearten the other prisoners he knew would follow after him. He was the Dinrhydan—the True Heart. You are his son. Can you not find in yourself some of his strength and courage? Truly it is there if you but search for it."

Gwenn rose slowly and hobbled towards him, and he saw for the first time the terrible bleeding ulcers that the iron shackles had rubbed into her ankles. She stepped closer and took his hand in hers. Her nails were black and crusted, but whether from dirt or blood, Tristan did not know. Although she still stood several inches taller than he, at that moment she looked so frail he wanted to put his arms about her and protect her from all harm. She must have sensed this for she whispered, "It is too late for me now, little brother, but you... you can still escape from this nightmare. Tell him you need to visit some far-flung corner of your kingdom. Then run. As far away as you can."

He sighed. "I cannot. I am the king of this godsforsaken country, remember? Anyway, in two weeks I am getting married."

Gwenn looked shocked at this. "At your age? Who to?"

"Roseberry Abelard."

"*Cousin* Roseberry? Is that even legal?"

Tristan shrugged. "It is now. I changed the law. I just told you—I am the king. Anyway, Maggrai..."

Gwen spat, "Do not utter his name. He is a demon. I have a lifetime of experience with them, so I should know. And he is far, far worse than Ketha ever was."

Her brother gave her a piercing glance. "But you defied her. You learned how. You even defied him—for a little while." He clutched at her arm in desperation. "Can you teach me?"

Gwenn gazed at him pensively. "Yes... I suppose I could try. But it takes time, and a lot of practice."

"I *will* practice, I swear it."

"All right," Gwen said softly, "then come and sit." She tried to demonstrate the correct position, but her shackles prevented her. Patiently she explained the methods that Arkady had taught her in Celeste long ago. She gave her brother a sad smile. "I had better tell you everything now. Who knows whether we will be able to have another lesson? So listen, and listen well. You need a mantra. Mine is *Ana Hana shawm tok duna*. It means 'Hana lights my way to heavens.' It is a very powerful tool. Now, let me see... What should yours be?"

Tristan smirked. "How about, 'King Tristan the Magnificent rules over all.'"

Gwenn gave him an exasperated look. "You have to be serious, or I won't tell you anything else."

"All right," he said contritely. "What should it be?"

"*Fess Tun Me Doha.*"

"What does that mean?"

Gwenn grinned. "I am an idiot."

"Gwenn!" Tristan said reproachfully. "You said I had to be serious."

She giggled like a young girl and then waved her hands about, though her shackles made the motion difficult. "All right! All right! It means, 'Freedom lies within.' Now repeat it after me until you have learned it off by heart."

As he said the words, following along with his sister, a little seed of hope started growing in his heart. Not to be free of Maggrai's influence altogether, but rather to use it—as he wished—to dominate the whole of Yr.

# 9

## Missad Quondam

You have returned, Lut. *Hana smiles at him, but he only frowns at her.*

She is in grave danger, I tell you. It is wicked for you to use her in this way.

Wicked for us, you mean? You are one of the Amaranthine. Why will you not accept it?

*He shakes his head firmly.* I am human. That is all I want to be.

*Hana shakes hers, just as firmly.* We need your strength, Mariner.

~~~~~~~~~~

When Katkin opened her eyes, the first thing she saw was a face. It hovered only a few inches above her own, filling her visual field with a blurry apparition surrounded by a halo of dark hair. Almost immediately it disappeared, and she heard footsteps clattering away across the wooden floorboards.

Poppy's voice drifted back down the hallway to her. "Patre! Come quickly. Patre Huw, her eyes are open." Katkin stayed very still, and wondered how it was she now lay in her bed at Brunner's house, instead of wherever she had landed when the bear chased her off a cliff. Soon, she gave up, frustrated. There was only a cold blankness in her mind and any attempts to penetrate it brought searing pain.

Huw hurried through the door and knelt beside the bed. Slowly, she moved her eyes to look at his face, and saw mingled fear and hope there. She wondered to herself if she was badly hurt. Experimentally, she wiggled her fingers and toes, as Huw asked her, "Katkin? Can you hear me?"

She did not know, at first, if she could answer. Her tongue felt gluey and stiff, and her brain seemed to have trouble forming the necessary words. Katkin tried instead to nod her head, and quickly closed her eyes as a wave of pain and nausea flooded over her. Concentrating hard now, she managed a hoarse, "Yes. I can."

He gave a cry of relief, and then put a hand over his mouth to stifle the sobs that immediately followed. Katkin's eyes opened again, and slowly, carefully, she slipped her arm out from under the covers and touched his hair. It was unbound, and quite unkempt. She said, "How badly am I hurt? Tell me the truth, Huw."

Huw struggled with his breathing before he could answer. "I... I do not know, Katkin. I have no medical training. You hit your head when you fell, and there was blood. So much blood..." He could not continue, and Katkin wondered if he might be lying, so as not to frighten her. But still, after a few more careful experimental twitches, she found she could move all her limbs, and she relaxed slightly. Her hand left his hair and traveled slowly to her own head, and she patted over it carefully to find the wound. Someone had wrapped a bandage tightly across her forehead.

She whispered, "Could I have something to drink, please?" He looked up quickly, and nodded, and Katkin saw, as her vision cleared, that Huw was now much thinner than he had been the day before yesterday when she set off to hunt for an offering to the eagles. His face was positively gaunt, and a scraggly black and gray beard covered his cheeks and chin. Something did not seem right about this picture, and Katkin tried to figure out what it was. Her mind did not seem to be able to process the necessary information, so she stopped trying.

He returned in a moment with a cup of water, and held her head carefully as she took a few sips. The coldness of the drink felt good going down, and helped to rouse her a little more. The question returned, about the beard, and once again she tried to connect it with her present situation. Huw had dragged a chair over to the side of her bed, and now sat silently, with his hands in his lap. Katkin said to him, "I want to sit up a little bit."

He stood and found another pillow, then tucked it under her head as she struggled to lift it. Once she was comfortable he sat again, saying nothing. Katkin wanted to ask about his face and the gauntness, but she did not know how she could frame the question. Instead, she enquired, "How did I get here?"

Huw sighed. "I was working outside when Varg came back to the house in the afternoon. I could see right away he was badly hurt. Half the skin was torn off his face, and he was very weak." His voice dropped to a ragged whisper. "I was so afraid for you. Ach, Katkin..." Katkin waited silently as Huw struggled again with his tears. When he was able, he continued, "I got Poppy up on Ajax and put Gwillam in his sling carrier and followed Varg as he limped back up the valley. It was obvious he was close to death, and I prayed to the Un-Named One he would lead us to you before he collapsed. He tried very hard, but he did not make it to the head of the valley."

"Varg is dead?" Katkin whispered, and Huw nodded his head. She closed her eyes, grieving for the dog whose courageous attack on the bear had probably saved her life. "What did you do then? How did you find me?"

"The sun was already low in the sky and I knew I could not stay out overnight, not with Poppy and Gwillam. I decided to come back to the house, and leave them behind, while I went on searching for you."

Katkin looked at him in shock. "Huw! What were you thinking? You should not have done that. What if something had happened to you?"

He shook his head. "I was not thinking—by then I was out of my mind with worry. I only knew I had to find you before the next snows came, and they were coming very soon. As I turned Ajax around, he snorted and reared, and Poppy had to hang on for dear life. There was a huge eagle on the path, looking at us, and waiting. I realized somehow that he had come to help, though he spoke no words to me. He took off and flew before us and I followed him, as best I could, until we reached the place you had killed the deer. While he attacked the carcass with his beak, I searched for you, and after an hour I came to the place you had fallen. By then it was almost completely dark. With Poppy's help I got you up on Ajax, and we came back here." He fell silent and looked down at his hands.

Katkin wondered what she should say now, since a simple apology seemed so inadequate for all the trouble she had caused. Another question came to mind, and she asked that instead. "How long ago was that, Huw?"

He met her eyes with his own and she could see only wretched misery behind them. "Two weeks, I think. Yes, that is right. Fourteen—no, fifteen days ago."

"Fifteen days? Is that what you said?" she whispered, and he nodded forlornly. The scope of the necessary apology was growing larger by the moment. She decided she had to try. "Huw, I know I should not have left like that. I am sorry... truly, truly sorry, for what happened. Can you forgive me?"

He did not look at her. "Of course, Katkin. It doesn't matter, as long as you are all right now." His voice was flat and almost expressionless. She could not help thinking somehow it did matter, very much, and her apology had done nothing at all towards making it right.

Poppy stuck her head through the door. "Patre, the potatoes are ready and Gwillam wants his supper. Shall I feed it to him?" Huw stood, wearily, and looked down at Katkin.

"Do you think you could eat something? I will mash some potato up with milk, as we do for Gwillam."

Katkin smiled and nodded as he turned away from her, but Huw did not smile back. He left the room with Poppy, saying only he would return in a few minutes after he had given Gwillam his dinner. But it was Poppy who came back bearing a cup full of mashed potato. She said stiffly, "Patre asked me to bring this to you. Can you eat it yourself?" Katkin slowly pushed her way up into a sitting position, and then held out her hand for the cup. Poppy passed it over without speaking further and turned to go.

"Poppy, will you sit with me while I eat? I would like some company." The little girl sat down primly on the edge of the chair, but did not speak. Katkin gazed at her and sighed. Her clothes were dirty and her hair unbraided. It was obvious, by the streaks left on her grimy face, that she had recently been crying. As Katkin took tiny bites of the potato she wondered what she could say to reassure her. "I know the last two weeks have been hard for you, but soon I will be well, and then everything will be all right."

Poppy's vehemence stunned her. "No it won't! You are a mean lady and I hate you!"

Katkin said quickly, "Poppy, I am sorry about what happened, truly I am. I know you must have been frightened, but you mustn't say you hate me for it."

"I *was not* frightened! That isn't it at all."

"Why then? What have I done to make you hate me?"

Poppy stared at her and said angrily, "You made my Patre cry. Lots of times."

Katkin looked horrified at this. "I did not mean to, Poppy. You must know that. My falling down was an accident. I got chased by a bear."

Poppy shook her head crossly. "Before you hit your head, stupid. When he got up in the morning and found the note you left on the table. He cried then, practically all day. I tried and tried to make him feel better, but he kept saying he had seen a note like that before. It was cruel, what you did. He loves us all very much—even you. But you don't love us." She stood and walked away from the bed, then turned back to say, "I will never ever forgive you, I don't care how many times you say sorry."

Katkin begged, "Poppy, don't go... Let me explain." But the girl ran from her, back to the warmth of the kitchen and her Patre. Katkin lay in bed, as the room grew darker and darker, wondering what Cara had written in the note *she* had left for Huw. It dawned on her that the girl, in an effort to delay his pursuit, probably would have written much the same things as Katkin had herself—reassuring him that she would be back soon and he mustn't worry about her.

After a time, she sat fully up in bed, and carefully swung her legs over the side. The pain in her head had eased a little, and Katkin wanted very much to join the others in the kitchen. She stood up very slowly, found she could keep her balance, and then shuffled down the hallway towards the water closet. After she had relieved herself, she continued to the kitchen but stopped just in the doorway, listening to Poppy's happy chatter and Gwillam's baby talk.

Huw stood up immediately when he caught sight of her. "You should not be out of bed. Tell me what you need and I will fetch it for you."

Katkin gave him a smile. "I don't need anything, Huw, except company. I just want to stay with you and Poppy and Gwillam for a little while."

"Of course," he said listlessly. "Come and sit here then, and I will make you some tea." Poppy sullenly cleared a space on the settle next to the fire and Katkin sank into it appreciatively. When she said "Thank-you," Poppy ignored her and spoke instead to Huw.

"Gwillam needs his wrapping changed. Shall I do it, Patre?"

He nodded vaguely, and Poppy carefully took her brother from his feeding chair. Once she left the room, Huw said, "Poppy has been a treasure from the Un-Named One. I could not have coped without her."

Katkin patted the seat beside her as Huw brought a steaming mug of tea and placed it on the table. Once he sat down, she took his hand and held it for many moments without speaking. Finally she sighed and said, "I should not have left you alone with Poppy and Gwillam. It was very wrong of me. I don't expect you to forgive me, not right away. I just wanted you to know that I never meant to hurt you, not like that."

He stared straight ahead, and pretended not to know what she meant. "Like what?"

"Like she did, Huw. I never thought how my note would make you feel. I am sorry, more sorry than I can say."

"I already said I forgave you," he said dully.

"I know what you said," she replied. "And I also know you don't mean it. But I will make it up to you and Poppy, I swear it." She squeezed his hand tightly and then brought it to her lips. Huw only sighed.

It was many more days before Katkin felt completely recovered. She spent a great deal of time in bed, alone, for Huw slept now in the spare room, though it was the one in which he had been tortured. Poppy rarely spoke to her, and Katkin found her only solace was the company of the baby, Gwillam, who seemed happy to lie on the bed with her for hours, as long as she gave him his toys to play with. Katkin assumed that once she was well again, things in the Brunner house would gradually return to normal. Indeed she soon had the place clean and tidy again, and the children's clothes washed and mended. But though she tried to cook Huw's favorite dishes to tempt his appetite, he continued to eat only sparingly. Several times she found him in the barn, sitting silently, staring into space, after she had sent him on some errand. Other times he wept, for no reason she could fathom. Whenever he did this, Poppy would look at Katkin accusingly, as if she was still somehow to blame for Huw's persistent unhappiness. Though Katkin begged him many times to tell her what troubled him, he would only shrug and walk away.

One day, as the snow fell thick and heavy, she sought him out in the barn. She found him sleeping on a pile of hay. Katkin shook him roughly. "Wake up, Huw! I sent you out here to feed Bessie and Ajax before the storm started. Why are you napping?"

He stood, sighing, and walked over to the hay rick, then placed a few lackadaisical forkfuls in front of each animal. Katkin watched with mounting impatience. "Don't you think they will need more fodder than that?"

"I don't know."

Huw's apathy was the most worrying aspect of the mysterious complaint that now gripped him. Whenever Katkin asked him a question, he almost always answered in the same way—*I don't know*. His apparent inability to make even the simplest of decisions bothered her much more than his previously intractable stubbornness. Now, in the barn, she seized his shoulder and forced him to look at her.

"Tell me what is wrong, Huw. It has been almost two months since my accident. Why can't you let it go?"

He shrugged. "I don't know."

Katkin gave a cry of annoyance, and shook him again. She shouted at him. "Don't say you don't know. Tell me the truth."

Though he threw off her hand, his voice did not rise. "I said I don't know. That is the truth."

"What on Yrth is the matter with you? Why will you not say? You don't eat, you don't sleep in our bed. You won't even talk to me. It is like living with a ghost."

He stared at the floor, but Katkin could still see the tears welling up in his eyes. He repeated, his voice a whisper, "I don't know what is wrong with me, but it has happened before. It begins in the winter, when the days are short. Not every year, just sometimes. I fight against it, I swear I do, but it is like a wolf stalking me, and I get so tired..." He raised his dark eyes to look at her face. "It started when we came here, and I tried so hard. But then you got hurt and I could not keep going. I wanted to die, Katkin. Only Poppy stopped me."

She gazed at him in surprise, then took his hand and led him back to the hay bale. They sat side by side. Katkin said, "Why did you not tell me all this before? I could have helped you."

"How? It is my own weakness that makes me behave so. My failing..."

She shook her head firmly. "That is not true. Melancholia is an ailment of the brain. You can treat it with herbs, like Goat's Weed. I am going to make you some tea, right now, and I want you to drink it all."

Huw's expression was wary. "What is this tea? Some kind of soporific?"

"I suppose so..." Katkin said, thoughtfully. "But it has been used for hundreds of years and it is very safe. It takes a long while to work, so you must be patient, and try to have faith."

"I won't take it," he said, with surprising firmness.

"What? Why not? I just told you..."

"It is of the lilies of the field," he continued. "It is forbidden by the Kyan*."

"Huw, listen to me," Katkin pleaded, but he walked away from her, with his head down and hands raised in defiance.

She shouted to his retreating back, "You are a stubborn fool, Huw Adaryi!"

He would not argue with her about it. Every overture was met with the same cryptic reply about the lilies of the field. Several days passed in which Huw's condition continued to worsen. Matters forced Katkin to do something she was loath to—confide in Poppy.

"So, Patre isn't well, do you see, Poppy? I need your help to get him to take the medicine he needs to get better. Can you do that?"

Poppy looked at her seriously and nodded. "I *will* help you, for

* Elders of the Firaithi

112

Patre's sake. Even though you are still a mean lady," she could not help adding. Katkin smiled and shook her head, thinking it did not matter what the girl thought of her as long as she was willing to help Huw recover.

They decided on a two-pronged approach. Poppy would make the tea twice a day, from the supply of dried herbs in Elsa's botanical cupboard. When she first brought the steaming mug to her Patre, he sniffed it suspiciously, but drank it down at her urging. He asked her on several occasions what was in the tea, and Poppy was resourcefully coy with her replies. She was, Katkin thought with grudging admiration, the most self-assured five-year-old on the face of the Yrth.

Katkin's own job was a little more difficult.

One day Huw found her in Jakob's old workshop, measuring pieces of wood.

"What are you doing?" he asked her, without much interest.

"I am going to make myself a vielle," she replied. "The house is too quiet these days. We need some music, and you never play your flute anymore." Huw expressed astonishment that she might try to make such a complicated instrument from scratch without any woodworking experience and only one hand. Katkin smiled and said, "I will just muddle through somehow, I expect."

He watched as she cut up the thin planks, and then wandered away again. Katkin sighed and kept working. Within a few days she had constructed a rough-looking box. Huw came back now and again to observe her, and bit by bit began to offer advice and instruction. After a week, he took the tiny saw that she had been using away from her, and carefully cut the first of the keyholes. Katkin backed away from the bench, and quietly left the barn. When he presented the finished instrument to her, in another week, Huw had begun eating again. That night, after they gave Poppy and Gwillam a rousing concert and saw them off to sleep, he stood uncertainly at the door of the bedroom as Katkin undressed.

She looked at him and smiled. "Come to bed, Huw. What are you waiting for?"

"I don't know," he said, and then gave a shout of laughter and ducked for cover as she threw a pillow at his head.

Huw had been on three more hunting trips for the eagles by the time the weather warmed up slightly. It remained below freezing at night, but now, during the daylight hours, the sounds of dripping and running water could be heard everywhere outside. Brunner's Valley was beginning its spring thaw. Though a lovely green mist seemed to cling to the trees and daffodil and crocus flowers peeked from the beds by the house, Huw did not view the changing season with much enthusiasm. He watched the farm track with anxiety, knowing that the Black Guard could invade their safe haven at any moment once the high drifts that blocked the entrance to the valley melted away.

One spring day, after he had returned from riding Ajax down the farm track, he announced, "The path is clear almost right to the main road. We should be making preparations to depart."

But although Katkin had once been concerned about spending the winter in Brunner's Valley, she had quickly grown to love the snug farmhouse that once belonged to Jakob and Elsa. She found the thought of taking to the road again profoundly depressing, especially with two small children in tow.

"The eagles are watching for us, Huw. Can we not just stay here a while longer? Maybe the Black Guard won't come back this way again."

He gazed at her quizzically. "I thought you wanted to go to Bryn Mirain and meet up with the Anandi and Gitashaen?"

She nodded unenthusiastically. "Well I do, but not just yet. Let us wait until the weather warms up before we leave. That way we won't have to worry so much about Poppy and Gwillam."

He had reluctantly agreed to this, and so they spent most of the spring in Brunner's Valley. Nevertheless, as the days grew increasingly warm and fine, Huw started worrying about the Black Guard again. Now, after the children slept, he and Katkin argued frequently over when they should leave for Bryn Mirain.

As they sat down to breakfast one morning, Huw gave Katkin a meaningful look and said to Poppy, "Soon, my little flower, we are going on a big journey. You and Gwillam will ride on Ajax, and we will travel south, to where it is always warm, and visit a very special place in the mountains."

Poppy looked at him hopefully. "Is Katkin coming too?"

He smiled at her. "Of course, Poppy. How can we go without her? I cannot cook nearly as well as she can."

"Oh," said Poppy, sounding disappointed. Katkin sighed and

handed the girl some toasted black bread. Poppy dipped it into a cup of milk and took a bite, and then her eyes went wide. She pointed and said, "Look, Patre! At the window. What a funny big bird!"

Huw whirled around and saw the eagle sitting on the sill outside. The bird tapped on the thick glass three times, and slowly flapped away. Huw and Katkin looked at each other in alarm. "Get Poppy and Gwillam and go down to the bolt hole," he barked. "I will stop them if I can." Already he was groping for his knife.

Katkin stood firm. "Don't be a damned fool, Huw Adaryi. *You* take Poppy and go down there. I can talk to them, and maybe convince them we belong here. They will not know who I am, but if they see you they will have no doubts we have been squatting." Huw wrung his hands for moment, unwilling to concede she was right.

"Are the Black Men coming? The bad ones who killed my other Patre and Ma?" Poppy began to cry and grasped Huw's hand, pulling him towards the door. "Let's go. Do as she says, Patre, please."

"Go on, Huw! Quickly now! We don't know how soon they will be here."

Huw picked up Poppy and ran for the barn as Katkin hurriedly tucked her long chestnut hair up into her scarf. She cleared the table and stacked the dirty dishes in the sink, all the while willing herself to stay calm. After five minutes she heard the horses, and went to the window. Three riders approached the house and dismounted in the muddy yard. It was only then that Katkin remembered that the intruders would most likely speak Secunian, and she did not—not without Lalluna's help anyway. As she bent to pick up Gwillam, arranging him so that his blanket draped over her artificial hand, she prayed, "Lalluna, please give me their tongue. I know you are still angry about Dai, but I need you now."

The heavily armed men, dressed all in black, were crossing towards the house. Katkin felt a rising dread, for Lalluna still seemed cold and dead inside her. "Please, my Goddess. Even if you will not do it for me you must not let Huw and the children be hurt." There was no response and Katkin grew angry, saying fervently, "I gave up my arm for you! Willingly, I did everything you asked of me. Is this how the Amaranthine repay the trust of the humans they use?" Katkin made a sound of disgust. "Dai was right about you."

The knock on the door made her jump. She took a deep breath and forced herself to open it. Three uniformed men stood before her. One spoke. She stared at him stupidly, understanding, at first, very little of what he said. Suddenly the words resolved themselves, as the familiar fluttering filled her chest.

"...looking for Bertram Barthonolay. Where is he?"

Katkin cleared her throat, and prayed the words would come. They did. "He ain't here, Master. Only me and the baby."

He gave her a suspicious look. "You his wife? I didn't know he was married. Where are Jari and Mick then?"

Katkin stared down at the ground. "We ain't been married long. Only since he took over this place. The other two men left late last year—didn't like the hard work. But me and Bert been taking good care of the farm, honest. He's up in the north paddock now, clearing some fallen trees. It's mighty muddy. Are you sure you want to go find him up there? Bert took dinner, said he'd be gone all day. Why don't you come back this evening? She peered up at the man, hoping he would decide to return later in the day. By then, she, Huw and the children would be long gone. But she watched helplessly as he pushed past her into the kitchen, and the others followed, tracking in quantities of mud across the kitchen floor.

"Make us some tea, wench. We'll wait a while."

Katkin filled the kettle and put it on the hob to boil. Then she said, very casually, "I'll just pop out to the barn and get some fresh milk. Won't be a minute." She strolled nonchalantly from the room, out the kitchen door, still clutching the baby tightly. Her heart sank as the leader barked to one of the others, "Go with her. See that she doesn't try anything funny."

She crossed the yard, desperately wondering what she might do now. Abruptly she said, "Goodness me, I've forgotten the pail. Go back into the kitchen and get it for me, would you? It's by the back door." The soldier nodded agreeably, and turned around. Katkin continued to walk towards the barn, slowly, as if she had all the time in the world. Once she passed into the shadows of the door she hissed, "Huw, Poppy? Hide yourselves."

The soldier came back almost at once, cheerfully swinging the pail. Katkin immediately turned her back on him, and placed Gwillam carefully down on the hay. He gurgled happily and waved his feet in front of his face. Keeping her artificial hand well out of sight she found the milking stool and sat down before Bessie. Normally Poppy milked the cow, as part of her regular chores, and Katkin was not at all sure she could do it now, with only one hand. The soldier came up behind her, and bent down. His hand came around to dig into the front of her blouse, fondling her breast. "Don't bother about that old cow. I would rather have some of this milk anyway, darlin'." She stood quickly, knocking over the stool, and backed away from him.

"Don't you dare touch me, brute!" she said furiously.

He snarled and reached for her. Katkin swung her artificial arm and caught him on the side of the head. The metal and wood hand flew off in the impact, as the soldier crashed to the floor of the barn. He rubbed his bruised temple and made to rise, growling, "Oh, you will pay dearly for that, whore. You can't fight all three of us. We'll all have you now, as many times as we want." Katkin gave a cry of relief as Huw dived from the shadows and slashed his knife deeply across the man's throat, before he could shout for help.

"You need to go," he hissed at her. Get Poppy and Gwillam and ride hard up the valley on Ajax. I will stop the other two from following."

Katkin shook her head in horror. She could see by his desperate expression that he meant to die in their defense. "I won't leave you! We will fight them together." She looked around the gloomy barn wildly. "Where is Poppy?"

"Hiding in the bolt hole," he said. "Fetch her and go, Katkin. You cannot help me now. The children have to come first." He took her hand and kissed it, then met her eyes. "Farewell, Queen of my heart."

Huw snatched his hand from hers as a voice rang out from the yard. "Brug? What are you up to in there?" Then laughter as he added, "Save some of that milk for me, you old goat!"

# 10

## Wanmoon + Zephur + Prox

*Fyn appears.* It is time, cousin. But take care. Maggrai is a dangerous beast when cornered.

So am I, *Lutyond growls.*

~~~~~~~~~~

Tristan returned to see Gwenn, to tell her about his increasing success with the practice of meditation. She sat morosely while he talked of that and his wedding, which had taken place two days beforehand. Then he whispered, with totally unexpected altruism, "I am going to take Berry on a honeymoon to the south of Beaumarais, by Lake Lisane. If I can manage it, I will help you get away before I go."

Gwenn's eyes brightened at this. "Do you mean it, Tris?"

He shrugged. "I said I will try. No promises though. I can't endanger myself, you understand. The country depends on me," he added grandly.

Gwenn thought this sounded more like the Tristan she knew, but still she asked, "You are going to escape as well, aren't you?"

He shook his head.

She gazed at him in confusion. "I thought you wanted to be free of Maggrai?"

Her little brother stroked his smooth chin pensively. "I do. It is just..." Abruptly he stopped talking and massaged his forehead as though it pained him. Then he said tersely, "We can't talk about it any more. Not right now."

Gwenn could hear the gaoler's panicked voice. "He's on his way down here now. Clear out, you lot. Gorr! That slitherin' black beastie makes my skin want to crawl clean off. Come on now, to the guard room. We'll come back when he's gone a'gin."

The drumbeat of many hurrying feet covered the sound of Maggrai's soft footfalls as he approached the cell door.

"Well, well. Having a nice family gathering, are we?" Maggrai asked with mock geniality. He stepped carefully through the narrow door, with his wings tucked close to his body. Tristan could see the anametronicus glowing in his cupped palm as he approached.

Maggrai shoved Tristan out of the way so that he could stand before Gwenn. He gave her an ugly, yellow-fanged grin. "It is time for our little visit, my dear. I know how you look forward to it all day." He tutted facetiously. "I hear from that sniveling gaoler that you have been vomiting up your meals in the corner again. That simply won't do, you know."

"I already told you that you could not make me eat. Anyway, the putrid food they serve down here would gag even a loathsome carrion-eating buzzard like you, Maggrai."

Maggrai raised his hand to strike Gwenn for her impertinence and Tristan only just restrained himself from coming to her aid. Instead, he interjected brightly, "Have you come to measure the anafireon, Master? How much longer do you think it will be until it is ready?"

But his clumsy attempt at distraction was fruitless. Gwenn took the blow without flinching, even though Maggrai's claws left three narrow strips of oozing flesh on her cheek. Tristan felt so proud of his sister. Why could he not summon the courage to defy his Master the way she did? Now he watched in trepidation as Maggrai slowly lowered the glowing blue ball towards their prisoner's slightly swollen belly. The color changed rapidly as the sound increased—blue, green, yellow, orange, pink—and then...

*Red.*

As red as the blood that now seeped from the cuts on Gwenn's face.

"No..." she whispered. "It can't be. Not now..."

Maggrai laughed in delight as he rapidly clicked his claws together. "It is time!" He turned to Tristan, who only just managed to conceal his horrified expression. "Go and prepare my sanctuary! Make sure everything is ready. I will bring her momentarily." Tristan stood still, blinking stupidly, and listened to the sound of his sister's broken sobbing.

"Master," he ventured. "Are you absolutely..."

Maggrai roared. "Go! Get out of my sight, worm." Tristan

howled as the all-too-familiar headache seized him, and ran from the cell.

He had paralyzed her again and placed her against one wall of the secret Vastness space he called his sanctuary. Though her muscles were as useless as limp hanks of string, Gwenn studied her new surroundings carefully as Maggrai bustled about the room. The sturdy-looking metal table in the centre loomed menacingly in her field of vision, so Gwenn resolutely ignored it.

Maggrai was putting surgical instruments on a white enamel tray, and counting them off as he went. "Scalpel, clamps, retractor, forceps..." Gwenn also tried hard not to listen to this gruesome inventory, though she knew full well that he intended to use all these instruments on *her*—without any ether. She swallowed thickly as bile rose to the back of her throat and prayed—*Please Hana, let it be quick—my end. Please...*

She gazed instead at the seated Uri'el crowding the room. Each one cradled the lifeless body of some poor soul who had died in the Infirmarie. The Uri'el's smooth, blank faces gave her no encouragement and so she allowed her eyes to wander over to the corner, where a glowing tank of some foul-looking liquid lay. A stream of bubbles rose from the murky depths, so that the turbid water moiled constantly about. An occasional flash of something dark passed close to the crystal wall of the tank, and Gwenn wondered if there was some unhappy aquatic creature trapped within. Close by the tank yet another Uri'el sat silently—only this one's lap was forlornly empty. And instead of the usual blank whiteness it had normal features on its face. Its expression spoke eloquently of its utter loneliness and despair. Gwenn quickly looked away.

Just then, Maggrai said testily, "Where is that boy? He should be here by now!"

Tristan hadn't been here when they arrived, and Gwenn could only hope that he had indeed escaped as she had urged him to. Maybe he would bring help? She discarded this optimistic thought almost immediately. If Tristan had run, it would be only to save his own skin.

A few moments later he arrived, out of breath, and rubbing his temples as though his head pained him. He began a fawning display over his Master that made Gwenn almost physically ill. It seemed his resolution to assist her had been lost somewhere along the way to Maggrai's sanctuary in the Vastness. Now, as Maggrai berated him, he cowered in submission like a terrified cur.

She felt her will crumbling to dust. Was there any point in fighting against despair? Nothing could help her now, or the child. They were both trapped in the Vastness with a madman who desired their total annihilation.

When it seemed all was lost a shaft of light flickered, from somewhere deep in her memory's darkest grove—dimly at first, then suddenly sharp and focused. A conversation she had once had with her stepfather returned, as clearly as if he stood before her now. She must have been about eight years old at the time. Jacq, huge and impossibly brawny in her young eyes, had been hammering horseshoes into shape with a sledgehammer that she could not even lift off the ground. But though his back and bulging arms dripped with sweat, a gentle gap-toothed smile lit his face as she waited next to him with the tongs.

Gwenn heard her own childish voice ask, "Papa Bear? Did they hurt you very much in prison?"

Jacq stopped the regular motion of the sledgehammer and wiped his face with the red-checked scarf he always wore about his neck. He looked at her with concern. "Who told you about that, Goldilocks?"

"I heard some of the guardsmen talking about it last week in the mess hall. They said you were a prisoner for five days, and that a bad man named Captain de Vigny tortured you until you almost died. Is it true?"

Jacq closed his eyes and Gwenn got the impression that he had traveled somewhere very far away without her. She tugged at the leather apron he wore and he flinched as though she had burned him. "Well, is it?" she asked again.

He sighed and put down the hammer, then took her hand and led her outside to the parade field, where a stone bench stood close to a cistern filled with drinking water. After taking a long draught of water he sat down on the bench and she sat beside him, swinging her legs back and forth in the warm summer sunshine.

"I was in prison a long time ago, Goldilocks. But it is true—the men there did hurt me, very much."

Gwenn observed pertly, "You don't have any scars!"

Jacq laughed at this and shook his head. "Well, I was lucky. Your mother and Lalluna healed my body, so that I was as good as new again afterwards."

She studied the thickly corded musculature in her father's shoulders before asking thoughtfully, "Why did you let them hurt you like that?" She could not conceive, then, of any man being able to best her magnificent father, the Dinrhydan.

His face grew somber. "I had to, Goldilocks. I made a promise to some people that I would keep them safe, and I could not go back on it just because I faced torture. Do you understand? There are things that are more important than any pain we might feel. More important even than death." Gwenn stared at him in confusion. Her father had never talked so seriously to her before and it frightened her a little.

She felt her face grow warm, as tears gathered in her eyes and threatened to spill over on to her cheeks. Gwenn grasped her father's massive arm. "Then how did you stop yourself—from telling, I mean? Did you not want to? Just to make the pain end?"

"I did," he replied gravely. "Sometimes I wanted to, very much. Then I would think about the things I loved—the things that mattered to me. I drew strength from them, and courage. Enough courage to fight for what was right. But still it was the hardest thing I had ever done, because I thought, at first, that I had nothing left to fight with. They had taken d'angwir away from me, you see." He gave her a look of frightening intensity. "In the end, I decided that I had to go on fighting anyway—right until the moment I dropped. I would not let them beat me."

Gwenn looked up at him with shining eyes. "You are the bravest and best Papa Bear in the whole world! But what *did* you fight them with, my Papa, if you had lost your sword?"

"My spirit," he answered quietly. "They could never take my spirit from me." He took her small hand in his rough one and squeezed it hard. "Always remember, Goldilocks—a strong spirit is the *only* weapon that anyone ever truly needs."

Returning to the present, Gwenn mentally gave herself a shake. With what weapon could she fight Maggrai? There was only one she could think of, and though it had failed her once before, she decided to try again. She began repeating her mantra, very slowly and quietly, in her mind. Maggrai was still busy, tugging on the leather restraints, muttering to himself. He did not seem to notice that his control over her might be slipping.

*Ana Hana shawm tok duna.*

*Ana Hana shawm tok duna.*

Somehow her father's voice blended with her own:

*Always remember, Goldilocks—a strong spirit is the only weapon that anyone ever truly needs.*

Even Tristan's high-pitched treble joined in:

*Be of good cheer, whoever finds himself here.*

The three phrases melded in her mind into a powerful, drumming rhythm that filled her, somehow, with exultant joy.

Gwenn listened intently to the conversation going on between her brother and Maggrai. Surprisingly, Tristan's transparent flattery seemed to have mollified his Master, and Gwenn wondered if she could somehow use his overweening pride against him. He had not frozen her vocal cords, desiring, he said, to be able to hear her screams when he performed the operation. So she was able to speak now, without fear of giving away her newfound sense of freedom. Meanwhile, in the back of her mind, the mantra that Arkady had taught her bubbled away, filling her with serenity.

"Why did you come here?" she asked, and tried to fill her voice with faux wonder. "Surely my child, Myriadne, was no match for your future strength and cruelty?"

"Indeed she was not," he said proudly. "But such was my fame that I had other enemies to deal with as well, such as the black creatures that came down from the Vortice."

"The Vortice? What on Yrth's that?" Tristan inquired gaily, and Gwenn wondered if he had somehow guessed her intention.

"The centre of the Gyre, idiot." Maggrai replied with a temperamental shake of his wings. "It used to be a passageway to the world beyond, it is said. The astral bodies of the dead traveled upwards with their keepers, the Uri'el. But I wanted the anafireon they possessed, to make corsfyre, so I blocked the shaft. But then the Angellus came down from above. They tried to stop my harvesting operation.

"Truly?" Gwenn asked. "They must have been very great to interfere with an all-powerful creature such as yourself. How did you manage to defend your lands?"

Maggrai shrugged with a leathery rustle of his wings. "My

123

kingdom was in no danger from *them*. They stayed in the Vastness, and fought only with my minions. As long as I had plenty, it did not matter."

"What was your kingdom like—in the future I mean?" Gwenn inquired.

Tristan chimed in with, "Yes, please tell us, Master. Was it very magnificent?"

Maggrai launched into a long-winded description of his total victory over his worthless Amaranthine brothers and sisters; his uncounted numbers of slaves; his abundant stores of corsfyre, and other weapons of destruction; his clever discovery of the anametronicus and the anafiremad.

As this hubris caused him to grow more and more animated, Gwenn felt his control over her body gradually slacken and then, suddenly, cease altogether. Now it took all her will just to remain standing stock-still, in the position in which he had propped her against the wall.

"But what brought you back here to us, Master?" Tristan asked, and actually gave Gwenn a sly smile.

"A mysterious illness was killing off my slaves, one by one. Nothing I tried would stop it. I worried that even I might succumb to it. What could I do?" he asked with a dramatic flourish.

"Come back in time and try to find a cure?" Gwenn suggested eagerly.

Maggrai snapped his fingers. "Exactly! I noticed that a very few of my slaves managed to hold out against the disease longer than others. Their blood afforded them some kind of immunity from infection. So I came back here, to a time when I knew there were more Autochthones. I needed to collect the blood of many healthy specimens."

"What... What are Autochthones?" Tristan asked him.

Maggrai gave a foul laugh. "You should know, little fool. Your Black Guardsmen are rounding them up for me even now!"

"The Firaithi?"

"Enough!" Maggrai said firmly. "I must prepare the ceptaculum. Tristan!"

Tristan jumped as Maggrai ordered, "Make ready to place the subject on the operating table."

*Ana Hana shawm tok duna.*

*Ana Hana shawm tok duna.*

Gwenn's eyes surveyed the room once more... quickly, hopefully—looking for anything she might use as a weapon. The surgical instruments were precisely lined up on the tray, where Maggrai had left them. He had his back to her, fiddling with another piece of equipment on the far side of the room, that he had called a ceptaculum. The blue globe stood in a transparent beaker next to it, glowing poisonously, like some slimy creature from the bottom of the sea, where sunlight is only a dreamy memory. It was the weapon Maggrai would use, Gwenn guessed, for the violent destruction of Myriadne's anafireon.

Over my dead body, Gwenn thought to herself, and then almost smiled. She knew she could not harm Maggrai. He would stop her long before she got anywhere close to him. But she could...

*There are things that are more important than any pain we might feel. More important even—than death.*

Gwenn mentally measured the distance to the scalpel, wondering if she could reach it in time, and then plunge it into her own abdomen, to kill Myriadne instantly. Tristan would not stand in her way, she felt sure. He might even help her, if it did not endanger his own cowardly skin. Slowly, so slowly, she moved towards the table, closing the gap as silently as a wraith. Maggrai still had his back turned to her, and she was able to edge about a foot closer before he turned around again. She froze. He searched briefly for something and then went back to his adjustments.

A flash of white and the iridescent shiver of wings caught her eye. The unusual Uri'el she had seen earlier—the one whose lap had been empty—now glided towards the tank in the corner of Maggrai's sanctuary. Gwenn watched in fascination as it pressed itself bodily against the side of the vessel, and scratched at the crystal with its alabaster hand. Silently, it circled the glowing tank again and again, tapping and stroking the crystal that separated it from whatever was inside. A thing it seemed desperately in need of. What could it be? Just as Gwenn resumed her inching progress towards the instrument tray, an agony-ridden face pressed briefly against the inside of the glass tank, and looked straight at her. The bleak, uncomprehending terror of its expression immediately robbed her of all her newfound determination.

"Dawa?" Gwenn whispered in horror.

Maggrai chortled from across the room. "So you have seen my little pet in the vivarium, have you? Yes, it *was* Dawa you saw, my lovely. I killed him, shortly after you arrived in Khalama and then placed his astarene in that tank, so it could not cross into the Vastness. A clever invention of mine, if I do say so myself. Quite painful for him, unfortunately, because the astarene decays rather quickly without the anafireon to sustain it. But never mind, it was all for a good cause. I needed to borrow his physical body, you see, so that I could keep an eye on you and that slovenly mate of yours, Grumar... Was that his name?"

Gwenn did not bother to reply to this provocation—she was still staring fixedly at the murky water of the vivarium, hardly listening. "I wanted to make sure it was he that went on that one-way trip to the Vastness." He smiled mirthlessly. "Leaving you and the dear old Seed Bearer to comfort each other. Both of you fell rather nicely into my trap, don't you think? You certainly did not waste any time before you spread your legs for him. And now," he said, with evident relish, "it is time for you to spread them even wider for me." Gwenn blanched, and felt the last of her courage draining away as surely as the blood from her face.

Then, like a breath of unsullied air...

*Ana Hana shawm tok duna.*

*Ana Hana shawm tok duna.*

As she watched in wonder, the despondent Uri'el beside the tank spoke, and although its lips formed the words without making any sound, Gwenn could hear the mantra repeating in her mind, strongly and cleanly. The other Uri'el scattered about the room somehow joined in the chant, though their faces remained as featureless as before. Their sweet-sounding voices echoed harmoniously in her mind, and a swelling sound like the ringing of many bells strengthened her resolve until it reached a breaking point inside her.

Dawa's guardian held out its hands in a gentle plea for help in freeing its charge from his noisome prison.

With a fearsome cry of rage, Gwenn strode forward. She seized on the heaviest thing she could find—a metal stool—and heaved it straight at the vivarium tank. The crystal shattered as Maggrai whirled, and flung his hand out protectively. A flood of noisome fluid gushed from the crack, along with Dawa's putrefied remains, which slithered to the floor in an oily, jelly-like mass. Tristan screamed in horror and retched uncontrollably when he looked upon the writhing, blackened remnants of Arkady's old teacher. The stench temporarily disabled them all, even Maggrai, but he was not still for long. He drew himself up, frothing with rage, obviously concentrating all his powers in an effort to strike at Gwenn.

Gwenn stiffened and then dove for the scalpel. She seized it and held it aloft, ready to slash her own abdomen wide open. As she did this, the Uri'el who had been waiting for Dawa caught up his putrefied body with a wailing cry. As it clutched Dawa to its chest, the astarene transformed—became whole again. The Uri'el now took to the air, shrieking in some strange tongue, beating its diaphanous wings madly in Maggrai's face. He screamed curses at it, and at Tristan—who stood stock still beside the table, looking at his sister.

He saw the hand holding the scalpel plunge downwards towards her belly and as he cried out, "Gwenn! No!" Maggrai dashed the Uri'el aside and screamed a command. The sound of it rolled through the Vastness like an earsplitting clap of thunder, creating a rippling blast wave that knocked over both Tristan and Gwenn.

As Gwenn lay on the floor, struggling to rise, a massive hand seemed to bear down upon her chest. Every muscle in her body went rigid as all her nerves fired simultaneously. The pain tore ragged screams from her, until she could no longer get the air into her lungs to make a sound. She could not breathe, could not even feel the beating of her heart. Blood spewed from her nose and mouth as veins and capillaries burst under the crushing pressure of Maggrai's rage.

Now a yawning black hole lay before her, and a glowing figure just beyond it, gesturing.

Gwenn's last conscious thought was a prayer of thanks that she would indeed be stone dead before Maggrai slit her wide open. Then the blackness swallowed her up.

Tristan stared blankly at the empty space. "Wait for me," he whispered despondently. "Don't leave me with him, please Gwenn. Come back..."

# 11

## Chind Prox

Hana tosses a Moonstone* down onto the table before Geya's mirror. It is the Wanmoon. She frowns, knowing that Katkin and Huw must make a long journey with the children, Poppy and Gwillam. The Redestone is Unda, and the Gyrestone—Prox. Hana doesn't like the look of this prediction, but she can do nothing to change it. There is only one Amaranthine who can help Katkin, and the Mebbain holds him prisoner. Hana tries to send a message to him anyway.

~~~~~~~~~~

"Brug? Where are you hiding? It's only old Danners. The Sergeant is still inside."

As the second soldier entered the barn, he could hear moaning coming from a pile of hay over in the corner. As his eyes adjusted to the gloom, he saw a couple stirring in the back, obviously in the throes of passionate love-making. He laughed again, saying; "Don't be all day. The Sergeant wants his tea." He strode forward into the darkness while suggesting playfully, "I outrank you anyway, *Private* Brug. Let me have a turn."

As he reached Katkin, he could see his comrade must have finished, for Brug looked curiously lethargic now as he lay slumped on top of the girl, with his uniform breeches down around his knees. As he bent to shake him by the shoulder, Huw exploded from another pile of hay to his right, and his curved blade flashed in a beam of light from the doorway. This soldier's reactions were much quicker than the unlucky Brug's. He dove to the floor and rolled away, and came up with his sword drawn. Huw circled him cautiously as Katkin, with a cry of disgust, threw the dead man off and stood up. She searched for a weapon, but could find nothing to help Huw.

Danner looked over towards her, and the body of his comrade.

---

* For more information on the Triske stones, see Appendices I and II.

He thrust his sword viciously towards Huw, saying, "Firaithi scum! You will die for what you have done, as slowly and painfully as we can manage it. Just like your farmer friend, that dirtbag Jakob Brunner." He laughed as Huw gave a scream of rage and threw himself forward. A slashing motion with the sword caught him on the wrist and he dropped his knife with a cry of agony. Katkin knew she must do something quickly. She closed her eyes and sent a desperate prayer to Lalluna. Then Ajax snorted anxiously, and bolted through the door of her stall.

The soldier, Danner, never even saw her coming. She trampled him down into the hay and then, as he sought to rise, kicked him hard with her back hoof on the temple. He fell back, twitching violently, and then lay still. Katkin hurried over to Huw, who was still on the ground, trying to stem the flow of blood from his forearm. She tore the scarf from her head and wrapped in around the six-inch long gash. Huw, still gasping with pain, said, "Go into the kitchen and bring the other man in here. Tell him there has been an accident with the horse. I will be waiting."

"You can't fight him. Not like that!"

"I will use my left hand. Hurry!"

Katkin ran from the barn, screaming, "Master... Master, come quickly!" The Sergeant burst out of the door, and caught her roughly.

"What is it? What has happened?"

"The horse kicked Danners!"

He shook her. "Where is Brug then? Answer me, wench?" Katkin said nothing else, and the Sergeant pulled his knife. Abruptly, he held her at arms length and looked at her face, and wild chestnut curls. "You! I have seen your picture in the guardhouse. The traitorous queen of Beaumarais." Katkin struggled wildly, trying to break his hold on her, but he held on tightly, then pulled her close and put the knife against her throat. "Roll up your sleeve, bitch. Let me see your arm."

Katkin did as he ordered, and he grunted in satisfaction as he saw the scarred stump that ended just below the elbow. "I thought so. Now heed me, whore! I will cut the other one off, so you'll have a matching set, if you don't tell me what happened to Brug and Danner."

"They are in the barn," she said dully. "I killed them both."

"You? All by yourself? I don't believe it. You must have had some help."

"Go and see then," she said simply. Pushing her before him, he headed for the barn, and Katkin prayed that Huw would be ready.

He kept the knife firmly at her throat as he stepped though the door. "I have the woman prisoner," he shouted into the darkness. "Come out with your hands up, or I will kill her, I swear it." A piece of horse dung came flying out of the rear of the barn, and struck him on the chest. "Don't play games with me," he roared, "or she dies. Come out and show yourself."

Poppy stepped out of the deep shadows, and threw another piece of dung from the pile she had collected in her apron. "Bad black man!" she screamed. "You killed my Ma."

Another hail of dung followed, and the Sergeant dragged Katkin closer to the girl, cursing as a piece hit him in the face. Katkin begged, "Poppy, run! Please, get away from here." But the girl stood her ground against the advancing soldier.

He made a grab for her with his free hand just as Huw dropped down from the rafters above and landed squarely on his back, forcing him to the floor. He thrust Katkin away with a cry of rage, and wrestled with Huw, who was trying to pin down his knife hand. A vicious head butt knocked Huw off him, and the Sergeant threw himself on top, and raised his weapon triumphantly. He was far larger than the Firaithi, but somehow Huw, his nose streaming with blood, managed to push him off before he could connect with the knife. The two men continued to grapple, and Poppy, frozen with fear, watched from the side.

The Sergeant made a grab for her and caught her leg as she squealed in terror, then held the knife close to her face. "Give up or I will cut her eyes out right now." Huw stopped fighting as Poppy whimpered in fear. "Drop the knife, and go stand by the woman. Do it!"

He ran the knife lightly down Poppy's cheek and the little girl screamed, then begged, "Do as he says, Patre. Don't let the bad man hurt me."

The blood dripped off her cheek and onto her pinafore as she wailed in pain. Huw dropped his knife, cursing under his breath, and looked around for Katkin. Just as the Sergeant raised the knife again, she stepped quietly from behind the stall divider and with all her strength smashed a heavy iron bar against the back of his head. He staggered and fell as she brought it down a second time, and then again, both times directly on his face.

A fourth blow would have followed, but Huw caught her arm. "That is enough, Queen of my heart. He is dead." She backed away from the body, gasping uncontrollably at the ruined pulp of his face, and turned away, taking Poppy in her arms so the girl would not see.

"You saved us," she cried, with her head buried on Katkin's shoulder. "I am sorry I called you a mean lady."

Katkin forced herself to speak calmly. "It is all right, Poppy. Everything will be all right now." Huw, after covering the dead Sergeant's body with an old sack, disappeared into the bolt hole and returned with Gwillam, who was also crying bitterly.

After Katkin had found her artificial hand buried in the dusty straw on the floor and reattached it, they went outside into the mild spring sunshine. Huw passed Gwillam over to her and unsaddled the first of the soldier's horses. Katkin said, "What are you doing, Huw?"

"We will take two of their horses as well as Ajax, and then you and I can both ride. Go inside and get the food together. We need to leave here as soon as we can. Poppy, go and pack some warm clothes for you and Gwillam." Poppy stopped crying and determinedly wiped the blood from the wound on her cheek.

"Yes, Patre. Shall I get Gwill's rabbit too? He won't sleep without it." Huw nodded at her, and she tore off into the house, her pigtails flying.

As Katkin dug through the saddlebags, Huw asked, "Did the men say how long they were going to stay, or if they had any reinforcements anywhere?"

"They just walked in like they owned the place," said Katkin angrily, still reeling from their close escape. "The Sergeant certainly did not confide in me about his plans."

"Then we don't know how long it will be before someone comes to check on them. We must make all haste."

Katkin pointed up to the sky. "Look! Huw, an eagle." The bird dropped down to land in the yard in front of them. She approached it warily, saying, "Have you any more news, my brother? Tell us quickly."

The eagle spoke gravely, "There are many more men at the road by the entrance to the valley. They wait impatiently for their leader's return. You will not be able to leave that way."

Huw, who heard only shrieking sounds, questioned Katkin about their meaning. Then he sighed. "We have no choice, son of Ben'aryn. There is no other way to leave this valley."

The eagle gave a piercing cry. "Foolish human. There is a way. A narrow track leads over the back of the ridge, and across a high saddle. Make ready and I will show you."

Katkin translated this and then hurried inside, returning in a few moments with the cloth sacks of dried foodstuffs she had kept in storage against the day they would leave Brunner's valley. Huw had already found their travel bags and blankets, and was loading them onto Ajax. The Guardsmen had each carried a full pannier of supplies, and Huw added these to their own meager store. Katkin was pleased to find the Sergeant also had a rolled-up canvas tent with his other gear. The eagle stood patiently, waiting for them to finish their preparations. She stared at it curiously, and said, "Why are you helping us like this?"

The eagle preened his feathers casually. "Because of the one whose spirit you bear."

"The Goddess Lalluna?"

"Not her," the eagle replied. "Dai Irrakai. He asked for our help and we give it willingly, for he is like to us a father."

"Dai Irrakai?" she repeated, softly, and her hand strayed to the crystal feather talisman she still wore under her blouse. As she touched it, she felt a shock, like a little discharge of static electricity. Was it her imagination, or did the periapt seem to pulse slightly, with the rhythm of her own heartbeat?

Poppy flew back out the door, lugging another canvas bag, full of clothes. As Katkin slung it onto Ajax's back, Huw said, "Come, Poppy. Jump up on this horse with me. Katkin will take Gwillam and we will ride together, to the place I told you of."

Poppy placed her hands on her hips firmly. "I can ride a pony. My other Patre taught me how ages ago."

Huw opened his mouth to disagree, and Katkin quickly came to the girl's defense. "We will be able to get away much faster if she takes the other horse, and anyway, we don't want to leave it here for the others to find." Poppy beamed at her.

He nodded and said, "Very well. Poppy will ride the smallest of the three and I will take this one." He pointed to the Sergeant's horse, which stood restively off to the side. After putting Gwillam in his carrying sling he helped Poppy mount. She grasped the reins with authority, and dug the heels of her boots into the horse's flanks. Huw leapt lightly onto the back of the second horse with Gwillam, leaving Katkin to manage alone, as best she could with her single arm, to mount the horse which still wore a saddle. In the end she led the horse to the fence and climbed on his back from the top of the highest rail. Huw laughed, "Well done, Queen of my heart. Now let us ride."

The eagle gave another cry and took to the sky, flying low before them on the track that led up Brunner's valley. They followed as best they could, although the rough ground made it hard to keep their guide in sight as he led them ever higher.

Although Huw felt a little trepidation at the thought of trusting the bird to lead them to safety, Katkin did not. She smiled and once again softly touched the talisman. *Dai Irrakai.* She did not know how his spirit had become melded to hers, but she had felt his presence ever since she left Starruthe, last year, and she felt it even more strongly now.

Her thoughts scattered as Huw turned around and said unhappily, "Look, behind you. They are burning the house."

Katkin saw the thick plume of black smoke from the valley below them, and spurred her horse forward to catch up with the others, who were now cantering up the sleep slope as best they could, following the eagle, who led them ever higher. Once they reached the top of the ridge and dived down the other side, the eagle sheared off, shrieking.

But she still heard its voice clearly in her mind, saying, *"They will not follow today, my Queen. We will prevent their passage up the valley. Ride hard for the east and you pass into a barren land where there are no more of your kind. May the wind lift your wings."* Katkin sent a silent prayer of thanks to the eagle and broke into a gallop.

That night, as the children slept, exhausted by the events of the day, Katkin and Huw huddled together under their shared blanket at the tent door. Katkin used catgut and a curved needle to place six sutures in the slash wound on Huw's forearm.

Just as she tied off the last stitch, she sighed. "I feel terrible about what happened, Huw. If I had listened to you we would have been gone from Brunner's long before the Black Guard returned."

He wrapped his arms tightly around Katkin. "It doesn't matter. Your plan to use the dead soldier's body as a decoy saved us, Queen of my heart."

She smiled in the darkness. "I think Poppy is the one you should be thanking. I still can't believe she did not run away when the Sergeant came after her with his knife."

He nodded. "She truly is a remarkable child. I told her to figure out a way to get him into the back of the barn, under my position in the rafters. She came up with the dung throwing all by herself." He stroked her hair and then murmured into the darkness, "I am sorry I doubted your story of speaking with the eagles. It must be a powerful gift that Lalluna has bestowed on you. I wish I could understand their talk. What does 'Dai Irrakai' mean? Is it some word of thanks in the tongue of Ben'aryn?"

Katkin, who had never told Huw about Dai's appearance and subsequent death in the forest, did not answer right away. Then she said slowly, "Yes. It means 'thank-you' in their tongue, Huw." Then, so he would ask her nothing else, she kissed him on the mouth.

Their journey to Bryn Mirain was long and difficult. King Tristan's soldiers were everywhere and Huw had to call on every shred of his knowledge on the hidden back ways of Yr to pass through without their being seen. They most often traveled by night. Katkin soon grew tired of the deliberate, careful pace he set, and complained bitterly. Only Poppy remained cheerful, always ready to light the fire or lend a hand with Gwillam. Katkin found herself both resentful and admiring of the little girl who had so effortlessly captured Huw's heart. She longed for the day when they could turn both children over to Elsa's kin, so that she and Huw could journey with the Kindred of Anandi in peace.

On the day they camped just outside the valley, she and Huw argued again. "Why should you go alone into Bryn Mirain? They are my people too!" Katkin glared at Huw, as Poppy went over and took his hand, trying to protect him, as she always did.

He sighed patiently. "It has been several years since I rode over the pass to the hidden valley, and I do not know if it is safe to do so now. You must stay here with the children until I return, Queen of my heart.

I know you wish to see your kinsmen, but one more day will not hurt, will it?" They had been traveling for most of a month, and it was the prospect of sleeping in a real bed that drove Katkin onwards, as much as the thought of seeing her grandmother and Uncle again.

Poppy said earnestly, "Listen to him, Katkin. He only wants to keep us safe."

Katkin bit back the angry response she had been about to make and just frowned. Huw rode off on Sergeant, as they now called the horse they had taken from the dead soldier, and disappeared over the hill, after saying he would return as soon as he could.

Katkin scanned the landscape around them to see if she could spot the entrance to the valley of Bryn Mirain. The geography was forbidding. The mountains were the highest she had ever seen, their naked flanks nothing but gray rock with occasional stark white patches of snow. But below, where they had made their camp, in the bottom of a gully with a stream hurrying down the center, the weather was pleasantly temperate.

After she and Poppy cooked supper, they sat quietly together, as Gwillam scooted about on the warm grass. She said to the girl, "You might meet some aunties or uncles tomorrow, and perhaps some cousins too. Won't that be nice? To have a family again?"

Poppy chewed a piece of grass thoughtfully. "I won't mind meeting them, but they will never be my *real* family. Not like Patre Huw. And you of course, Katkin," she added, after a sly glance. Katkin gave her a worried look and hastily changed the subject.

In the morning Poppy woke early and shook Katkin's shoulder, as the sun was just rising. "Katkin, wake up! I had a dream about a nice lady. She told me that Patre is in trouble. We have to go and find him." Katkin gazed at her blearily, wondering what on earth she could be talking about.

"You had a dream?"

"Yes! Get up, Katkin. We have to go to the secret place, now." Poppy looked on the verge of tears, so Katkin got up and dressed herself, while trying to get more details from the little girl.

In reply to her questions, Poppy said, "A very pretty lady with long dark hair came to see me. She said her name was Eira and she was Patre's sister. She said we have to go, right now."

Katkin objected, "But Poppy, we can't do that. I don't even know how to get to Bryn Mirain."

But Poppy insisted, "I know the way. She told me." As Katkin put Gwillam in his carrier, Poppy seized her hand and urged her forward. Katkin hobbled the other horses together in a patch of grass and set off behind her, wondering if she had lost her mind. To follow a five-year-old into the mountains seemed a ludicrous folly, if not actually dangerous, even if she had been guided by a dream. But Poppy pattered ahead, and never faltered, until they reached the end of a long ravine, covered in boulders and loose scree. There looked to be no exit from the rocks piled haphazardly at the top, and Katkin sighed, regretting her impulse to give in to Poppy on this early morning trek.

She said, "Come on, Poppy. We had better go back down to the camping place. Huw might be back soon, and he will wonder where we have gone. Anyway we should not leave the horses..."

Poppy ignored her and continued to climb until she reached the top of the slope. Then, quite abruptly, she disappeared. Katkin broke into a run, puffing up the slope with Gwillam, until she reached the last place she had seen Poppy. There was nothing but solid rock ahead, but as she walked closer, the boulders turned to mist and disappeared, and she could see down into a perfectly round grassy dell, surrounded by high green pine forest. Katkin rubbed her eyes in amazement. Many paths led down into the dell from all sides. Twenty or thirty caravans clustered at the bottom, and the smoke from the cooking fires gave the air a pungent haze.

When Katkin caught up to her and grabbed her hand, Poppy had almost reached the outlying caravans. "Slow down, Poppy. Let us go and talk to the Tane of these caravans, and find out what he knows about Huw."

She walked slowly to the largest of the brightly painted caravans, and knocked on the door. An older man with graying hair answered, and broke into a smile. "Katkin! Remember me? Ikor* Ander?" He hurried down the steps and embraced her. Ander was her mother's brother, and she had met him once before, many years ago, when her grandmother paid her a visit at Acorn. He was also Cara's father, Katkin suddenly remembered. She wondered belatedly if this had anything to do with the trouble Huw had found himself in.

Poppy spoke breathlessly. "Where is my Patre? What have you done to him?"

---

* Uncle

Ander bent down to speak with her. "Your Patre? What do you mean little one?" Poppy did not answer, so he said to Katkin, "Is this your little girl? Who is she looking for?"

"This is Poppy—Jakob and Elsa Brunner's child—and this is her brother, Gwillam. We brought them with us to Bryn Mirain." She patted the baby, who was sleeping contentedly in his sling.

Ander's face darkened. "I know what happened to her father then. There are rumors flying through Yr of the persecution of our Catena."

Poppy snorted impatiently. "Not my other Patre. He was killed by the Black Men. I mean Patre Huw. Where is he?"

He gave her a sharp look. "Huw Adaryi? Is that who you mean?"

Katkin nodded and her uncle's expression became grim. "He has been made captive until we can hold a clanning with the Kyan of the Chandrathi. They should be here soon."

Katkin stared at him in shock. "Captive? Why on Yrth would you do that?"

"For the murder of his wife Cara, and their daughter, Maia. He has been named by Rha Tane, Neirin Mare."

She could not believe her kindly grandmother would do such a thing, so Katkin asked anxiously, "Where is my Kymatre?* I need to get to the bottom of this right now." Poppy had started crying, and Katkin reassured her. "Don't worry. It is all just a misunderstanding, I am sure."

But later, as she sat with Neirin in her tiny caravan, Katkin's certainty crumbled. Her grandmother nodded her head firmly when asked if she was sure that Huw had committed the crimes of which he had been accused. "We have been searching for him many years, Kitty. Always his Kindred came to Bryn Mirain on the years when we, ourselves, did not. At last he may be brought to justice, by the grace of the Un-Named One."

"But Kymatre, how do you know he killed them? No one witnessed the murder, did they? He told me that Cara ran away with a man called Shiqaba, and took the baby with her. I believed him."

"No, there were no witnesses, but I do not need the eyes of others to show me the truth. I have the stones and..." The old woman paused and seemed to be considering whether to share anything

* Grandmother. Grandfather is Kypatre. "Ky" means elder.

else with her granddaughter. After a moment she asked, "Are you his woman, Kitty?"

"We are traveling together, and I care for him a great deal. But we have no formal bond, other than the responsibility for Elsa and Jakob's children. What difference does that make?"

"If you were his woman, you would be allowed to speak on his behalf at the Clanning. He is lucky that he is not one of the Anandios. The punishment for blood is blood, and he would already have been executed."

Katkin's eyes went wide. The customs of her people seemed barbaric indeed. "What happens after the Chandrathi come to Bryn Mirain?"

Neirin looked stern. "After the Kyan give their permission he will die." Poppy, who had been sitting quietly, burst into tears.

Katkin hugged the little girl and said firmly, "Don't cry for your Patre. I will find a way out of this, I promise. He is innocent, Poppy. We just have to prove it." She turned back to her grandmother. "I want to see him, right now. Where is he being held?"

Neirin wagged a wrinkled finger. "I cannot say. Only his family will be allowed to see him. You said you were not bonded."

Katkin scowled, rapidly losing patience with her grandmother's slavish adherence to the laws of her people. "I was lying. I am his woman and Poppy is his daughter. Now take us to him." Neirin stared at her a moment, her expression unreadable. Then she shrugged.

"Very well. Ander will show you the lock-up."

Ander led them up to the side of the dell, to a tumble of boulders that hid a narrow but high cleft in the cliff side. A stout set of iron bars had been bolted to the rock, and Huw sat behind it, looking very dejected. Poppy rushed forward with a cry, and thrust her hands through the bars.

"Patre! Are you all right?"

Huw nodded and squeezed her hand. "Of course, little flower, I am fine." But Katkin could see a fresh welt on his cheek, and knew that Huw had not gone willingly into his cell.

She spoke to reassure him. "Don't worry, Huw. I am going to get you out of here."

He grasped her hand feverishly. "You do believe me, don't you? I did not kill Cara and our daughter." His eyes filled with tears. "I loved her. I never would have..."

"I know, Huw. I will speak at your trial. They can't convict you just on the basis of what my Grandmother saw in the stones. It is ludicrous." Huw quickly shook his head, casting his eyes over to Poppy, who sat disconsolately by the lock-up, obviously fighting back tears.

"Let us not talk about it anymore right now, Queen of my heart. Tell me how you managed to find me. You must know by now that it is the power of the Un-Named One that keeps Bryn Mirain hidden from prying eyes."

Katkin smiled brightly, saying, "That was all Poppy's doing. She must tell you the story while I go back for the horses and our tent. Tonight we will camp here beside you, and keep you company." Poppy brightened up as she began to tell Huw of her dream.

Katkin left them with Gwillam and walked hurriedly back up the side of the dell towards their campsite at the bottom of the ravine. The horses were where she had left them. After she packed up the tent and stowed everything in their travel bags, she picked her way back up the mountainside.

After guiding all three horses down into the hidden valley, Katkin set up their camp as close as possible to the lock-up. A guard appeared shortly thereafter, standing casually just beyond the last boulder. Katkin smiled grimly at this and wondered how they thought she might help Huw escape when the bars covering the cave were at least an inch thick and made of solid iron. She passed several blankets through to Huw, as well as some lentil patties wrapped in flat bread for his supper. As they ate, she said earnestly, "As soon as Poppy and Gwillam go to sleep I am going back down to talk to Ander and my grandmother. They cannot possibly make you stay in here until the Chandrathi arrive for the Clanning."

He sighed and sadly met her eyes. "I will not have to stay in here long after they arrive. Once the Anandios find out that my own Kindred have banished me, then they will have to wait no longer for my execution. It will be carried out immediately."

"What! You cannot be serious. That is so unfair."

"It is our way, Katkin. The Kindreds must have swift justice, for there is no time to waste when we are always on the move. My brother Arkady once saved me from a similar judgment, but now he is dead, and there is nothing you can do to stop it."

"I *will* do something, I swear it." She reached through the bars to hold his hand, and he stroked it softly.

"You must leave here, my Queen, before the Chandrathi arrive. They might file a charge against you for your actions in helping Gwenn escape. Do you not understand the danger? I can no longer protect you." He kissed her hand, and said, "Promise me you will leave here with Poppy and Gwillam, before they come."

She frowned. "I am not going without you, and that is final." He opened his mouth to argue further, and then Poppy appeared, asking for a bedtime story. Katkin brought her a blanket and she curled up close to the bars of the lock-up. Huw stroked her hair and told another of the many Firaithi legends he knew by heart. Katkin, watching his face in the twilight, saw the tears on his cheeks, but Poppy did not.

"Kymatre, you are wrong! Huw did not kill his wife or his child. You must let him go at once." After putting Gwillam to bed, Katkin had hurried down to her grandmother's caravan, and now she stood, with her fists clenched, glaring.

Neirin shook her head sadly, and avowed, "There can be no doubt, Kitty. I have seen."

Katkin gave a derisive cry. "With the stones? That proves nothing."

Her grandmother stood. "Come, let me show you something." She hobbled over to the tiny table that stood in one corner of the caravan, and picked up a hand mirror with an ornate frame. Age had blackened the edges, but the centre remained bright and reflective, though the wavy glass distorted the image a little.

Katkin looked baffled. "It is a mirror, Kymatre, nothing more."

Neirin smiled. "No, Kitty, it is much more. It is my scrying glass. With it I can see what the Un-Named One sees. I simply breathe upon it—like this..." She exhaled on the glass and the mirror fogged, then cleared. Katkin watched over the old woman's shoulder. Though she could still see her grandmother's reflection, a different picture superimposed itself in the mirror, of a stony ford, surrounded by beech and oak trees. A shallow river flowed lazily over the shallows, but the scene looked strangely inert, and devoid of life.

"That... That is the Sharm River ford," Katkin stammered.

Her grandmother nodded softly as the mirror once again reflected only her face. "Yes, and Cara and Maia are there, do you not see?"

Katkin peered closer and saw a woman, clutching a baby, on the far side of the ford. She was standing still, and in the flickering image from the mirror it appeared she might be shouting something unintelligible. A tall man, with iron-gray braids, came to stand beside her and put an arm across her shoulders.

"The glass shows her leaving with Shiqaba, nothing more. Huw cannot be convicted by this." Katkin said.

"But there are Uri'el there. See? Here, here and here." Her grandmother's wrinkled finger, twisted with arthritis, pointed out the seated figures, scattered among the trees. Katkin drew a deep breath. There could be no doubt—Cara and Maia were in the Vastness.

"But Kymatre, even if they *are* dead, it doesn't mean that Huw killed them. Perhaps that man Shiqaba murdered them, after they left the Chandrathi Kindred. It doesn't prove anything!"

Neirin lost patience. "She begs for vengeance! Cara cries out the name of her executioner. Be quiet and look, girl!"

By staring intently at the glass, Katkin could easily read the girl's lips as she continued to cry out, "Huw! Huw!"

# 12

## Pellunis Nowhen

They have thwarted him for now, but he will soon try again. What can we do, Fyn?

*Fyn shrugs.* We must depend on Lutyond to come to his senses. He is the only one who can protect the child.

But this is terrible! The stones say...

Whisht, Hana. Even if Moera has decreed his fate to you, I do not wish to know it. *Fyn shakes his head unhappily, knowing he can do nothing to protect his cousin from the dangers that lie ahead.*

~~~~~~~~~

Gwenn woke slowly from a deep sleep, as if she were rising to the surface of some still and silent lake. She wondered, as she did so, what happened to you if you died while you were in the Vastness. After all, dead people were supposed to go there *after* they died. Did it mean you had to go somewhere else instead?

Not that she cared that much about finding the answers to her questions. The crushing weight had left her chest, and she could no longer hear Maggrai's howls of fury. Strong arms cradled her close. And even though the arms rocked and swayed, as if the person or thing holding her was walking or perhaps flying—she felt safe and utterly at peace. But that was wrong, was it not? Uri'el always sat perfectly still—they did not move about. All except for the sad one who had been waiting by the vivarium. Gwenn remembered the jubilant look of happiness upon its face when it had at last gathered Dawa up into its arms. She felt glad that she had been able to help it—even more glad that Dawa no longer suffered endless festering decay in Maggrai's vivarium.

Then she wondered briefly about Myriadne. Had Maggrai managed to get to the child before Gwenn herself had died? Somehow, she did not think that he had. Her abdomen felt smooth and unbroken as far as she could tell, but maybe all your defects were healed when you died and went to sleep in the arms of your Uri'el?

Which brought up another rather inconvenient point... Why was she awake at all?

Death did not feel at all like she had supposed it would—an endless slumber without dreams. But as long as she was stirring, she thought perhaps she ought to open her eyes and have a quick look around.

But she did not, not right away. What if she discovered that the comfortable tranquility she felt was some horrible delusion created by Maggrai to further destroy her will? No, she decided she would travel quite happily with her eyes closed—on this peaceful journey with Death, to wherever he wanted to take her.

It *was* strange though, how Death kept muttering to himself.

"Fareon, Tilde, Ornex Prox."

*Ornex Prox?* What did that mean?

"Benichise leads to the inner ring of pellicula," the voice droned on, sounding strangely familiar.

But she could not imagine the owner of that particular voice saying anything like what he was saying now.

"Mayfe, Endymia and then the last six."

*No. It can't be. Gunnar would never... Anyway, he is lost in the...*

Gwenn's eyes snapped open and she squinted against the bright light pouring down from the sky. At first she could see only a halo of unruly reddish-blond hair. But then, as her vision cleared, a cleft chin appeared, nearly obscured by a scruffy beard, as well as the front tooth she had chipped when she punched him in the mouth a few months ago. Last of all, his bright, bright blue eyes—narrowed, at the present moment, in deep thought.

She cried out, "Gunnar!"

He looked down upon her and grinned. "Just a moment, Faircrow. This part is a bit thorny. I have to concentrate..." He went back to his recitation. "Jerrun, Haplia, Greyshoals and Vale."

As he spoke the bright light around them flickered and died, to be replaced by subtle hues of blue and green, then purple, then yellow. To Gwenn it seemed as though many lands flashed rapidly by, and she viewed them through a narrow windowpane.

"What are you...?"

"Shhh..." he cautioned, and Gwenn fell silent.

After a few more minutes, he exhaled heavily and slowly lowered her to the ground. "I think we can rest here a moment. Can you stand?"

"Can I stand? Can I stand?" Gwenn threw her arms around Gunnar and then shook him violently. "Where have you been, you great lummox? How did you..."

He did not answer, only looked at her with concern. "Are you sure you are all right? Your nose and mouth are all bloody. Did that vile beast hurt you?"

Gwenn paused to rub her face, and her hand came away rusty red. She rapidly checked herself for other wounds.

"I... think I am all right," she said. "My chest hurts a bit, that is all." Then she added, "But I thought I was dead, Gunnar. I truly did."

Gunnar closed his eyes. "No, you are not dead, thank the gods," he murmured. "I got to you just in time." Then he stopped talking because she was kissing him.

Thirty seconds passed before Gwenn remembered the twins. She tore her lips from his with an agonized cry. "Jakob and Arvid! We have to go and rescue them. They are..."

"All right," finished Gunnar firmly. "You need not worry, love. Inky has them and they are safe."

"Inky? Who is that? And how do you know they are all right?"

"Come on," he said, and held out his hand. "I will take you to them. You can see for yourself."

As they journeyed on together through the worlds between worlds, Gwenn caught glimpses of lands whose existence she had never dreamed of before. Flashes of towering trees and misty mountains, of garishly hued skies, of watery places replete with leaping silver fish—all filled her with wonder. She was awed, too, at Gunnar's ability to navigate unerringly through these trackless spaces of light and color. How had he learned it?

"Gunnar? When did you..."

He shushed her again. "Not now, Gwenn. Wait until we get there."

She stole a glance at him, wondering now about his five months alone in the Vastness, and how it had transformed him. He seemed much more... pensive, for one thing. And there was another difference she could not quite put her finger on—a quiet authority which she had never seen in him before. Physically he had always been powerful; Gunnar was undoubtedly the strongest man she knew, other than her step-father. But there was something lurking below the surface of that power now, a hint of magic—or transcendency. She had just opened her mouth to ask him about it when, with a rush of displaced air, they issued back into the living world, landing with a splash in the rolling tide of some shingled strand.

"Sorry about that," Gunnar said, and smiled sheepishly as they sloshed their way out of the freezing water towards the beach. "Navigating in the Continua is not like sailing, exactly. Each azimuthal pellicula has its own interior level so I am still trying to get the hang of landing. Are you all right?"

Gwenn looked at him and blinked.

Yes, there was something very different about Gunnar.

She gave a cry of recognition when she caught a glimpse of the high pines clothing the mountain rising darkly before them. "I cannot believe it. We are in Feringhall! How did you bring us here so quickly, Strong Arm?"

He shrugged modestly, but Gwenn had already left him far behind. She tore up the path between the sand dunes, wondering where Jakob and Arvid could be. Feringhall lay in one of the remoter parts of Starruthe, and there were no villages within thirty miles. Although Gunnar's grandmother had once had a house here, it had been burned to the ground in the terrible fire that had also taken her life.

Gunnar hurried to catch up with Gwenn, but she had stopped, and was staring in shock at the tumbledown cottage nestled under the pines, with deeply overhanging eaves and many odd-sized windows.

"What on Yrth? It burned... I saw it with my own eyes! Did I not?" She turned to Gunnar, her eyes full of confusion.

He laughed at her shocked expression. "You did. I did too. But yet, when I returned three weeks ago, it was here again, just as if the fire had never happened. I cannot explain it."

"And Eydis?" Gwenn asked eagerly. "Is she..."

Gunnar sadly shook his head. "Nay, not she. But the house remains and we can make of it a safe haven, at least for now."

The door to the cottage opened and Arkady appeared, with Jakob and Arvid in his arms. As Gwenn sprang forward with a happy shout, he drawled, "So, what took you so long, Strawhead? I was beginning to think I was going to have to rescue you both!" Arkady put the boys down, and they immediately scurried across the yard towards their mother, shrieking excitedly.

"Sorry, Inky," Gunnar answered in the same bantering tone. "I had to take the long way round, to make sure we were not followed."

Arkady left the doorway and went to stand beside Gunnar. He looked at Gwenn, who had fallen to her knees on the sand and was hugging her children with wild joy. "Is she all right? There is blood all over her shirt." he said to Gunnar softly.

"I think she is. But it was a near thing. A very near thing."

Arkady's voice lost its lightness. "I *told* him we should not have waited until the last minute. If that monster Maggrai hurt her..."

Gunnar growled, "He will pay. I will see to that, believe me. I will hunt him down—through every stinking azimuth between here and the outermost shell, if I have to."

Gwenn, oblivious to their conversation, gathered up the boys happily. "Is there any food inside? I am starving!"

The three of them sat at the worn pine table. Gwenn ran her fingers along the surface, scrubbed white and satin smooth by centuries

145

of use. "So? Who will be first? I want to hear the whole story." She gave Arkady a black look. "Properly this time. No lies."

He studied his fingernail intently. "Strawhead should start. He is the hero here—not me."

Gunnar gave him an exasperated look. "We both had our parts to play, Inky. Fyn said..."

Gwenn smacked her fist down on the table, and then looked guiltily over her shoulder to where the twins lay sleeping on the floor, bedded down in wide bureau drawers. Arvid snorted and rolled on his side, but slept on. "At the beginning, if you please," she urged. Gunnar glanced at Arkady, who waved his hand in an exaggerated invitation for him to embark upon the tale.

After pouring himself another cup of tea, Gunnar leaned back in his chair and clutched the tin mug in both hands. He said, "After I said goodbye to you that morning, I crossed over the threshold into the Vastness. I hunted around Dawa's house, as he said I should, and I finally found Inky, lurking in a grove of trees not far from the back door."

"Why do you call him that?" Gwenn interrupted.

"Inky. For Inkhorn," Arkady answered. "Strawhead seems to think I am too clever for my own good sometimes. Just because I can speak five languages..."

Gunnar cut in caustically, "Look, who is telling this story—you or me, Egghead?"

Gwenn looked at the two of them, amazed. Last time she had seen them together they had wanted to kill each other. When had this rough camaraderie begun? "Just get on with the tale," she said evenly to Gunnar.

He began, "I explained, very politely..."

At this Arkady snickered loudly and Gwenn aimed a kick at him under the table. "Kadya, please!"

Gunnar cleared his throat. "As I was saying, I explained why I was there, but Inky did not believe me. We had a little discussion, of a physical nature. I was about to prevail..."

"Hah!" said Arkady.

"...when your father arrived."

"My father?" asked Gwenn. "What was he doing there?"

"Looking for us, apparently. And he was plenty mad when he found we were fighting. He grabbed us both by the scruff of the neck and banged our heads together so hard my ears were ringing for ages afterwards."

"Mine too," Arkady seconded, grinning proudly.

Gwenn shook her head in amazement. "Then what happened?"

"Well, Cousin Tomas said he could not believe that we were arguing about such selfish and petty concerns when there was a war going on. He said we needed to stop acting like little boys and take a look around us." He sighed and rubbed the back of his neck. "At first, neither one of us wanted to listen to him. But then he dragged us over to a house in the village and we saw..."

Gunnar fell silent, and Gwenn looked at him questioningly. "Saw what, Strong Arm?"

Arkady unexpectedly came to his rescue. "We saw—something that made us decide that we needed to work together. You don't need to know anything else."

Gunnar continued, "Then Tomas explained to us about Maggrai."

"How did he find out?" Gwenn wanted to know.

"Apparently Lalluna told him," Gunnar answered. "The three of us talked a long time. At the end of it we had come up with a plan to fool Maggrai into thinking we did not know about his presence this turn of the Gyre." He turned to Gwenn, and his eyes were sad. "I fought against it to the very end—because of the risk to you, love. Keeping you in the dark like that..." He sighed. "But Tomas convinced me there was no other way, and Arkady went back alone."

Arkady took up the tale. "Once I awoke again in the living world, I could tell right away that Maggrai had already taken over the body of my teacher. It grieved me terribly, but of course I could say nothing." He gave Gwenn a worried look. "I hope Dawa is all right, wherever he is. Did you see him when you were with Maggrai?"

Gwenn shivered, remembering the Vivarium. There was no need to upset Arkady by telling him the whole truth. She said reassuringly, "I saw him resting peacefully in the arms of his Uri'el. You need have no worries for him."

He flashed a grateful smile. "Once I found out that Maggrai had put spying devices all over the house I knew I could not tell you about Gunnar. I had no choice but to play out my part—pretending I could not remember what had happened in the Vastness."

"I think I knew, even before I found that strange bottle, that there was something wrong with Dawa," Gwenn said thoughtfully. "But what happened after he caught me snooping in his cupboard and pushed me into the tunnel to the Citadel?"

"When you did not return after an hour I went to look for you. The twins were very hungry by then, so I gave them their gruel and put them back to bed. Then I searched the whole house for you and Dawa. When neither of you could be found it did not take me long to decide he had made off with you somehow."

"What did you do?"

"I sent a message to Gunnar in the Vastness, via Hana. Both of us were ready to abandon the whole charade and ride to your rescue. But once again your father said we must wait, and let the game play itself out. He said you were in no immediate danger."

Gwenn took Gunnar's hand and squeezed it. She asked, "What were you doing in the Vastness all that time? The boys and I missed you terribly."

"I mostly stayed with Fyn. He taught me how to move between the continua. I learned a lot about him..." He paused and looked off into the distance. "And about myself. We did a bit of hunting too. But a day never passed in that cursed hole that I did not think of you and the boys. I wanted so much to..." He brought Gwenn's hand up to his lips and kissed it. Arkady looked away, obviously annoyed, and Gunnar blushed deep red.

"I understand, Strong Arm," Gwenn said softly. "You don't have to say anything more." Then she yawned cavernously. "I am so tired I think I could sleep for a week. You two can finish the story tomorrow over breakfast." Gwenn stood and stretched, and then waited uncertainly, wondering what would happen next.

Arkady and Gunnar remained at the table and a look passed between them that left Gwenn in no doubt that the issue of who she was to sleep with had already been determined. It angered her a little, but she quickly decided this arrangement was an improvement over the previous one—when they had fought over her. Gunnar stood and picked up one of the drawers. Gwenn took the other and they walked to the back hall, and then beyond into the bedroom that had once belonged to Gunnar's grandmother. A curtained canopy bed took up most of the floor space, but there was room for a wardrobe and the bureau from which Arkady had taken the drawers to create make-shift beds for the twins.

Gunnar brought in a steaming jug of water so that Gwenn could wash away the blood and grime of her three-week ordeal. She stripped her prison garment off and looked at it distastefully. Gunnar took it from her and shoved it in the fireplace without a word. Eydis had owned many soft robes made of brightly dyed reindeer hide, and Gwenn selected the longest one she could find. She slipped it over her clean skin with a satisfied sigh, and crawled into the double bed. Gunnar slid in beside her and blew out the candle.

It was very quiet—only the distant roar of the sea and the soughing of the pines could be heard. They lay side by side for a long time without speaking. Gwenn knew she must now confess to Gunnar what had happened between her and Arkady—and about the child they had created together. Somehow, what had seemed so reasonable in Khalama—that the three of them might live together as a family with their children—now seemed like utter insanity. He would never agree to it. Would he?

Gwenn took a deep breath—and began.

He did not say anything. Not until she had run out of words and lay silent and still beside him. Then he sighed deeply. "I knew all the long that if I went to the Vastness that you and Inky would..." Gunnar left that sentence unfinished. "I decided I had to go anyway, for your sake, and for the sake of the child." Gwenn made a questioning sound in the darkness. Gunnar explained, "Hana had already told me about the Dawnmaid, and how important she was to your people." He spoke with finality. "It was the only way. I have no regrets."

She turned to face him, not quite able to believe his words. "Do you mean that, Gunnar?"

"Yes," he said, in a way that brooked no argument.

Now she sought his embrace and gave him a lingering kiss on the mouth. Gunnar responded eagerly. But before she let him make love to her, Gwenn had one more question to which she wished to have an answer: "What has happened to you? You seem... so different."

"Do I?" he answered softly. "I don't feel very different. But maybe it is because I saw so many things in the Vastness—things so deep and dark that the remembrance of them frightens me, even now. I learned a thing or two there, you see. Knowledge I wish I could run away from. I don't want it to be so, but it is."

"What on Yrth do you mean?" Gwenn asked, a little nervously.

"All my life I believed in the hallows of Skyre, over the bridge of Atenfy, where the fallen brave go to feast with Ods, and Faysta and the rest. It was the reward that me and my felag* lived for, what we fought for, even what we died for." His voice grew sad. "But I found out that it doesn't exist. When we pass on, our anafireon rests with the Uri'el, like everyone else."

"I am sorry," she said. "To learn such a truth must be hard indeed."

"It was harder still to learn the rest of it. For Ods and Brigga and the rest don't exist either. They are just shadows on the walls of my dreams, Gwenn. Nothing more."

She touched the golden anchor that Gunnar wore on a chain around his neck. "What about Lutyond? Surely he..."

Gunnar growled, "Especially him."

Gwenn sighed in the darkness. "Are there no Gods left to fight Maggrai and the Angellus?"

"There is your father, Fyn. And Hana. And..."

"And?" Gwenn repeated curiously.

"Nothing," Gunnar said dully, and turned away from her. Gwenn curled her body against his, wondering what he had been about to say.

After a while she offered, "I never thanked you, properly. You saved my life, and the life of a child that isn't even yours. How can I ever make it up to you?"

He made a sound of impatience. "I swore allegiance to you, remember? You have no call to repay me for that."

"Only because you thought I was a Goddess. Now you know better, why do you still put up with me?"

"I love you," he answered softly. "I need no other reason."

But his voice sounded sad and so she asked, "Are you sure you are still willing to try this? The three of us living together, I mean."

His answer was immediate. "I have no difficulties with *that*. Inky and I seem to have reached an understanding."

"Then what is it, Gunnar? What is bothering you?"

"It is just..." he began, and then said, "Nothing," again in a way that left Gwenn convinced that he was hiding something from her. But she gave up trying to find out what it was, for now anyway, and settled on stroking his back softly, offering reassurance

* A brotherhood or fellowship

without the need for words. He sighed with pleasure and arched his body towards her, so she let her hands wander lower, running her fingertips teasingly over the downy skin of his buttocks until she felt gooseflesh rise. Gunnar hurriedly turned to face her again and wrapped his arms around her waist as Gwenn sat up and tugged the bulky robe off over her head. She shivered violently as the cold night air hit her naked skin and dove back under the covers, seeking the comforting heat of his flesh against hers. Gunnar smoothly rolled on top of her, blanketing her completely, then clasped her tightly until she stopped trembling. Neither of them was in a mood for delicacy, so he joined with her immediately, beginning a quickly escalating rhythm that soon had them both breathless. Gwenn buried her face in the angle of his shoulder and neck, trying to muffle her cries of ecstasy, for she could not quite forget the presence of Arkady, who was sleeping in the curtained alcove just beyond the wall. Neither, it seemed, could Gunnar. When, at last, the final passion took him, it took him as silently as a mournful ghost.

Gwenn sipped a mug of strong black coffee as she watched over the feeding of Jakob and Arvid. Gunnar and Arkady each held one of the wriggling twins on their laps, and tried to shovel oat gruel into their uncooperative mouths. She gave a hoot of laughter as Arvid, on Arkady's lap, sneezed suddenly just after being fed a heaping spoonful of gruel—spraying both his father and his brother with food. Gunnar, cursing roundly, reached for a rag as Arkady said laughingly, "Don't wipe it off. It is a definite improvement to your looks, Strawhead!" This prompted Gunnar to toss a handful of the sticky paste at Arkady and the two men were soon involved in a food war, to the delight of the twins, who clapped and giggled in delight.

Gwenn rapped on the tabletop sharply with the porridge spoon and shouted, "Stop this at once. What kind of example are you two numbskulls setting for the children, I would like to know?" Even though Gwenn was only eighteen, at that moment she felt like the only adult in the room.

Arkady grinned sheepishly and raised his hands high. "Truce?" he asked Gunnar.

Gunnar nodded, and after a curt command from Gwenn started to tidy up the mess.

"That is better," Gwenn continued. "And while you clean up you can finish the story from last night. What happened after I was captured?"

Arkady, who had gone back to feeding Arvid the remaining gruel, explained. "Once I sent the message to Gunnar, I began making arrangements to escape from Khalama with the twins. When Maggrai was around, still pretending to be Dawa, I acted like I believed his ridiculous story that you had run off without me or the twins. As the days passed, he spent less and less time at home, I guess because he had you imprisoned in the Citadel. But he was still adamant that I not leave the house, so I had to be very careful with my planning."

"He wanted to use you and the twins as hostages, to ensure I would not escape," Gwenn remarked bitterly.

"I did wonder why he kept us around," Arkady said softly. "But in any case, I got them out of there as soon as I could. After Maggrai had been away for several days, Strawhead took a chance and stepped back into the living world. We managed to escape without being seen by the spying devices, and made our way to Feringhall. He had already been here with Fyn, so we knew that the house had reappeared. We thought it would be the perfect place for me to hide out with the twins while Strawhead went to rescue you."

Gwenn said wistfully, "I am very glad that you and the twins got away safely, Kadya, but I suppose you did not have time to..." She stopped, thinking that it was very ungrateful of her to be asking about her sword, when she should just be thankful that he and the boys were all right. Arkady grinned at her and went in to the sitting room, then returned with a long bundle, still wrapped in its silk brocade sheath.

He knelt down and handed it over to her, saying, "I believe this is yours, my lady." Gwenn jumped up with a cry of delight, thanking him profusely for remembering keth'fell, the sword that her stepfather had given her on her sixteenth birthday.

Gunnar continued the story. "After Fyn showed me the way to gap shift between the continua, I went to Isle St. Valery, though it took me a long time to get there." He grinned as he admitted, "I kept getting lost. Your father insisted that you not be rescued until we knew just what Maggrai's plans were, so I spent a lot of time skulking just outside the Vastness, listening to him talk with your brother. I had just traveled back from meeting Fyn with my latest round of news when I discovered that Maggrai had taken you from your cell in the Citadel. It was terrible, thinking I had returned too late to save you."

"But you came just in time," Gwenn declared.

"Not soon enough to stop that beast from hurting you. A few more seconds..." he grimaced and left the rest of the sentence unfinished.

Gwenn stepped forward and kissed him warmly on the mouth. Then, feeling slightly iniquitous, she did the same to Arkady. Both men stared at the ground in embarrassment. "It is all right," she said brusquely. "I won't make a habit of it. But I just wanted to thank you both for what you did. And now," she continued brightly, "what have the two of you got planned for today?"

As the weeks passed, the increasing closeness between Gunnar and Arkady both surprised and pleased Gwenn. They spent the days together, hunting and fishing or working on the house, always trading genial insults. She was amazed at how quickly they seemed to have been able to put their former hatred aside. Indeed, as the summer wore on, and she grew increasingly round, she often felt a little jealous of her two husbands out tramping around the wilds of Starruthe while she stayed at home with the twins.

One day, as the three of them sat around the kitchen table, still littered with the remains of breakfast, Gunnar announced happily, "Inky and I going to build a new boat to replace the Fire Drake." Arkady nodded in agreement.

"Really?" Gwenn asked, smiling at Arkady. "But what do you know about building boats, Kadya?"

Arkady grinned back at her. "Quite a bit, actually. I worked on a lot of vessels as a fisherman's jack during my travels. But Strawhead has to get to work felling some trees first. I am *way* too smart to do the heavy work."

"No chance, pretty boy," Gunnar shot back. "If you cannot handle an axe, then you will have to learn."

Gwenn watched in bemusement as they walked out the door together, already arguing good-naturedly. Arkady came back a few moments later, saying, "Strawhead wants you to come up to the building site with some lunch for us, around noon. I came back to get some tools from the shed, and then I will head over to help him with stripping the trees. You know the cove just behind the next headland to the west?"

Gwenn nodded.

"That is where we plan to construct the boat. Will you be able to manage everything?" He gave her a questioning look and she smiled.

"Of course, Kadya. Don't worry about me."

Arkady stepped forward as he softly brushed a stray lock of hair from her cheek. "I *do* worry about you, my crow girl. All the time." He grasped her around her thickening waist and pulled her close. "Our baby will be here soon. You need to take extra good care of yourself." Then he kissed her and strode off towards the shed, whistling cheerfully.

After selecting a sturdy shovel and a small hatchet from Eydis' store of tools, Arkady walked back through the dunes, towards the beach, still whistling. As he made his way back towards the cove he reflected that this unlikely arrangement of Gwenn's had somehow turned out all right, despite his original misgivings. He still missed the rootless existence he had once had as a traveling scholar, but settling here in Starruthe had its rewards as well. His meditation practice had never been better. The beauty of the landscape reminded him of T'Shang, and the weather, too. Though it was now high summer, the grass in the deep shade was still white with frost and his breath made a steaming cloud in the crisp air. But he could tell by the brilliant blue sky that the day was shaping up to be a warm one.

As he followed the path around the rocky headland he saw a tall pine swaying violently back and forth up behind the beach. Figuring that Gunnar was toppling the first tree for the new boat, Arkady stopped well clear of the cove, wanting to be outside the zone where the tree might come down. A few seconds later it did fall, with a resounding crunch, and he could hear Gunnar's annoyed curses shortly thereafter. After rounding the last bend in the path, Arkady saw that the tree, which was over sixty feet high, had dropped directly over the pit they had dug to fire harden the planks for the keel. Arkady hurried forward, a sarcastic jibe already on his lips, and then stopped dead in utter astonishment as Gunnar bent low, picked up the offending tree and dragged it aside as if it were no more than a branch.

# 13

## Dardisea Prox

Welcome back, Moonlight. This place has seemed empty without you.

*Lalluna looks about her, and then shivers.* Where are my sisters?

Gone. The Numen sent them far away to the outer pellicula.

*Lalluna looks distressed. Hana strokes her wings softly.* It was for the best. Geya has caused enough trouble for one turn of the Gyre.

*Lalluna nods in grudging agreement and then asks casually,* Have you seen Fyn around anywhere?

*Hana gives her a sly smile.* Yes, I think he is looking for you. Why don't you go to him?

Moonlight quickly disappears with a happy shiver of her bright dragonfly wings.

~~~~~~~~~~~

Huw crawled to the very back of his cell, and wrapped himself in a blanket. He said morosely, "So you think I have been lying to you? I tell you I did not kill them."

Katkin sighed and said, "Come on, Huw. The evidence is pretty incontrovertible. My grandmother's scrying glass..."

"Is deceitful!" he interrupted vehemently. "I don't know why it shows Cara in the Vastness with Shiqaba. I suppose you think I killed *him* as well?"

She studied the bars of the lock up intently. "I don't know what to think anymore. But if you are guilty you should just admit it. Perhaps you can claim insanity as a defense. You might have been afflicted with melancholia."

He shook his head angrily but said nothing.

Katkin stared at him, trying to make up her mind whether or not he could be trusted. How well did she really know Huw? Was it possible he had murdered all three and hid their bodies by the ford? Neirin seemed to think so, but there was something about the story that did not make sense. If Cara and Maia were dead, why did they not rest in the arms of Uri'el? Could there be any other explanation? Katkin asked suddenly, "Is there anything you can remember about this man Shiqaba? Anything that might help prove your innocence?"

Huw looked at her hopefully. "Does this mean you believe me?"

Katkin nodded, albeit reluctantly. "You stood by me, the day your Kindred banished you. What kind of a friend would I be if I abandoned you now?"

Huw crawled up to the bars of his cell and pressed his face against them. Katkin embraced him awkwardly, and kissed his lips. Huw said sadly, "I cannot think of anything else. I told you everything I remember already." Then his face brightened and he snapped his fingers. "There is the book that the Gruagá girl left behind when she ran away. My father gave it to me right after Cara and Maia left, in case it might have some clues to their whereabouts. It turned out not one of us could read the strange tongue in which she wrote, but I have kept it all these years. It is in my saddle bag, with my other things. Perhaps Lalluna will give you the understanding, Queen of my heart."

She hurried to the tent and found the book, carefully wrapped in a piece of worn cloth. It was exquisitely bound with red leather with a stamped border of leaves and flowers. Katkin untied the thong that held the book closed and squinted at the first page, still just readable in the dim twilight. She said excitedly, "This is Elisabeth Benet's journal, Huw. See the name written here – Penro? I was right! The girl with Shiqaba must have been Jacq's mother."

"How can you be sure?"

"Because Thad's middle name was Penro. Thaddeus Penro Benet!" Katkin wrapped herself up in a blanket and read the first few pages. She said, "The writing is Secunian. It begins in April in the year '49. In the first few pages Elisabeth is talking mostly about school and her friends. She has just turned seventeen, and this book was a present from her mother. Her father is a wealthy merchant and trader, and isn't home very much. They live in a big house by the harbor, in Scarfinda."

The fading light made it difficult to read further so Katkin went back to the tent once again for a candle lantern. After skimming a few more pages she said, "Listen to this...

'Today my father came home rejoicing! A ship of his—the Briny Leviathan, thought lost forever, has just come limping into port bearing all manner of strange and wondrous goods. Even stranger is the passenger that traveled back with them. When the Captain, Josiah Tavish, made for an uncharted island, after sustaining damage to the ship in a storm, a foreigner begged passage from him for the return trip to Yr. Now he is coming to stay with us, and my father says he is very tall, with olive-colored skin.'

"In the next entry she talks about meeting Shiqaba.

"'Dearest diary. I am in love! The man who came back with the boat is so very handsome, and though he is the same color as my father's uncouth sailors he is in no way like them. He is tall, as tall as I imagine the gods must be, and his shoulders are broader than the doorways in our house, so that he must bend his head and turn sideways to enter a room! His black hair is long, with silken braids. I felt so shy when I met him I could hardly curtsey or say a word, but it doesn't matter, for he speaks little of our tongue anyway. After he shook my hand he handed me a curious gift. It is a feather carved of the most pure crystal, and Shiqaba pointed at his chest as he gave it to me. I think this must mean that his name in his own tongue is Feather.'"

Katkin continued to read, as night fell. She snuggled deeper into her blanket, and Huw wrapped his arms about her through the bars of his cell. "Now she is telling all about a ball at her house, that her father held to introduce Shiqaba to society. She danced with him all night, and although he still speaks little Secunian, he managed to let her know that her interest in him was returned." Katkin smiled wryly, remembering Jacq's awkward shyness the first time he declared his love for her. "There is no need for words when two people are attracted to one another. But goodness, what happens next is very shocking!

"'I suppose you will think I am terrible, my diary, for what I have done with Shiqaba. He came to my room last night, after father and mother had gone to bed. When he kissed me for the first time I felt a scalding flame that rose from the soles of my feel right up to the top of my head. He lifted me into his arms and carried me to my bed, with his lips still on mine, and I could do nothing but allow myself to be taken. I wanted him so badly and he wanted me too.'"

Katkin paused and cleared her throat, trying to reconcile this passionate discourse with the staid, gray-haired lady she had known as Elisabeth Benet. Shaking her head, she continued. "Now the story gets rather sad. Elisabeth writes that her father discovered them together a few nights later and shot Shiqaba in the abdomen. Then he threw them both out of the house. Her mother managed to slip a single piece of gold to her as they left, but the money soon ran out and she and Shiqaba were forced to take to the road, sleeping wherever they could. Poor Elisabeth!"

Huw said, "That must have been when they came upon my people and were taken in."

Katkin nodded and read another entry:

"'The Firaithi treat Shiqaba like a long lost brother, for he speaks their tongue. Now he has been given their physics his infection has cleared and he is very much stronger. I suppose I ought to be grateful, but I don't want to stay here with these people another day. Though my father crewed his ships with darkies, he taught me never to trust one.'"

Huw snorted in disgust at her casual use of the Gruagá nickname for his people. Katkin said, "I wonder why Elisabeth's father always used Firaithi sailors. Are the Kindreds especially good crewmen?"

"Not that I have ever heard."

Katkin continued to peruse Elisabeth's diary. A later entry made her eyes go wide.

"'I have decided I must leave here, as soon as I can. Though I still love Shiqaba with all my heart, I can remain with him no longer. Diary, is he of the race of the Gods? He speaks secretly now of his home in the West and how we will someday pass beyond the Vastness to go there. To me this means we must die, and though he says it is not so, I do not believe him.'

"Here is the last entry, Huw. She says:

"'The worst possible thing has happened. I am with child. Now I must run away, before he learns of it. I have no money and no friends. Oh Diary, what shall I do?'"

Katkin shut the book with a snap. "That is it! The clue we needed. He says his home is beyond the Vastness! That is why Cara and Maia are there. Do you see, Huw?"

He nodded in the darkness, but said despairingly, "Your Kymatre will not believe this story, Katkin."

Huw was right. When Katkin told her grandmother of the diary, she merely wagged her finger and asked how Master Penro's trade-ship had crossed into the Vastness in the first place. Were not all the men on board living and breathing souls? They could not have found Shiqaba in such a place, so the account must be false. Katkin gave a cry of frustration, and left the caravan in tears. For several days she prowled the hidden valley of Bryn Mirain like a trapped beast. She knew Huw's time was running out, but she could not think of any way to help him. Then, at last, she had a sudden inspiration.

"Poppy, I have to go away for a few days, and I cannot take you and Gwillam with me, for I must travel as quickly as I can. Patre Huw's life may depend on it."

Poppy nodded bravely. "Where are you going, Katkin? Will you be able to help my Patre?"

"To Scarfinda. I hope I can find the answers there that I need to save Huw. Will you and Gwillam be all right while I am gone? Now that the Gitashaen kindred are here, you will be able to stay with your Ikora Betrys for a few days. She has a little girl, named Aeronwy, who is just your age."

Katkin left on Ajax, after delivering the children to Elsa's sister, and saying good bye to Huw. It took her many days of hard riding to reach the prosperous port of Scarfinda. As she rode through the crowded streets she eyed the magnificent cathedral and remem-bered that the Fynära had once sacked it, with Gwenn at the helm. Her connection with Gwenn made her visit to the city somewhat hazardous but Katkin did not think anyone would recognize her as the former queen of Beaumarais. She had cut her long, chestnut hair before she left the secret valley and now her head sported a mop of tight curls, dyed very dark red with henna. Of course she could do nothing to hide her injury, so she bandaged her prosthesis carefully, and placed her arm in a sling, making it look as though her left arm was merely broken rather than missing altogether.

After finding a room with board in an inn called The Wind-lass, Katkin unpacked her small bag and splashed some water on her face before heading back down the stairs to the big tavern that occupied most of the first level of the Inn. It was lunchtime and a sullen cook was ladling portions of stew onto wooden platters. A small bread roll completed the meal.

Though the other residents looked at the greasy broth with disgust, Katkin ate hers with relish, thoroughly enjoying the unfamiliar taste of meat. She felt herself relax in the comfort of the tavern, which reminded her poignantly of the Compass in Isle St. Valery. A bright bit of fire blazed in the hearth, filling the room with warmth. The folk sitting around her held murmured conversations about their trades and farms. As she sipped a cup of red wine, she felt the warmth settle right to her toes.

Then Poppy's face intruded on her thoughts. The little girl had come to her as she prepared to mount Ajax for her trip to Scarfinda, and handed a small package up to her.

She said earnestly, "I made some oatcakes for you to take on your journey, Katkin. Please hurry back. Patre needs you." Poppy's eyes were filled with tears. "Ikora Betrys doesn't love me and Gwill, not like he does. Even though she doesn't say so, not properly. She frowns when she has to give us something to eat."

Katkin had reassured the girl, saying she would be back soon. Now, in the dining room of the inn, she angrily shook her head, trying to erase the picture from her mind. The ruddy-cheeked man beside her, dressed in the rough clothes of a farmer, kept trying to start a friendly conversation, so Katkin, in an effort to forget her unhappy errand, questioned him about the port of Scarfinda.

"Do many ships come and go?" she asked.

"Ay, they do, Marm," he said, and his broad accent indicated he had come in from the country, probably for trade.

Katkin gave him a winning smile. "With so many ships they must have to keep records of all the ships and cargoes and suchlike. Where would I find them?"

He looked over at her, a little suspiciously. "Funny thing to be interested in, if you ask me."

Katkin quickly made up a story. "I am searching for a long-lost relation of mine, Captain Josiah Tavish. He was the Captain of a tradeship called the *Briny Leviathan*. Have you heard of it?"

The farmhand shook his head. "Not me! I don't live here in Scarfinda. I only comes in to sell my turnips at the Saturday Market. But you can finds what you be wanting to know at the Custom's House, on the Marketplace."

"How will I know it?" Katkin asked.

He smiled, revealing a broad expanse of toothless pink gum. "Just look for the unicorn over the lintel. 'Tis a fancy beast for a fancy building."

Katkin thanked him for the information and excused herself, then made her way back up to her room. Though it was still early, she wanted to have a nap, hoping that the pillow would provide the counsel she needed to make plans for the future. She threw herself down on the bed with a sigh. The mattress sagged in the middle, and was probably swarming with lice, but after so many weeks on the road it felt heavenly to be lying on a real bed again. The room was cozily decorated, with an overstuffed armchair in the corner by the fireplace. Several framed prints of idyllic pastoral scenes rendered in watercolor hung haphazardly on the walls, probably to hide stains in the wallpaper. The room was warm, and the noise from the wharves outside sounded somehow distant and inconsequential.

All at once, Katkin felt an overwhelming desire to forget the errand that had brought her to Scarfinda—forget Huw and the children and make a new life for herself here in this city, where no one knew her or her traitorous past. Money would not be a problem, at least for awhile. Huw had insisted she take all the coins they had found among the dead soldier's possessions and she had more than enough to last until she could find employment. The realization that she could so easily free herself from her overwhelming responsibilities brought tears to her eyes, and she cried out to Lalluna in her heart for guidance.

To Katkin's very great surprise the Goddess answered her. "*You must do what you know to be right, my vessel. To abandon those who depend on you now would be a grave betrayal. I do not believe you would even consider such a thing.*"

"How is it I can now hear your voice in my mind, my lady? It has been many years since you have spoken to me so strongly."

"*My strength in this world depends on the belief of my people. I feel, here in Scarfinda, a powerful current of prayer and worship that has given me new life. I almost wish...*"

"You wish what?"

"*I wish I could leave you, my vessel. If I did, then I could travel once more across the heavenly plane and see Fyn. I would tell him of Dai's return to Yrth, and his grave predictions of the future beyond this turn of the Gyre.*"

"Then why don't you go, Lalluna?"

"*When Fyn brought me to you, in the dungeon of the Citadel, he*

161

*told me that you might not survive another separation. Each time we join and part, your human frame is weakened, my vessel."*

"But you must go! Perhaps Fyn and the others can do something to stop this Maggrai creature from seizing power."

*"Even if it means your death? What of the information you hoped to gather here in Scarfinda? Without it your friend Huw may die. I would not have your two lives on my brow, for I do not wish to become as callous as Dai believed we Amaranthine are with your kind."*

Katkin said firmly, "So much depends on you, Lalluna. You must go."

*"You must be very sure. When I leave you this time, I can never return. For even if you survive this parting another joining would surely be your end."*

As Katkin nodded her agreement, she felt a pain in her chest that began as a burning sensation, and quickly progressed to a crushing weight. She gasped as she felt the Goddess leave her, and the fire engulfed her throat and mouth. As her sight faded, Katkin lay back in the bed and closed her eyes, thinking that if she was dying at least she would have to make no more difficult decisions. Her hand groped instinctively for the feather talisman that had once belonged to Jacq, and as she wrapped her fingers around it, her vision abruptly cleared and she found she could breathe once more.

Now Lalluna stood at the bottom of her bed, a wavering smoke-white female form with magnificent wings. "Farewell. I go now to Fyn, but I will never forget you, my vessel. Many turns of the Gyre will pass before another soul such as yours comes to be born. You are truly the brightest jewel in all the heavens."

Katkin watched the outline dissipate, and then Lalluna was gone. She lay on the bed and waited for the pain in her chest to pass. After a time, she slept.

Now she wandered aimlessly through a light and airy space. Bracken crunched under her feet. Trees, like silent sentinels, reached high on either side, their drooping branches soughing in the gentle breeze. She looked up and up, but could not see the tops of those trees. Katkin had a memory of this place. Was it from another long-forgotten dream?

*No, it was no dream... What was it he said? The third azimuth of the eighteenth pellicle—Rythis.* Yes, she was in Rythis. Leafy twigs brushed her face, though there was no wind. She stared at the trees, sensing an ageless intelligence within them, like nothing she had ever encountered. "Who are you?" she cried, and the song increased in rhythm.

A single voice, soaring high above the others, made itself clear. "Deres. Emma na Deres." The sound was utterly entrancing and she closed her eyes, letting it fill her with solemn joy. Now there was a different voice—Jacq's voice—whispering her name. It seemed to come from everywhere, from nowhere. Katkin turned and turned, seeking the source, until she grew dizzy and her thoughts incoherent. "Jacq!" she cried, but her voice did not seem to penetrate the singing of the trees. The word fell, heavy and dull, at her feet. Something made her try again—only this time she said, "Dai?"

His wings shimmered with light as he appeared before her. He said, "You have come. At last, you have come. Tell me how it is I still live."

Katkin wanted to rush forward, wanted to throw herself in his arms, but she did not. Who was *this* Dai? The Dai of Brunner's Valley, whom she had seen dead and burned? Or was he the Dai who had been Jacq Benet? He could even be the Dai who had flown with her to Rythis once before. Katkin asked him warily, "How should I know if you do not? I am not of the Amaranthine. First tell *me* who you are."

He stared at her in confusion. "You do not know? I am Dai, known as the Irrakai—the seeker of paths between the stars."

"You are the third creature I have met who calls himself by that name. I am beginning to wonder if you have brothers, Dai Irrakai."

He shook his head. "I have no brothers. You must tell me everything you remember of those who bear my name."

So she described both her dramatic mid-air rescue and her encounter in Brunner's valley with the Amaranthine who had poisoned himself. Dai listened without interrupting. "...then after he died I burned his body. Do you know anything of these others, Dai? Can you explain what is meant by a paradox in the gyre?"

"Part of this story I remember. I did take poison after I transferred my essence to the woman, because I knew it would be wrong to exist on two planes at once. I thought with such care I could avoid interfering with your continuum, but it seems I was much

163

mistaken. This creature, Maggrai, must be the offspring of Jacq and the demon Keth Dirane." He paused, obviously distracted. "The other Dai, who saved your life, I have no memory of. That means he came from the future, from a time beyond this turn of the gyre. Since my past self knew that the tyrant Maggrai destroyed all the other Amaranthine, then this appearance by a future form of Dai ought not to be possible. Thus the paradox."

Katkin found this all very confusing so she asked, "This place we are in now—it is Rythis, is it not?"

"Perhaps it is, but I am not sure. It seems I am trapped in some world between the worlds, and I have been here for some time, alone."

Katkin was just about to ask him about the Deres, when a sharp rap on the door woke her, and she sat up with a start. A male voice shouted something unintelligible that might have been the Secunian word for dinner, but Katkin was not sure. She did not want to have to make conversation with her country admirer again, so she ignored the announcement and instead spent the evening in bed, reading through Elisabeth Benet's journal, looking for clues. She found nothing that would help Huw, and she could only hope that she might be more successful when she visited the Customs House on the morrow.

When the candle in the brass holder by the bed burned low, she extinguished it and lay in the darkness, waiting for sleep and hoping that it might carry her back to Rythis—and Dai Irrakai. Unconsciously her hand found the talisman again, and as she clutched it tightly a dizzying sensation of dislocation assailed her. When she moved her hand the vertigo stopped. Katkin carefully grasped the feather again, and closed her eyes. When she opened them, she found herself once more in the tree-filled space of her dream—although this time she was absolutely sure she was not asleep. Dai sat cross-legged on the bracken-strewn ground, his wings gracefully folded.

He said, "You have returned to me. Can you now tell me how I came to be in this place?"

Katkin looked around her and then said slowly, "I know it sounds absurd, but I *think* you are in Jacq's feather talisman—the one he got from his mother, Elisabeth. I found myself here with you as I held it in my hand. But I still don't see how you came to be trapped within it, unless it happened when I was with Eydis in Starruthe. Perhaps your anafireon was released when I cut the thread binding Gwenn and Keth Dirane."

Dai said sharply, "You have been with Eydis, whom we call the Numen? She is the most powerful of all the Amaranthine. Shiqaba is her brother."

Katkin nodded. "Yes, for she is also Gunnar's grandmother." Here, she sighed. "And Tomas de Vigny's as well."

"Then the talisman is a *Mebbain,* a gateway to the worlds between worlds. Only she amongst us has the power to create such a thing. But why has she trapped me here?"

"I do not know. She said nothing to me of this Mebbain before she left us. Tomas told me that she went back across the heavenly plane with Raven and would not return in this turn of the gyre. Do you know why Raven desired your death, Dai?"

He sighed and studied his hands. "I have no doubt Geya acted through her. She and I have been enemies for many turns of the gyre. When the others discovered that I had come to Yrth, she saw an opportunity to revenge herself on me."

"The other Dai told me that you came... *for me*? Is that true?"

Dai spoke offhandedly. "I only wanted... I mean, I did not understand then what it meant to be human. Perhaps in my selfishness I hurt you and if I did, I am sorry." He gave way to his frustration, and stood, clenching his fists. "It seems I have a great deal to be sorry for and I can do nothing to make it right, not while I am imprisoned here."

Katkin looked at him in confusion, surprised by the lack of warmth in his voice. She could not reconcile this Dai with the one in Brunner's Valley. After a moment she decided it was all in her imagination. "Use me," she said softly. "I can be your vessel, Dai. I love you, as I loved Jacq." She walked forward, with her face upturned, hoping he would put his arms about her, but he did not. Instead, he stepped quickly away again.

"You cannot be my vessel, nor do I wish you to. I am trapped here, within the Mebbain, and here I must stay. Nothing you do will change that."

"But... But Dai, in the forest you said..."

His interruption was cold. "Do not take the broken ramblings of a dying man to heart, my dear. Your place is on Yrth, not with me."

She stared at him, unbelieving. "But I want to be here with you. I don't care about the living world! There is nothing there for me."

"Do you know what will happen to your body while your spirit rests here? Without your anafireon to sustain it, it will soon die. You must leave here. Now."

Katkin did not move.

"You think that I am your husband," he continued in a hard, pitiless voice, after a moment had passed in which they stared at one another in silence. "I am not. Jacq Benet is dead. You do not belong here, not now—or ever. Go away." She backed away from him, abjectly miserable, her hand covering her face. For a moment his expression softened, and he raised his hand towards her, but quickly dropped it again.

Dai closed his eyes, and waited for her to leave him. When he opened them she was still standing there, crying bitter tears. He stared down at her face for a long moment and then leapt high. His wings stroked powerfully, until he was high above her—the only point of darkness in the blurred field of white that filled her vision.

In the morning, Katkin rose, sighing, and went reluctantly about the task of finding the proof she needed to free Huw, though she was still not sure she would return with it to Bryn Mirain. It was early, just after cock's crow and no one else was present in the dining room for breakfast. The dour cook gave her a ladle full of gummy cooked oats and left the dining room. After finishing her breakfast, Katkin pulled a cap firmly over her curls and made sure her artificial hand was well-bandaged, then set off towards the Market Square.

She let her feet carry her along with the crowds of people streaming along the road edges. It was Saturday, market day, and the town was filled with carts and horses piled high with goods. She paused on the edge of the paved square, daunted by the mass of people and animals milling about within. The farmer from the inn was there, minding his stall. He gave her a friendly wave from behind an enormous mound of turnips and she smiled at him.

After studying the imposing buildings that enclosed the market on all sides, she spied a gray stone edifice on the west side, near the waterfront. It had a magnificent carving of a unicorn over the door, and some strange words carved on the lintel. Katkin passed under them without much thought. A man stood behind a writing desk just inside the double front doors. He wore a pince-nez on the end of his bony nose, and looked down it rather impatiently.

Katkin gave a curtsey and said in what she hoped was serviceable Secunian, "Pardon me, Sir. I am looking for the *Registrumhallen*."

He did not speak, merely jerked a thumb backwards over his shoulder towards a fancy set of cut glass doors. Katkin thanked him and passed by, wondering why he seemed so unfriendly.

A wooden counter, obviously worn by long years of use, bisected the inner office. Behind this stood rows and rows of shelves, each home to hundreds of leather bound journals and ledgers. A young clerk stood behind the counter, busily writing in another such ledger. He did not look up as she entered.

Katkin cleared her throat and said, "I wonder if you could help me?"

He raised his head sharply and spoke to her. It took Katkin a few seconds to realize she could not understand a word he was saying. She cleared her throat and tried again. Still nothing. She framed another panicked question. He gave her an impatient look and hurried away from the counter.

Then he returned with an older man, who said slowly, in heavily accented Maraison, "May I help you, Miss? Are you lost?"

The understanding finally hit her—she could no longer speak or understand Secunian, now that Lalluna had left her. Katkin quickly considered her options. Should she turn and run? But the old gentleman was waiting patiently for her response, and she thought his face looked kind. Although having to communicate in her home patois was the last thing she had wanted to do, she decided to state her request briefly and hope the man would not recognize her face.

"I am looking for the records of a voyage made by the tradeship *Briny Leviathan* in the year of '49."

The old man gave her a curious glance. "Who was Master of the ship?"

"Josiah Tavish, I think." Katkin held her breath as the man translated her enquiry to the clerk. He nodded and disappeared behind one of the shelves.

The older man said genially, "So, what brings you to Scarfinda? We don't see many Beaumaraisians these days. Your king hasn't made himself very popular around here, you know."

Katkin smiled and nodded vaguely, not wishing to reveal any more information than she had to. But the man continued to ask questions, so in the end she repeated the story about Josiah being a long-lost relation. At that moment, to Katkin's relief, the younger clerk returned lugging a heavy canvas bag filled with documents and dusty books. He dumped them out on the counter, and then turned back to his colleague. He began a low and hurried monologue that made the older man's eyes go wide. They disappeared behind the shelves again, holding an animated conversation in Secunian.

While they were gone she pawed through the various books and papers on the countertop. She found something that looked very like a journal, with Josiah Tavish's name stamped on the front. Just then the two men returned, carrying a small printed flyer. The younger man pointed at Katkin and then the picture on the flyer. His colleague shook his head in confusion, but Katkin did not wait to see anything further. She recognized the flyer as one of those distributed throughout Yr by her son, King Tristan, showing the face of the traitorous Queen of Beaumarais. Snatching up the journal, she turned and fled.

The younger clerk agilely vaulted the counter and was at her heels, shouting for the doorman, "*Eska, Eska! Dammen ni scapa!*"

Katkin, seeing her exit blocked, fled the other way down the hall and into a stairwell. She slammed the door shut behind her, and wedged the handle with her shoe. Frantic pounding on the door indicated that her pursuers were close behind. She pelted up the stairs to the top floor, three flights in all. A locked but flimsy wooden door lay at the top and she broke it open with her shoulder. She could hear the sounds of heavy footsteps on the stairs behind her.

Out on the open rooftop she looked desperately for some cover, or some other door through which she might escape back down into the building. There was nothing but trash and a waist high stone parapet circling the roof edge, home to a few roosting pigeons. Katkin peered over, eyeing the long drop straight down to the pavement below.

The men following her were very close now. Another building's rooftop, across an alley, beckoned her and she mentally measured the distance. Could she make the jump? As the first of her pursuers stepped onto the rooftop of the Customs House she decided she had no choice. She turned and started to climb up onto the parapet, but she never made it. A jagged rock, hurled by one of her pursuers, caught her on the back of the head. Katkin staggered and fell to her knees as the first man reached her. He hauled her up roughly, and then stepped back.

She looked on desperately as the circle of men closed in around her. Three Constables had joined the clerks. They wore blue uniforms and carried long wooden truncheons. She saw nothing but implacable hatred in their eyes. With a cry she rushed at a gap between them, and two men threw her back into the center. Slowly, for they knew they had all the time in the world, they searched the pockets of their rough linen breeches and produced knives. Some larger, some smaller – all wickedly sharp, with course serrations on the blades.

They jeered at her in Secunian, probably telling her what they had planned, and she felt glad now that she could not understand their tongue. She screamed at them, "Come on! Get on with it. I am not afraid to die, cowards." But in truth, she felt very afraid— a fear that filled her throat with bile and made her light-headed. Panic overtook her as the first leering man stepped forward and raised his gleaming knife.

# 14

## Nundael Sequent

*Hana stares at Moonlight in shock.* Who let them cross the heavenly plane?

*She shrugs.* I do not know, but whoever it was, I thank them with all my heart.

How can you say that? They have ever been our foes.

*Lalluna looks unrepentant.* Then why did the Angellus save her, when I could not?

*Hana sighs.* You are right I suppose. But now that they are here, what will we do with them?

~~~~~~~~~~

*Clicking...*

Like the sound of withered seed pods in the autumn. A gentle sound, so peaceful. It made Katkin think gratefully that being dead was not so bad after all. Much better than being in the living world, where there had been so much pain... Her mind recoiled from the memory of that agony, as the men on the Custom's House roof had flayed her alive with their eager knives. Like the swooping and pecking of many iron-beaked birds, only each little peck had bitten deep—deep into flesh and bone—leaving a gouged wound behind. She had screamed and struggled until they could no longer hold her upright. Then the knife birds stopped their plunging attacks, but the men remained. Katkin could see only the tops of their heavy boots as she writhed agonizingly in the sticky red lake of blood that widened across the tarred roof top.

*Clicking...*

A touch of something soft, like velvet on her skin. It tickled and before she had time to think she brushed it away with her hand. Light flooded her eyes. The softness had been some sort of a covering on her face. At first, she could not see, and she brought up her fists to rub her tearing eyes.

*Clicking, now louder, with a change in pace. Fast and then slow again, in little bursts of two or three. Another timbre joins in, a bit higher.*

She rubbed her eyes again, and opened them slowly. Now the light was not so blinding. She could see, blurrily, two flesh-colored blobs in front of her face. Blinking brought them into focus. They were *hands.* Her hands. Two hands...

*Clicking...*

Wait a moment! *Two* hands? That was not right, was it? Katkin felt sure she had lost one of them long ago. Hy... Hythea. The volcano Hythea had taken one of her arms, hadn't she? She stared again at the left hand, thinking perhaps that when you passed away Death magically healed all your wounds. Certainly, the times she had visited the Vastness, all the corpses resting in the arms of the Uri'el had looked whole and perfect, their faces at peace. But the faces of the Uri'el were blank. She had been told that the dead person could see the image of the person they loved most in life.

*Click, click-clickety-click. Soft and encouraging sounds, like a mother might make to a newborn child.*

Katkin wondered and then looked up, wanting to see whose face her Uri'el bore.

But she saw no Uri'el at all. Her eyes took in sky, and clouds, and overhanging trees. But something about the trees seemed wrong. They were black, with many naked branches that moved strangely, though there was no wind. Oddly enough, Katkin did not feel afraid, even when she found, after more study, that the black things she took for trees were actually beings, stooping low around her.

*Click clack. Click, click. Clack. Clack.*

As hard as she tried, Katkin could not grasp her situation. The men on the rooftop had killed her. She should be in the Vastness, lying in the arms of Uri'el. But instead she was in some strange place, surrounded by black creatures whose soft clickings she could now recognize as a language, though a completely incomprehensible one. Carefully, she raised herself onto her elbows and saw the grassy curve of a meadow, studded with many small blue flowers. Katkin lay on some sort of table that was soft, and pliant, like a hammock.

One of the black things moved closer. It was tall and thin, more like a shapely young sapling than anything else. Save for one glowing circle of green that might have been an eye, it was featureless. Somehow, the Sapling could move its branches wherever it wanted, and Katkin watched as a spindly black arm with two pincer-like fingers slowly telescoped out towards her. It clicked questioningly as it touched the talisman she wore. Other Saplings came forward and sent out identical appendages, until there were ten or twelve of them, each lightly touching the feather that rested in the hollow of her throat.

*Concentrated clicking, building in volume. Faster. Louder. Reaching a fever pitch.*

A powerful burst of light surrounded her and she felt the heat flash beating against her neck and chin. As the feather vibrated into a high pitched whine, Katkin jumped up and away from the table, afraid, for the first time, of what the Saplings might do to her. Irrelevantly perhaps, she noticed first that the surface on which she had been lying was in fact created by other Saplings, who were now slowly straightening themselves and withdrawing their interlaced branches.

"Katkin... Katkin..."

Dai had to call her name several times before she turned and saw him standing behind her. With a cry of fear she threw herself at him, and he caught her up in a fervent embrace. Neither of them noticed as the Saplings, with many satisfied clicks, rose into the air with a fiery exhaust that stirred and then quickly blackened the grass below them. A second later they had disappeared.

"Dai! How did you... I mean, how did I... Are we both dead?" Katkin took several deep breaths to clear her head, trying to make sense of it all. "Where is this place and what were those... *things*?"

He said, "We are neither of us dead, although with you it was a very near thing." He spoke angrily. "I will find the men who made you suffer, Katkin. They will know ten times the agony before they die, I swear it." She shook her head numbly, knowing it would cause more harm than good for Dai to exact his revenge on her behalf.

"But how is it that I still live?"

"I am not sure," he gravely replied. "But I think the Angellus saved you."

Katkin scratched her curls in confusion. "Those tree creatures were the Angellus? But I thought they were the enemy. Everyone else seems to believe so."

Dai sighed. "For myself, I do not know what to believe. You told me once that my counterpart from the future denied that they were the true enemy. As we have seen ourselves just now, they are capable of healing and acts of great power, like the breaking of the Mebbain. But in truth, they are a mystery to me. I do not understand their tongue, if the clicking is indeed a language, and they are like no other life form I have ever seen in all my journeys between the stars."

Katkin looked around her. "How did we get here?"

Dai answered. "As you lay dying on the rooftop and your ana-fireon grew weak, those creatures came, dropping from the sky like black spears. Your attackers ran like frightened children. Then the Angellus gathered you up and brought you here. This place is one of the worlds between, but not one I recognize. After they laid you down on the living bower, the rest of them formed a circle and extended many arms around you, until you were completely covered. The most amazing energy began pulsing through the appendages, such as none I have ever felt before." He shook his head in amazement. "Within a minute you were completely healed."

Katkin laughed as she held up her left hand. "Yes! They even gave me back my missing arm."

When he caught her hand and fervently kissed it, she looked at him in utter bewilderment. "What are you doing? I mean... Last time we were together you told me to go away. You were very cruel to me, Dai."

He sighed. "I know—I hurt you terribly. How could I let you stay with me? Your anafireon would have wasted away. But everything has changed now that I am free. I don't have to hide..."

Suddenly, a searing bolt of lightning assailed the heavens, and a deafening thunderclap followed an instant later. Katkin screamed as Dai leapt up, looking wildly at the sky. The wind howled, but some powerful force drew it upwards, through a jagged hole that had appeared in the green firmament above them. Something was coming towards them, a black-winged something, dropping down in lazy arcs. Dai grabbed Katkin and thrust her behind him, but he had no weapon and nowhere to hide. The black creature furled its wings and came screeching out of the sky, before landing heavily in front of them.

"Sorry, Father," he said sarcastically as he touched down. "Was I interrupting something?" Maggrai laughed unpleasantly as Dai stared in disbelief. "Don't you see the family resemblance? They say I am very like you, old man." He continued, boastfully, "But I am stronger, of course. Much stronger."

Katkin's eyes widened in disgust as she beheld the being before them, and smelled his decaying stench. She said, "Who... Who are you?" But she already knew the answer.

Maggrai moved forward a pace, and Dai stepped backwards, pushing Katkin along with him. He said, "Don't come any closer. Return to the lake of fire that spawned you, hell child. You are no son of mine."

The black-winged creature laughed raucously. He stared at Katkin, still cowering behind Dai. "I have no quarrel with you, old man. Just give me the woman and I will allow you to go free. For now, anyway."

Dai said casually, "First tell me what you want with her." Katkin stiffened behind him, stunned at this seeming capitulation.

"Dai, what are you..." she began, and he thrust back a hand to cover her mouth.

Maggrai took no notice. "My minion Tristan wants her back. They have some unfinished business to attend to, I believe."

Katkin recoiled in shock and dismay. Was Dai contemplating sending her back to the Citadel so that her son might have another chance to torture her? She tried again to speak.

He turned and grasped her bodily, then thrust her forward, saying, "Go ahead and take her. She means nothing to me."

Katkin screamed in shock. A powerful wrath overtook her. She turned her head and viciously sank her teeth into Dai's forearm. With a strangled cry of pain he let her go, and she ran blindly from him. The ground gave easily under her bare feet as she threw herself forward and a little to the left. She felt a moment of sickening vertigo and the turf seemed to rise up to meet her. But then it dissolved into a spinning mist as she gap shifted into another of the continua.

She fell hard into another world. This place was gray and completely featureless, except for some oddly shaped crystals scattered here and there on the ground. After listening for a few minutes she relaxed slightly; there was no sound except the soughing of a thin biting wind.

Katkin shivered and dug her hands deep into the pockets of the silvery garment she now wore. What had happened to her other clothes? Her fingers encountered a heavy, smooth object. Curiously, she removed it. It was a clear globe that had many colored bars floating on the inside. Katkin stared at it for a moment without comprehension and then shoved it back in her pocket. Whatever mystery it represented would have to wait.

A long-ago conversation came back to her, when Dai had spoken of the worlds between:

*"Are there many of these... continuums?"*

*"Continua," he corrected gently. "Maybe an infinite number. They are all around you, and you part them like a sea of long grass as you move about in your world. Do you see?"*

If she kept shifting between them would her pursuers be able to follow? She decided it would be prudent not to find out. Several more jumps in quick succession left her feeling shaky and nauseated, and she decided she must rest awhile before traveling further. Fortunately, the world in which she found herself now was hospitable and somewhat Yrth-like. There was a stream of clear water flowing down by her feet, and after she had drunk deeply her nausea disappeared.

Katkin scanned her surroundings for shelter and spied an old gnarled tree, standing all alone on the edge of a meadow. Bending low, she squirmed her way inside its hollow trunk and curled up on the sandy floor. The interior of the tree was cool and dry and very quiet. Though it seemed she had escaped, she could not help crying bitterly for many minutes.

After carelessly wiping her nose and eyes on the silver dress, she settled back to take stock of her circumstances. They were grim. So grim, in fact, it took her a few moments to notice that the robe had turned a brownish color, to match her surroundings, and had somehow developed long sleeves and a cowl to ward off the chill. She raised the hood to cover her face partially, and snuggled her hands deep within the sleeves. Thus warmed, it did not take long for exhaustion to win over her anxiety. She fell asleep.

When her eyes snapped open, after what she thought was only a few moments rest, it was completely dark in her hiding place. The patter of rain broke the silence and Katkin wondered if it was that sound which had woken her.

"Katkin! Please, you must answer me. Where are you?" The voice was Dai's and he sounded utterly miserable. Katkin huddled in the tree and did not speak. He went on, "I know what it looked like, but you have to believe me. I never intended to give you to that monster. It was a trick. A trick to make him lose his guard. Katkin, please. Don't hide from me, I love you..."

From within her hiding place Katkin struggled with indecision. How could she now be sure Dai was telling the truth? Perhaps Maggrai was with him, and they waited only for her to reveal herself before they would fall on her again. As Dai continued to call her name, she grimly made a vow to herself.

*I will have no more dealings with any of the Amaranthine.*

Not Lalluna, whose petulant withdrawal of her boons had almost cost Katkin her life, nor Dai, whose erratic behavior left her bewildered, if not actually endangered. Over her former lover, Tomas de Vigny, now the Amaranthine Fyn, she hesitated momentarily. But Fyn loved Lalluna, she knew that well enough.

Meanwhile, outside in the driving rain, Dai's frantic calls had ceased. After a few moments, she slept again.

This time when she heard a voice, she was sure she was dreaming, for the inside of the tree had disappeared and she was floating inside a faintly glowing space. Katkin saw the light came from her own robe, which had turned a luminescent shade of green. Just then, she felt the unmistakable sensation of movement behind her, making the hairs raise on the nape of her neck. She slowly turned and beheld a very tall man, standing quietly a few meters away from her, waiting for her to notice his presence. He had long silvery hair, braided with many colored beads and feathers. His high cheekbones and prominent nose made her think at once of Jacq, and so Katkin approached the stranger without fear.

"Shiqaba?" she asked, very quietly, and he gave a quick nod.

Katkin decided that now might be an excellent time to put her recent vow into practice. She tucked her arms up into her glowing sleeves and said firmly, "Go away. I no longer wish to serve you, or any of the others. Leave me in peace to die here, if that is my fate."

Shiqaba sighed and his voice sounded troubled. "Though I do not blame you for hating us, it cannot be as you ask. You are bound with the Amaranthine, this turn of the Gyre. We need your help, Katrione."

Katkin laughed bitterly at this. "And what is to be my reward, Shiqaba? Another knifing? Will I lose my other arm? How will you Amaranthine betray me this time?" Then she repeated coldly, "Go away. I say again, I will not help you."

Shiqaba shook her gently. "Listen to yourself. You are angry, rightfully so, but would you condemn the whole world to death? Now we know the true nature of the menace that lies before us, the Dawnmaid is ever more important. The future depends on the choices you make now."

"Of course, the fate of the world always lies in my hands," she replied sarcastically. "What is it you want me to do this time?"

"You must go back to Yrth and free the human, Huw."

Katkin asked, before she could stop herself, "Huw? What does he have to do with all this?"

"He is the Father. The first of the Autochthones."

"And if I don't wish to free him?"

"Come with me and you will know," said Shiqaba. He held out his hand and, after a moment's hesitation, she took it.

A jarring moment of dislocation meant they had gap shifted,

and Shiqaba released her hand. They stood on the top of a wide cliff, sheltered by a copse of gnarled and twisted pines. Katkin could see it overlooked a beautiful rolling land of forests interspersed with lakes that sparkled in the mid-morning sun. The air was warm and softly scented of resin. Katkin looked up at the tall Amaranthine by her side and asked, "Where are we? Why did you bring me here?"

Shiqaba shaded his eyes with his hand and continued to stare at the tranquil panorama before them. "What you see below us is the Dawnmaid's kingdom."

"So this is the homeland that the Kindreds have dreamed of? When will they be able to come here?" She thought how beautiful the lands before her were, laid out like a deep green counterpane replete with shining blue lake jewels.

*How happy Huw and the others would be if they could see this...*

Shiqaba's voice interrupted her thoughts. "They will never see it, unless you return to save the Autochthon known as Huw. He is needed." And yet Katkin could clearly see the smoke of several fires against the horizon.

Katkin sighed. Though Lalluna had left her, and Dai had betrayed her, it seemed that the Amaranthine were still not prepared to let her do as she pleased. Angry now, she spoke sharply to her companion. "What else can I do? I cannot translate the journal I stole from the Registrumhallen nor can I defy the whole Kindred of Anandi alone. Why don't you Amaranthine get someone else to fight your battles? I am tired."

Shiqaba placed a hand lightly on her shoulder. "What has happened to you, my Elleranne? Your spirit is weak. Have courage! Never before have the Amaranthine placed so much trust in one human. But you are worthy of that trust. You will not fail us."

She looked at him, bewildered. "Why did you call me that? My name is Katkin."

Shiqaba said only, "Elleranne is the healer."

Katkin wanted to question him about the Firaithi legend—the one that Huw had told her as they walked to Brunner's Valley— the tale of Elleranne and Ben'aryn. But he said, "We must go now," and then took her hand.

"Wait!" she cried. "If I am to save Huw then you must help me. I cannot do it alone."

As the world spun away she heard Shiqaba's voice saying softly, "There is a friend waiting for you. Look for him by the bridge."

Her landing was hard and awkward, leaving her to stagger over to a rough brick wall. When Katkin opened her eyes again she found herself in the alleyway close to the back yard of the Windlass. The high buildings on either side of her blocked the sun, and the abundant piles of refuse made the space cold, dank and rather smelly.

Katkin gazed down at her miraculous robe, wondering how it had known to transform into a perfectly serviceable Secunian maid's uniform, complete with tattered shawl. Just then, remembering the glass globe, she thought to have another look at it. But when she pushed her hand down into the uniform seam, she could find no pockets at all. Sighing, she pulled the wrap closer and stood quietly, wondering if it would be safe to go inside and retrieve her traveling bag. Katkin stepped deeper into the shadows as two black-uniformed Guardsman rode up to the back door.

One of them pounded on it, saying sharply, "Open the door, in the name of King Tristan."

Cursing softly, Katkin quickly crossed back into the Vastness. She made her way through the silent inn, carefully stepping around several seated Uri'el. Her bag was where she had left it, on the bed, and Katkin dug through it, looking for the special change of clothes she had brought from Bryn Mirain. A few moments later she was back on the street, wearing Huw's spare shirt and breeches, and leading Ajax by her halter. A thin black moustache, affixed with spirit gum to her upper lip, and a wide-brimmed hat pulled low over her forehead, completed her disguise. The strange clothing her rescuers had given her now resided in the bottom of her valise.

Nothing hindered her progress as she made her way through the busy lunch time traffic, out of the city of Scarfinda, though she spied many Guardsmen scurrying about, obviously engaged in a house to house search. After she had followed a broad avenue for several miles, the built-up district gradually petered out, and Katkin found herself in a neighborhood of small houses separated by weedy empty lots or common gardens. Up ahead lay the Scar Bridge, and once over the river Katkin knew she would have to make up her mind whether to turn north, towards Starruthe, or southeast, to Bryn Mirain. As she rode along she lost herself in a happy dream, of a snug harborside house in Einar, with her two grandsons, Jakob and Arvid, playing in the front garden. There would be no more hiding—no more fear. Only peace...

"Oi! You there!" There was a shout and a piercing whistle from somewhere behind her.

Ajax snorted in fear as Katkin abruptly abandoned her daydream and sat up straight in the saddle, looking about wildly. She jerked the reins, making ready to jump down from the horse if she had to gap shift again. Katkin watched as several policemen appeared, and passed her by, chasing a fleeing urchin who was clutching a pair of red apples in his grimy fists. She sighed her relief and gave Ajax a gentle nudge with her boots to get her moving again.

As she joined the throngs of people crossing the narrow iron suspension bridge, Shiqaba's last words came back to her.

*There is a friend waiting for you. Look for him by the bridge.*

Katkin scanned the faces of the passersby anxiously, but she did not recognize anyone. Whom could he have meant? After a moment she abandoned her search, thinking sadly that she had only a very few friends left in Yr anyway. Many of her former subjects now hated her, and she was not any more popular with her own kin, the Firaithi.

Once on the far side of the Scar Bridge, Katkin slowed Ajax while she tried to make up her mind in which direction she should proceed. Try as she may, she could come to no decision. Looking ahead, she saw that the road north was the lesser traveled of the two routes. She decided to make camp a little further up that way. Perhaps a quiet sleep would give her the certainty she craved.

Once on the North Way she relaxed a little, and started to enjoy the pastoral scenery around her. A line of low purple hills in the distance made her think of Beaumarais, and she wondered what new devilry her son, King Tristan, might be planning next. She rode for several miles, lost in grim contemplation—wondering about the future of Yr, and all her peoples.

Some ways beyond the bridge there stood a comfortable caravansary, with long and low wings spreading out either side of a thatch-roofed tavern. It was getting on for noon, and the thought of a decent meal and some coffee cheered Katkin a little. She tied Ajax loosely to a post and left her to graze on the verge. After a quick reconnaissance showed no black guardsmen were present, she stepped inside the common room. A long wooden counter

179

took up one wall, and the innkeeper, dressed in an immaculate white apron, stood behind it, pulling mugs of frothy dark ale. Diners occupied all the tables, so Katkin headed for the bar, and sat down on a stool. The innkeeper barked an order to a young lad.

Katkin, remembering her disguise just in time, gruffly asked him, "D'you speak Maraison, lad?"

The boy smiled and said cheerfully, "Yes, Sir. How can I help you?"

Katkin quickly perused the menu, scribbled on a slate to one side of the bar. "I'll have a plate of roast meat and some bread, and a beaker of black coffee, if you please."

The lad brought the food almost immediately, placing it before her with a flourish. As she thanked him, a strident voice began shouting curses and she looked down the bar to see what the disturbance could be. She saw a rather unkempt man, wearing a heavy, travel-stained cloak. He was slumped over the bar, with quite a forest of ale bottles before him. Though she could not understand the conversation, it seemed obvious that the innkeeper had decided to stop serving the drunken stranger, who was arguing vociferously in Secunian for more ale.

The serving boy grimaced, saying, "He orta throw that'un out. Been staying here three days he has, and hasn't once stopped drinkin'. Never says a word except askin' for more booze."

Katkin ignored the boy and listened intently to the drunken man's voice. Why did it sound so familiar? As she ate her dinner she kept glancing at him, but he had shifted on his stool so that his back was half to her. His broad-brimmed hat covered his hair, and most of his face, but a stray lock had slipped out—and lay, long and silver-white, against the black wool of his cloak. Suddenly the identity of the man sitting beside her was very clear, but Katkin did not greet him. Instead she thought back to the last time she had seen her brother-in-law, Arkady Svalbarad—*alive...*

He had saved her daughter Gwenn's life and then... well, then, he had died. Everyone had *seen* him die—Huw, Gunnar Strong Arm, Arvid, even Gwenn herself. All of them had helped her wash the body and wrap it in a linen shroud. Then Gwenn and Gunnar had taken Arkady back to T'Shang for interment, to the home of his old teacher, Dawa Tinley. Now he was here, once more amongst the living, and Katkin wondered who or what had brought him back to life, and whether or not he was even aware of his own identity. How could she find out without giving away her disguise?

Just then, Arkady staggered to his feet, and weaved through the tables towards the outside doors, bawling out a vulgar Maraison drinking song. Katkin gulped the last of her coffee, threw a few silver coins down onto the bar, and hurried after him. Her quarry shuffled down the path to the road, but stopped singing abruptly when he saw the horse still grazing on the grassy margin.

He shook his head in disbelief and then slurred, "Ajax?"

The horse nickered in recognition, and put her head down so that he might scratch behind her ears. Arkady leaned heavily on the horse, stroking her mane awkwardly as Katkin joined him by Ajax's side.

She said softly, "Hello, Stranger. Do you like my horse? She seems to know you." Then she added, "Will you walk with me awhile? I am traveling north."

Arkady stared down at her groggily, with no recognition in his bloodshot eyes. He swayed from side to side, opened his mouth to speak and then slumped down on the grass, in an alcoholic daze. Katkin looked down at him, reflecting that if this was the friend whom Shiqaba had indicated might help her, he was going to have to do a lot of sobering up first.

# 15

## Cendemar Sequent

*Hana and Eira sit together. The stones lie on the table before them, and Eira is shaking her head.*

Do you see? *she says sadly.* The future seems so grim. And all because of that demon Maggrai.

*Hana gazes thoughtfully at the stones.* Maggrai? *she whispers.* Now I am not so sure...

~~~~~~~~~~

*Tis true, without lying, certain and most true. That which is below is like that which is above and that which is above is like that which is below to do the miracles of one only thing. And as all things have been and arose from one by the meditation of one: so all things have their birth from this one thing by adaptation. The Sun is its father, the moon its mother, the wind hath carried it in its belly, the earth its nurse. The father of all perfection in the whole world is here. Its force or power is entire if it be converted into earth. Separate thou the earth from the fire, the subtle from the gross, sweetly, with great industry. It ascends from the earth to the heaven and again it descends to the earth and receives the force of things superior and inferior. By this means you shall have the glory of the whole world and thereby all obscurity shall fly from you. Its force is above all force, for it vanquishes every subtle thing and penetrates every solid thing. So was the world created. From this are and do come admirable adaptations where of the means (or process) is here in this. Hence I am called Hermes Trismegist, having the three parts of the philosophy of the whole world. That which I have said of the operation of the Sun is accomplished and ended.* [*]

Tristan stared down at the ancient book that lay open before him on the table and rubbed his tired eyes. He read the passage again and again. The secret lay within those mysteries written on its yellowed pages, of that he was most sure.

*By this means you shall have the glory of the whole world and thereby all obscurity shall fly from you.*

But how to unlock those words, to make them work for him?

Maggrai had said that most chymike was rubbish; nonetheless Tristan did not believe him. He had caught the scent of its potency in the moments of stillness he achieved as he practiced the arts that Gwenn had taught him.

*And as all things have been and arose from one by the meditation of one: so all things have their birth from this one thing by adaptation.*

* Sir Isaac Newton's translation of the Emerald Tablet.

He would yet bathe himself in the full perfume of its power, and then...

Maggrai would kneel before him, and so too...

The Yrth.

*Its force is above all force, for it vanquishes every subtle thing and penetrates every solid thing.*

The supremacy beckoned him, called his name.

Tristan...

Tristan...

"Tristan!"

His head snapped up. Roseberry's increasingly impatient voice broke through his reverie.

"When are you coming to bed? I won't wait up for you if you don't hurry. I need my beauty sleep, you know."

Tristan ignored her. As he turned the heavy vellum pages, the brilliantly colored illustrations filled him with wonder. A dragon, with scales like green jewels, eating its own tail. A golden salamander, glowing on the blazing fire known as the Quintessence. A tall king, dressed in magnificent purple, bearing the very Sun as his crown. But the most intoxicating of all—a woman, with regal bearing, naked and comely. She was the Moon, and the partner of the sun-crowned king. Tristan drank in her dusky beauty as his wife continued to call his name at intervals. Where could such a woman be found? To join with her—to deposit his essence within the deepest recesses of her vessel—that would be true magic, and the fruition of all his fantasies of power.

His body stirred and grew warm at the thought. *He would find her...*

"Tristan?"

At last he stood and closed the book with a sigh. "Coming, Berry," he said, without much enthusiasm. Though they had been married just a few weeks, Tristan already found his new bride profoundly unsatisfying. She had so many needs. His time, attention, money— even sex became just another tiresome gift to be lavished on his increasingly demanding wife. Tristan would not have thought it possible. What had happened to the simple Unity Juvenie he had once known?

"What are you studying over there anyway?" she asked him, her voice petulant. "You have barely said two words to me all evening. Come on, Trissy-wissy," she pouted. "Why don't you come to bed?" Tristan shuddered at the use of this nickname, and hoped the guard contingent outside the door hadn't heard his wife use it. "Come and make love to me," she purred. "I am ever so much more interesting than that dusty old rubbish."

"It is *not* rubbish," Tristan said sharply. "This is the greatest chymerical text ever produced. I found it amongst King Benedict's papers. Once I decipher it..."

Roseberry yawned hugely.

Tristan let his voice trail off. What was the point, anyway?

"Listen, Berry," he said briskly. "I am going to be very busy the next few days. Why don't you go to Belladore and visit your mother? I am sure she would like to see you."

She sniffed in return. "But it is boring there, and Mother's house is *so* small—it is only two rooms, you know. Where will all my retinue stay?"

"Well, ask her up to the Citadel then," he suggested in what he hoped was a reasonable tone of voice.

"No chance of that, Silly-Billy," Roseberry replied, using another of her favorite cringe-worthy nicknames. "She says she will not come to St. Valery until you allow the Deputies to reconvene, Tristan. Mother is very upset that you..."

"Fine!" he barked. "Then I will requisition the Inn in Belladore for your use. Your ladies-in-waiting and footmen can lodge there. You will leave in the morning."

"But Trissy..."

He spoke over his shoulder as he retreated from the room. "I am going to my laboratory. Don't wait up for me."

Once down among the retorts and beakers of his chymerical apparatus, he relaxed again. He noted that Maggrai had moved several more cramped cages into the room, containing various sorts of unhappy looking birds. A dove cooed at him mournfully. Tristan ignored it. A series of drawings occupied a large worktable, and he dragged a lantern over so that he could study them. As he did so, he recalled a conversation he had shared with Maggrai a few days beforehand.

Maggrai had been pacing back and forth in this room, like a

caged beast. He slammed his fist down on the table and snarled, "How many Autochthones have the Guard brought in?"

Tristan spoke quietly, less afraid now of his Master's moods, thanks to Gwenn. "About thirty-five all together, I believe. They all belong to the Kindred of Chandra." He hummed vacantly, but inside his mind he was turning over the mantra his sister had taught him like a diamond-spoked wheel. "Why do you ask, anyway?"

Maggrai bad-temperedly waved his hand, and Tristan assumed a carefully crafted expression of agony.

"Don't bother me with your vapid questions, idiot! It should be obvious that I need more subjects for my experiments." Maggrai turned away again, and Tristan's face relaxed.

"My men are combing Yr, my Lord, but the Firaithi are expert wayfarers. They have a web of secret paths and safe camping areas. We have not been able to catch up with all of them just yet."

Maggrai muttered to himself. "Travel in this benighted plane is too slow. We need some way of chasing them down. Something they cannot hide from..."

"What do you propose?" Tristan asked, with unfeigned interest.

"I have designed a flying machine." Maggrai pointed to the rudimentary drawings he had already created on the big laboratory work table. "It is somewhat pathetic, but it cannot be helped. There is not much in the way of raw material here—no plastics, or composites, even Aluminum has yet to be discovered in this backward age. Even a master craftsman such as myself has trouble with such an underdeveloped manufacturing base."

"My Lord? What is al-u-minum?" Tristan asked, confused and a little awed by this list of unknown substances.

"Never mind, dolt. Your job is to set about collecting this list of supplies for me. And we will need corsfyre—lots of corsfyre. Select the fifteen strongest Autochthones. Make sure they have wives and children that we can torture to ensure they stay in line. Bring them to me at once."

Now Tristan lingered by the table, studying the drawings, remembering the next part of the conversation, which had been so very, very interesting.

He had turned to Maggrai, all innocently wide-eyed, and said admiringly, "Please teach me about corsfyre, my Master. I remember that you mentioned it to Gwenn, but I would like to know more. Such a substance seems too miraculous to be true."

Maggrai's head had swung up sharply. "You doubt my words?"

Tristan quickly waved his hands. "Of course not! But I would like to see for myself the magnificent manifestation of your glory and power through the medium of the corsfyre."

As was usual, this transparent flattery soothed Maggrai, and he patted Tristan's shoulder almost paternally. Tristan had recently learned to suppress the shudders this gesture used to cause him and so he was able to say brightly, "Could you not take me with you—to the Vastness, I mean? I would dearly like to see how the corsfyre is collected. Is it very difficult to do?"

"Very well, little Tristan," said Maggrai obligingly. "We shall go now. It will be good for you to understand the methods involved." He walked over to the corner of the room, and picked up a long-ish metal pole. A wide blade, glinting evilly in the dim light, was securely lashed to the top with rough twine. At Tristan's questioning glance he explained, "This is a voulge—the only tool you need to harvest corsfyre. It is not difficult, but it can be..." Here he lavished a wide yellow-fanged grin on his protégé. "Dangerous. Oh, yes. Very dangerous."

A small step forward and to the left had carried them into the Vastness. Nothing moved, excepting themselves, although Tristan felt sure that the fearsome pounding of his heart was creating ripples, like heat waves, in the dead air around him. Maggrai strode confidently forward, out the laboratory door and into the hallway.

"We will go to one of the torture suites," he whispered. Tristan noted with interest that even the god-like Maggrai was not immune to the oppressive silence of the Vastness. "There will be plenty of raw material there."

He opened a door at random, on the left side of the hallway, and peered inside. The noise that issued forth was like nothing Tristan had ever heard before. It was as if someone had decanted all the anguished screams of the damned into one, powerful all-con-suming wail. Tristan covered his ears in terror but Maggrai merely tutted. "No good, I have already done this one." A second door proved more successful, and Maggrai stepped through, followed by Tristan, still shaken by the shattering noise issuing from the other room. Abruptly it died away, and he found he could think again.

Eight or nine Uri'el sat about the suite, cradling their charges in peaceful repose. Maggrai approached one, and positioned himself at its side, so that he stood facing the astarene in its lap. The Uri'el holding it did not look up.

Maggrai laughed callously. "You see? I told you they did nothing to protect those in their care. Now watch carefully." He grasped the metal pole with both hands and swung it upwards above his head, then sent it whistling down, right on to the serenely sleeping face of the astarene. Tristan forced himself to watch, though the dull smacking sound of the blade's impact tied his stomach into knots.

The head split asunder, like a paper bag of full of rotten bread pudding. The Uri'el clutched its arms towards its chest convulsively and made the same wailing scream Tristan had heard previously. He stuffed his fingers in his ears and shuffled forward, as Maggrai shoved his hand down into the wide open gash that was all that remained of the astarene's ruined face. Carefully he retrieved a softly glowing object, the color of wild poppies, yet perfectly faceted, like a jewel.

"Behold!" he said, triumphantly. "The epiphysis cerebri. Seat of the soul."

Tristan gazed at it. His fascination abruptly overcame his horror. The Uri'el continued to shriek in the background, but he hardly heard it. After a moment he implored, "Can I have a turn? Please, Master?"

Maggrai stared at him doubtfully. "Did I not tell you it was dangerous? Why do you think I usually employ slaves in the harvest? They are of little consequence."

"What... What do you mean, Maggrai?" Tristan asked with trepidation.

"Have you not been listening to me, my little fiend?" his Master said, and then struck him soundly across the face. "Then by all means pay attention now. If the stroke goes awry and splits the epiphysis then the resulting explosion will destroy this room and everything in it. I don't wish to risk my life for your idiotic amusement. If you wish to try, then so be it. But I will not be so foolish as to watch." He handed Tristan the voulge, and stepped away. "Bring me whatever corsfyre you can. I will show you a most interesting use for it, if you survive." With a flash of his yellow fangs he was gone.

Tristan stood in the torture suite, thoughtfully rubbing the stinging welt on his cheek. Maggrai was going to pay, someday, for all his abuse—he, Tristan, would see to that, with relish. He allowed himself a happy moment to imagine ever more ingenious retributions, each one more agonizing and humiliating than the last. Then he shook himself and hefted the voulge, trying to get a feel for its weight, and the sweep of its action.

Though it was undoubtedly the most dangerous thing he had ever attempted, Tristan felt no fear as he approached another of the Uri'el and took up a place at its side.

It had worked. Gloriously. After a couple of heart-stopping miscues Tristan had managed to split open the astarene's head cleanly, and dig out the epiphysis hidden inside it. Now it lay in his palm like a quivering pomegranate seed, and Tristan could feel the power pulsing from within, like a beating heart. With a trembling finger he poked at it, and felt its gelatin-like softness. Within a few seconds the skin on his palm began to tingle and then burn, so Tristan quickly transferred the epiphysis to his pocket and turned to the next Uri'el.

He had taken most all the corsfyre in the room, until the colossal sound of the Uri'el's collective anguish forced him to flee back into the living world. Maggrai was waiting.

"Still with us then, little Tristan?" he had asked, with evident pleasure. "How much have you collected?"

Tristan allowed himself a downcast expression. "Only three pieces, Master," he lied. But another five lay securely in the inner pocket of his jerkin, wrapped in his handkerchief.

"Let me have them," Maggrai commanded sharply. Tristan dug into his pocket and handed over the anafireon, wondering what his Master would do with it.

"First, it must be smelted, to harden it and remove the impurities," he said briskly. "Hand me that alembic, will you? Is the athanor ready?" Tristan nodded. He had lit the fire in the furnace sometime ago, and now the clay was perfectly primed with heat. Maggrai looked around the cluttered worktable impatiently. "What have you for lute?"

"Powdered glass and clay, Sir," Tristan answered promptly, and handed over an earthenware pot full of the greasy mixture necessary for sealing the joints between various pieces of chymerical apparatus. Maggrai very carefully pierced the soft anafireon with a round wooden dowel, and then assembled the alembic, with anafireon resting in its belly. "Watch carefully. I will add *lapis infernalis*,* and then *arcana corallina*.† Now, we place it in the athanor, thusly."

After a few anxious moments, he removed the glass vessel from the furnace and shook out its contents. A perfectly round stone, smoking hot and as hard as diamond, lay on the table, creating a circular scorch mark. The dowel had burned away, leaving a hole through its heart. Maggrai left it on the workbench to cool, and then strode to one of the cages. He retrieved a smallish brown owl. It struggled and screeched briefly, then lay limp in his hands.

"Watch now, little Tristan." Maggrai tied the ruddy corsfyre about the dead owl's neck with a strand of twisted wire and carelessly threw it down on to the floor.

Even now, though he had seen it with his own eyes, Tristan still could not believe what happened next.

Maggrai had left shortly afterwards, taking the reanimated aviscet with him. He was gone for several days and in that time Tristan managed to secretly smelt the rest of the anafireon and hide the resulting corsfyre. Not that he had any idea, yet, what he might use it for.

When his Master returned he was thoroughly annoyed. Tristan hovered just out of range of his anger, noting that one of Maggrai's wings hung at an odd angle. "What happened?" he asked cautiously.

"Nothing!" he snapped back, but Tristan saw a bleeding scratch across his face as well.

"Have you been injured?" he asked again, and this time Maggrai's fervent denial almost knocked him to his knees. Nevertheless, the knowledge that the Prime God was not all powerful filled Tristan with undisguised glee.

---

* Silver Nitrate. Silver nitrate crystals can be produced by dissolving silver metal in a solution of nitric acid and evaporating the solution. The equation is as follows: $3\ Ag(s) + 4HNO3(aq) \rightarrow 3\ AgNO3(aq) + 2\ H2O(l) + NO(g)$

† Mercuric Oxide. The red precipitate of HgO.

# 16

## Dunmoon + Zephur + Sequent

*Eira watches as Hana rolls the stones again. Dunmoon shows, black and ugly, followed by Zephur. She asks, What does that mean?*

*Hana rolls the third stone. Sequent.*

It means that our friends will be unhappy with each other for awhile, but mutual need will eventually forge a partnership of sorts. It is good. Dunmoon is good—for the hunted.

~~~~~~~~~

"Gods on fire, my aching head! Where am I?" Arkady groaned and sat up, clutching at his temples. A second later he doubled over and vomited, and the putrid liquid ran in rivulets into the fire, which hissed and spat.

Katkin helped him sit up again and said brusquely, "Drink this—it will help with the pain." She handed him some tincture of opium poppy and willow bark mixed with hot sweetened water. Arkady sipped it carefully and asked nothing else. He did not seem at all curious about his new traveling companion. Katkin busied herself making some supper out of the dried ingredients she carried in her pack. Once the soup was heating in an iron pot over the fire, she turned back to Arkady.

She asked gently, "Do you know who I am, Arkady Svalbarad?"

He stared up at her blearily and took another long draught of tea, as she carefully peeled the false moustache off her upper lip and removed her hat.

"Katkin," he whispered. His eyes seemed to focus on her properly for the first time. "But, I must still be very drunk," he added. "Because I could swear you only used to have one arm. Now you seem to have two."

"That is good," she said. "I was starting to think you might have lost your memory in whatever uncanniness brought you back to the living world." She smiled encouragingly and held up her hands.

"And you are right—I did have only one arm for awhile. Then I met some friends and they... fixed it for me."

Arkady blinked at this but then seemed to accept her explanation without question.

"Now," she said briskly. "Why don't you tell me what happened with you?" He shook his head numbly, and continued to sip the tea. Katkin sighed in resignation. "All right, we can talk after you recover from your three-day bender. Whatever possessed you to..." She stopped herself and went back to stirring the soup, thinking that Arkady, who had never in the past been much of a drinker, must now have some powerful demons hounding him. She was brimming with questions—about Gwenn and Gunnar and her grandsons—but she bit them back resolutely and handed Arkady a bowl of soup.

They sat together silently in the dusk. Katkin had set up camp in a grove of chestnut trees, some distance from the North road, well away from prying eyes. She continued to feed dry branches into the fire as she waited for Arkady to say something more. He stared into the glimmering flames, watching as the sparks rose on glowing wings into the darkness. After a long time, he said, "I have been drunk for much longer than three days, Katkin."

She glanced over at him. His face looked quite haggard in the firelight, and for the first time she wondered if perhaps something terrible had happened to her daughter or her family. She put a hand to her mouth and began to frame a question. He must have guessed her thoughts for he said, "Nay, do not worry. Gwenn is fine and so are the twins. Or they were when I left them in Starruthe a few weeks ago." He smiled mirthlessly. "She was large with child though. She may have had it by now."

"Another baby? So soon?" Katkin could not hide her dismay. "Who is the father, Kadya?"

"I am," he answered, tonelessly, and got up. He wandered over to Katkin's food bags and rifled through them.

"What are you looking for?"

"Wine," he answered, and then cursed her violently when she said she had none.

He had gone to sleep in a sulk, and Katkin, worried that he might slip away in the night, had knotted his bootlaces together and hobbled Ajax very firmly to a small patch of grass near the campfire. But in the morning when she woke he was still sleeping soundly, curled up by the remains of the fire, wrapped in his tattered cloak. She studied his face, thinking that he looked nothing like Jacq, for all they were half-brothers. His father, Nicholas Reynard, had come from the principality of Ruboralis and Arkady's wide set eyes and olive skin tone reflected this.

As she busied herself poking up the fire and boiling water for tea, he rolled over and stretched. After she had warned him about his bootlaces, Katkin went back to making breakfast. Arkady wandered off behind a tree, and returned a few moments later, wiping his filthy hands on his equally filthy clothes. They reeked of vomit and urine. Katkin wrinkled her nose in distaste. Arkady had once been a handsome man—and a proud scholar who spoke five or six different languages. He had even followed the difficult meditation disciplines of Hana, the Eastern Star. What had happened to change him so?

But this morning, at least, he seemed disposed to talk, and after breakfast he told her the whole story of how he came to be among the living again.

"So after Gunnar rescued Gwenn, and met you in Feringhall, what happened then?"

Arkady sighed, and stared down into the dregs at the bottom of his tea cup, as if he were practicing tasseomancy. "Gwenn wanted all of us to live together, as they do in T'Shang," he finally answered.

"What do you mean, Kadya?"

"The women there can have two husbands," he explained. "She thought it would work, and even Strawhead... I mean, Gunnar, was willing to try it. So was I, at first."

Katkin stared at him in shock. "Forgive my prurient curiosity, but how on Yrth did you manage... I mean, what were the sleeping arrangements like?"

"Nothing too out of the ordinary, despite how exotic it sounds," he replied dryly. "Strawhead and I built a one-roomed cottage behind the main house. I lived in there. He and Gwenn lived in Eydis' old house. We all got along great."

"So what happened to make you change your mind?"

"I found out that Strawhead could not be trusted, that is what!" he rejoined angrily.

"Why ever not?" Katkin asked him gently.

He spat angrily into the fire. "I saw him move a huge tree that by rights he should not have been able to budge. It must have weighed fifty tonnes."

Katkin's eyebrows shot up. "Are you sure? That is not possible."

He nodded grimly. "Gunnar tried to pretend it didn't happen, but I know what I saw," he said stubbornly. "I went to Gwenn, to warn her that Strawhead had been turned into some kind of monstrosity in the Vastness, but she would not listen. She said she would always trust him, no matter what he might become."

"Well, she cares about him, Kadya," Katkin offered reasonably, but he only shook his head.

"I wanted to prove to her that I was right, so I tried to provoke Strawhead as often as I could, to see if I could crack his facade. I thought if I made him angry enough to attack me, then she would see how dangerous he was. But somehow he managed not to take the bait, so I started in on Gwenn instead."

After Katkin said "Kadya!" he shrugged guiltily.

"That got him mad, and we had another fight." As Katkin shook her head in disgust he continued with a smirk, "I guess he did not want her to find out about his supernatural powers because he let me beat the shite out of him." Then he added petulantly, "But Gwenn got angry at *me* instead, when I was only trying to help her! She gave me a black eye and then threw me out."

"It sounds as though you richly deserved it," Katkin said matter-of-factly. "Now tell me the truth. What is this about, Kadya?"

He stared moodily into the fire. "How can I compete with Strawhead if he has turned into some kind of heroic God? Gwenn is always going to love him more. I might as well not even bother."

Katkin looked at him in shock. "I cannot believe you would say such a thing. You love Gwenn, I know you do. And you have a responsibility to take care of the child you created with her. You cannot just run away from your problems when things get difficult." She stopped talking, belatedly realizing that the advice she had just given Arkady applied equally to her own situation. She felt her cheeks color, and cleared her throat awkwardly. "Anyway... This child—yours and Gwenn's—is she not supposed to be important to the Firaithi?"

"Yes, she is—the Dawnmaid. But Gwenn and Strawhead can raise her without my help."

Katkin was firm. "No, they cannot. And you don't want them to. Otherwise, why did I find you drowning your sorrows in a roadside tavern yesterday? Look at you, you are obviously miserable! Stop being childish and admit it, Kadya. You lost your bearings for a while, but it is not too late to make it right."

He sat for a long time staring into the fire. Finally he scratched the rough salt and pepper whiskers on his chin and grinned at her wryly. "Hana came to me in a dream, as I was sleeping off another binge about a week ago, in Beaumarais. I thought she said I must come to Scarfinda—that someone needed me to right a great wrong. I only came because I thought the weather would be better for sleeping out of doors the further south I went, not because I wanted to help anyone. But I believe I must have misunderstood her anyway. She must have meant that you were going help me, Katkin."

Katkin insisted softly, "No, you were right the first time. You have helped me, Kadya, very much." Though he gave her a questioning glance, she did not say anything further about her own persistent unhappiness, or her recent indecision about leaving Huw to his fate. Instead, she told Arkady of the reason for her journey to Scarfinda, and of Huw's trial and possible execution.

"My gods, Kat! Then we need to translate that journal and get back to Bryn Mirain right away," he said urgently.

She sighed. "I don't know if it will do any good, Kadya. My grandmother's people are very proud and stiff-necked. They may not believe the evidence we present. But anyway, now I have you to help me, maybe we can rescue Huw from the lock-up. First of all though, we need to find another horse for you, *and* some cleaner clothes."

Arkady gave her a devilish smile. "As to the first, ma'am, I have a horse, by the name of Ceres at the inn stable. And for the second," he paused to sniff his sleeve and grimaced, "I will steal something fresher to wear on the way. All right?"

Katkin nodded happily and gathered up her cooking utensils. Arkady watched her in thoughtful silence. He opened his mouth as if to speak, and then shut it again. But soon afterwards, he asked, "If you were on your way back to Bryn Mirain with the journal, then why did you camp on this road? You should have been heading east, not north."

Katkin gave an uncomfortable shrug. "I was only—that is to

say, I did not..." her voice trailed off and although Arkady gave her a sharp glance she did not elaborate. Huw was Arkady's adopted blood brother, and she did not want him to know how close she had come to not returning at all. But it was not long before he guessed. His face darkened.

"You weren't going back to Bryn Mirain, were you?" he asked accusingly. "Don't lie to me. I can see it on your face." He glared at her though narrowed eyes and she blanched.

"Kadya, I..." she began, but he cut her off furiously.

"So that pretty speech you gave me, about not running away from my responsibilities, does not apply to you, is that it? You stinking hypocrite." He stood and backed away from the fire.

Katkin began to cry softly. "I promised myself I would make up my mind today. I had not actually decided..."

Arkady looked down at her. "I would love to hear your charming explanation, dear Sister, but I don't have time. Since you obviously have other plans, I will gladly go and rescue Huw—alone."

She stood and clutched at his sleeve. "Kadya, wait!"

"Go to hell, Katkin. Oh, and I am taking Ajax, by the way." He turned away and gathered up his cloak and traveling bag.

He would have ridden away, but Katkin caught Ajax's halter and held on as Arkady dug his heels into the horse's side. "Get out of the way, bitch, or I will ride you down, I swear it," he said angrily.

Katkin did not let go. She said, through gritted teeth, "Look, I don't give a damn what you think about me, but we have to save Huw together."

"Why?" he spat back. "You don't seem to care about him, or the Brunner children."

She looked stricken at this but did not dispute it. "Maybe you are right—but remember this, Kadya. You don't know *how* to find Bryn Mirain. You will never get there without my help."

Abruptly he checked the horse and climbed down off the saddle. He stared down at his muddy boot tops and then said slowly, "Well then... a truce... for now, anyway. But when Huw is free, then we go our separate ways, understood?"

"But... But what about Gwenn and the baby?" Katkin asked softly. "Won't you go back to Starruthe? That is where I was thinking of heading before I met up with you. Maybe we can all live there together in peace."

Arkady gave a short humorless bark of laughter. "Yes, dream on, my dear. Dream on..."

They rode together for many days in virtual silence, always trying to stay ahead of the Black Guard. Although Katkin still wore her hat and moustache disguise they decided to take no chances. Arkady often rode ahead into the towns and villages, scouting for trouble, and would return for her when it was safe for the two of them to pass through. The countryside seemed on edge, and there was little activity on the roads. Farmers and villagers hurried past, keeping their heads down, and did not speak. Katkin longed for a sound of laughter or a snatch of song, or even the trill of a bird. The weather turned cold, and as they climbed up into the Altas Range, endless days of drizzle made travel thoroughly uncomfortable. They dared not stay the night at the various inns they passed. Instead they camped out of doors if the weather permitted, or passed the hours of darkness secretly in barns or sheds, always making sure to be gone before dawn when the maids came to milk the cows or gather eggs.

Katkin's spirits sank lower and lower. Her traveling companion, Arkady, was perpetually dour. Although he had unwillingly decided to help her free Huw, he made no pretense of friendship. He also made it quite clear that he did not intend to return to Starruthe when they finished their business at Bryn Mirain. She had no doubt that Arkady would tell Huw of her seeming betrayal once they had rescued him. Then they would probably go off together and leave her to make her way back to Starruthe alone.

These bitter thoughts occupied her mind as the horses picked their way east up a long valley, littered with huge boulders. The road they followed was little more than a track that wound alongside a rushing stream. The water was milky blue—colored by the crushed stone suspended in it—and ice cold, straight from the terminus of a glacier somewhere up ahead. Katkin watched the path carefully, looking for a patteran. She knew there was a Firaithi camping ground in the valley, where they might find a snug cave to sleep in, some firewood and perhaps a cache of supplies. Her own supplies of food were running low, and although Arkady ate heartily he had done nothing to help her replenish them. As the evening wore on, the light grew longer, bringing the boulders into sharp relief. The water of the stream was tinted a delicate rose by the sunset at their back.

A series of broad stepping stones spanning the stream just ahead caught her eye and she signaled Arkady to halt. Katkin jumped down from Ajax as Arkady reined his horse, Ceres. She crossed the stream and studied the muddied ground on the other side.

She called back, "Many horses have passed this way only a day or two ago, along with men wearing heavy boots. There must be some Firaithi camping in the side valley I was making for. I definitely don't want to meet up with them, so I think we should just keep going and find another place to spend the night."

Arkady stridently disagreed. "Don't be such an idiot. They might have information we need." He added smugly, "Anyway, I am not their enemy—you are. Wait here for me while I go and talk to them."

He led Ceres across the stream and then rode up the hollow without a backwards glance. Katkin wondered if he intended to ask them the way to Bryn Mirain, and whether he really would return for her. But to her surprise he came hurrying back after she had been waiting only a few moments and called for her to follow him into the glen.

A strange sight met her eyes. A motley collection of caravans stood in a half-circle around a fire pit, ringed by blackened stones. Goats and dogs wandered freely through the campground, rooting through the bags of dried foodstuffs and clothing haphazardly scattered about. An iron cauldron lay tipped on its side, mutely bearing witness to whatever disaster had befallen those Firaithi who had been camped here. Katkin looked around her, almost overcome by a creeping horror.

"They seem to have been defeated without a struggle." Arkady's voice, sounding shrilly in the silence of the dell, made her jump. "I can't find anyone—man, woman or child—living or dead."

Katkin looked around her in disbelief. There is no way the Black Guard could have captured the proud Firaithi men without a fight. Maybe they had left for some other reason? But she did not think they would leave their brightly painted caravans behind without posting some sort of guard over them.

She went to stand beside Arkady, who had squatted by the ring of stones while examining the ashes from last night's fire. "What do you think happened here, Kadya?" she asked him softly.

His hazel eyes were melancholy. "I think a force of Black

197

Guardsmen attacked them here in this dell, while they slept. There must have been so many of them that the men could mount no defense. I guess they were all made prisoner or worse yet, taken away from here and killed. There is no telling what those evil minions of Tristan would do." He sighed as he rose and brushed the ashes from his hands. "Do you know whose caravans these were?"

Katkin did not answer, though an awful certainty had already settled over her like a dark shroud.

"It was the Kindred of Chandra, Kat. Huw's people."

Neither Katkin nor Arkady wanted to stay in the deserted camp. But as they talked, a fine rain began to fall, and the sun sank below the level of the hills, taking with it the last of the warmth. Katkin broke into one of the caravans and used the spirit stove to boil water for tea. There were plenty of dried foodstuffs in the cupboards, and she replenished her own food bags—though she felt more than a little guilty in doing so. Arkady joined her in a few moments and they sat at the tiny table sipping tea in silence. Stale lentil flour bread made a cheerless supper, but Katkin had little appetite anyway.

"I am going to sleep in here," she announced after Arkady's dejected expression grew too much for her to bear. "You can take the first watch. Wake me in a couple of hours," she added, and then yawned pointedly. Arkady left the caravan, slamming the door behind him. Katkin slipped into the narrow compartment bed, and shut the sliding door about halfway. The bed was warmer and more comfortable than anything she had slept in lately, and she soon dropped off.

A violent thump woke her, and she scrambled out of bed in alarm, after almost cracking her head on the low ceiling. As someone wrenched the door wide open, Katkin felt around frantically for anything she might use as a weapon. She screamed for Arkady as a dark menacing shape filled the doorway.

"Yesh?" he said and stumbled into the caravan.

Katkin sat down abruptly. "What in the hell are you doing? You almost scared me half to death," she chided him.

"Shorry," he slurred. "S'time for you t'watch, s'all."

She gave him a disgusted look. "Are you drunk again?"

She could just see the flash of his teeth in the darkened caravan as he grinned broadly. "I might have foun' a bottle or three of wine, yeah. J'want some? I din't drink it all, I swear." Arkady waved a bottle towards her, after carefully wiping the top with his filthy sleeve.

"No, thank you," she said firmly. "You are completely hopeless, Kadya. Now I will have to keep all the rest of the watches tonight. Thanks a lot," she added sarcastically.

"No prollem—any time," he replied, and then took another long, self-satisfied swig from the bottle. Katkin snatched it from him, and hurled it out the door.

He blinked stupidly. "Hey! Wadja do that for?"

She shouted. "Get out! Go and sleep it off somewhere," but Arkady did not move. Katkin, finally losing her temper completely, gave him a shove towards the door. He stumbled, and caught hold of her for balance. She held him up for a second, and then tried to extricate herself as his arms tightened around her.

"Whash your hurry? Les' just stay in here t'gether an' get nice n'cosy. Plenny of room."

As she struggled against him, his hand grasped her jaw firmly and twisted her face up to meet his. His lips tasted of sour wine and tobacco. She gave a cry of disgust and jerked free of his embrace. The tiny caravan gave her little room to maneuver, and as he weaved towards her again she could only back away towards the bed. Luckily, the chair she had abandoned tangled in his legs and he fell heavily. Katkin sidestepped him adroitly, and then fled out the door, locking it behind her. After a couple of minutes, the handle rattled violently and she heard him yelling for her to let him out or at least bring more wine. Thus satisfied that he had not injured himself when he fell, she slumped down by the fire to watch for the rest of the night.

One of the abandoned dogs settled by her side, and she stroked his rough fur, saying softly, "Well now, old fellow. Wonder what your name is? I guess I'll call you Chan, since you came from the Chandrathi. Wish you could tell me what happened to everyone, Chan. You probably saw the whole thing, did you not?"

The dog whined mournfully and licked her hand.

In the morning, though Katkin was very tired, she forced herself to build up the fire and make some tea. She rummaged through one of the caravans, finding a cache of eggs and some more flat bread, and then made herself and her newfound friend Chan some breakfast. The dog wolfed down his share of the scrambled eggs and lapped some water from a cup. Just as she sat down to eat her own breakfast, she heard a timid tap at the caravan door and Arkady called her name from inside. Katkin unlocked the door and he stumbled out, before collapsing next to the fire in a heap.

She went back to her breakfast, after handing him a cup of tea. He sipped in silence for a few moments before saying, "What happened last night? Please tell me I did not try to..." His voice trailed off and he peered at her through half-closed, bloodshot eyes.

"You did," she answered briefly and then, because Arkady looked so stricken, she added, "But you were quite drunk, so you did not get very far."

He gave a mortified groan and covered his face with his hands. "Gods! I had hoped it was a dream. I am so sorry, Kat."

"No harm done, Kadya, but you must get a grip on your drinking."

"I know," he said humbly. "And I will, I promise. But... you won't say anything about this to Huw, will you?"

Katkin gave him a serene, sunny smile. "Well now. It seems to me that we might be able to work out some kind of a deal, don't you think?"

He stared at her blearily. "What do you mean?"

"Just this, Kadya. You don't tell him which road you found me on, and I don't tell him you made an amorous advance to me last night. Fair enough?"

Arkady considered this for a minute, then nodded and held out a grimy hand. "All right then. Partners in crime forever." As Katkin shook his hand he gave her the first genuine smile she had seen from him in a long time.

# 17

## Cendemar Prox

*Can we do nothing? Moonlight shakes her lovely head in horror. She speaks hurriedly, in a rush of words that she hopes will wash away the image she has seen in Geya's mirror. Let me go to Fyn. He can stop it.*

*Hana takes her hand. There is nothing Fyn can do, not in the living world. Lutyond is on his own, until he accepts who he truly is.*

~~~~~~~~~~

"Are you *sure* you will be all right?" Gunnar asked for the twenty-fifth time as he shoved the last items of clothing into a leather traveling bag.

Gwenn smiled and ruffled his untidy hair affectionately. "Of course I will, Strong Arm. You are only going to be away for a few days."

He looked at her worriedly. "But the baby could come at any time. What if I am not here to help you?" He gently touched her swollen belly, and then smiled as he felt a strong kick from within. "You see? She is as eager as Faysta's steeds to be born. Maybe I should..."

She pushed his hand away and said resolutely, "Don't be silly, Gunnar. The baby is not due for another three or four *months*. And anyway, you have to go. Arvid sent a message to say he needs your help. You would not want to disappoint your old shipmate, would you?"

"No, I guess not..." he said pensively, wondering what Arvid was wanting, so suddenly, after all this time. It was eighteen months since Gunnar had last trod the sandy hills of the principle city of the Fynära. He knew that many people in the capital still resented the Faircrow for her part in the disastrous expedition to Beaumarais that had killed many men, so he and Gwenn had avoided visiting Einar since coming back to Starruthe, by trading for supplies with the neighboring coastal villages.

He sighed as he slung his bag over his shoulder. "I just wish I knew what Scar Brow wanted. It had better be important. Are you sure...?"

"The boys and I will be fine," she repeated firmly. "Get moving, Gunnar. You know you have been dying to take the *Able Drake* out on a proper voyage since you finished her. Go to Einar and see what Arvid needs." She kissed him lovingly on the mouth. "But hurry home. I will miss you, love."

Gunnar backed out the door, never taking his eyes off Gwenn. She smiled and waved to him, then bent down awkwardly, hindered by her ungainly waist, to see to Jakob, or was it Arvid? Gunnar still could not tell them apart. He shook his head, a little ashamed of his foolish need to protect her and his boys. As long as she had keth'fell he knew she could look after herself, but still—it was a long way to the closest village, Syver Beck

As he proudly surveyed the recently completed deck of the *Able Drake*, Gunnar reflected that his new vessel was both blessing and bane. On the one hand, he was never truly happy without a boat to call his own. The loss of the *Fire Drake* had been one of the hardest trials he had ever borne and he still missed her. Building another boat had been his main concern once they had all settled in at Feringhall. Of course this new boat was nothing like her sister, the *Fire Drake*. She had been made to carry forty Fynäran raiders on voyages across the rough open sea, for conquest and plunder. The *Able Drake* was a far smaller craft, both shorter and shallower. She was really only suitable for sailing along the quiet coastline of Starruthe with a crew of one or two, but Gunnar was pleased with her all the same.

But on the other hand, the *Able Drake* had been the beginning of the trouble between him and Arkady.

*Naught but a cog boat*, the Inkhorn said, and his voice had dripped contempt. But he had been contemptuous about everything in the days before he left.

If only Arkady hadn't seen him shift that tree on the day they started building the *Able Drake*. No explanation Gunnar had given him was satisfactory, and in the end they had fought. And he had let Arkady win, in part because he still felt guilty over that time in Celeste when he had been the victor in an unfair contest. But his other reason was far more compelling.

He no longer knew himself or his limits.

*That tree must have weighed fifty tonnes*, the Inkhorn had repeated, again and again.

What could someone who had successfully lifted fifty tonnes with one hand do to a man if he balled up his fist and smashed him in the face? Gunnar did not want to find out, so he had let Arkady hit him, many times, until Gwenn had angrily intervened on his behalf. She had landed a couple of solid punches, despite her pregnancy, and then sent Arkady packing. That too was a mixed blessing. Hana had told him once, in T'Shang, that Gwenn would eventually choose him over Arkady. Gunnar had not believed her then, but it made him very satisfied to think he was Gwenn's only lover now. But since he had left her, heavily pregnant and with two little ones to look after, would it not have been better if Arkady could have been there too?

Gunnar raised the sail and guided the boat away from the jetty. As he headed out to sea, the gentle swell of the waves filled his heart with unfettered joy. The summer sun beat down on the wide boards of the deck, and he kicked off his boots in delight, and then pulled his linen shirt off over his head. As he stood by the rudder, guiding the *Able Drake* down the coast towards Einar, Gunnar studied his right arm and shoulder. They looked just the same as before and yet he knew there was now some mysterious power buried within his limbs.

He had discovered this quite by accident when Gwenn had asked him to clear a patch of ground for a garden. A large boulder, probably abandoned there by a retreating glacier, stood right in the middle of the proposed plot. Gunnar had half-heartedly tried to lever it out with an iron bar, and almost killed himself as it shot out of the ground and landed five or six feet away. Curious, but not believing, Gunnar had given himself a test. Afterwards he stood still, trembling and sweaty, in awe of his own might and wondering fearfully what he had become. For although that rock weighed five or six tonnes, without a doubt, he had been able to squat, wrap his arms around it and lift it high.

After a few more experiments, carried out in the deepest secrecy, Gunnar decided that he wanted no part of this newfound strength. The balance of power between he and Arkady and Gwenn stayed nicely in tune as it was, and Gunnar did not want anything to upset the delicate equilibrium that allowed them all to live together in peace. But if he took the time to probe within himself—which he steadfastly tried *not* to do—the motive ran far deeper. *Fear...*

Fear of the uncanny, fear of the unknown. Fear of becoming something he was not. Fear, when it got right down to it, of power—power that he had neither the knowledge nor discernment to use properly. Yes, Hana had given him to understand that he was the grandson of the Numen, and therefore possessed of the wisdom of the ages.

*Look to your heart*, she had urged him.

Well, he had looked, and looked some more. The only wisdom he had found was of the most ordinary human kind—he loved the sea, he loved his wife and his sons, he even loved the child that Gwenn carried now. That was enough for Gunnar—to be human and to love. It was all he wanted and more than he thought he deserved. So after Arkady had caught him, that day in the cove, he had sworn, on the Mariner's anchor, that he would never use his superhuman strength again. The irony of this might have been funny if it had not also been so thoroughly ridiculous.

The bay was strangely quiet as Gunnar put into the port of Einar; nothing like the old days, when raiding ships came and went with holds full of slaves and booty. Nowadays his brethren were traders, like the Dalvolk, though nowhere near as successful. Too many people still harbored a deep distrust of the Fynärans, as if they expected the soberly dressed merchantmen to suddenly produce swords and axes from somewhere within their fur-lined cloaks. It would take a generation, at least, thought Gunnar, before the predations of the past might be forgiven. He doubted they would ever be entirely forgotten.

He stared up at the hill called Sandymount, rising impressively above the town. Arvid had taken over the Magnus' residence there, when he alone had returned from the disastrous raid on Beaumarais that had cost the lives of almost five hundred of Starruthe's finest warriors. Gunnar's eyes narrowed as he saw that a very large building with a peaked roof had been constructed beside it.

After he left the *Able Drake* tied up to a surprisingly shabby jetty, Gunnar walked up the Market Street towards the square. He looked curiously at the passersby, who were dressed identically, in a manner quite unlike the ordinary Fynärans he remembered. He had been away for some time, it was true, but from whence had come this appetite for severe black and white clothing? And every women who scurried by him wore a snow white headscarf, intricately knotted—designed to cover the hair, as well as most of the face and neck.

Gunnar saw a diminutive, black-robed man hurrying down the main street. His high-peaked cap was a somewhat comic echo of the new building on the Sandymount, but Gunnar was far too polite to smile. The man drew up, obviously out of breath, and gave him a clipped bow.

"Gunnar Strong Arm?" he inquired, and received a wary nod in reply. He spoke passable Dalvolk, but his accent placed him as a Southerner, and Gunnar was not inclined to trust him.

"Welcome in the Name of Prime. I am Proctor Janus Verbik. The High Priest asked me to keep watch for you, so that I might conduct you to his residence as soon as you arrived." He looked curiously over Gunnar's shoulder. "You are alone? I understood there were others in your family." His eyes were very small and sharp, like a bird's. They seemed to drill into Gunnar's in a very disconcerting way.

He answered only, "There is no one but myself."

Janus did not seem perturbed, although his eyelids drooped a little. "No matter. Will you accompany me to Sandymount?"

Gunnar shrugged and fell into step with him, thinking that they may as well walk together. As they passed along the main street, he inquired of his companion, "What is that new building by the Magnus' house?"

Janus answered promptly, and with pride. "The edifice of which you speak is the Most Holy Tabernacle of the Prime God, completed in the Year of our Redeemer '86, for the grace and good of the people of Einar."

Gunnar looked over at him in shock. Prime God? What had happened to Ods, and Faysta and the rest? He was about to question Janus further when a young boy of perhaps ten or twelve, running flat out, almost bowled into them.

"What is the meaning of this, Lars?" Proctor Janus demanded.

The boy immediately dropped his eyes and crossed his hands behind his back. "Prime's Blessings to you, Proctor," he said timidly. "I was hurrying so I would not be late for Consecration."

"That is a poor excuse," Proctor Janus snapped. "And have you no greeting for the gentleman at my side, young Master? What does Prime God teach us?"

The boy spoke, his voice curiously singsong, as if he had learned the words off by heart. "Treat a stranger as a brother and you lead him willingly to the Bounty, as a thirsty horse is led to water." Janus gave an approving smile as he bobbed his head respectfully and mumbled, "Prime's Greetings to you, Stranger."

The boy stared in obvious fascination at Gunnar's smocked and ruffled "town" tunic, made of starched linen, carefully hand-stitched by Gwenn. The boy's own tunic was boxy and plain, poorly made, with a heavy, black leather belt fastened around the middle.

"May... May I go?" he asked Janus, after a moment had passed in heavy silence.

The black-robed man frowned. "Indeed you may not. There is chastisement due for your insolence. On your knees, Sinner!"

Lars dropped down, babbling a confused apology. "Proctor Janus, I did not mean to..."

The Proctor said implacably, "Your girdle, if you please, young Master."

Gunnar decided it was high time he intervened. "Why not let the lad go about his business? There was no harm done." Janus ignored him.

Lars fumbled with the wide leather belt he wore, and handed it back to the Proctor. As soon as he did so, the back of his shirt gaped wide. Before Gunnar could react, the strap whistled down and left a brutal red welt on the boy's shoulder blades. He gave a strangled cry of pain. A second blow would have followed, but Gunnar caught the Proctor's wrist and held it, none too gently.

"That is enough," he growled, and nudged Lars with his foot. "Get going, lad. He is finished."

Lars looked back at the Proctor with tear-filled eyes. He nodded dismissively and tossed him his belt. He quickly fastened it and ran off towards Sandymount.

Janus rubbed his wrist and snapped, "The Exalted One will not be pleased by your interference. It is my holy duty to chastise those in need."

Gunnar fell prey to his mounting exasperation. "Who or what in the name of Ods is an Exalted One? Look, I just came here to see the Magnus, Arvid Scar Brow. We used to be shipmates, before..." He stared at the Proctor thoughtfully. "Before the likes of you showed up."

"If you are a friend of the High Priest as you claim, then doubtless he will show you mercy." He looked up at Gunnar, and his gimlet eyes were bright once more. "But I give you this warning, Stranger. To mention the name of any idol in this place is punishable by death."

"It was like this, Strong Arm. Remember I told you that I escaped from St. Valery by hiding in the lake all day? I was frozen to the bone and close to collapse when a farmer and his wife found me clinging to a log by the water's edge. They took me home with them and warmed me up, then gave me food and drink. I was stunned. Obviously they knew by my clothes that I was a raider, but they did not seem to care. So I asked them why they would show such deference to an enemy. They explained to me about Him, and how one must always show mercy and kindness to a stranger, so that he might be willing to receive the Bounty of Prime."

Gunnar stared at Arvid. He looked the same—more or less, but there was something profoundly unsettling about the burning conviction in his eyes when he spoke of Prime God.

Arvid continued, "Once I understood the Bounty, I saw the error of my ways—killing and stealing, and worshipping idols are all anathema to Him. So when I returned and found Einar to be the selfsame loathsome pit of sin and depravity, I knew I had to do something. Prime God demanded it of me, and I willingly complied."

"So what exactly did you do, Arvid?" Gunnar asked. "There seem to have been a lot of changes around here, and I am not at all sure I approve of them." He sipped his tea and nibbled some of the unsalted dry bread his host had offered him. Arvid had already explained that such fripperies as ale and cakes were now forbidden, because they encouraged indolence.

Arvid smiled indulgently. "But that is only because you do not yet share in the Bounty. Soon you will know," he added confidently. "As for me, I merely did what Prime God requires. I made myself Magnus, so I could lead the people of Einar from the thorny paths of unrighteousness on to the straight and narrow way. Then I cast down the idols and reliquaries of their sinful past and together we built the magnificent Tabernacle."

He left the carved throne that had once belonged to Per Drake's Son and strode about the room, as he described the conversion of Einar to the Bounty of the Prime God.

"Of course, at first, there were some who did not wish to abandon their sinful natures. So Prime God directed the method of holy chastisement you witnessed on your way here. Everyone, even I, wears a girdle and whipping shirt. That way, we can be immediately punished for our transgressions. It has been very helpful."

Gunnar noted silently that Arvid did not seem to be wearing either the girdle or whipping shirt at the moment. His wide-sleeved black robe, though severely plain, was made of heavy silk brocade, undoubtedly imported at great expense from Cherumea. Such opulence would not have appealed to the Arvid Scar Brow of old, who had steadfastly fought at Gunnar's left hand in every battle. Gunnar shook his head, thinking that this new Arvid was far less agreeable. He decided that perhaps it might be best if he cut this visit short and headed back to Feringhall—today.

He said briskly, "What did you need to see me about, Arvid? I have responsibilities to tend to at home..."

Arvid interrupted. "Yes, of course, Gunnar. We won't keep you any longer than necessary, I give you my word. But what is your hurry? You have not yet seen the Tabernacle, nor sat down to a proper meal with me. Surely you plan to stay at least one night as my guest?"

Gunnar considered this and could think of no polite way to decline. "Very well. But I must sleep on board the *Able Drake* tonight, so that I may make an early start in the morning."

Arvid answered coolly. "As you wish, Strong Arm. Why don't we visit the Tabernacle now? I would not want you to miss that."

Gunnar had no interest in seeing the place of worship for this God to whom allegiance had changed both Arvid and Einar so unpleasantly. He gave a heavy sigh.

They walked together across the top of Sandymount, staring into the westering sun. Black-robed figures strode back and forth across a wide paved square. Arvid commented, "I am pleased to say you have arrived in time for our Festival, my friend."

"Is that so?" Gunnar answered vaguely. A tall, cast-iron column in the center of the Plaza had captured his attention. Arvid passed by it without comment, but Gunnar had an inexplicable feeling of creeping horror when he saw four heavy iron rings, one on each face of the column, about half-way up its sides.

And from inside his mind a voice spoke urgently—*something is not right.*

"It is held only once a year," Arvid continued. "For two weeks. You are so very fortunate to be able to see it."

Gunnar slowed to examine the flagstones. They were stained or burned black underneath. The feeling of horror intensified, though Gunnar could not for the life of him understand why.

Arvid called back, telling him to hurry, as the evening service would soon begin. Wide double doors opened directly onto the square. The inside was dark and cool and quiet. Gunnar looked up at the ceiling that soared thirty feet above his head. Some cunning craftsman had designed it to look like the upturned keel of a boat.

"Striking, no?" Arvid said proudly, and Gunnar had to agree that it was.

They walked up the main aisle, passing through rows and rows of uncomfortable looking straight-backed pews, made of a kind of dull black wood utterly lacking in beauty.

In front of them stood a wide circle with four prongs set equidistant around it. It was suspended from the ceiling by two chains. Probably made of iron, Gunnar thought to himself, and wondered out loud what its function could be.

Arvid explained. "That is the symbol of the most holy Prime. The Naught. It represents the goal we all strive for—the purity of perfection. The Naught helps us to empty ourselves of sin." He smiled encouragingly.

The voice in Gunnar's head suddenly shrilled, *Get away from here.*

A huge curtain, dull and black, like everything else in the room, covered the back wall. What was hiding behind it?

*Now. While you still can.*

Proctor Acolytus Janus joined them at the front of the Tabernacle. He bowed to Arvid. "Will you be showing your esteemed guest the back rooms, High Priest?" Gunnar saw a look pass between the two men, and his hand instinctively strayed to his sword, before remembering that Arvid had demanded he leave it outside the door.

*Run, you fool. Run!*

Gunnar tensed himself, and turned from them, only to see that the center aisle of the Tabernacle had quietly filled with heavily armed men in black tunics. "My blessed Abaryanites," Arvid said casually. "Shall we continue the tour, Strong Arm?"

Gunnar stared at him and licked his suddenly dry lips.

"What is this, Scar Brow?" he asked hoarsely.

Janus looked on with undisguised glee as Arvid replied, "Welcome to the Bounty of Prime, my friend. Here you will find atonement for all your transgressions."

He would have fought then, and with all his strength—oath be damned—but a curious lethargy seemed to overtake his muscles even as he swung his right arm up, intending to crush the face of that boil-brained little codpiece Janus. The high beams above his head were spinning as the Abaryanites closed in.

They caught him as he fell, and the last thing Gunnar remembered for a time was Arvid's face bending low over his, saying solicitously, "Carefully now. Take him to the number three cell, the one I have specially prepared for our guest."

When he woke and found he could move, without restraint, Gunnar breathed a silent prayer of thanks. He sat up and rubbed his stomach, still queasy from the drug with which Arvid had laced his tea. Then he looked around him. The cell he occupied was maybe fifteen feet square, with one barred wall that seemed to end in blackness. A very solid-looking iron door took up part of another wall, and it was through this door Gunnar planned to escape. As soon as he had gap shifted into the Vastness, he knew he would be able to step through it freely.

He stood, waiting patiently until his legs felt a little less rubbery, then stepped forward and a little to the left. Instantly a searing bolt of pain shot through his head, and tore a ragged scream from his lips. It felt as though his forehead—no, his brain—had been skewered with a red-hot spike. After a few seconds of this unbearable agony, Gunnar crashed to the stone floor of his cell, unconscious.

The next time he came to, Gunnar stood even more slowly, rubbing his cheek where it had grazed the bench as he fell. He did not understand what had happened to him when he had attempted to gap shift, but he was determined to try again, even though every muscle in his body ached like fire.

Gunnar lifted his foot, intending to take another step forward, when Arvid said, "I would not try that again if I were you. The pain gets worse every time, I am told."

Gunnar turned bit by bit, until he saw his old first mate looking at him through the barred wall at the far end of his cell. He shuffled forward, grunting with the painful effort of movement, until he stood directly opposite Arvid. The bars, when he grasped them and held on, were very, very solid. "Why in the name of Nung am I locked up in here, Arvid?" he asked angrily.

"You are in the cells of the penitents," Arvid replied mildly. "Although we had to make certain modifications to this one, as you have already discovered."

Gunnar said contemptuously, "I don't care what you have done. You cannot keep me in here."

Arvid smiled. "Such pride. But you always were a stubborn one, were you not? Well, then, go ahead and try. You will learn, soon enough." He waved a hand in Gunnar's direction, inviting him to proceed.

He did. And Arvid was right—this time the pain, at least until he passed out again, was much, much worse.

Coming to, this time, was like waking from a nightmare, only to find that reality was far more terrifying. He sat up slowly, only as far as his elbows, and found that Arvid or one of the Abaryanites had placed him back on the bench again. His gummy, cold breeches prompted the humiliating awareness that in this last attempt to leave his cell via the Vastness he had fouled himself. He stripped then off, circumspectly lying on his back, and threw them away in the farthest corner. Gunnar did not try to stand up because he knew, this time, his legs would not hold him.

Arvid spoke from his position just outside the bars, saying gently, "I expect you would like an explanation. It is quite simple. There is a substance called corsfyre, which comes from the Vastness. It has many useful properties, I am told, amongst which is the ability to act as a magnet for anafireon. There are four pieces of it hidden in this cell. When you tried to leave, the corsfyre exerted a tremendous amount of pressure on your anafireon. As you have seen, each time it does a little more damage to your brain, until soon, if you persist in these foolish attempts at escape, you will be nothing but a drooling half-wit. Do you understand?"

Gunnar nodded, very carefully, and asked quietly, "What do you want from me, Scar Brow? Why are you doing this?"

Arvid said solemnly, "I am only trying to save you from your transgressions, my dear friend."

"And if I don't wish to be saved?" Gunnar growled back.

"But you do. We all do." Arvid's voice rang with earnest self-righteousness. "I know you will want to be free of the crushing weight of your sins once you have experienced for yourself the Bounty of Prime."

"What are you going to do to me?" Gunnar asked. Arvid patted his hand encouragingly through the bars.

"Nothing, for now. For a little while, you will watch and learn as others accept the Bounty. Then soon, very soon, it will be your turn. That day will be a blessed one, Strong Arm, for you..." Arvid met his eyes, and Gunnar saw only undisguised menace, "...and your lovely little family." He smiled and a sudden spasm of fear raked Gunnar's chest. Not for himself, never that—but for Gwenn and his children, utterly alone at Feringhall.

"Come on," Gwenn said to the boys, as she took each one by the hand. "The tide is coming in. Let's go look for Daddy. It has only been five days, but maybe he is coming home early." Two little faces smiled up at her happily. "Da Da." lisped Jakob, always the more advanced of the two.

"Yes," agreed Gwenn softly. "I hope so."

She walked slowly down the path between the dunes with them, to the quay that Gunnar had built in the sheltered cove close to the house, hoping all the while that a square sail might be visible on the horizon. He had sent no message, but that was hardly surprising, since it would take as many days to get to this isolated beach as Gunnar would himself.

But the sea looked gray and empty, and a cold wind blew in off the whitecaps. Gwenn shivered but spoke cheerily to her sons, to hide her own disappointment. "Tomorrow, I expect." She nodded and smiled at them. "Yes, tomorrow, for certain."

*The Festival of the Bounty of Prime.* Fourteen days of hell.

Once Proctor Acolytus Janus swept the great curtain aside, Gunnar's cell looked directly out on to the altar of the Tabernacle. He could observe everything that happened and every member of the congregation could see him as he watched. As Janus intoned the list of sins, the struggling victim was stripped and brutally spread-eagled on the metal ring. The Abaryanites made sure there was no

212

escape possible by tying the penitent securely to the wicked metal prongs. Arvid came forward, now wearing a pure white chasuble, and strode amongst his congregation, shouting and waving his arms, whipping the crowd into a frenzied froth.

*The Bounty of Prime.* Einar reveling in the punishment of one of their own.

A thief would be flogged by the Proctor Acolytus. A man who gossiped against his neighbor might have his tongue nailed to a board. A storekeeper accused of cheating would be made to swallow hot coins. The list of sins was endless, the list of punishments barbarically innovative—until Gunnar wanted to vomit out these scenes of depravity like pus from a festering sore in his gut. He had stopped watching, after the second day, but he could not get away from the sound of the torture, from the screams of the penitent, from the ecstatic cries of the congregation.

And all the time he was thinking, soon it will be *my* turn. *The Bounty of Prime.*

One evening, when the High Priest paid him a visit, Gunnar asked curiously, "What of your wife, Scar Brow? Did she embrace this nonsense so willingly?" He could not imagine the acerbic Gudrun meekly following the regime of the Prime God, nor had he seen her among the faithful in the Tabernacle.

Arvid looked a little discomfited. "Gudrun accepted the Bounty—of course. She was transported by it." Gunnar did not understand, then, what he meant. Arvid continued, pensively, "Her sharp tongue was ever her undoing. Once it was removed she was able to curb her impious wickedness. For a time, anyway."

His Captain stared at him in horror. "You cut out Gudrun's tongue? Your own wife? My gods, how could you do that, Arvid?"

Arvid shrugged and said defensively, "Better to lose a tongue than your soul, Strong Arm."

"And what of your sons? Did they consent to this torture of their mother?"

Now Arvid's smile was proud. "They are all high in the ranks of my Abaryanites. It is Prime God's blessing and reward that I should have such fine offspring."

On the sixth night the Abaryanites carried up a wailing woman that Gunnar recognized—Nanna Storm Bringer. Gwenn had killed her husband, Stig, when he joined a group of mutineers on the *Fire Drake*. Now Nanna was here, facing some sort of charge. She cried and begged for mercy as they stripped her and tied her down. The scroll was read—adultery in thought, adultery in word, and adultery in deed. Arvid, as always, moved among the congregation until the roar for vengeance filled the Tabernacle to the roof. Then Gunnar listened in horror as he invited all the men to come forward, to take part in Nanna's Bounty.

*No, they can't possibly be going to...*

But they did. Every man, including the Abaryanites, took his turn with Nanna, with shocking sadism, until her screams grew course and ragged—until finally her voice gave out—until her body sagged limply on the circle—until...

She was dead. It took a long time. And still the congregation clamored for more.

Gunnar crawled to the back of his cage, and covered his head with his hands, rocking back and forth, moaning gutturally. Trying, at first, to shut out the noise and then later, the awful ghastly silence.

It had been late, near midnight, when Arvid, flanked, as usual, by four burly Abaryanites, visited him. Gunnar was weak now, from six days without food, and the mysterious effect of the corsfyre, but his captor would take no chances.

"Did you watch the Bounty tonight, Strong Arm?" he asked brightly. Gunnar, lying on the bench, with his face to the wall, did not reply. Arvid, undeterred, went on. "Of course you did. I wanted you to have the benefit of that one, especially. Do you know why?"

Gunnar turned over, suddenly afraid, and Arvid gave him a satisfied little smile. "I thought you might guess. Because, of course, when we find your wife, that is the selfsame Bounty that she will receive and enjoy. I can only hope it transports her as quickly as it did Nanna." He leaned forward confidentially and whispered, "Sometimes it takes a lot longer." Gunnar leapt up from the bench, fists raised in fury.

"Leave her alone!" he cried, and the Abaryanites stepped forward and shoved him back down. Gunnar lay there, panting hard, wondering why they had not found Gwenn already. Arvid had visited Feringhall several times in the old days and knew where on the coast it lay.

"You could make it a lot easier on her, you know," Arvid said reasonably. "If you tell me where she is, I might be able to get the charge reduced to lascivious conduct. The Bounty for that is only one hundred holy chastisements." He paced around the cell, musing, "I thought she would be at your Grandmother's old place. When I heard you had come back to Starruthe I sent some Abaryanites there, but the house was just as it was when we left it—burned down to the ground."

Gunnar stared at him, and then quickly dropped his eyes, wondering what in the name of Ods was going on. "When was that?" he asked cautiously.

"A month or more ago," he replied, and Gunnar felt a sudden surge of hope in his heart. Was this another of his Grandmother's subtle magics, to protect Gwenn and the children? Arvid said, "I knew you must be somewhere close, so I sent a message to the storekeeper in Syver Beck. I had hoped that perhaps you would all come, but no matter. We will find her, Strong Arm."

"Go to hell, Arvid," Gunnar growled, and turned back to face the wall again.

Gwenn woke from an afternoon nap as the boys drowsed on beside her. The heat and the flies buzzing in a desultory manner against the window glass made her feel as though she was still dreaming. She had been, a moment ago—a dream in which Gunnar had been shouting her name, urgently, painfully. She had been running, desperately searching for him, until another voice called for her. Very loudly and clearly, she had heard someone speaking her name. And now, even though she was awake, she heard it again.

# 18

## Wanmoon + Zephur + Sequent

*Hana looks angrily down at the stones.* My people have become stiff-necked fools! I cannot help them anymore. Now comes the time for reaping.

*She sits in silence, as her tears fall unchecked.* O, my little ones. That you should have to suffer in this way...

It was only as they camped together in the valley below Bryn Mirain, where Poppy had had her dream about Huw, that an unhappy thought occurred to Katkin—Arkady might not even be able to enter the hidden meeting grounds of the Firaithi with her. After all, Hana had cast some veil of invisibility over the entrance to the dell, and who knew whether they would be able to pass through it together, since Arkady was not of the Kindreds.

Apprehensively, she asked him about it. He replied, "I don't know if what you say is true or not, but you had better take the translation of Tavish's journal with you tomorrow. If I can't enter Bryn Mirain then you will have to show it to Ander on your own."

Arkady had been poring over the journal for the better part of a week, sitting close to the fire in the evenings, trying to make out the crabbed writing. Katkin had taken down his translation as he spoke it aloud. They had only managed to interpret the first twenty pages, and there was much more still to finish. She stared down at the sheaf of parchment he laid in her outstretched hands. "Do you think it will do any good?" she asked.

He shrugged. "Well, all we know so far is that Tavish thought it important to crew his boats with Firaithi, because otherwise they could not seem to navigate towards the chain of islands that they knew lay to the west. I believe the islands might have been one of the worlds between, but we have no conclusive proof until I finish the journal. Maybe what we have translated will be enough to convince them, but somehow I doubt it. We will probably just have to fight our way out with Huw."

Katkin groaned aloud at this. For all their pig-headed ways, the Kindred of Anandi were still her family and she was loath to think that she and Arkady would have to draw weapons against them.

Arkady shot her an angry look. "We have no choice. They mean to execute Huw. We cannot let that happen."

"Of course, Kadya. You are right. But I hope it doesn't come to that." She sighed in frustration. "We should all be united against the Black Guard, not fighting amongst ourselves like foolish children. No good can come of it." With this unhappy thought she wrapped herself up in a blanket and tried to sleep, after telling Arkady to wake her after the first watch. The night passed uneventfully and after an early breakfast they set off again, climbing high up the mountainside, heading for Bryn Mirain.

They left the horses at the bottom of the stony draw. Katkin patted Chan and told him firmly to stay behind. The dog dutifully laid down and put his head between his paws.

Arkady looked up towards the top. "Are you sure this is the right way? That looks like a dead end up there."

Katkin scrambled up the slope, confidently calling back over her shoulder, "I told you, Bryn Mirain is under Hana's protection. It is completely hidden."

But it was not. As they reached the lip, the basin lay wide open before them, utterly bleak—and totally deserted. The blackened ground and broken tree stumps stretching out below left them both temporarily speechless with shock. Then Arkady cried, "Gods beyond! Huw!" and pelted down the steep slope. Katkin ran behind him, looking around her in alarm. Piles of refuse lay about, along with many fly-encrusted dead goats, making a powerful stench in the warm summer air. There were no caravans in sight, and she could only hope that the Kindreds camped here had been able to escape before this devastation took place—and had taken Huw with them.

Arkady followed her to the lock-up. Katkin gave a cry of dismay when she saw that the iron bars remained bolted in place. She pressed herself against them, eyes straining in the dim light. With effort, she could just make out an untidy pile of rags in the very back of the cavern. Katkin felt her mouth go bone dry. "Huw?" she whispered. The rags fluttered briefly, and then were still again.

"Help me!" she barked to Arkady. "We have to get this door open somehow. He is in there, I can see him." She shook the bars in frustration, calling for Huw, but he did not answer her.

"We will need some sort of lever," Arkady said, after examining the fastenings holding the bars to the mountainside. He scurried back into the camping ground, and returned a moment later with a stout iron bar, probably a cast off wheel axle from one of the caravans. "Stand back," he warned her, and then wedged the bar in between the iron bars and the rock. But in the end it took both of their combined strengths to pry the door open.

Only one of them could fit into the narrow cave at a time, so Katkin crawled forward on her hands and knees to where Huw lay curled up in a fetal position. She quickly called back to Arkady to fetch some water. Arkady hurried to where they had left the packs and water skins, and carried them to the lock up. He filled a small cup and handed it to Katkin. She lifted Huw's head and trickled a few drops of the water between his cracked lips. He coughed and choked in his eagerness to get the water down, and she said, "Easy Huw, just try to swallow it slowly."

Katkin backed out of the cave so that Arkady could move Huw out into the sunshine. This he did with some difficulty, since the space was impossible to stand up in, and only a few feet wide. When Huw finally lay on the blackened grass Katkin examined him while Arkady kept watch. He was suffering from extreme dehydration, but had no visible wounds. Katkin sat back on her heels, relieved. "I think he will be all right," she told Arkady. "But we must watch him carefully to make sure he does not drink too much water right away."

Huw groaned and tried to sit up. His voice was a parched whisper. "Poppy... Where is she? I have to..." Katkin gently pushed him back down.

"You must rest first, Huw. Here, have a little more to drink and then tell us what happened, if you can." She trickled another half-cup of water into his mouth. Huw closed his eyes and began to sob quietly, though his eyes could make no tears. The bitter, broken sound of it was too much for Arkady, who got up and walked away with his hands clenched.

"A few men of the Chandrathi came... to warn the Kindreds here. Padarn was with them," Huw finally said.

"How long ago was that, Huw?" Katkin asked gently.

His dry lips pulled back in a painful grimace as he mumbled, "I don't know now. Maybe six or seven days ago. I lost track of the time." Katkin squeezed his hand tightly, trying to offer what comfort she could.

Arkady squatted down by Huw's right side, forgetting the shock that his presence was likely to cause. "What happened after the Chandrathi came?"

Huw squinted as he looked up at Arkady, and raised a trembling hand to touch his shirt. "What is this miracle? Am I dead? Why are you here with me, my brother? And how has my queen now two good arms? Nothing seems right in this world."

Arkady shook his head. "Nay, it is I who has returned to the land of the living, Huw. But that is a story for another time, along with the tale of Katkin's healing. Right now you must tell us what happened here."

"The men said that Black Guardsmen had attacked their caravans. Only a few of them managed to escape. The rest were taken." He paused to accept another sip of water from Katkin. "So the Elders decided that the Kindreds should leave right away for Shadion. Then Poppy... Poppy—my sweet little flower," Huw said brokenly. "I could hear her shouting to Neirin and Ander, saying they must let me go. Padarn stood beside her and added his voice to hers. But your Kymatre paid no attention to them. She and Ander decided that they would carry out my execution before they left. Poppy tried to stop them, and then I heard someone strike her and she screamed. Ach... What have they done to you, my little flower?" He stopped talking for a moment, and an anxious glance passed between Katkin and Arkady.

He carried on doggedly. "When Ander and Neirin came to the lock up, Padarn stood before the door and drew his knife, though I begged him not to. I did not want him to risk banishment for my sake, but he would not listen to me. By the tears of the Un-Named One, I wish he had."

"Why? What happened?" Arkady asked.

Huw started to weep again, softly. "Three men of the Anandios attacked him. They knocked Padarn to the ground and held him there. And then..." He closed his eyes, recalling the dull, wet sound of the Tane's knife plunging deep into Padarn's chest. After a shaky breath, he continued. "Ander murdered him, in cold blood. I never thought my people could kill like that, without any justification, but I have seen it. I have seen it."

"Oh, Huw..." Katkin said sorrowfully, remembering the tall horse-master who had once gone against the will of his Kindred to take pity on her. "That such a thing should happen at Bryn Mirain."

He looked around him sadly. "Yes, the Un-Named One was very angry that her sanctuary should be defiled in this way. As soon as Padarn fell, and his blood stained the ground, she sent a huge bolt of lightning flashing across the heavens. The lightning struck a tree, and soon the whole dell was ablaze. The horses went wild with fear and the men of Anandi and Gitasha had to chase them down. After a time, I think I must have fainted from the heat and smoke, because I remember nothing more."

Katkin closed her eyes in horror, thinking how frightful it would be to be locked up with no hope of escape, while all the world burned all around you. "By the time I came to, everyone was gone. They left nothing behind except the animals that had died in the fire."

"So you have had nothing to eat or drink for six or seven days?" Arkady asked in wonder. "You are very lucky to be alive, my brother."

Huw gave him the ghost of a smile. "I held my shirt out of the bars when it rained a few days ago. I was able to suck a few drops of moisture that way. The rain was a gift from the Un-Named One. Otherwise I am sure I would be dead by now."

Katkin had been busy cutting up an apple from her food sack. Now she helped Huw sit up and fed him the apple one tiny sliver at a time. Already he seemed much stronger. After he had finished the fruit he said softly, "Thank you for coming back for me, Queen of my heart. I am very happy that your arm has been returned to you." He did not see the sudden angry expression on Arkady's face, nor Katkin's guilty one, for he had closed his eyes once again.

"Let us get you out of this horrible pit," Katkin said after a moment had passed in silence. "We have horses down by the stream and a place to camp." Huw tried to stand, but fell back almost immediately. Arkady knelt by his side and picked him up, and Katkin thought sadly that the emaciated Huw looked like no more than a child in his arms. Slowly they made their way back up the dell, and passed over the lip. Huw looked back.

"The Un-Named One has taken her blessing from this place forever," he said forlornly. "No more will the Kindreds shelter here in beauty. What will happen to my people?"

Later, after Katkin had made a fire, they sat together by the stony draw sipping tea. The dog Katkin had called Chan now sat pressed against Huw, who absently stroked his ears. "His name is Caleb," he offered presently. "He belonged to me, once upon a time, before the Fynära attacked us in the dunes of Secuny." At the mention of his name, the dog looked up expectantly. Katkin passed him a piece of hard bread from her pack and he crunched into it eagerly.

"What do you want to do now, Huw?" Arkady asked. "The way I see it, we can either follow the Black Guard who took the Chandrathi or we can try to catch up with the Kindreds who have the children. Either one is a difficult task."

Huw said despondently, "You mean an impossible one, my brother. We cannot fight the Black Guard—with just three. And Poppy and Gwillam are long gone. I will never be able to find them now." Katkin looked on helplessly as Huw buried his face in Caleb's rough fur and cried.

"We will find them," she said firmly. "You know the routes they would take to Shadion, and Caleb will help us track them too. Won't you, boy?" The dog stood up and barked excitedly. "As for you," she said to Arkady, "You are wanted up north. Huw and I will rescue the children." Swiftly she explained to Huw about Gwenn's pregnancy and the coming birth of the child they believed to be the Dawnmaid.

Arkady opened his mouth to argue, but Huw said, "You must go, Kadya, and take Katkin with you. Every minute she spends in Yr she is in danger from the Black Guard. But if you can spare one of the horses then I will go after my little flower and Gwillam as soon as I am able."

Katkin said vehemently, "No! I won't leave you again."

"Neither will I," Arkady added. "So it is settled. We will go together or not at all."

"But this is absolute madness!" Huw retorted angrily. "One can move much more quickly and silently than three, especially when there are only two horses between them. And if the Dawnmaid is truly to be born soon, then your place is with her, both of you."

Katkin admonished, "You are very weak, Huw. How far down

the road would you get before you collapsed? You need someone to look after you."

He set his lips in the stubborn line that she knew so well. "No, queen of my heart, the danger is too great. Go north, while you can, and help your daughter with the birthing." He sighed. "Kadya can come along with me, if someone must." Though Katkin argued against this for many hours, he was intractable and Arkady, of course, took his side as well. By the time night fell, they were all barely speaking to one another. Katkin stretched out by the fire and fell into an exhausted sleep.

When the bright sunshine of early morning woke her, they had already gone, taking one horse and the dog, Caleb, with them. Only Ajax remained, tied to a tree, with Katkin's food satchel and travel bag draped in the branches. After studying the ground carefully, she found she was unable to tell for certain the direction in which they had set off. Huw or Arkady had carefully erased every sign of their passing, no doubt to prevent any pursuit. She stood and looked around the empty valley, thinking of the bitter irony of her situation.

*Had she not wanted to be released from her responsibility to Huw and the children? Had she not wanted to go north and find Gwenn and Gunnar?*

But now the way was clear before her, she felt a curious reluctance to take it.

She lingered over breakfast and a cup of tea, wondering what she ought to do. Her daughter needed her, without a doubt. Yet, seeing Huw again had rekindled feelings for him she had almost forgotten she possessed. Which road should she choose—towards Huw and the danger from which he wanted to spare her, or back north to Starruthe, where she could help Gwenn? She sat still for so long while she pondered this riddle that a rabbit, emboldened by the silence, hopped cautiously out onto the short, springy turf. He nibbled contentedly, followed a moment later by his mate, and two little ones.

Katkin's eyes filled with tears as she watched them and abruptly her mind cleared. Somehow she would find Huw, and tell him everything, and beg for his forgiveness. Together, they would search for the children. Then, perhaps, if he and Poppy were willing to give her another chance, they could be a family again...

A second later the rabbits scattered in panic as a dog, barking joyously, sped across the grass and into Katkin's open arms. "Caleb! Good dog! You came back for me, did you not?" The dog licked her face ecstatically, and then ran back down the path, looking over his shoulder expectantly. "Just a minute, boy, while I saddle Ajax," Katkin called to him happily. She hurriedly packed the remains of her food, and kicked dirt over the smoldering fire.

By the time she mounted Ajax and rode up the path behind Caleb, the sun was high in the sky. The dog ran unerringly southwards, following narrow and little used paths of the kind that the Firaithi love. But Katkin saw no sign of Huw and Arkady, though she followed the dog all day and well into the evening. By rights, she knew she should have caught up to them by now, for they had not had more than a few hours head start on her. That night, she crept into a thicket of trees to sleep, and hobbled Ajax close by. The weather was warm, and she lit no cooking fire, eating only some of the twice baked bread she had taken from the empty caravans of the Chandrathi.

Caleb looked at it hungrily. "Go off and catch your own dinner. You would not like this anyway." He shot off into the bushes and returned with a brightly plumaged grouse.

In the pearled light of dawn they set off again, although she was rapidly losing hope that her guide would actually lead her back to his master. He traveled along a broader track now, and Katkin could see wide ruts had been dug into the soft ground, as though by many caravans passing. As she followed Caleb further she recognized the cast off bits of harness and gear along the wayside as those belonging to the Firaithi, though normally they passed without a trace. Obviously this Kindred must have been in a great hurry. But loaded caravans move much more slowly than a single horse and rider, and by late evening Katkin had caught up with them—the Kindreds of Gitasha and Anandi, making their way down to Shadion.

She knew they would certainly have set a watch, so she halted Ajax and Caleb just to the north of the camping ground. The last thing she wanted was for her uncle or grandmother to capture and question her, so Katkin decided to approach the camp in complete darkness. She settled down to wait for midnight, secreted in a dense grove of holly. Caleb sat beside her, panting restlessly in the humid night air.

After a drink of water and quick snack of dry bread for both she and Caleb, Katkin left the holly grove. The dog whined unhappily when told to stay, but sank obediently down onto his haunches. The moon was at three quarters, the Waxmoon, and it lit her way as she crept towards the deserted camping area. She had hoped she could locate Poppy and Gwillam quickly, and spirit them away without attracting anyone's attention. But her plan quickly went awry, as every dog in the camp barked noisily as she approached the outlying caravans. Katkin swore softly and gap-shifted.

She stood now in the Vastness, surrounded by ghostly trees, deeply shadowed at the base. The stars shone dull and insubstantial above her, as though they possessed only a faint memory of the blazing luminosity that was theirs by right in other worlds and times. Katkin shivered, unhappy, as always, with the profound silence and loneliness of Death's realm. The darkness here seemed so... well, dark, compared to the living world. She forced herself to concentrate on her objective. How could she tell which of the forty or so caravans scattered in a rough semi-circle held Poppy and Gwillam? The children would not be visible to her from her vantage point in the Vastness, and if she crossed back into the living world she would almost certainly give away her position.

Katkin was just creeping between two caravans when she saw a tall, blond-haired figure standing with his back to her on the other side of the empty fire pit. She quickly stepped back into the gloom and watched in breathless fear as he slowly turned to face her.

"Come out, Katrione," a voice said. "I know you are there."

Katkin knew that voice. She hurried forward, crying, "Tomas!" but stopped in confusion when she got close enough to see who it was that had called her name.

He did look like Tomas, more or less, but he no longer wore the faded cuirassiers' uniform she knew so well. "Who are you?" she asked softly, remembering the many incarnations of Dai Irrakai, and wondering if Tomas also had been reborn.

His silver tunic, girt with a wide sword belt, seemed to glow faintly in the darkness. He moved towards her but did not answer her question. "Who do you think I am?" he asked instead.

"I thought you were an old friend of mine—Tomas de Vigny," Katkin said, wondering now how she could have possibly confused this grim-faced Amaranthine with her former lover. "I guess I was wrong though." But when he stood face to face with her and gave her a wry smile, she was not so sure.

"Tomas I was, once upon a life," answered Fyn. "But my memories of him have grown dim. That is why I asked you his name."

"Do you remember me then?" Katkin asked him curiously.

"Of course," he said softly, and brushed the tips of his fingers against her cheek. "Of you I have many memories, both bitter and sweet. We have traveled the Gyre together for many turns, with our hearts sailing ever on parallel seas." He sighed and dropped his hand to his side. "But I did not call you here to speak of what is past."

She stared up at him uncertainly, thinking that there was still something of Tomas in his sad and noble face. "You called me? How?"

"I placed my thoughts in the mind of the dog, and asked him to bring you here. He was a most willing servant."

Katkin smiled, understanding now why Caleb had not led her to Huw as she had asked him to. "But why did you send for me?" she asked.

"There is work to be done. The Autochthones have taken the child called Gwillam, and we have need of him and his sister."

"What for?" Katkin asked him, a little too sharply. She was not at all sure she wanted Gwillam to become an implement of the gods in the way she herself had.

"He is the servant of the Dawn," Fyn said. "She has called him."

Katkin sighed at this opaque explanation, so typical of the Amaranthine. "How do you expect me to rescue him? I don't even have a weapon," she asked crossly.

Fyn pointed to the last caravan on the end of the semi-circle. "He and Poppy are there, locked in a cupboard to prevent their escape. I will create a distraction to give you enough time to free them. Then bring them here, to me, so I may examine the boy. Do you understand?"

She nodded, while mentally questioning whether Tomas understood that Gwillam was only a year old. "But..."

He interrupted harshly. "There is no time for argument! Go at once." Then his voice softened again. "Please, Katrione, I place my trust in you now, as I have done in so many lives before. Do not fail me."

"Of course, Tomas," she agreed, but already she had decided to rescue Gwillam and Poppy from the Gitashaen—but not to return with them to the Vastness as Tomas had instructed her to do. Their experience in the dell would likely have traumatized the children, and bringing them to Death's kingdom would only add to their terror. The Amaranthine could wait—indefinitely, as far as Katkin was concerned.

She walked towards the distant caravan, carefully stepping around any seated Uri'el in her path. There were a lot of them clutching dead Firaithi men and women and Katkin wondered if there had been some kind of battle between the Kindreds here some time in the past. Once she reached the end of the line, she gap-shifted back into the living world. This time the dogs were silent, no doubt because Fyn had so commanded them. She waited in the shadow of the caravan, until several hobbled horses nearby snorted and reared. The dogs exploded into a torrent of barks, and she could hear excited shouts from the caravans in her vicinity. Doors flew open and men emerged, pulling on shirts and trousers as they ran to see what had disturbed the horses.

Once the occupant of the caravan holding Poppy and Gwillam had exited with the rest, slamming the door behind him, Katkin crept up the steps. She listened intently but could hear no sound from within. Grasping the handle, she turned it silently, grateful that the man had not locked it as he left. Inside it was as dark as the inside of a stone. Moving stealthily, with her hands out in front of her, she crossed the tiny interior space until she reached the far wall.

Katkin hissed, "Poppy, it is Katkin. If you can hear me, bang on the door."

She strained to listen over the various shouts and whinnies filtering through the walls from outside. Nothing. Again she whispered Poppy's name, this time a little louder. A muffled thump from the far end of the caravan gave her the answer she was listening for. Katkin dropped to the floor and wrenched at the handle of a long and low cupboard built in underneath the sleeping compartment. It was locked, but she could hear whimpering from the other side.

The noise outside was dissipating and Katkin knew she had little time left. She urged Poppy, "Kick the door with your feet as hard as you can when I count to three." Then she grasped the knob firmly with both hands, while planting her feet on either side of the door to brace herself.

"Now, Poppy... One, two, three!" As she said three, Katkin pulled on the knob with all her strength. The lock broke with the additional force of Poppy's kick and the children tumbled free. Gwillam immediately burst into life, wailing angrily. Katkin quickly caught him up, and covered his mouth whilst saying to Poppy, "Don't make a sound. Get ready to run as fast as you can." The little girl nodded calmly and picked up Gwillam's stuffed rabbit, which lay on the floor at her feet.

They reached the door just as it opened, and Katkin looked into the face of her Ikor Ander, brightly illuminated by the moonlight. He stared back at her in shock, and said, "Katkin! What on Yrth are you doing here?"

Katkin drew Poppy up close beside her. Her voice was harsh. "I have come for these children, Ander. They belong to me. Now, please get out of my way." To her surprise, he backed willingly down the steps and let her pass.

"I am so glad you have come back to us, Kitty," he said. "Rha Tane said that you would. The stones told her so. She is in her caravan. You must go to her now."

"Why?" Katkin asked, a little mystified by the sorrow in his voice. "I don't..."

"She is dying," he interrupted sadly. "And she wishes to see you before she crosses the moon gate." Ander seized her arm, quite firmly, and dragged her and Gwillam along the row of caravans to the largest one. Poppy followed unwillingly behind. Katkin opened her mouth to protest, and then decided it would be better to go with him—for now. She could easily sneak away later, with the children, if she did not arouse his suspicions.

When they stepped through the door, the interior of the caravan smelled foul, like decaying meat, only somewhat masked by the odor of carbolic soap. Neirin lay in the compartment bed, deeply shadowed by the light of a single candle that burned on the table in the center of the room. Katkin put Gwillam down and approached her grandmother's bed. Her face looked ashen and mask-like in the dim light.

"Kitty..." she groaned. "Is that you?"

"Yes, Kymatre."

Her grandmother's smile hardly raised her sunken cheeks. She muttered, "I knew you would come. Justice has been done to the murderer, and you are free to take your place among us once more. It is well."

Katkin pressed her lips together tightly and did not speak, though the thought of Huw—abandoned like a starving dog in a kennel by her grandmother and Ander—filled her with rage.

Neirin's claw-like hand reached out to touch her chest as she cackled toothlessly. "My little Kitty-Kat. You are meant to be the Rha Tane—the stones told me so," she said proudly. Katkin stared at her, wondering if the old woman was raving. But her next words were chillingly reasonable. "My boy Ander's woman has been past Tsmar'enth these last ten years. He is lonely, Kitty. You will make for him a fine wife."

As she said these words, Ander came to stand very close behind her, so close she could feel his hot breath on the back of her neck. She shivered in revulsion.

"Kymatre! He is my blood relation. Surely you know that such things are forbidden."

"Pah! Gruagán law," the old woman said dismissively. "It means nothing to us. We of the traveling peoples must have our own ways. Any man who desires a woman may take her as his wife, if she is not already married, even if she be his kin. The wedding will take place at the next full moon. I have spoken."

Katkin shook her head in horror, remembering Huw's graphic description of Padarn's death at her uncle's hand. "But..."

Ander's arm snaked round her waist, very possessively. "Do not worry, Kitty," he whispered to her. "I am a gentle man and a good lover. I will take good care of you, and the children, too. We will find happiness together as a family."

"Don't listen to him!" Poppy wailed. "He hit me, and Gwillam, and locked us up. You saw where we were when you came to get us."

Ander growled. "Silence, little brat! You were beaten and locked up for misbehaving. Now do not try my patience or you will feel the sting of my belt on your backside again this night."

Katkin stood silently, trying to decide what to do. After a split second, she took a deep breath and purred obediently, "Very well.

Of course I will marry Ander, if you think that is best, Kymatre." Poppy burst into tears, and crawled into a corner, screaming protests. Katkin ignored her and yawned hugely. "Now I would like to get some sleep. Is there a caravan where the children and I can stay tonight? In the morning we can see about planning the wedding," she added brightly.

Ander's fingers crept upwards to her breast. Katkin only just managed to suppress a shudder of loathing.

"Your place is in my bed," he whispered huskily. "Let me show you what a lucky woman you are right now."

She pushed his hand away. "Wait until the after the wedding, my love."

Ander did not drop his hand. "You sound like a lily Gruagá," he said mockingly. "In our world if a man wants a woman he takes her." He grasped her elbow and made to push her out the door.

"Wait!" Neirin commanded, her voice surprisingly strong. "There is a binding gift I would give Kitty, which is hers by right. Ander, my mirror."

Ander reached into the drawer under the bed. "Are you sure, Rha Tane? This should wait until after the wedding, I think."

The old woman disagreed. "I will not be here then. Tsmar'enth waits and the road is clear before me. Now I have seen my granddaughter betrothed I can die in peace. You will watch with me the rest of this night, my son. I have spoken."

Ander sighed disappointedly. "Very well, *Matre mi*. I will return when I have seen Kitty to her room." He handed Katkin the mirror, and she tucked it away carefully in her pocket. They left Neirin's room, breathing deeply of the softly scented night air, glad to be free of the sickening stench inside.

He led them to a dilapidated caravan, close to the end of the half-circle. "This used to be Old Lonner's. He died in the fire at Bryn Mirain. You can stay here until the wedding." Ander paused and cleared his throat. "Please don't be offended, but I have to lock the door behind you. That brat Poppy is quite the little escape artist. But I will return in the morning. Good night, Kitty." She had to let him kiss her lasciviously, and fondle her breasts once more in order to assuage any lingering distrust. Finally he left them alone, and locked the door.

Katkin gave a sigh of relief and wiped her mouth vigorously on her sleeve. "Thank the gods," she said out loud, and bent down to see to Poppy, who was still weeping miserably. "Stop crying and listen to me," she whispered. "Don't fret. I have no intention of marrying that filthy swine."

Poppy looked up at her with wide eyes and spoke out loudly in her excitement. "You don't?"

"Shhh... Not so loud." Katkin smiled. "Of course not. He is my uncle, for one thing, *and* at least sixty years old. But even if he was not, he is a murderer, and a cruel man. I just pretended to agree so that he would leave us alone for tonight. Now we are getting out of here."

"We are?" Poppy's look of joy was undisguised. "But how? The mean man said he was going to lock us in."

Katkin picked up Gwillam and took Poppy's hand. She said reassuringly, "The door won't matter in a moment. But to open it we are going to have to go to a scary place for a little while. We won't stay there long, I give you my word." Poppy nodded bravely, and Katkin dragged her forward and a little to the left.

Once they were in the Vastness, the caravan door swung open easily. Katkin quickly crossed the sleeping greensward with Poppy and Gwillam in tow, heading for the woods. Behind her, she thought she heard Fyn's voice, calling her name, but she resolutely ignored it. As soon as she could, within the shelter of the trees, she gap shifted back into the living world. Ajax and Caleb thankfully remained just where she had left them, in the holly grove.

Poppy clambered on the horse's back, and Katkin handed up Gwillam, who started to cry loudly. After climbing up on to the saddle, she gave Ajax a kick that sent her tearing through the forest. Caleb followed, barking madly. Katkin had hoped that they might be able to escape without detection, but she was disappointed. The sound of many following hooves soon filled the night air, and Ajax, already overburdened, was obviously flagging.

When it was clear that they would not be able to outrun their pursuers, Katkin reined the tired horse and leapt down from the saddle. She put up her arms for Gwillam and then Poppy jumped down to stand beside her. The child looked around her fearfully, begging Katkin, "Don't let them take us back. We can't go back there. We can't."

"We won't. I already told you—there is no way I am marrying

that murderer." Katkin said firmly. They crossed back into the Vastness, just as the first of the Firaithi horses thundered into sight.

The silence of Death's kingdom settled on them like fine dust. Poppy looked around her with interest. "When are we going to get to the scary place you keep talking about?" she inquired presently, and Katkin smiled.

"I thought you might find this place frightening," she answered, as she perched on a fallen tree to rest, and placed the squirming Gwillam down at her feet.

"Here?" said Poppy, squatting down beside her brother and handing him his rabbit. "Why ever for? I have been here lots of times."

Katkin stared at her, profoundly shocked. "You have been here before? To the Vastness?"

Poppy nodded proudly. "The nice lady, who is Patre Huw's sister, brought me here." Then her expression changed back to one of tearful concern. "Is Patre all right? The mean man and that wrinkly hag were going to kill him. They didn't do it, did they? I tried to stop them and so did Patre's friend."

Katkin gathered the girl up into a reassuring hug. "Don't worry Poppy; your Patre is all right. You were a very brave little girl to try and help him like that."

The little girl smiled and dried her tears with her filthy pinafore. Then she focused on a spot just over Katkin's shoulder and said amiably, "Hello, Uncle Fyn. What are you doing here?"

The tall Amaranthine strode forward and joined them in the dell.

Fyn was staring at her, and Katkin dropped her eyes, with the sure knowledge he was angry. She asked Poppy, "How do you know Fyn?"

The little girl smiled. "Patre's sister has another sister—a nice lady with a green face. She introduced me to Uncle Fyn ages ago. Sometimes he tells me stories when I come here in my dreams." The little girl ran over to Fyn and took his hand. "Will you tell me one now?" She gave a disappointed sigh as Fyn shook his head.

"I have something important of which I must speak to Katrione, little one," he said, as he patted her hair with obvious affection. "But look, I have these sweets for you and your brother to share. Will you watch over him while we talk?" He dug in the pocket of his tunic and produced, somewhat incongruously, a small paper packet of sugar plums. Poppy squealed in delight as he handed them to her. She hurried back over to where Gwillam sat playing with his rabbit, and plopped down beside him, after solemnly handing him one of the sugary treats.

Fyn went to stand before Katkin, who had taken shelter behind an outcropping of rock.

"I requested that you return to me with the children. Why did you run away?" he asked her, with a hint of irritation.

She stared up at him defiantly and spat back, "How dare you ask me that? Do you know how much I have endured for your sake—for the sake of all the Amaranthine? I just don't want Poppy and Gwillam to suffer the same fate. Why can you not leave us alone?"

He stood for so long without speaking that she wondered if he had been struck dumb by her angry words. But at last he said, "You have changed, Katrione. When I came to you, in the Citadel dungeon, you told me you were overjoyed to be the vessel of Lalluna once more. But now I feel in you an anger, as though we have treated you unjustly. I greatly rue this."

She gave a brief, bitter laugh. "Unjustly? Nay, I am sure I only received what I deserved. But I am tired."

"You no longer wish to help me or any of the Amaranthine?" He gave her a piercing glance as she nodded slowly. "Will you tell me why?"

She shook her head dully and would have turned away, but Fyn caught her by the shoulders. He said sadly, "I remember a time when you and I were close—as close as two of your kind could be. I moved within you, and felt your spirit entwine willingly with mine. It was strong, burning with the desire to mend all the hurts of the world. Where has that spirit gone, Katrione?"

"Shiqaba asked me the same thing," she answered dully. "The truth is I don't know. Somehow, I don't believe I can trust you—or the others—any more."

"Why?" he asked her. "What has happened to make you feel so?"

"I thought Dai..." As Katkin spoke this name, Fyn frowned darkly. "At least, until just a little while ago, I thought Dai was Jacq, returned to life again. But he betrayed me! He was going to give me over to Maggrai." The memory of this made Katkin weep, and Fyn put his arms about her in a comforting embrace.

He said softly, "Of Dai, you already know my feelings. He has ever been a traitor to our kind. But do not ascribe to all the Amaranthine the same black heart. We only want what is best for you—and I most of all, Katrione. Though much of what I once was is lost to me now, I will never forget the night we spent together at Acorn."

She looked up at him and saw the desire in his eyes.

"Tomas, I..." she began, but he was already lowering his mouth to meet hers.

A moment later, no more than a moment, as Katkin and Fyn stood close, and he kissed her eyelids with tender passion, Poppy called out, "The sugar plums are all gone, Uncle Fyn. Do you have any more?" Fyn sighed regretfully and dropped his arms.

"In this life we have many leagues to sail in bitter loneliness, my love," he whispered. "But know you are ever in my heart." He caught up her hand and kissed it, just as Poppy rounded the corner of the rocks they had stepped behind. She gave Katkin a disapproving look.

"I don't think Patre Huw..." she began, and Katkin smiled.

"Don't worry, Uncle Fyn and I are friends, Poppy. Just old friends who have a great deal in common, nothing more." She squeezed his hand tightly for a few seconds and then let it go. Then she said quietly, "What would you have me do, Tomas?"

He looked at her questioningly, and she nodded in silent agreement. "Our hopes and dreams rest now with the Dawnmaid," he said. "We must protect the child, at all costs, in the coming turn of the Gyre, as Maggrai bends his mind to her destruction. Our daughter will soon be ready to deliver her into the world. Will you go, with Poppy and Gwillam, to Starruthe? She will need your help, Katrione."

"Of course," she said resolutely. "But how will we get there? And what about Huw and Kadya? They are searching for the Firaithi, even now."

Fyn smiled as he picked up Poppy and placed her on his broad shoulders. She clapped her hands in delight at this high perch. "We will travel the worlds between. The faithful dog and horse that wait for you in the living world can carry a message to the Autochthon and the Seed Bearer. Later, when I have seen you safely to my grandmother's house, then I will return for them. All right?"

She grinned wickedly at him over her shoulder as she went to retrieve Gwillam and his rabbit. "I hope you don't think all that sweet talk is what made me change my mind. I am only doing this for Gwenn, you know."

Fyn laughed and shook his head. "Welcome back," he said and took her hand.

# 19

## Varden Prox

*Oh, Lut, my stubborn northern brother. All our prayers are with you now.*

*Let his heart not fail him...*

~~~~~~~~~~~~

It was the evening of the fourteenth day of his captivity in the cells of the penitents. Gunnar lay on the bench, with his hands behind his head, thinking about Gwenn. He wondered if she would come looking for him in Einar after another few weeks went by and he had not come home. It seemed likely, and he could do nothing to warn her away. He could only hold on to the hope that his grandmother, from her place across the heavenly plane, was somehow protecting Gwenn and his children, as well as the precious infant she carried. Gunnar himself would be dead by then, of that he had no doubt—and Arvid meant for him to die in some hideously painful way. All he could do was try to face this death with courage, as a true Fynäran should. He would not give Arvid or his puking Prime God the satisfaction of seeing him beg for mercy.

Sighing in resignation, he rose and paced the cell, back and forth, back and forth, trying to think of some way to...

*...each time it does a little more damage to your brain, until soon, if you persist in these foolish attempts at escape, you will be nothing but a drooling half-wit.*

There was that.

Why should he not gap shift, many times, until he no longer

knew who he was? Maybe it would even kill him. Gunnar smiled grimly at the thought of robbing Arvid of his Bounty. The Tabernacle behind him was filling up with people, some loudly chanting prayers for mercy and forgiveness.

*Time to get on with it then.*

Just as he was about to step forward, the shutters hiding his cell were thrown aside, filling the dimness with light. The worshippers packed the space outside the bars, pushing and straining for a better view of him. They crowded forward until their faces were pressed against the bars by the crush of the bodies behind them, and still they kept on, until everyone was as close as they could be. Proctor Acolytus Janus was before them all, and gave him a viciously self-satisfied smile. Gunnar turned away from him with a sinking heart, just as the cell door opened. Arvid stepped through, along with six of his strongest Abaryanites. One was carrying an anvil. Another—a sledgehammer. Gunnar's heart raced in fear, but there was nowhere to run.

"Sorry, Strong Arm. I am afraid you will not be able to experience your Bounty on the Altar as is right and proper." Gunnar backed away from him and the Abaryanites moved swiftly. The crowd behind him gave a roar of approval as they roughly seized hold of his arms and legs.

Arvid continued smoothly, "If I take you from your cell then your legendary strength might return, and we could not have that, now could we? You would fight against the Bounty, and we both know that would be very wrong. So I have invited the congregation to watch from outside as you receive it." Gunnar, struggling assiduously against the Abaryanites as they ripped his clothes from him, suddenly stopped.

"How do you know about my strength?" he asked sharply.

But Arvid ignored him, addressing instead the crowd outside the cell.

"Brothers and Sisters! Welcome to the most holy Bounty of Prime."

As the others cried, "*Princeps! Primus!*" High Priest Arvid Scar Brow led the opening prayers. One woman persistently inched her way forwards until she was close to the front. Her posture was the same as every woman there—head well down, shoulders rounded in deference to the men around her. She looked heavily pregnant, and clutched at her stomach protectively as the people behind her strained forwards.

Arvid cried, "My Brothers and Sisters in Prime! Before you is a creature so befouled in sin that he can no longer comprehend his filth. Raise him up, Abaryanites!" The six men holding Gunnar picked him up and turned him so that he faced the crowd. The congregation cheered as he continued to struggle wildly, until the sweat rolling off his skin made him almost too slippery to hold on to. His captors responded by pounding him almost senseless with many brutal blows, until Arvid cried, "Stop! He must remain awake and aware so that he may fully participate in the Bounty."

"Prime shows mercy to all, even those who would set themselves up in His place. This creature is one such fool. For he is a God, my Brothers and Sisters—a God so weak and frail that even now he cannot escape from his redemption, though he struggles against it. His sins are many, red and nefarious. Nay, scarlet, not red. But Prime has brought him before us to demonstrate His power and mercy. I give you Lutyond, believers, the pathetic last remnant of the Gods you once worshipped. Now let him receive the Bounty."

Gunnar's head, bloody from many small wounds, snapped up at this introduction, and he said hoarsely, "You cannot have known. I told no one."

Arvid turned to him and smiled. "Prime knows all, my friend. Every thought, every sin. Now, let us begin."

When the hammer came down for the first time, the pregnant woman, who had been shouting along with the rest for the start of the Bounty, suddenly slipped to the floor in a dead faint, probably from the heat. Four men carried her back to the small room especially reserved for such occasions, back behind the cells of the penitents, and left her on a long wooden bench. She did not stir.

Gunnar faced the crowd, who hungrily waited for the next swing of the hammer. His eyes burned with the outrage and pain. "What are you staring at?" he cried to them. "Look to yourselves instead. You were once honorable people—Fynärans—men of the sea. What are you now? Nothing but cowardly children, who take sick pleasure in the punishment of their brothers and sisters. *Felag*! Do you even remember what that means?" Gunnar stared at them, and some dropped their eyes. Then he screamed in agony as the Abaryanites broke his other thigh bone.

236

Arvid stood close by, a queer smile playing on his face as he occasionally stroked his victim's head and murmured vague encouragements. Gunnar fought for air as his heart pumped desperately, trying to keep his failing body alive—trying somehow to deal with the pain that was drowning him. But all the air in the world would not help him now. He tried to speak, and only the guttural sounds of a wounded animal came from his mouth. There was something Gunnar had to say, so he frantically tried again, after the hammer had finished its crushing work on his right tibia. He stared up at Arvid, his face now transfixed with the greatest suffering imaginable, and gasped out the words, "My... Gods..., Arvid. How could you... do this? I... named my first... born... son... for you. We were... brothers." The hammer was raised again as he spoke. When his left tibia snapped in two places, he slipped into a torrent of incoherent babbling and vomited up a pool of green bile.

Arvid, unmoved, gave him the gentlest of smiles. "We are still brothers. Brothers in Prime." He looked to the Abaryanite holding the sledge hammer and said coldly, "Now the arms. Start with the right humerus."

In the resting room, the woman who had fainted began to stir as another loud anguished scream filtered through the walls. She stood and threw off her headscarf. Anyone who had seen her face at that moment would be forgiven for thinking that another of the old Gods was also in the Tabernacle with them—Sif, of the golden hair, now looking just like an avenging angel in white as she quickly drew her shining sword.

After they had broken one of Gunnar's arms, Arvid called a halt to the evening's proceedings. His captive was still alive, barely, and the High Priest hoped he might live on, for a day or more. Tomorrow his Abaryanites could break his ribs one by one, until he could no longer breathe. But the crowd outside had grown restless, after Gunnar's speech, and he thought it would be wise to let them go for tonight. With a dismissive gesture, Arvid signaled to Proctor Acolytus Janus to close the shutters and recite the collect.

He sent the Abaryanites away with a curt command to clear the hall, and stood looking down at Gunnar, thinking on the lovely purity of pain, and how it washed away all sin.

Gunnar was on the ground, where the Abaryanites had dropped him. Already his arm and legs were grossly puffed up—the skin thick and blackened, like the putrid hide of some long dead animal. He looked less than human laying there, now only a mass of agonized flesh, still whimpering a little. But the mighty god Lutyond would never again be a threat to Prime. His servant Arvid had seen to that, and he hoped to be rewarded for it. *Princeps Primus.*

A sharp rapping startled him, and he crossed to the heavily reinforced iron door, turned the ring and opened it. One of the men stood on the other side, looking slightly bemused. "Well?" Arvid said abruptly. "What is it, man? I haven't got all day."

The Abaryanite still did not speak, so Arvid stepped forward to tap him on the shoulder. As he did so, the man suddenly collapsed forward into his arms, driving him back into the cell and off his feet. Arvid quickly pushed the unconscious figure off him and stood. He noticed the dagger sticking out of the man's back first—and only then did he think to look to the doorway, where Gwenn stood waiting, with keth'fell in her hand. The blade was stained red.

She stepped through unhurriedly, and closed the door behind her. "Key," she snapped coolly to Arvid, and held out her hand.

He eyed the distance between them, wondering if he could push past her and make it to the door alive. A second later he was rolling on the floor, clutching his head in agony. Gwenn stood over him, with the point of keth'fell against his nostril.

"The *key*, Arvid," she said again, and this time he did not hesitate. He scrabbled in his pocket with a sticky, bloodied hand and handed over the key. Then he lay still, nursing the profusely bleeding hole in his head that had once had an ear attached to it. Gwenn locked the door. Only when she was sure that they were secure in the special cell did she cross the floor and squat down beside Gunnar.

"Oh, love," she said softly and stifled a moan with her hand. "I came as soon as I could, but it was not soon enough, was it?" Gunnar's eyes opened, only a little. Only enough that she could see a sliver of blue in the purple-red of his swollen lids. He coughed, and a trail of spittle ran down his chin and lay shining like a silver thread on his beard. She did not wipe it away, afraid that even this small touch might cause him more pain.

His voice was as quiet as the distant echo of the ocean in a whorled shell. "Love..." She bent her head close, so that her hair fell softly down upon his face and bathed all his hurts in the cool scent of the sea and of pines. Gunnar felt, just then, that he could die and be utterly at peace. "You should not have come here. Not for... not for me. Now leave, quickly, before the Abaryanites return."

Gwenn kept her face close to his and whispered, "They are no more, love. I killed them all, with keth'fell." Gunnar, incredibly, somehow, raised the corners of his mouth in an ethereal smile.

"My Sif of the golden hair... So beautiful you are, and so deadly, my goddess. Grant me a boon, before you go..."

Gwenn's eyes filled with tears, wondering if he even knew who she was anymore. "What do you want, Gunnar? We need to get you out of here, back to Feringhall. My mother is there. She is a doctor, she can..."

He coughed again, and his face twisted in a spasm of agony. "Not going back. You must... You must end it, for me."

Gwenn's eyes went wide as she understood the nature of his request. "You want me to... kill you? Gunnar, no!"

An anguished groan escaped his lips. "Can't bear it. Love, please..." Gwenn shook her head in utter dismay. He whispered, "When it is finished, bear me back to the *Able Drake*. We can escape together, love. When you are safe, only then, return me to the sea, and let the fire take my soul."

She cried, "Don't make me do this. I won't..."

Arvid lay behind her on the ground, completely forgotten. He groped in his other pocket, and retrieved a short-bladed folding knife. His fingers nimbly eased it open, while it was still concealed amongst the folds of his clothing. He drew his knees up under him, coiling like a snake, ready to strike. Then he threw himself forward, and plunged the knife into Gwenn's back as she bent over her dying husband.

She felt the motion just before he landed the knife, and stiffened her shoulders. The metal blade rang and snapped as it pierced her robe, leaving Arvid holding half a blade in his hand. Gwenn stood up slowly and turned towards him, with the broken blade still protruding from her back. Arvid lunged again and slashed the other half of the blade down her belly, ripping her robe wide open. He looked on in utter bewilderment as a cloud of pure white feathers filled the cell between them. Gwenn grabbed his wrist and twisted hard, so that he was forced to drop the weapon. Then she shoved him back against the wall, and raised her sword threateningly.

"One more move like that and I will cut off your other ear and

239

then stuff it up your nose, understood?" He nodded dumbly and slid down to a sitting position, while protectively covering his remaining ear with his hand.

Gwenn pulled the remains of the robe off, and threw down the feather bolster she had used to create her false pregnancy bump. Underneath she wore a shining corselet of steel mail, leather leggings and high black boots.

Arvid swallowed as she took two steps towards him. "Go ahead," he offered softly. "Kill me. You know you want to. I am not afraid. *Princeps Primus*. I have earned my place in his kingdom today." She gave him a smile, but her eyes were as cold and pale as glacial ice.

"Oh I will, Arvid. As slowly as I possibly can. You will suffer ten times the torment you gave him, I swear it on..." Gwenn had been going to say "Lutyond's Anchor", but given what she understood now about her husband, she fell silent instead.

Behind her she could hear the rasping moan of Gunnar's breath and knew she had little time left in which to save him. She placed the tip of her sword by Arvid's eye. "Now," she said decisively. "We already know you can move with one ear, shall we see if you can still walk with only one eye?" Arvid shook his head in terror. "No? Well then, on your feet. You are going to carry Gunnar back down to the *Able Drake* for me. If you drop him or cause him any more pain, I will stab you in the buttocks with keth'fell. Not hard enough to do much damage, but you will feel it, all the same."

Arvid laughed in derision. "You will never get past my Abaryanites, fool. They will cut you to ribbons."

"Will they?" Gwenn answered him softly. "Well, we will just see about that, won't we?"

When Arvid bent to take Gunnar into his arms, Gwenn had to turn away. She knew this journey back to the *Able Drake* would only add to his already unbearable anguish, but there was nothing she could do to lessen it. He screamed and screamed, his voice thin and high, like a child's, until the moment he passed out from shock. Gwenn looked at his ashen face and felt very afraid. "Don't die, please, love..." she whispered.

"Why are you doing this, Gwenn?" Arvid asked her as she unlocked the cell door. "You are taking the Bounty from him. If you truly loved him then you would want him to be transported. It is Prime's way. He only takes those who are..."

"Shut the hell up, Arvid." Gwenn growled at him. "Or I will cut your tongue out."

But Arvid looked back at her and said callously, "He won't thank you, you know. Even if you manage to keep him alive. Nothing you can do will cure the wounds inflicted in Prime's name. He will be a twisted cripple for the rest of his life."

Gwenn shook her head furiously, even though she knew that Arvid was right. If Gunnar could not walk again, or even worse, could not sail, then he would undoubtedly rather be dead.

She was sorry she could not see the look on Arvid's face as he entered the main hall. The soldiers of Prime were still where they had fallen, piled in random heaps. He stopped and stared fixedly at the corpses, until a heartless thrust from Gwenn forced a pained scream from his lips.

"Get moving, or feel it again," she threatened.

They crossed the new plaza, Arvid in front carrying Gunnar, who lay absolutely limp in his arms, and Gwenn behind, still using keth'fell occasionally if her captive did not move to her satisfaction. No one approached them. By the time they reached the Magnus' house Arvid was panting with exertion. Though Gunnar had been starved for fourteen days, he was still quite heavy and Arvid's back was bent almost double.

"Have to... rest," he gasped. Gwenn did not press him, lest he lose all strength in his arms and drop Gunnar. But neither could she allow him to put her husband down, in case he tried to escape once he was relieved of his burden. As she stood, wondering what she might do, a motion caught her eye. A man timidly approached, pushing a large two-wheeled wooden barrow before him. When he was within twenty feet of where they stood he stopped and carefully put the barrow down, then backed away. As his lips moved in prayer, he never took his eyes off Gunnar, lying hushed and still in Arvid's arms.

Gwenn could not be sure, but she thought she heard him say: *Hail to thee, Lutyond.* As she looked around the plaza, she could now see more people, hidden behind the columned porticoes of the Magnus' house. No one spoke a word, but now as they passed, with Gunnar resting in the barrow, some bowed their heads—and others looked away in shame.

Suddenly a voice screamed from across the plaza. "Murdering

harlot! Prime will flay your flesh for desecrating His Holy Tabernacle." Proctor Acolytus Janus shook his fist at Gwenn, but stayed well out of the range of keth'fell. Gwenn prodded Arvid. He had slowed down almost to a halt at his deputy's words. She kept close behind him, while keeping a watchful eye on Janus. Though he had quickly left the Tabernacle when the fighting started with the Abaryanites, she did not trust him not to try something now that her back was unprotected.

"Come on, coward," Gwenn taunted him. "Come and fight me, in the defense of your puny Prime God." She hoped she might lure Janus closer, where she could slay him with keth'fell. But he did not take the bait. He turned instead to the crowd, still watching Lut's silent progress across the plaza.

"In the name of Prime, I order you to stop her!" he exhorted. "She has interfered in the Holy Bounty. Look at the High Priest." He pointed to Arvid, whose once-white chasuble was now dyed scarlet with the blood from his ragged ear hole. "He has been gravely wounded by this irredeemable sinner. She must be punished accordingly. Get her!" He waved his arms encouragingly, but no one moved—except for the little procession with the barrow containing the fallen God, Lutyond, passing now beyond the plaza and onto the road back down into Einar town.

Gwenn called over to him. "If you wish to see your High Priest live until the morrow, you had better fall in step with him... Now! Come on, one hand on the barrow." Janus stood still, his mouth working in fury, as Gwenn stabbed Arvid extra hard, making him cry out again in pain.

"Get over here, Janus! She is turning me into a pin cushion." Arvid ordered, but his assistant was unmoved. With one last angry look at the motionless people lining the plaza, Janus turned and ran past them; back down the hill towards the wharf.

It took about fifteen minutes to get back to the *Able Drake*, and with Gwenn unable to leave her watchful position behind Arvid, she had no idea whether Gunnar had survived the trip. Once they reached the jetty, she made Arvid move Gunnar on to the boat. He did not stir, and Gwenn did not know whether to be pleased or fearful.

Arvid stood on the deck, with Gunnar at his feet. Gwenn ordered, "Sit down with your back to the mast." He instantly complied, thinking happily that she meant to tie him up, and that she would have to drop keth'fell to do it. As Gwenn approached, with a rope in her hand, he readied himself to strike, knowing it would not be difficult to drive her over the side with a well-timed attack. But Gwenn stopped well before she reached his side, and unexpectedly swung the knotted end of the heavy mooring rope at his unprotected ear hole. Arvid's head exploded in pain as the knot connected solidly with his wound, and he slumped down, almost unconscious. By the time his head cleared he was soundly trussed—hands and feet—and bound tightly to the mast.

Gwenn had raised the square sail and was guiding the Able Drake out into the harbor. As she turned to make sure there was no sign of pursuit, an arrow came whistling out of the dunes and pierced her cheek. She gave a cry of absolute agony, and dropped down to the wooden deck. Arvid saw Janus, dancing up and down with glee on the shore, the bow still in his hands.

He called out to him, "Well done, my Acolytus!" but his joy was short-lived.

As he watched in dismay, a crowd surrounded the Proctor, and Arvid caught the flash of many knives. He did not see what happened next, because just then the wind carried them out of sight of the land. But he could guess well enough.

Gwenn yanked the arrow from her cheek. It had pierced the flesh cleanly and broken the tooth inside. Though it was very painful, she did not think the damage was serious, so she gathered up a handful of rags from the deck and scrunched them up against her face. The wound bled freely, and she was soon forced to look for another bandage. Arvid watched her, with an amused expression on his face, so she kicked him hard in the stomach as she went past. He made a sound like a bladder suddenly deflating and doubled over, as much as the ropes would allow.

By the time he sat up again she was at the rudder, sitting on a wooden box. Gwenn looked worriedly down the coastline, hoping the wind held long enough to get Gunnar back to Feringhall. She wiped her face again. The constant trickle of blood from the arrow wound was making her feel dizzy and a little ill. Why would it not stop bleeding? To distract herself from the pain she asked Arvid, "How did you find out about Lutyond, anyway? And don't give me that Prime God knows all rubbish. Who told you?"

"I had a visitor one day—maybe a month and a half ago. The white-haired Beaumaraisian who used to be your thrall."

Gwenn stared at him in shock. "Kadya?"

He nodded. "He sought me out to tell me he was very worried about you. That Gunnar had changed in the Vastness into a God. I did not believe him, not at first, but when he told me about the tree..."

"I cannot believe he would betray us like that," she said unhappily.

"Once I knew the truth about Lut, I knew I had a responsibility to help him break free of his sinful past." He gave her an angry glance. "Until you interfered. Now his soul will be lost forever."

Gwenn snarled irritably, "Shut up, Arvid." Then she rubbed her eyes with her hands. Two Arvids sat before her, both smirking. She got up and splashed some water on her face. The rocking motion of the boat made her feel suddenly nauseous and Gwenn had to sit down again very carefully. The two Arvids continued to grin at her.

Then he asked sweetly, "Not feeling well? That will be the poison taking effect."

Gwenn's head snapped up and she looked at him blearily. "P... poison?" she stammered.

"Oh, yes," said Arvid cheerfully. "Janus always uses poison on his arrows. He used to be a chemist, you know."

"You are lying," she protested, but already her racing heart and sweaty hands proved the truth of what he said. Gwenn made a quick decision. Whatever happened to her—and to Gunnar, there was a task she intended to complete first. Unfortunately, the poisoned arrow wound meant she would not be able to linger over it as long as she would have liked. She picked up keth'fell and staggered forward. Arvid shrank down in fear as she muttered, "Time for you to die then. I will not have you outlive me, you scumbag."

Gunnar's voice, hoarse and broken, drifted down from the prow of the boat, "No."

Gwenn slowly lowered keth'fell. "What did you say?"

"No," he repeated. "Don't kill him. Put the boat in close to shore and let him swim for it."

"What?" she cried. "Gunnar, after everything he did to you, why would you want him to live?" She staggered over to him, and squatted down by his side.

He raised his unbroken arm to touch the wound on her face. "Are you all right?"

"Yes," she lied. "I am fine. Just a flesh wound." But in truth she felt worse with each passing minute. She said firmly, "Arvid is a monster. He deserves to die, Strong Arm."

Gunnar shook his head, very slowly. "He... He saved you. And the boys. You would not be here now, if not for him. I owe him that." Gunnar raised his voice a fraction and addressed Arvid. "Do I have your word, if Gwenn lets you go, that you will allow her and our children to leave this island, without hindrance?"

Arvid paused for a moment, staring pensively at Gwenn's back. He seemed to be listening to some inner voice. After a time he said, "Yes, Strong Arm, I give you my word."

"Swear on your God," Gunnar demanded, and Arvid did so. Gwenn sat back on her heels, trying to breathe slowly and deeply, so that the poison would not work its way through her body too quickly. Gunnar said, "Now let him go, love. He has promised."

"Gunnar..." she began.

"Please," he begged her softly. "I am in too much pain to argue with you."

Cursing, Gwenn cut the ropes that bound Arvid to the mast. He stood unsteadily, eyeing the distance to the shoreline. Gwenn shoved him towards the gunwale and said, "Sit on the edge. I am not cutting the rest of your bonds until right before you go in. I don't trust you, Scar Brow. I don't give a damn what Gunnar says."

Arvid gave her a gleeful smile. "I will keep my word, not that it matters. That poison Janus uses works very quickly. You will be dead in a few hours anyway, without any help from me. Good-bye and good riddance, you little whore."

Gwenn looked at him coldly. "It is time for your swimming lesson, Arvid." She grabbed him by the collar and lowered him down into the water, then held on as the motion of the boat dragged him forwards.

"Wait!" he said, panicking. "You have not cut the ropes. How can I make it to shore like this?"

"I know," she said softly, and let him go. He struggled violently, screaming curses. Gwenn watched as his head disappeared below the surface of the water, and then popped up again. He sank a second time, and Gwenn rubbed her eyes, trying to correct her blurring vision. Something black was quickly approaching from the south—no, a pair of somethings, far too large to be birds. Just then two black creatures, with wingspans of twenty feet or more, swooped down from the sky, passing low over the deck. They called raucously to one another, and to the struggling figure in the water.

"No..." Gwenn shrieked, dropped to her knees by the gunwale and covered her head with her hands, more afraid than she had been since before Ketha left her. The birds dove down to the ocean's surface and plucked Arvid from the water. They hovered, wings pumping madly, as he raised his fist high in a gesture of triumph.

"I will be coming for you, bitch!" he shouted exultantly. "You and the baby. Whatever magic is hiding you won't last forever. I will be waiting..." The bird creatures swooped quickly out of sight. *Maggrai.*

Gwenn screamed and then retched—her stomach emptying itself completely in one violently painful outpouring. The liquid left a bright red stain as it flowed down the slanting deck. A massive cramp made her head swim as she slowly crawled back over to Gunnar, on the verge of collapse. If she was going to die then she did not want to be anywhere other than by his side.

And perhaps death was for the best... yes, now that she knew who was in control of Arvid.

"Gwenn?" Gunnar whispered. "Who is steering the boat?"

"I am... sorry, love," she whispered back. "I don't think I can keep awake much longer. I am so tired. So tired..." her voice trailed off, and she began to shiver violently.

Gunnar called her name again and again but she did not wake up. Her face was cold and clammy under his hand. The answer came to him at once. *Poison.* And now there was no one to get the boat back to Feringhall—back to Katkin, who might be able to save her.

No one but him.

Getting back to the steering oar was the hardest thing Gunnar had ever done. He clawed his way along the wooden planking with his one good arm, though every movement was torture for his broken bones. Several times he had to stop and rest, when pale spots danced in front of his eyes like fireflies, and his hammering heart felt as though it might explode with the effort. But he could not stop for long. If the *Able Drake* ran aground, or went too far out to sea, then Gwenn's life would be lost.

Somehow he managed to traverse the deck, one painful inch at a time, and then hook his arm up onto the gunwale. Pulling himself into a semi-sitting position was even worse, as the smashed bones in his legs ground against one another. It was incredibly agonizing. And yet, somehow, he felt more alive now than he had at any time in the last few months, ever since he had found out about Lutyond. A new spirit buoyed him—made him want to test himself against the pain and see who would be the victor.

*Look to your heart*, she had said.

And there, suddenly, was the understanding and acceptance of what he had become—Lutyond, the divine Mariner. The pulse of the waves coursed through his broken body—the heartbeat of his mother Ocean washing him clean. Gunnar thought of his people, in Einar, and their deadly allegiance to the Prime God. Here was the redemption they sought and would never find—for the sea forgives all and takes all with equal fairness and mercy.

At last, after much cursing, he managed to hold on to the oar, and keep her steady, though he could not see much of the shoreline from his low position. But the Mariner knew every inch of this coast, as well as he knew his own hands. He could keep the boat on course for Feringhall, as long as he had the strength to grip the rudder.

# 20

## Chind Nowhen

Hana turns and addresses Fyn and Lalluna, who sit close together, but without touching each other.

*She says*, I have seen a thing in Geya's mirror, the likes of which I do not understand. They should not be able to make such an object, not in this time. And what powers it? My heart is troubled. Maggrai has had a hand in this, I fear.

*Fyn hammers the mirror with his powerful fist and it shatters into many gleaming shards.* Where in the hells is he getting corsfyre from?

*Moonlight and Hana both look at him in alarm.* Corsfyre?

~~~~~~~~~~

"What should we do now, Kadya? We have reached another dead end." Huw's voice sounded almost despairing. "Without Caleb we will never be able to track the Anandios. I wish he had not run away." He jumped down from the back of Ceres and dug amongst the bags for a water skin. Arkady continued to study the ground, looking for clues as to which way the caravans had turned. There was evidence of traffic on both branches of the forked path before which they had halted.

He scratched his head. "Well, all we can do is pick one of the forks, and look for traces of their passage further down. Is there a stream or beck to the east?"

Huw nodded and then passed the water to Arkady, who drank deeply. "In this hot weather they may very well head for a water source," he agreed. "I, too, think we should follow the eastern fork first. But we must be far behind them now," he added sadly.

"But at least in the mud around the river ford we might find a sign. It is worth a try. We should get moving again."

Huw said solicitously, "Why do you not ride, my brother? You have been walking all day without a break. I can use my legs for a while." But he swayed tiredly even as he said this, and put his hand on Ceres' flank.

"All right," said Arkady. "But there is no need for both of us to go. I will take Ceres as far as the stream and see if there is any evidence that the caravans went that way. You stay here and rest."

Huw objected to this, but Arkady cut him off saying, "It has only been two days since we rescued you. You were practically dead. Stop being such a hero and sit down. I won't be long." He mounted the horse and gave him a kick before Huw could start arguing again.

Huw stood still and watched, until a bend in the path hid Arkady from his sight. Then he found a sturdy chestnut, with a deep and inviting grassy space underneath. He settled down with his back against the tree, where a gap in the branches allowed light to warm the ground. The sun beating down against the rough linen of his breeches felt good on his weary muscles. He closed his eyes and a red haze filled his vision, as red as the setting sun. It seemed to swallow him up, until he felt as though he was floating in a sea of fire, rippling, flowing with a warmth that sank right into his bones. In a few moments Huw was asleep, with his head resting peacefully on his chest.

A woman entered the grove. She was diminutive, but stunningly beautiful, with velvety waist-length hair. With a sigh, she knelt before Huw and reached out a hand to touch his knee. The sound of soft footfalls behind her made her quickly draw back again. Another woman came to stand beside her. "How dare you?" she said. "It is not your time."

"Why not?" the other woman said petulantly. "I have been waiting for fifteen years. We… have been waiting fifteen years. When is he coming?" The beautiful woman turned away with a pout. "Tell me, Eira. Why should I keep waiting?"

"You have always been spoiled, Cara. Huw loved you, so he was blind to your faults, but I am not, believe me. But the Un-Named One needs him, so you will have to wait a little longer. And now you *must* go. If he sees you, he might be tempted to stray from the path ordained for him."

Cara turned her back and walked away, but called over her shoulder, "Next time I find him alone I am going to tell him the truth. You cannot stop me, Eira."

"Yes I can," Eira muttered, under her breath. "You won't find him again, not where he is going."

Huw was still sleeping when Arkady galloped up on Ceres and hurriedly swung down from the saddle. He knelt down and shook him by the shoulder.

Huw's eyes popped open. "What is it, my brother? Did you find anything?" he asked anxiously.

Arkady shook his head. "I rode as far as the stream crossing on the east track. No one has passed that way for several days. I don't think we are going to find the Anandios down that path, Huw." He sighed. "I will ride a little way on the southwestern trail and see if I can pick up any clues. Wait here for me." Arkady mounted Ceres and went off again in a breathless hurry.

Huw settled back against the tree. Soon sleep overtook him once more; as if his brother's coming had been naught but a dream. The sound of the retreating hoof beats blended seamlessly in Huw's tired thoughts, until he dreamed of many horses passing—passing into the west, until they reached the sea. The ocean filled him with its songs of roaring and booming tides, as he skimmed like a sea bird, carried on a fresh breeze. He flew and flew, over waves with no beginning and no end, until he reached a crescent of sand, with dark cliffs rearing high behind. A lonely cottage stood on the beach. A place filled with memories—of loneliness, hunger and despair.

*Asaruthe...*

The door to the cottage opened and Poppy ran out, followed by Gwillam, who toddled behind her, clutching his rabbit. They both threw themselves down into the warm sand, laughing and playing together happily. Huw watched them from his perch on top of the chimney and his heart was filled with longing. Somehow, Poppy seemed to see him, for she shouted, "Patre Huw! Hurry up and come home, we are waiting for you..." He tried to speak, to tell her he was searching for her, but his voice sounded like the harsh shrieking cries of a tern. After a moment, Poppy turned away, though he called and called her name.

This vision so upset Huw that he woke up crying.

Arkady squatted down before him. "Are you all right, Huw?" he asked as he saw the tears in his brother's eyes. "What has happened?"

He spoke in a wistful monotone. "I dreamed of my little flower.

She tells me to hurry." Then Huw seemed to wake up properly, for he asked, "What did you see to the southwest, my brother?"

"Nothing that will help us, Huw. The path that way is stony and dry. I saw some evidence of traffic, but whether it was caravans and people I do not know." Arkady sighed and then peered at Huw anxiously, wondering what to say next. On his way back to the junction, he had all but decided that they should abandon the search for the Anandios and make their way north. A single horse between the two of them was proving to be too much of a handicap in trying to catch up with Poppy and Gwillam. But he thought it might be very difficult to convince Huw of this, especially after his dream just now.

He tried anyway.

Huw frowned. "But what about my little flower? I just can't..."

"We need to go back to Starruthe. The Dawnmaid has to come first, Huw," Arkady avowed, but Huw stood firm.

"I won't leave her," he said stubbornly. "Or Gwillam. I gave Elsa my word on her deathbed that I would care for them. What kind of a man would I be if I broke it?"

"One who was easier to live with," muttered Arkady under his breath. A sudden desire—to see Gwenn, and even Gunnar again and to make things right with them—made him ache inside. He spoke aloud, with determination. "Well you can keep up this fool's errand after the Anandios if you truly want to, but I am going back to Starruthe. Katkin was right; I never should have left there. My place is with Gwenn and our child."

They both looked at Ceres at exactly the same time.

Huw stood and quickly closed on the horse. After grasping the bridle he said, "I need the horse, Kadya. There is no way I can catch them without it." Arkady walked slowly over to where his brother stood, wondering what he would do when he reached him. They eyed one another. Arkady was six inches taller than Huw, and—as a result of his brother's ordeal in the Firaithi lock-up—a good deal stronger, but he was loath to take the horse from him by force. He tried to reason with him instead.

"I have the further distance to travel, my brother," he said softly. "And my errand is the more important of the two, by far. You must let me take Ceres."

Huw set his jaw. "No."

Arkady took a deep breath and fought to control his mounting annoyance. "Listen to me, you stubborn ass. That horse is mine anyway, so I am taking it."

"No," he said again, and grasped the bridle more tightly as Ceres grew restive in the face of Arkady's anger. They scowled at one another for a minute or more, then Arkady threw up his hands and walked away. Huw opened his mouth to speak but said nothing as Arkady flung himself down on the ground under the chestnut, with his arms crossed.

"Well?" Arkady snapped. "What are you waiting for? Get moving. I won't stop you. You will have to answer to Hana for your actions, not me. She would want you to protect the Dawnmaid of your People, Huw. Will you betray her?"

"It is not a betrayal," said Huw, anxiously. "I am always ready to serve the Un-Named One, you know that. But I have to do this first. I gave my word." He unloaded the horse, sorting through the various bags to find his things.

"You would choose the safety of one little girl over the whole Yrth, Huw? Sounds like a betrayal to me." Arkady said heartlessly. His brother looked stricken but continued to make two piles on the ground. Then he packed his own things into a tattered bag and threw it over his shoulder. With a last lingering look at Ceres, he set off falteringly down the right hand path without saying good-bye.

Although Arkady called his name several times, he did not look back. The trees soon swallowed him in their dappled shadowy jaws.

Arkady watched him disappear, shaking his head guiltily and wondering if he should have let Huw take the horse. In fairness, how could he weigh the needs of two children against his own pressing need to return to Starruthe? Obviously Huw had decided with his heart, but Arkady knew he must use his head. The Dawnmaid had to come first.

He checked his pocket watch and then settled back against the tree, in the same spot Huw had been resting. Arkady decided to give his brother an hour or two to cool down and come to his senses. Surely he would see that Arkady had been right all the long? When he returned then the two of them could travel to Starruthe together. The time passed slowly, and Arkady drowsed in the heat. Flies hummed quietly, the only sound in the woods.

Just then, something swept in front of the sun, large enough to make a sinister undulating shadow on the ground. Arkady, somewhat alarmed, stood up and shaded his eyes. A huge rounded shape, obviously man-made, was passing silently overhead. It had objects—most suggestive of weapons—bristling from its sides, and many small round apertures that might have been windows, with tiny faces looking down at him. He threw himself down into some low brush, abruptly aware of his vulnerability. Arkady stared upwards from his hiding place, marveling at the impossibility of its flight, with equal parts of fascination and terror.

"Holy Gods of the beyond," Arkady whispered involuntarily.

What was this thing that hung so effortlessly in the sky, against every law of nature? It seemed both menacing and miraculous, like a fortress brought to life and given wings. Subsequently it passed out of sight beyond the brow of a hill, but it had been losing altitude as it passed westward, in almost the same direction in which Huw had been traveling. Arkady wiped his suddenly clammy hands on his shirt, picked up his things and threw them on the back of Ceres. He mounted the horse and dug his heels in, so that Ceres reared and then bolted off down the right hand track. Arkady hung on tightly, intent on stopping Huw before he blundered right under whatever...

*Whatever it was.*

Fifteen minutes down the track, and still well under the shelter of the trees, Arkady met Huw, hurrying back towards him—mounted on Ajax, with Caleb running alongside. The brothers both dismounted and hurried towards one another. Neither felt the need for explanation or apology, but they embraced with the implicit understanding that wherever the two of them went next, it would be together. Arkady patted Caleb, and then gave Huw a worried look.

"Where on Yrth has Katkin gone off to? We left Ajax for her to ride. And did you see..."

Huw interrupted, "She is all right. Look, here. There was a note attached to the saddle." He dug in the pocket of his breeches and passed Arkady a crumpled piece of parchment.

It said:

*I have Poppy and Gwillam with me. We are traveling to Starruthe with Fyn. Meet us there as soon as you can, but be careful of the flying aermaran. They carry Black Guardsmen and can spy you from many leagues away in open country. K.*

Huw looked questioningly at Arkady. "It is good news indeed that my little flower and Gwillam are safe with Katkin and Fyn. But what does she mean when she warns us of the aermaran? Is this some new kind of weapon?"

Arkady shook his head. "Worse than a weapon, Huw. That is what I was just trying to tell you. I have seen one. A flying fortress, carrying men inside."

Huw said, incredulously, "Come now, my brother. Surely the heat has addled your brain. Fortresses cannot fly."

"I know what I saw, and it was no dream," Arkady exclaimed firmly. "It passed right over my head and headed that way." He pointed to the southwest. "I think it was going to come to the earth somewhere over there. Is there a clearing or field anywhere around?" Huw scratched his head thoughtfully, and then nodded.

"About three leagues from here there is a meadow, with a boggy place in the centre, with many rushes and cattails. But how do you think this fortress can be made to fall, Kadya? Won't everyone inside be crushed under its weight?"

"I don't know how it works, but I want to find out. Let us ride as close as we can to the meadow, under the cover of the trees. Maybe we can learn more about this aermaran, before we head north. It could be very important."

Huw agreed to this and they set off in a westerly direction, cutting across the forest, and avoiding any clearings. The trees were mostly ash and rowan, and the ground was quite open underneath them. After they had gone about ten miles, Huw raised his hand. Up ahead the trees thinned, and they could see a patch of bright sunlit ground beyond them. Arkady thought he caught the hint of something black blocking out the distant view, but as the ground was sloping upwards it was difficult to tell for sure.

He whispered to Huw, "We should leave the horses here, with Caleb, and go on foot."

Huw breathed back, "Very well, but we must not try to get too close, Kadya. We cannot help the Dawnmaid if we are captured by the Black Guard."

They slunk through the fringes of the forest, with Huw in front picking the path. Arkady marveled at his brother's ability to flit silently between the trees, almost like a shadow, while he himself blundered along, seemingly snapping every twig. Several times Huw stopped and held up a warning finger. In this way they worked their way right up to the top of a small crest, which gave them a good view of the marshy lands below.

Huw reached the top first and his sharp intake of breath let Arkady know that the aermaran had indeed come to rest in the meadow. He joined his brother, who had sprawled flat on the ground behind a clump of bracken. Neither spoke. The aermaran lay below them, vast and menacing, like some bloated silver-finned creature of the primeval sea. It had two black teardrop-shaped gas chambers for lift, attached together with a delicate tracery of bright silver girders and framework. On one end, encased in a round band of brazed metal, hung an enormous propeller, now stationery. A nacelle, with many round windows and several doors, occupied the space under and between the gas chambers. One of the doors was open, with a gangplank leading down, and from this portal many Black Guardsmen came and went, some leading horses.

One called out, "Make sure the forward ropes are secure!" and two others scurried over to follow his command. Other men walked about on the superstructure, and they looked like baby rabbits clinging to some futuristic mountain warren.

Arkady and Huw stared at the aermaran for many minutes in silence, before crawling like beaten dogs back into the relative safety of the forest.

"What are we going to do?" Huw whispered. He shook his head in dismay. "What can we do, against yon... evil beast of prey?" His eyes were wide with fear as he gripped Arkady's sleeve. "There will be nowhere to hide now—all the secret paths and shelters of my people will be laid bare under the unblinking eye of the Black Guard. Nowhere to hide. Nowhere..."

Arkady shook him hard and hissed, "Stop that, right now! Panicking isn't going to help us. We have to think rationally; find a way to outrun it. Now shut up while I try to figure out how it works."

Huw squatted with his head bowed, breathing hard, fighting to control his unreasoning fear. "Surely it is magical, my brother. The work of that monster, Maggrai. How can we hope to understand it?"

Arkady sat silently for a few moments. Then he said thoughtfully, "No, I don't believe it is driven by magic, Huw. At a scientific demonstration in St. Ekaterina, I once saw a man fill an animal bladder with some lighter than air gas. The bladder floated, just like the aermaran does. Not for very long, because the gas leaked away. But if you could build something that would hold enough gas, and make it strong enough—so that it could not escape—you would have a vessel something like the one we have just seen. And all you would need is an engine to power it with, to make it go in the direction you wanted. Do you understand?" He looked over to Huw questioningly.

"No," said Huw sheepishly. "Not at all. But I believe that you do. Still, I don't see how that helps us, not really."

Arkady said patiently, "The gas inside those huge bladders must be controlled by the pressure outside. It can only rise to a certain level and then it will stop. I don't believe the aermaran will be able to float very high. Maybe not high enough to cross a mountain range. Neither will they be able to fly at night. Too much risk they would blunder into something. That is why they landed here in the meadow. The sun is about to set and they could not safely cross that range of hills to the west of us."

Huw smiled. "I wish I had your cleverness, and then perhaps I would understand, my brother. But are you saying that if we travel at night, and keep to the high country, then they will not be able to find us?"

"Yes," said Arkady. "But I don't know how we will find our way to the coast in the dark."

"Leave that to me," said Huw, confidently. "I know nothing of science, but I do know the ways of Yr. Light or dark, I will find the path for us."

"What of your brethren, Huw?" Arkady asked quietly. "If we go to Starruthe now, then you may never see them again. The aermaran will make it easy for the Black Guardsmen to hunt them down and pick them off one by one."

He sighed and stroked Caleb. "I cannot help them now. The Dawnmaid is their only hope, so I must do what I can to protect her." He looked fearful again. "Do you think yon beast is capable of flights over water? Perhaps she is already in danger."

"I don't know for sure, but I doubt it, somehow. Something that large would be at the mercy of strong winds. But come; let us not worry about anything else—except getting to Starruthe. We should get some rest before nightfall, if we are going to travel far under the cover of darkness."

Huw nodded. "You are right. There is a cave a league from here, with a cache of supplies inside. We can rest there until it is fully dark."

Arkady laughed softly. "I may know more about science, but you have the knowledge we need the most at this moment, my brother. Lead on!"

*I must ask everyone in the audience to extinguish all pipes and smoking materials. The vapor I will use for this demonstration is extremely flammable and the slightest spark could spell danger for everyone in this room. Now observe closely as I...*

Arkady woke up with a jerk. It was pitch black inside the cave, but the trees outlined in the door were silvery with moonlight. He could hear Huw's gentle snores on the other side of the small, low-ceilinged cave they had taken shelter in. Not wishing to provoke another argument, Arkady rose quietly and made his way over to Ceres and Ajax. The horses stood sleeping, hobbled in a patch of grass close to the mouth of the cave.

"Shh..." he said to Ajax, as she woke and snorted softly.

After digging through his brother's bag for the items he needed, Arkady took Ajax, and led her through the silent forest. The bright moonlight helped him pick his way back to the bluff where they had first seen the aermaran. It still rested peacefully, like some huge somnolent spider, down on the meadow below. But if Arkady had any plans to draw closer to it, he had no choice but to abandon them now. Some mysterious light source, far too bright to be mere lanterns, lit the aermaran brightly on all sides. He reconsidered his firm denial to Huw about the use of magics, but he had no time to investigate the lights further.

He had gone to sleep wondering if there was any way they might disable the aermaran, so as to give the fleeing Kindreds a better chance of escape. A dream had given him the answer, perhaps, if he could get close enough to it. Arkady took Huw's short crossbow, and selected a bolt. He ripped several strips of cloth off his own shirt and smeared them liberally with the oil he had found amongst the cooking gear. Now came the tricky part. He had to light the bolt quickly, before he was seen, stand and fire it straight at the nearer of the two gas bags. Whether the flaming bolt would pierce the envelope and ignite the gas inside he had not the slightest clue.

The brightly illuminated aermaran was guarded by many men, patrolling back and forth, some with muskets propped on their shoulders. He could only hope that the strength of the lights would blank out the view beyond the meadow. Arkady heaped twigs and dry moss into a pyramid. He carefully struck tinder against flint, and started a small blaze on the ground before him, then curled his body over it, so that it could not be seen from below. Once it caught properly, he thrust the wrapped arrow into the midst of the flames, drew it out and stood. One chance—that is all he had.

*One chance.*

He stood and fired, then turned and ran for Ajax as the world exploded behind him.

# 21

## Mysteny Prox

He lives!

Is he coming here, to help us?

*Fyn growls.* No! Yrth needs him more. The Dawnmaid has need of both her fathers now.

<hr />

Katkin sat, clutching a cup of coffee, more exhausted than she believed she could feel while still being wide awake. The sun was rising, illuminating the mists that clung to the shoreline in pastel harmonies of color. It was beautiful, but to Katkin's tired eyes it represented just the start of the day—another long day in which she would try to keep her daughter and son-in-law alive, in the face of almost insurmountable odds. She could only pray for strength, and give thanks that she now had two good hands with which to care for her patients. The weather continued unseasonably fine, which was another blessing, but she knew this Old Wives' summer wouldn't last.

When the square sail appeared over the horizon—three... or was it four days ago now?—Katkin had been overjoyed. After Gwenn had left her with a week-old squalling infant and her young twins, saying she would be back with Gunnar as soon as she could, Katkin had, at first, been kept happily occupied with the business of grandmotherly attention, as well as the care of her own two adopted children, Poppy and Gwillam. But when two days turned to three and then to four, the pressures of dealing with five children on her own had rapidly eaten away at her reserves of patience and calm. Poppy had tried to help, as much as she could, but Katkin had been loath, then, to leave a six-year-old in charge of younger children, even one as resourceful as Poppy.

But when she had hailed the *Able Drake*, as it bumped roughly on the jetty, she had been a little worried when she could make out no one standing at the steering oar. After she climbed aboard to find the mooring rope, then she had seen...

Well it was a miracle that either of them was alive at all.

She could not move Gunnar. He was far too heavy, and too hurt. Gwenn, she might perhaps have transferred into the house, with a little help. But she did not have any help, unless you counted the five children age six and under, who clamored to see what it was that kept Katkin so busy on the *Able Drake*.

Katkin had rigged a shelter, of sorts, over the stern of the boat, with the canvas tent that she and Huw had taken from the dead Guardsman in Brunner's Valley. She dragged Gwenn's practically comatose body underneath it and arranged her next to Gunnar, after she had prised his stiffened fingers free of the oar and helped him to lie flat. He could talk, and did, when he was not sleeping off the copious draughts of opium she gave him. Unfortunately, she could understand little of his rambling explanation, since he spoke only fragments of Maraison.

"Arvid," he said. "Hammer me."

She looked at him with horror. "He hit you with a hammer?"

"Not he," Gunnar shook his blond head mournfully. "Make others hit lots."

"What about Gwenn?" she asked him, and tried to disguise the urgency in her voice. "Do you know what happened to her?"

"How Gwenn?" he asked her plaintively. "How my Gwenn? Janus arrow poison?"

Katkin's heart sank. If Gwenn had been poisoned then there was almost no hope for her. For Gunnar himself the prognosis was a little brighter, but it was obvious to Katkin, even at this early stage of his recovery, that he would never walk again. She had set the broken bones in his arm as well as she could, but both his legs were a hopeless mess of crushed bone.

After that first exhausting day, Katkin sat wearily in the bow, bathed by the last rays of the setting sun and took stock of her situation. She had to make poultices and compound medicines from Eydis' store of herbs. She must drop tinctures and water into Gwenn's slightly parted lips every hour. Bandages and bedpans also required her attention several times a day. And how could she ignore the needs of the children? It was not humanly possible to do it all and yet, if she failed, then Gwenn and Gunnar would die.

*What on Yrth could she do?*

"Poppy?"

"Yes, Katkin? Why did you wake me up? I was sleeping."

"I know. I am sorry. Please come with me, and don't disturb the others. I have something to show you."

She had no choice now but to trust the little girl with the care of all the younger children, except the baby, Myrie. Katkin kept her on the boat, in the old cradle that had once been Gunnar's own. It swung now from the yardarm, and rocked the child with the ageless touch of gently lapping water. She lay quiet and still, with a preternaturally watchful expression, as if she was waiting for something to happen.

Poppy came and went, bringing fresh goat's milk for Myrie, and food and drink for Katkin. She did not seem bothered by the sight of the critically ill grown-ups under the tent.

"You will make them better, won't you, Katkin? Just like you fixed Patre when he was sick. You are the best doctor in the world."

"I will try my very best. Now you had better get back to the boys. Make sure they wash up before you give them their breakfast."

Poppy followed her instructions with a combination of military discipline and childish cajolery, leaving Katkin free to go about the business of doctoring, as well as she could, Gwenn and Gunnar.

With Gwenn it was never going to be anything but a losing battle.

Her only hope was that she might keep her alive long enough for Kadya and Huw to arrive. If Kadya still had the ability to heal, then perhaps he could make Gwenn whole again. But even that was only a faint chance. She was sinking quickly.

Katkin finished her coffee and stood, before crossing the deck of the *Able Drake* towards her makeshift hospital. She would check on her patients, give Gwenn another few drops of a strong herbal tincture that she hoped was counteracting the poison, and then go inside to help Poppy make breakfast for the other children. Gunnar, if he was awake and aware enough, could give her a teaspoon of water now and then with his good hand, while Katkin was away.

Excited shrieks from Poppy drifted down the dunes. Katkin, despite her exhaustion, nimbly vaulted the low gunwale, fervently praying that she would have no other patients to look after. But when she rounded the last turn, at a dead run, she saw Poppy ecstatically clutched in the arms of a small, very dark-skinned man. Caleb bounded about happily, barking.

*Huw...*

Arkady looked on, smiling. He hailed Katkin. "Ahoy! Where are Gwenn and Strawhead? Has the baby come yet?" He looked somehow different, and his clothes were even more tattered than before, but Katkin was far too distracted to properly notice.

She slowed her steps, but did not speak. Huw quickly stood, with Poppy still in his arms, and crossed over to her. He could tell from her expression that something was not right. "What has happened, my Queen? Tell us quickly."

As he put his free arm about her, she almost collapsed with the relief of knowing that help had come at last. She blurted out, "Come to the *Able Drake*, both of you. I will explain on the way. I am sorry, but Poppy will have to stay here and make breakfast for the others."

Poppy rubbed her eyes, tiredly, and nodded. Huw put her down saying, "I will return to help you in a few moments, my little flower. But now I must go with Katkin. Don't worry, everything will be all right."

Katkin could only shake her head, knowing how misplaced Huw's optimism was. Arkady peppered her with questions all the way to the boat, but she gave him no answers, except to say warily that Gwenn had given birth to the baby two weeks ago and called her Myriadne Elisabeth. According to Gunnar, Arkady had played some role in his capture, and until she understood what it was, Katkin did not think it wise to give him any further information.

Carefully, one at a time, they stepped over the gunwale, and then Katkin led the way to the tent. Both Arkady and Huw gave cries of dismay when she threw aside the hanging door flap. Arkady was the first to speak as he fell to his knees by Gwenn's prone form.

"What in the God's names happened here?"

"She has been poisoned, Kadya. By an arrow wound. See—it is there, on her cheek. I am sorry, but I don't know much beyond that."

He looked up at Katkin and his eyes were wild with shock and grief. "And Strawhead? What happened to him?"

"He has multiple fractures on his legs and a fractured left humerus," Katkin continued dully, and watched Arkady's face carefully for his reaction. He seemed genuinely dumbfounded.

"Has there been some sort of accident? Why won't you tell me?" he asked angrily, and then shook Gwenn, urging her to wake up.

Huw whispered sorrowfully to Katkin, "Oh, my queen. You have had nothing but grief since you returned to this place. I wish I had been here to help you."

Katkin stepped forward, intending to pull Arkady away from Gwenn, since he was obviously close to losing his self-control. But to everyone's surprise Gwenn's eyes snapped open. She squinted, trying to focus on Arkady's face.

"You!" she whispered hoarsely. "Get your murdering hands off me."

Arkady sat back as if she had slapped him. "Murdering? What on Yrth?"

She turned her head with difficulty and blinked at him. Her eyes were pink, and runny with sticky mucus. "Don't even look at me!" she rasped through bloodless lips. "Show him," Gwenn ordered her mother. "Show him what he did to Gunnar."

Katkin bent down slowly, as Arkady continued to protest his innocence. She pulled away the light woolen blanket that covered Gunnar, as he slept on peacefully, too drugged to be bothered by the disturbance around him. Underneath it, he was naked, as he had been when he arrived. Katkin could not have dressed him in anything else without causing him more pain.

Arkady went pallid when he saw the livid broken flesh covering his grossly swollen legs and arm. "Sweet mother of the Gods," he whispered. "Is she fey? Why does Gwenn think... I mean, I had nothing to do with..." But even as he said this, a fierce prickling feeling in his solar plexus filled him with dread—a reaction that alleged he knew very well what he had done when he left Feringhall.

Gwenn coughed painfully at his side. "*Arvid*," she spat, at last. "Your new best friend..."

A sudden horrified look of comprehension crossed Arkady's face, as he stood, and backed away. Seconds later he vomited over the side of the boat, as Katkin described Gunnar's torture at the hands of the Abaryanites. She finished by asking him, urgently, "Have you still the gift of healing from Hana? Both of them need it now."

He shook his head uncertainly, still reeling from his own unforeseen complicity. "I don't know. I have not tried since I came back from the Vastness. Gods, I never meant..."

"Try," Huw urged him. "You must, my brother. There is no time now for recriminations. Whom should he heal first, Katkin?"

"Gwenn," answered Katkin, firmly. "She needs help the soonest."

"No!" Gwenn croaked. "Gunnar. *Only* Gunnar. He has suffered by far the most torment at that stinking traitor's hand. I don't want his touch, ever again, for any reason. Keep him away from me."

"Gwenn, no," said Arkady, and he sounded utterly broken. "Please let me help you."

"Go... to... hell..." she gasped, and then began to jerk spasmodically. Within seconds she was thrashing madly on the deck, as Huw and Katkin tried to hold her down. Gunnar jerked awake and screamed as her foot lashed out and hit him on the leg.

"She is having a seizure!" Katkin cried. "The stress could kill her. Kadya, you must..."

But he was already drawing on his centre, trying to find the mystical source of the healing power given him by Hana, long ago. Within seconds, a white fireball appeared within his cupped hands. He dropped it over her, just as she cried out, "No! Not me!"

Within seconds the fire had engulfed her in pulsating white tongues of flame. She rose up, spiraling gracefully away from the deck of the *Able Drake*, as Huw, Katkin and Arkady looked on, entranced as always by Hana's healing grace. Thirty seconds passed.

She landed on the deck and looked around her, panting hard. She spied Arkady first. With a scream of rage, she snatched up a boat hook and launched herself forward. Only Huw's quick-thinking intervention saved his brother's life. He tackled Gwenn and held her, with Katkin's help. Katkin shook her daughter until her teeth rattled.

"Stop this childish behavior at once, Gwenn. He won't be able heal Gunnar if you kill him." Gwenn subsided, albeit unwillingly, and then crawled over to where Gunnar lay on the deck, sobbing quietly. She kissed his mouth, tenderly, and wiped the tears from his face. Then she looked down at his broken body and stifled a moan. Her eyes, now clear and blue once again, lifted up until they met Arkady's. He saw nothing but hatred there.

"Well, what are you waiting for?" she hissed. "Why don't you fix him, the way you fixed me? Go on, you sniveling weasel."

He tried. Everyone could see the effort on his face, as he drew deeply on his core, to find the magic once again. After a moment, when it became patently clear that he could do nothing at all to help Gunnar, Gwenn spat in Arkady's face, and went to see to her children.

The four of them moved Gunnar inside with little difficulty, and installed him in the sick bed in the alcove. That night, as the children slept, and Gunnar lay on the kitchen table, deeply anaesthetized with ether, Katkin amputated his left leg just above the knee. The wound created by the compound fracture of his tibia had become acutely infected, leaving his foot blackened and putrid with gangrene. With Huw's help she rigged up a traction device for the other leg, and splinted the shattered bones as well as she could. Later, as he lay once again in the alcove, Gwenn bustled about, making him comfortable, while Arkady sat, still and silent, with little Myrie in his lap. Occasionally the others talked to him, and he answered as if in a dream, but he never took his eyes off Gunnar, and the flat place under the covers where his lower leg should have been.

A few days passed. Katkin stayed busy with the children, and watching over her patient. Huw followed her around, trying to help, and engage her in quiet talk. She rebuffed him as gently as she could. Though she knew she must eventually confess to him all her doubts and indecision, Katkin told herself it could wait until Gunnar was stronger.

But Gunnar improved steadily, now that the infection was under control. Surprisingly, it was Arkady who took over the better part of his care—fussing endlessly with his pillows, bringing him food and sponging his wounds with the antiseptic poultices that Katkin had taught him to prepare. The rest of the time he spent with Myrie, and often he had the baby with him while he kept Gunnar company in the alcove.

But Gwenn ignored him when she came in to check on Gunnar or the baby—looking through him as if he did not exist, speaking loudly over the top of his frequents attempts to apologize.

After her last visit had left a definite chill in the room, Gunnar gave Arkady a tired smile and said lightly, "Don't let it bother you, Inky. She will get over it one of these days."

Arkady sighed. "I don't think so. You did not see how she looked at me when I tried to heal you and could not. She hates me now. I think she always will." He gave Gunnar a sidelong glance and said, "There is something I don't understand. You ought to hate me too. Why don't you?" He sat back and watched as Gunnar closed his eyes, obviously lost in contemplation.

In a little while he said thoughtfully, "Why should I hate you? I don't believe what happened was your fault. Perhaps you brought it about, indirectly, but the true cause goes back much further—to my own days as a raider. And for that I can blame no one but myself." His bright blue eyes grew hazy with remembrance. "I butchered many innocent men—aye, and sold women and children as slaves to the Haba. My men stole the lifeblood and livelihoods from thousands of people over the years." Gunnar shrugged. "Arvid believed that I needed to be punished for those sins, and he was right. Not because of his fraudulent Prime God, but because of what I am."

Arkady stared at him, a little disconcerted, and then touched his hand, very gently. "What are you now?" he asked softly. "Not the man I thought I knew in Celeste. Not anymore. That man is dead."

"Nay, he still lives—in here." He touched his chest once with his good hand. "But there is more of me now than I ever dreamed there could be. Fyn tried to tell me so in the Vastness, but I did not want to believe him. I was... afraid. Strangely enough, it was Arvid who gave me the strength to find myself, and to accept who I truly am."

"Lutyond," whispered Arkady, reverently. "The Mariner."

An ironic smile played on his lips as Gunnar said, "Yes, I suppose I am a God now. The very same God I used to call upon in prayer, before me and my crew set off across the ocean on a voyage, when I wore his symbol on my chest so proudly." He touched the gold anchor that rested in the hollow of his throat. "Then I found that Lutyond was there inside me, all the long."

"I know. I wanted to hate you for that," said Arkady, remembering that day in the cove.

"But why? There is a God in you, too. You have only to look to your heart. Hana has given you great power for good."

Arkady shook his head sadly, and declared, "There is nothing good left in me—not now." His eyes filled with tears, as his lower lip trembled. "Hana has taken her gift away, and I cannot heal the very person I have hurt the most. How can you ever forgive me?" He bent his head, so that he could bury his face in the soft wool blanket covering the bed, and cried bitter tears of remorse and shame.

Gunnar stroked his shorn head, and said softly, "Forgive yourself, Kadya. That is all that remains. You and I have made our peace."

Katkin, Huw and Gwenn sat at the kitchen table. The children slept around them, in various drawers and boxes, except for little Myrie, who rested peacefully in Huw's arms. He looked upon her tiny face, framed with a fringe of dark, dark hair, and said softly, "Here is the savior of our people. That I should be so fortunate to hold her in my arms is a miracle for which I can never thank the Un-Named One enough.

Katkin smiled. "She is more of a miracle than you know, Huw. Gwenn is quite certain of the date she got pregnant, and I delivered Myrie two weeks ago."

Huw looked puzzled. "Is there some small discrepancy?"

"Not small, no," Katkin remarked. "Huge. Myrie was born after only five months gestation. There is no way a child that premature should have survived, but as you can see, she appears to be a healthy, full-term infant, apart from her tiny size. I cannot explain it, except to say she must have known she needed to be born, so that Gwenn could go and rescue Gunnar."

"The ways of the Un-Known One are not always clear," he said confidently. "But they are always right." He looked down at the baby in his arms and smiled as she yawned widely with her little rosebud mouth. "What now shall we do to protect this little one? I don't believe we should stay here in Starruthe."

Katkin nodded. "Even though Gunnar says this place has some divine protection, Maggrai will not rest now that he knows she is here."

Gwenn spoke up in agreement to this, but said, "Gunnar is not strong enough yet to be moved. How are we to travel? He is the only one among us who has the skill to navigate across open water." Gwillam cried out in his sleep and Gwenn distractedly bent to give him back his rabbit. He snuggled against it and started snoring. "And with so many children, how can we possibly travel over land, even if we make it back to Yr?"

They all looked at one another and sighed.

"Yr offers no shelter for us anyway," said Huw, despondently. "The Black Guard will see to that, now they have that cursed aermaran to menace the skies."

"But I thought you told me that Kadya destroyed it in some sort of fire?" Katkin asked. "He certainly looked as though he had been through hell when he arrived. What happened to all his hair?"

Gwenn sniffed and got up from the table, saying she would check on Gunnar.

"I was sleeping in the cave, and I heard the explosion, though it was a league or more away," Huw explained. "When I found that Kadya had gone, and taken Ajax, I was very afraid. I rode back through the woods, towards the place we had seen the aermaran, but I could not get close. The whole forest was on fire. Suddenly Ajax appeared out of the smoke, dragging something behind her. It was Kadya—luckily his foot had caught in the stirrup when the explosion knocked him from the horse. He was out cold, and his clothes were burned, as well as most of his hair."

Huw paused and closed his eyes, remembering the approaching inferno, and the nightmarish screams of the horse.

"Ajax was very badly injured, and I had to cut her throat to stop her suffering. Ceres had bolted as well, dragging his picket with him, so I did not know what we would do. But then Fyn appeared, out of nowhere. He picked up Arkady as though he was a sleeping child, and I grabbed Caleb. Fyn took my hand and we traveled from the forest, through ways I cannot fathom. But I saw glimpses of such beauty and wonder. Our journey here seemed to take no time at all."

"It took you a *long* time to get here," Katkin answered softly. "I have so much I need tell you, Huw." She looked around the crowded main room of the cottage with trepidation. "Why don't we go for a walk along the beach," she suggested. "The moon is high and it is a warm night." He nodded resignedly and followed her out the door.

A warm breeze swept in from the ocean, but the water was flat and almost dead calm. Tiny wavelets lapped the sand. A bird, hurrying across the moonlit sky, called briefly before settling in a tall pine. The peace and quiet of the night sharply contrasted with the tumult that Katkin felt inside as she walked with Huw, silently wondering how much to say—and how to say it.

He surprised her. "Let me help you, my Queen."

"What?" Katkin had been so lost in thought that she did not, at first, understand what Huw meant.

"You want to tell me something, yes? Something you think will hurt me?"

Katkin stopped walking. "How did..." Her voice grew abruptly sharp. "Did Arkady say something to you?"

Huw shook his head. "No, he has said nothing. But I have eyes, Queen of my heart, and ears, too. I can see when someone I love is suffering. I can hear the catch in her voice when she speaks my name."

She took a deep breath, knowing the moment had come for her to confess her doubts and indecision. So she told Huw all about meeting Dai in the forest, and about her journey to Scarfinda. She left out no detail, from her misplaced trust in Dai to her terrible hesitancy about returning to Bryn Mirain. She even told him about her initial refusal to help the Amaranthine. Throughout this long soliloquy he remained silent, and kept hold of her hand tightly.

When she finished, the waves continued to slap gently against the shingle, but that was the only sound to be heard. Though she expected Huw to be angry he only gazed at her with sadness in his eyes.

"I have known all the long that you were unhappy," he said, after a moment. "And how could I blame you? I should have told you about Cara at the beginning, and given you a proper choice about whether to stay with me or not, rather than selfishly waiting until we were practically snowed in at Brunner's. You never promised me anything, Queen of my heart. And yet I treated you as I have seen other Firaithi men treat their wives—telling you what to do and expecting you to obey without question. No wonder you did not wish to return to me."

She sighed. "What I did was still wrong, Huw. I was just being self-centered and cruel to both you and the children. I don't know how you will ever forgive me for it."

Huw smiled gently. "There is no need for forgiveness between two people who have erred equally." Quite unexpectedly, he dropped to his knees in the sand before her. "Will you give me another chance? Do you think we could start again, from the very beginning?" he asked earnestly.

Katkin nodded slowly, but still thinking she ought to be the one on her knees.

"Good," he continued softly. "Then will you do me the honor of becoming my partner? Equal in all things, and cherished above all things, until we stand before Tsmar'enth?" He dug in his pocket and produced a slender ring of gold set with a single clear jewel, then held it out to her.

Katkin looked at it, shining in the moonlight on his dark palm, thinking it seemed somehow familiar. "Huw, where did you get that?"

He smiled. "Strangely enough, Fyn gave it to me as we traveled the worlds between. He said a good friend of his, named Tomas, had once wanted you to have it. I did not want to take it, at first, but he insisted. Will you accept this ring as a long-overdue token of our esteem for you, my Queen?"

"I will," she said softly, thinking once more of Tomas, fondly, but not with longing—not anymore. "And will you accept my solemn word that you also will be equal in all things and cherished above all things, until we stand before Tsmar'enth?"

"I will," he said.

She placed the ring on the third finger of her left hand and smiled ruefully. "Long overdue? It is just as well you waited, Huw. I wouldn't have been able to wear it properly before now."

Huw stood and held out his hand and then said, joyfully, "You and I have not shared a proper bed since we left Brunner's Valley. Shall we see if we can find one now?"

Katkin laughed merrily and pulled him into the moon-dappled shadow of the trees, where a deep cushion of dry pine needles lay warm and inviting under their bare feet.

"Was it a whole month?" Arkady asked in amazement, the next morning at breakfast.

Katkin nodded.

He shook his head. "To me it has seemed like a few days at most. But perhaps traveling the worlds between twists time, as well as space."

Huw sighed audibly. "I wish I knew how to return there. Somehow I know that our own land lies that way, beyond the hearts of the blazing stars."

Katkin took his hand and squeezed it. "You are right, Huw, and it is very beautiful. But none of us mortals understands how to travel the worlds between, except for Gunnar." Her eyes went wide with sudden inspiration. "But do you think perhaps we could hide there, if he could take us?"

Huw's answer to this was surprisingly fervent. "It is a place of peace and tranquility! We must not carry the troubles of Yrth there. For better or worse our difficulties must remain here." Arkady nodded in agreement.

She sighed resignedly. "You are right, of course. But now we still have to decide what we must do. Do you think there are any more aermaran?"

"Kadya believes so, almost certainly."

Arkady added, "But I don't think they can travel any great distance over water. If only there was somewhere..."

Poppy sat up just then and called out, "Patre Huw? Can I have a drink of water?"

As Katkin drew the girl some water from the pump, Huw snapped his fingers and said excitedly, "I know where we can go to keep the little ones safe. The Un-Named One told me in a dream, as I slept under a tree. I have only just remembered."

His cry brought Gwenn running. "Where?" she asked him eagerly.

Now they clustered around the foot of Gunnar's bed. "Asaruthe?" he said skeptically. "I thought you said there was little food to be had there. You certainly looked like a starved dog when you got back to Starruthe."

Huw said confidently, "But we did not have a boat then, to make fishing easier. This time we would—the *Able Drake*. And we could bring with us seeds and tools to work the soil. There used to be a settlement upon the island. We could make a new one, in secret, and the Black Guard would never be able to find us. Sven Red Beard told me that the island is uncharted."

Gwenn interrupted Arkady, who had just started to speak up in agreement with Huw. "But how on Yrth will we get there? Gunnar isn't..."

"Yes—he is," he growled. "I can get us there, as long as there are people on board to man the oars and raise and lower the sail." He glared fiercely at the ring of faces surrounding his bed, and no one dared disagree with him.

Arkady put in quickly, before Gwenn could interrupt him again, "Good, then. We will go to Asaruthe. It is settled."

"The hell it is," Gwenn said stonily. Four pairs of eyes turned simultaneously to look at her.

"Why ever not?" Katkin asked her daughter. "I think it is the best thing we can do to keep Myrie safe."

"I do too," she agreed. Then her voice grew hard as she stabbed her finger in the air towards Arkady. "But not with him. I won't go anywhere with that spineless jellyfish." Arkady looked devastated at this, and Huw rushed to his defense.

"He is sorry for what happened, Gwenn. He has said so many times. Can you not find it in your heart to...?"

"No," said Gwenn, flatly. "I cannot."

"I once had a grave wrong to forgive," Huw continued softly. "Do you remember, my dear?" He gazed at Gwenn. "Will you not do the same?" She shook her head and quickly looked away.

Gunnar tried next. "He is Myrie's father, for the God's sakes. We cannot take her away with us and leave him here, Gwenn. It would not be right."

"I don't care!" Gwenn drew herself up and faced them all. Her voice rose to a scream. "If that murderer goes, then I will not. Do you hear me?"

"Calm down, Gwenn," Arkady said gently. "I won't go if you don't want me to." He stood and wiped the tears from his eyes. "All I ask is that you take me with you on the *Able Drake* and put me ashore somewhere on Yr."

"Kadya, don't," Katkin said. "None of us wants you to be left behind."

"I do," Gwenn went on callously. "We can leave him in Danica, across the Straits of Angar'et. I suppose I can bear to be in a boat with him for that long. But no further."

Arkady turned and shuffled out of the room, with his head bent low.

They spent the next days busily gathering everything anyone thought they might need to live comfortably on Asaruthe. Tools, seeds, dried foodstuffs, bedding and clothes were packed away in the clinker-built hull of the *Able Drake*, until she sat low in the water with all the ballast.

"Did you get the medical supplies?" Katkin asked anxiously, with her eye on Gunnar. "I need all of Eydis' herbs and opium. There is no telling when I might be able to get more." Gwenn packed each of the phials in a canvas bag, after carefully wrapping them in tissue. "And don't forget the bandages." Her daughter nodded, and packed a dozen rolls of gauze on top.

Huw passed by and added, "I have taken all the useful tools from the shed, but I cannot find a sledgehammer." He dropped his voice and winced as he saw Gunnar's expression. "Oh dear," he said ruefully. "I will go and look in the cellar."

Arkady stayed resolutely uninvolved in these preparations, other than spending time with Gunnar to tell him what he remembered of the route to Asaruthe. Sometimes he could be found in the cellar at Feringhall, carefully working away on some mysterious objects made of wood, with the rapidly dwindling supply of tools. Other times he took the baby, Myrie, out in a sling carrier, walking along the beach, alone with his unhappy thoughts. The high pines cast long shadows, and the air beneath them was chilly. He was reminded that fall was passing, and then winter would arrive with unsheathed claws of ice. The *Able Drake* must leave Feringhall before that ice locked the seas away from them—a matter of a few more weeks at most, according to Gunnar.

He sighed deeply, wondering what he would do once he returned to Yr, alone. Though everyone had tried to reason with Gwenn about her decision, she remained intractable. Arkady still loved her fiercely; as he loved the little blue-eyed mite of a child she had borne with him. But he could not force her to forgive him, nor to love him in return.

A few days before they were all due to depart, he came quietly into the alcove, carrying something under one arm. "I have a present for you, Strawhead," he said, and smiled, though, as always, his eyes looked sad.

"What have you got there?" Gunnar sat up, jovially, and looked at the long wooden objects Arkady had placed across the bed.

"Crutches," he answered. "Soon you will be up and around, and you will need them to help you. See you put them under your arms, like this..." Arkady demonstrated. "And I put a special bracket on this one, to rest your broken arm on while it is healing." Gunnar ran his hands across the satiny-smooth wood and admired the deeply padded leather arm rests. Arkady was a natural craftsman, and anything he took the time to make he would make with the utmost care.

"Thank you, my friend," Gunnar said softly. "I wish..."

"I know. You don't have to say anything." The two men looked at one another for a long moment.

Gunnar broke the unhappy silence. "Can I try them out now, do you think?"

"You had better ask the doctor, not me." Arkady called out to Katkin in Maraison.

"Ask me what?" Katkin chimed in, as she passed by with an armful of blankets.

After she had examined the crutches and found them to be sturdy, she spoke carefully as Arkady translated. "I don't know if you are well enough to move around just yet, Gunnar. Let me check your legs." But when she inspected his wounds and his stump, she found them to be improving far more quickly than she would have thought possible. She gave him a thoughtful glance. "Well now. I believe you might be able to try them after all, but only a few steps. All right?"

With Arkady's steadfast help, and a great deal of colorful cursing, Gunnar sat up and swung his legs over the side of the bed. After wedging the crutches carefully under each armpit, he stood, slowly, and took three wobbly hopping steps, with Arkady's arm firmly around his waist. Then he turned and hopped back towards the bed, before spying Gwenn, who stood in the doorway, with tears in her eyes.

"Gunnar, my love" she said softly. "I did not believe I would ever see you walk again. It is a miracle."

"Nay," he laughed. "'Tis only good doctoring, and these excellent crutches." He held one out to Gwenn, who examined it with interest.

"Did you make these?" she asked Arkady. He nodded warily.

"Oh," she said mildly, and left the room. Gunnar and Katkin exchanged a look. It was the first time Gwenn had addressed Arkady directly in a very long while. They could only hope that perhaps more than Gunnar's broken bones had begun healing at last.

## 22

## Varden Sequent

*Silently, Ben'aryn drifts, on the edge of Night. Here in the Nowhen he already sees the flow of time dividing, like a forked stream. One way leads to devastation—the other to the unknown. He has given himself the task of closing the left way, to protect those he loves. That variant of the future will cease to exist, leaving them free to live in a world untroubled by the interference of others.*

*The irony of this—that he must interfere in order to bring this about—is not lost on him.*

~~~~~~~~~~~~~~

Poppy, clutching her favorite rag doll, walked beside the tall, sad-eyed man that her Patre called brother. She had decided to take him in hand after watching him leave, day after day, for lonely walks on the beach, with no one but baby Myrie for company. It was obvious he needed a friend, someone to make him smile again. So, today she had tugged on his tattered cloak and asked if she might walk with him, and bring Dotty and Caleb too. As he strode along, she chattered about the coming voyage, her dead mother and father, how much trouble it was to have a little brother. Arkady listened with grave attention, and answered her many questions about passing birds and the sea with knowledgeable ease. He even explained how he and Patre had come to be brothers—an exciting story that made her eyes go wide. Arkady had actually *killed* someone to protect Patre's sister, Eira, and then had almost been killed himself. No other grown-up she knew had ever confided a thing of such adult import to her.

She looked up at him with bright eyes and asked, "So, you are my Ikor now? Ikor Kadya?"

Arkady nodded.

Poppy gave him a captivating smile and squeezed his hand. "I am glad to have a nice uncle like you. When we get to the island, I promise that Caleb and I will go for walks with you everyday. Then you won't be sad anymore."

He stopped walking abruptly, and then knelt down so that his head was level with hers. "I am not coming to Asaruthe, Poppy," he said quietly.

She looked distressed at this. "Why ever not? Myrie is coming with us, and you are her Patre, aren't you? It is sad to grow up without a Patre. I am so lucky to have Patre Huw."

He sighed and tried to explain. "I did something very wrong, and Gwenn... Well she is angry with me—rightfully so. She asked me not to come. I don't blame her and you must not either." Arkady stood up and started walking again, so Poppy fell into step beside him, very pensively.

Presently she asked, "Did you say you were sorry and try to make amends? Patre says you must always do so when you have hurt someone." Arkady smiled inwardly at this bit of homespun wisdom from Huw, thinking that Poppy was lucky indeed to have his brother as her father. Then he replied, "I did, lots of times. But it was not enough, somehow."

"Oh," said Poppy, and bent down to retrieve a piece of driftwood from the tide line of the windswept beach. She threw it end over end, and Caleb took off after it, barking excitedly. But then he bypassed the driftwood, and continued down the beach, still barking wildly. Poppy looked into the distance and cried, "Look, Ikor! What funny birds. Caleb wants to chase them instead."

Arkady's head flew up in alarm. He saw a flock of black birds, flying in a v-formation, obviously searching the land below them.

When they spotted Gwenn, sitting outside the house with Gunnar, they sheared off, shrieking, and headed back the way they had come. With a muttered curse, he grabbed Poppy up in his arms and ran with her back towards the jetty, where the *Able Drake* was berthed. As he passed the house he cried out breathlessly, "Get to the boat. They are coming!"

Huw and Katkin came running.

"What is it? What have you seen, my brother?"

"A flock of crows. Messenger birds, sent by Maggrai to spy out the land."

"Hold on a moment, Kadya." Katkin said skeptically. "How do you know they were messengers?"

He answered breathlessly as he unwound Myrie from her sling. "I just know. They spied Gwenn just now, and flew swiftly away to the east. Don't waste time!" Arkady bent before Poppy, and said, "I need to borrow Dottie for a little while, all right?" Poppy nodded, more than a little mystified. She handed him the doll and Arkady carefully placed Myrie in her outstretched arms, saying, "Take her to the boat, little one. Hide under the big tent that Katkin made, all right?"

Poppy nodded, her eyes solemn, and then walked quickly towards the jetty, with Caleb trotting protectively beside her. Arkady quickly placed Dottie in the carrier, to look as though he still had the baby with him.

"Come on!" Arkady said. "Get the rest of the children on board. I will help Gunnar." The urgency in his brother's voice convinced Huw, who hurried towards the house. Katkin caught up with Poppy, and helped her board the *Able Drake*.

Gunnar struggled to his feet as Arkady tore up the path. "What is happening?"

But he needed no answer to his question. The much larger winged minions of Maggrai had just come into view over the hill. Gwenn screamed in terror and picked up Jakob and Arvid, who had been playing at her feet.

"Get them aboard the *Able Drake*," Arkady commanded her, and she took off running. Gunnar threw an arm over his shoulder and they hobbled together towards the boat, but at a hopelessly slow pace. Huw passed them, running swiftly with a screaming Gwillam in his arms. They met him again in a minute, as he raced back towards the house, pointing to the sky in alarm. The first of the minions would be over their heads in no more than a minute.

"Take him," Arkady cried.

Huw took his place under Gunnar's arm, and hurried with him down the path to the cove. After dropping Jakob and Arvid in the boat, Gwenn ran back down the jetty to help Huw with Gunnar. Between the two of them they managed to lift him over the gunwale, and onto the wildly rocking boat. "Get the children stowed," he roared. "Raise the sail!"

Once Arkady was sure that they were all safely on board, he turned back towards the house. "Hurry!" he cried over his shoulder. "Cast off and get out to sea. I will draw them away from you." He broke into a run down the path to the beach, clutching the carrier to his chest as though it still contained an infant. The winged minions took the bait and followed—ten at least, swooping low with wicked talons outstretched. Their horrible screeching cries rent the air.

Huw looked on helplessly from the *Able Drake*. "He will be killed! I must help him." He struggled to disembark as the vessel pulled away from the jetty. Katkin held on to him, as the first of the huge birds attacked Arkady, and knocked him to the ground. He rose and continued to run doggedly, his feet slipping and sliding on the loose shingle.

Katkin cried, "You cannot save him now. We have to get Myrie away from here. He knew what he was doing when he ran away, Huw. He is giving us the only chance we have to protect her." Huw fell to the deck, sobbing, as three birds converged on Arkady and drove him down to his knees.

Gwenn stood at the gunwale, watching with the rest. The boat slipped further away from the dock—ten feet; fifteen; twenty. The wind picked up, and filled the sail. She saw Arkady struggle to rise, saw a bird land directly on his back and try to lift him into the air.

"Kadya!" she screamed, and executed a perfect knifing dive off the side of the boat. Gunnar called for her, cursing wildly, but she did not surface. Seconds later, her blond head exploded out of the waves and she hit the beach at a dead run. Keth'fell gleamed in her hand.

Gunnar brought the *Able Drake* around, intending to head back to shore, when he caught a glimpse of a longboat, oars stroking in unison, moving smoothly up the coast towards them. He gave a cry of dismay.

On the shore, Gwenn slashed upwards with keth'fell and brought down the first bird that tried to attack her. The second managed to drive its claws into her back before she cut its legs off, with a whistling backwards hack of her blade. It rose, wings beating in agony, as its blood splashed down in red runnels onto the sand. She fought her way over to where Arkady lay, face down, and kicked at him with her boot. He moaned weakly but did not move. Gwenn slew two more of the attacking creatures with vicious upwards thrusts of keth'fell as they dove down. The other birds fell back, evidently now convinced that Myrie was not with Arkady and Gwenn. They headed out to sea, towards the *Able Drake*. Gwenn roughly shouldered Arkady and ran back into the waves.

Arvid stood at the helm of the rapidly converging longboat, with his hand on the dragon prow. It was a magnificent ship, far more opulent than any dragonship Gunnar had ever seen before. The elaborately carved figurehead and tail were solidly gilded, and the reflected sun was almost blinding. Red runes festooned the bows, saying her name—*Long Drake*—along with many other enchantments of death and protection. The sail featured the black Naught symbol.

Without a doubt, Arvid's vessel was far superior to the *Able Drake* in every respect, but Gunnar was not afraid. He called reproachfully over to Arvid, "You said you would let us go, Scar Brow. You swore on your God."

The long boat reached the *Able Drake*, and pulled up alongside, so that the hulls were parallel. Sixty seasoned warriors stood ready, with their hands poised over their swords and halberds, waiting for the signal to attack. Huw went to stand next to Gunnar and drew his knife, ready to die in defense of his family and friends, though the fight seemed a hopeless one. Katkin crawled back into the tent to comfort, as well as she could, the terrified children.

Arvid called back, "Perhaps I did, Strong Arm. But there has been a change of plans. I need that baby. Give her to me."

"No," said Gunnar, and his voice was as cold and hard as blue steel. "Leave us alone. I kept my word. You must keep yours, or die, Arvid. I shall not warn you again."

Arkady's unconscious form flopped over the gunwale on the

shoreward side of the *Able Drake*, making her rock wildly, but Arvid took no notice. He was laughing too hard. "Really, you are too much, Gunnar. You don't even have a weapon. What will you do? Beat me to death with those pathetic crutches?"

Gunnar whispered over to Huw, "Help Gwenn get on board, and tell her to hold on to Kadya. Then make sure the children are secure." He cleared his throat and addressed Arvid's sixty companions on the boat. "Listen to me! I am your God—Lutyond, the Mariner. Why should you die in defense of this slithering worm, who has made a mockery of all we believe? You owe him nothing. I don't wish to have your blood on my hands, my brethren."

As the men behind him murmured, Arvid cried, "He is not a God! Look at him—he is hardly even a man anymore." His voice rose to a scream. "I destroyed him, I tell you. In the end he was begging the Prime God for mercy."

Gwenn angrily scrambled to her feet. "Liar," she cried. "You never broke him! I was there."

"Sit down, Faircrow!" Gunnar hissed urgently. "Sit down and hold fast!"

"Attack!" screeched Arvid. "Kill them all, except the baby. Bring her safely to me."

Gunnar closed his eyes and sighed in resignation as the first rank of warriors swarmed forward, grappling hooks at the ready. "So be it," he said softly.

Without warning the *Long Drake* exploded, heaving up into the air with the sharp reports of many cracking and rupturing timbers. The keel buckled under the pressure, and the dragon figurehead snapped free of the boat, falling back with a resounding splash. The ice-toothed jaws of the sea opened wide to receive it—as well as the warriors who fell chaotically from the splintered vessel as she continued to rise, borne upwards by a vast dark shadow.

The huge wave that broke against her side drove the *Able Drake* rapidly away, and came close to swamping her. Gunnar lost his footing, falling back on to the deck with a cry of agony. It seemed the little boat might capsize in the maelstrom that followed, but somehow she kept upright as the sperm whale that had breached under the Long Drake continued to flail at the remaining shards of the boat with its mighty tail. The few survivors floundered about, screaming with fear and panic.

Gunnar dragged himself over to the side as the boat bucked and swayed underneath him like a wild horse. With great difficulty he raised himself up to the edge of the gunwale, just as Arvid's head broke the surface of the water next to the smashed gilt figurehead. The high priest of Prime cried out, "You haven't beaten me! There is nowhere you can hide, Strong Arm." Then he looked up at the three massive avisceti that circled the remains of his ship. "My minions! Come to my arms. Hurry!"

But the swooping birds were denied another dramatic water rescue. Arvid's voice ceased abruptly as the sperm whale opened its huge jaws and swallowed him whole. It sank back down to the bottom of the sea, leaving nary a trace of its passing. Huw felled two of the remaining minions with deadly shots from his crossbow. One dropped, shrieking, on to the deck of the *Able Drake*. The other landed in the sea, and disappeared. The last bird flew away to the southwest, crying mournfully.

Gunnar stared down in to the moiling black waters and whispered, "Thank you, good beast." Then he turned and sat briefly with his back resting against the side of the boat. He was almost completely exhausted, but there was work yet to be done.

The aviscet on the deck had just ceased its death throes as Huw cautiously approached it, curious to see what manner of outlandish creature he had brought down. It looked something like an owl, he thought, but with a strange and disturbing human caste to its face. He bent to close the sightless eyes, and noticed the bright red jewel strung cruelly tight about its neck with a piece of wire. Feeling strangely drawn, he cut the wire with his knife, and tucked the talisman in his pocket. When, a moment later, Gwenn called to him to throw the dead beast overboard, he did so with a lingering sense of regret, as though it had cried out to him for a respectful burial.

Gwenn helped Gunnar to stand as Huw came forward with his crutches. Once he was upright, he began issuing orders. "Gwenn, man the oars with Huw. Get her about, and see if we can pick up the survivors." Then he called towards the tent, in Maraison, "Katkin, leave the children. They are safe. Come and see to Kadya."

Katkin staggered from the tent, and looked with horror at the remains of the *Long Drake*. "What in the God's names did that?" she cried, but everyone was far too busy plucking the surviving warriors from the water to answer her. Poppy joined her at the gun-wale, where Arkady rested, in exactly the same position in which Gwenn had dropped him. His sodden form lay so still and silent that Katkin was utterly sure he was dead. She turned him over carefully, and then put her hand over her mouth to stifle a cry.

"Get back to the tent and make sure the children are all right," she said hurriedly to Poppy in Firai. "Go on!" But Poppy had already seen the bloody shredded wreck that the attacking birds had left in place of Arkady's handsome face. She screamed at the sight of his empty eye sockets and crashed to the deck in a dead faint.

Gunnar watched over the sixteen remaining warriors as they huddled at the stern of the *Able Drake*. They looked back at him bleakly, with utter dread, sure that this vengeful God would slay them all. But as he limped among them on his crutches, soothing their fears with soft words, they soon touched his broken body reverently, with many whispered pleas for mercy. No one heard what Gunnar said to them in response, but when the *Able Drake* drew up to the shore, and the grim-faced warriors disembarked, there was no doubt in anyone's mind that the edifice that Arvid had built for the Prime God would be gone from Einar as soon as they returned there.

"Farewell, my brothers," said Gunnar to them, as a gentle wind filled the sail of the *Able Drake* and swept her away from the island of Starruthe once more. "Take care of those amongst you who have fallen, if our Mother, the sea, doesn't. I will return to you, if I can. But for now I must protect the child on whose life all of ours depends."

As a man, they fell to their knees, and gave a cry of "Hail to thee, Mariner!" as Gunnar turned from them and limped back to the rudder.

Gwenn sat huddled next to the tent, sobbing bitterly. Gunnar drew her into an embrace. "Don't cry love. If he is gone from us, then he did not die in vain. His quick thinking saved us all. You cannot mourn for one who so desperately needed the redemption of a great deed. Now he can rest in peace."

She buried her head on his chest. "But I never told him. I let him die while he still believed that I hated him. How could I have been so cruel, Gunnar?"

"Whisht, Gwenn. He knew you loved him. He knew..."

Katkin came to stand beside them. As she rooted through a box of medical supplies she said briskly, "He is not dead, Gwenn. And he *won't* die, not if I have anything to do with it."

Gwenn gave her mother a disbelieving look.

"Yes, the damage to his face is serious, but all the wounds, with the exception of those to his eyes, are superficial. The salt water bath you gave him should help to prevent any infection, though it must have been terribly painful for him. No wonder he passed out." Gwenn quickly translated her mother's news into Dalvolk. Katkin patted Gwenn on the arm as Gunnar gave a whoop of pure elation.

Then she said, "Come and help me bandage him up."

# 23

## Sisciot Nowhen

Has she a part to play in the coming battle?
Indeed, Hana. Hers may be one of the most important roles of all.
Will she become one of us?
*Eira shakes her head.* The stones seem to be saying that powers far greater than ours will adopt her. But who could that be? We have always ruled the Yrth.
*Hana looks vaguely troubled.* Do the stones say anything more?
Only this, my sister: listen for the song of the trees.

~~~~~~~~~~

Poppy walks alongside her Ikor Kadya, holding his arm, and murmuring instructions as he steps carefully over the rocks that line the shore of Asaruthe. Gunnar has made roped walkways to most of the places he needs to go, but Kadya likes the beach, likes to sit and listen to the sounds of the sea.

"Such beautiful voices, Poppy," he says. "They sing to me. But do you know what? I never heard them until I lost my sight."

She has kept the promise she made to him, that day on Starruthe.

Every day they walk together, and she tells him all she can see with her eyes. He still listens with grave attention, still answers her questions and tells her stories. Caleb is long gone now, but another dog, with rusty colored rough fur trots along beside them, and Poppy throws a stick for him to chase now and then.

"Here, Bax. Come on, boy," she whistles, as the dog occupies himself with his favorite pastime, trying to catch the puffins that nest within the rocks on the cliff side. Their booming growls of protest are much louder than the waves, and a familiar springtime sound.

"That dog..." says Kadya, reprovingly. "Why can he not leave those birds alone?"

He is blind, and his face is terribly scarred; still Poppy believes that her Ikor Kadya is the best and most handsome uncle in the world. But Poppy is a girl of extraordinary grace and perception, as her parents are quick to say. Katkin and Huw live on one end of the tiny island called Asaruthe, in a stone cottage they built themselves from the ruins of a bigger house. There had once been other inhabitants on Asaruthe, but they went away long ago. Poppy doesn't understand why—she loves the island, with its high brown cliffs and desolate spaces. Though not as desolate as it once was—Gunnar and her Patre have planted many saplings, mostly spruces and cedars, and now the hills are clothed with patches of deeper green.

"How are the new trees we put in last winter faring?" Ikor asks her, as they pass beside a grove of young *Pinus Sylvestris*[*], sheltered by the lee of the cliff. "Has the dry weather hurt them at all?"

Poppy studies the trees before replying. "I don't believe so, Ikor. A few have died, but the rest are growing well. And the sheep have not been in again since Gunnar put the fence up."

She glances up to the top of the cliff where sheep and a few cows crop the deep turf. The animals shelter through the long winters in the byre that lies below Ikora Gwenn's big house, on the other side of the island. Gunnar lives in the house with Gwenn, and Arkady has his own little cottage close by, but they are all one family, and share equally in the care of their three children—the twins and Myrie. Poppy doesn't question this unusual arrangement, since her Ikor explained that it is common in other places on Yrth, like the country of T'Shang.

* Scots Pine

Poppy sees the twins watching from the top of a sand dune close by, and she hails them. "Hello, Jakob! Hello, Lut!"

Both of them are blond and very tall, like their mother and father. They tower over Poppy's brother Gwillam, who is the same age. Jakob comes down first, and greets her with a stiff, "Hello, yourself." He is ten, and so like his brother that Poppy often gets them confused. Lut comes down more slowly, and only nods at her. He is shy, much more so than Jakob. Once upon a time, Lut had been called Arvid, but Gunnar had said, once they reached Asaruthe, that he never wanted to hear that name again as long as he lived.

So Arvid had become Lut, after his father.

"Can't chat," says Jakob, importantly. "We have a sailing lesson with Dad. And guess what? Next month he says we can go to Minbeorg with him." With a flash of a grin he hurries down towards the dock, where the *Able Drake* is berthed. Lut trails behind him after waving solemnly to Poppy.

Poppy has heard much of Minbeorg. It is a town on the coast of Cittern, where Gunnar takes Ikora Gwenn's wool and round red-waxed cheeses for trade. When he returns the *Able Drake* will be full of exciting things—cambric for new clothes, books to read, special fare like sugar and tobacco, coffee and wine. These staples will be carefully stored away, and used frugally through the coming year. Gunnar and Gwenn think it is not good to visit the mainland too often, because they do not want people asking questions about where they live.

Ikor Kadya and Poppy leave the beach and walk back through the dunes, along a well-worn path. They come across Myrie and Gwillam, playing together in the lee of a big sand hill, amongst stalks of nodding oat grass.

Gwillam calls out jauntily, "Ahoy! Where are you bound?" as Bax leaps up to lick his face.

"Home for dinner," says Poppy. "And you should be weighing anchor and coming along if you don't want to get in trouble again, Gwillam Brunner."

Myrie, who is filling and emptying a cup of sand with machine-like precision, says nothing at all, even to her Patre. But Kadya doesn't mind. He lightly strokes his daughter's long black hair and she gives him two clicks with her tongue.

"She says 'Hello, Pop,'" declares Gwillam, and Arkady smiles.

Gwillam is Myrie's constant playmate, interpreter and guardian. Her half-brothers Jakob and Lut are sometimes jealous of this special relationship, but when they try to separate the two of them, Myrie begins an awful earsplitting keening that soon drives her brothers away. She never speaks, does Myrie, only makes a clicking sound with her tongue when she is happy, or screams when she is not. Her deep blue eyes are strange. Though she gazes straight ahead with a sometimes disconcerting stare, she never seems to notice anything much. But everyone loves her anyway, and Ikor Kadya most of all.

Kadya and Poppy begin the slow walk back to Ikor's cottage. Poppy asks, "Will Myrie ever come to school with us?"

Arkady sighs. "I don't know—Myrie is a very special child, with special abilities, but she might never be able to speak or learn things the way that you can."

Poppy knows this already, for she has seen Myrie stacking objects into impossibly high columns as she clicks away happily. She wonders, but only to herself, if Ikor Kadya is disappointed that Myrie is the way she is. He never says so, but Poppy has heard him talking to Ikora Gwenn about someone called the Dawnmaid and how important she is for the future of Yrth, and everyone living there. If Myrie cannot communicate, they say, then how can she possibly be the child the Firaithi have been waiting for?

Such talk is confusing and a little frightening for Poppy, who would like to think that the tiny island world she inhabits is a place of peace and safety. But many whispered warnings intimate to her that it is not. She listens and digests far more information than the adults give her credit for, and Patre's sister Eira often visits her dreams. Eira died many years ago, and Patre never talks about her in front of Ikora Gwenn. Poppy would like to know the story of how she came to die, but she is a little afraid to ask. The grown-ups around her have so much confusing and conflicting *history* and Ikor Kadya is only one who ever speaks of it openly. She cannot help thinking that all of it is wound tightly about the thing Ikora Eira calls the Gyre, and her own life is deeply intertwined with the rest.

*The wind doesn't change direction by chance*, Eira once said to her, in a dream.

Poppy wonders how long it will be before the gentle winds that embrace her haven will sing a different, more strident song. A song of war—of the battle against Maggrai, and the Angellus. She understands that one day she will leave this sanctuary, that great and terrible things are happening in Yr, and her cousin Myrie is a part of it all. And where Myrie goes, Gwillam will surely follow, and Poppy must be there to protect them both.

# Appendix I

## History and Practice of the Triske Stones

The Firaithi use an array of three Triske stones for divination. The stones are made from spinel*, a naturally occurring mineral, often ruby red in color, that fractures naturally into a perfect octahedral shape. The three stones are called Moonstone, Redestone and Gyrestone. Each has its own set of four symbols, repeated twice on the eight faces of the octahedron. The history of the Triske is largely unknown, although it is believed to be the oldest and most accurate of all the mantologies of Yrth. It is surmised that the Firaithi originally came from the mountainous east of Yr—the only location where spinel stones naturally occur, and brought lithomancy with them when they migrated westwards.

Each Kindred boasts a single lithomancer, always female. They call her Y'dane, a title of great respect. The Y'dane keeps the stones in a special soft leather pouch, tucked between the breasts, so that the female energy of the body (the flux) may permeate it. The Y'dane always has several apprentices and she imparts to them the secret understanding of the stones. When the Y'dane is about to die, she will name her successor—usually, but not always, the most adept of all her tyros.

To practice the art of lithomancy, the Y'dane tosses each spinel individually, so as to prevent damage to the precious stones, which are extremely costly to replace. She begins with the Moonstone, which foretells the predominant character of the roll by its correspondence with the phases of the moon. The Firaithi name the moon phases Halemoon, Wanmoon, Dunmoon, and Waxmoon.

**Halemoon** represents the lunar orb at its fullest aspect, a time of plenty—but dangerous for the hunted and the insane. The season most closely associated with the Halemoon is summer.

---

\* Magnesium Aluminium Oxide (MgAl2O4)

**Wanmoon** is the shrinking moon, calling for a drawing inwards, and conservation of energy. It is the autumn season—a time of reflection, old age, and dying.

**Dunmoon** is the new moon, the blackest night. Associated with winter. A time of dearth, and darkness for the spirit, but the hunted find safety within its inky mantle.

**Waxmoon** is the emergent moon, gathering strength towards its full aspect. The season of spring—a time of fertility, passion and unruly behavior.

The Y'dane then tosses the Redestone. It clarifies and enhances the prediction by adding the effects of The Wayfarers—the naked eye planets visible from Yrth. The Wayfarers are Ruber, Unda, Zephur, and Hurd. They roughly correspond to the elements fire, water, air and earth.

**Ruber** presides over matters of the spirit and also the health of the physical body.

**Unda** is the controller of love, passion, birth and fertility.

**Zephur** touches on territory, battle, aggression and sanity.

**Hurd** rules the home, hearth, partnerships and industry.

Lastly, the Y'dane will toss the Gyrestone to place the prediction within the span of time, either present (Prox) past (Quondam) future (Sequent) or the Firaithi indeterminate Nowhen.

The stones, their associated symbols and meanings are outlined in Appendix II.

# Appendix II

## Connotations and Significance of the Triske Stones

The stones are tossed in the following order: Moonstone—Redestone—Gyrestone. Some noteworthy combinations are given special names, which are also specified below.

Moonstone/Redestone Combinations:

### *Halemoon*
(Associated season—Summer)
Tossing the Halemoon indicates a position of strength. Things are ripening, becoming fulsome, gravid or meaningful. Births, beginnings, journeys, partnerships, marriages and contracts are imminent and favored. Although tossing Halemoon is almost always a positive sign, for the hunted it spells deadly menace and exposure.

Ruber+Halemoon= A powerfully energetic spirit is coming or already amongst the Kindreds. A time for undertaking long journeys on the Greater Ambit, while health and spirit are strong. (Nundael)

Hurd+Halemoon= Look for completeness in matters of kith and kin. Hearth and family are well-knit, steady and secure. Wealth and food are abundant. (Sisciot)

Zephur+Halemoon= A time of peace and tranquility. Aggression wanes in the heat. (Mysteny)

Unda+Halemoon= New births and marriages are favored. Satisfaction, satiety and completeness bring joy to the Kindreds.

### *Wanmoon*
(Autumn)
Tossing the Wanmoon indicates a position of decay and potential weakness. Things are losing strength and influence, slowing

down, dying out or losing favor. Relationships may sour, marriages founder, journeys will be slow and tortuous, or lead to dead ends. Consequences of earlier actions, both good and bad, are to be expected.

Ruber+Wanmoon= Energy flags, illness may afflict, growth is slow or non-existent.

Hurd+Wanmoon= A time of foolish waste for some. If the storehouse lies empty then it is too late to save for the lean times. (Pellunis)

Zephur+Wanmoon= Courage is rapidly dwindling. Battles are inconclusive, with many casualties on both sides. Misfortune will befall the unprepared.

Unda+Wanmoon= Love is weak and untrusting. Passion's flame is dying. Fertility is low, but, on a happier note, births are at their peak. (Chind)

### Dunmoon
(Winter)

Tossing the Dunmoon indicates a position of stagnation or inertia. It is impossible to proceed with any journey or with the accomplishment of goals. Though to toss this stone is almost overwhelmingly negative, it does provide protection for the hunted, or any creature that thrives in darkness.

Ruber+Dunmoon= Growth is at a standstill. It is time to take stock and dream of better times to come. The hunted may lie safely in hollows and rest. (Methuit)

Unda+Dunmoon= Passion is cold and dead, or perhaps sleeping—like the heart of a seed, waiting for the warmth of the sun and the kiss of rain. Babes are lost to stillbirth. Partnerships will fail. (Dardisea)

Zephur+Dunmoon= Insanity and melancholia become rampant, as thoughts are scattered and useless. Battles will be lost. Death comes prowling, and creates fear rather than acceptance. Aggression is tamed by apathy and want.

Hurd+Dunmoon= Energy and food stores will be depleted, savings drained. Times of famine and dearth. (Cendemar)

## Waxmoon

(Spring)

Tossing the Waxmoon presages a time of awakening. The sap will rise, the ice melt, and tightly furled buds begin to open in the gentle rays of the sun. But all is not beneficent—Waxmoon is a time of thunder and storms, when spirits are wild and violence common. Marriages and partnerships will flourish with passion and zeal, but are sometimes short-lived. Weary travelers will make great headway.

Ruber+Waxmoon= Growth begins anew, spirits rise. The sun warms the dead Yrth, and brings forth life. New enterprises begun with anticipation and fervor must be carefully tended to prevent exhaustion. (Pindaen)

Unda+Waxmoon= Passion rises to new heights. Babies and plans will be conceived and thrive. The reawakening beauty of Yrth provides inspiration and happiness for all.

Zephur+Waxmoon= Pent-up anger is unbridled at last. Battles for territory and property are fierce and reckless. Daring deeds are accomplished by those who find the courage to attempt them. (Varden)

Hurd+Waxmoon= Material gains will begin anew. The Yrth stirs and the Kindreds become industrious once more, just as the bees leave their hives and seek for nectar amongst the flowers. (Missad)

## The Gyrestones

Nowhen—The enigmatic Gyretime. May mean all the time, no time at all or all together outside the passage of time.

Quondam—It has been said that the past is a different land, and it would seem useless to predict things that have already happened. But due to the cyclical nature of Firaithi existence, all of time becomes the ground for further being, and a toss of the Quondam Gyrestone can mean a great deal to the present and the future.

Prox—The events predicted will take place at once, or very soon.

Sequent—The future, near or far. Could be at a future time in this life or possibly a different life all together.

# Appendix III

## The Annals of the Firaithi Elders

The following accounts were taken down by Arkady Svalbarad on his first journey with the Firaithi Kindred of Chandra, after he was adopted by Tane Grigor Adaryi. During the three weeks he rode with the Chandrathi, Arkady questioned the Elders of the Kindred on the original homelands of the Firaithi. The Elders have no written histories, but Arkady developed a simple alphabet to transcribe their tales, and they are set down here as he heard them.

### *Kyan Dewi's account of the Quondam—the time before the Firaithi came west to Yr*

In the time of aza'thuwlas, there were many more of the Kindreds than there are now. We were innumerable as the stars in the sky, or the grains of sand on the beach. Of our original name it is not permitted to speak, but we were not called the Firaithi. That came much later.

We had proper homes then. Homes of stone and wood, with roots in the Yrth. We shared our land with the Sentinels, who towered over us. They watched over us, and in return we made many sacrifices to them. Lathie mostly, and some Ky too, left on the shoulders of the Sentinels, so that they might serve their new masters beyond Tsmar'enth. It was considered a great honor to lose a child to the mountains, even though they were never seen again, for it meant propitious rebirths for everyone in the family in the next turn of the Gyre.

Our lives were simple, for we lived the way of Asparitus. We herded cattle and goats, and made our fare by the gifts of the Un-Named One. Her bounty gave us all we needed, and never did we raise our hand against another living creature. The milk, the barley, the lilies of the field, all provided our sustenance and our grace.

In those blessed days we traveled only twice a year, and never did we go very far. In the summer we and the animals camped on the high green meadows on the sun-drenched sides of the Sentinels. Our cattle and goats grew fat and glossy on the rich green grass there. In the winter we moved back to sheltered houses tucked well down in the deep valleys, and our animals shared their milk and wool with us in return for the warmth of the hearth, and the dried stuff we set aside for them.

Rain and snow were our brothers, and the winds sang a song just for us. Many turns of the Gyre found us there, happy and at peace.

## Kyan Glaw describes the Dardisea

Perhaps we were foolish to think that our good fortune might last forever—for it did not. First the winds changed, and sang a different song—one of discord and unrest. Then the kylathie* whispered against their parents. Husband and wife argued bitterly with one another over the practice of the sacrifice. After a time no one wanted to give up their lathie to the Sentinels, and then our guardians withdrew their boons. Brother fought brother to the death over the lilies of the field, and made from them a potent poison instead of food. Whosoever took this poison did not grow strong, but wasted away in ill-health, and yet, oddly, this only made them desire it more and more. Soon there was no joy or contentment anywhere to be found.

We were a people cast adrift.

Then a stranger came. He was tall, as tall as the Sentinels, or so it seemed to us, because by then we had been reduced to crawling on our bellies in the dust, in disease and filth. His hair was gray, like iron, and braided with many sparkling stones of blue and green. As he looked upon us, in all our misery, his eyes were filled with stern pity. His voice thundered like the voice of the mountain storms.

"Leave this place at once!"

Jagged rocks rolled from the shoulders of the Sentinels, crushing our homes to dust. Our cattle and goats fled in terror as the women begged for mercy. The stranger's breath set fire to the lilies of the field, and a great smoke consumed the hills and valleys.

We were left with nothing and yet...

We had regained everything which we had lost before the coming of Shiqaba.

* Older children.

So we took to the way west and did not look back at the glowing valley of flames that had once been our home.

### Kyan Haul recounts the first Ambit

Walking was all we could do—at first. Many of our people suffered terribly from a sick need for the poison of the lilies of the field which made them sweat and groan in agony. But as we traveled further away from our valley the need lessened, until it became only a ragged nightmare. This is when we understood that we had walked away from death, and back into life again. We swore then that we would never return to the valleys of the east—nor ever consume the lilies of the field. Our eyes remained on the setting sun, and he guided us faithfully.

Soon we found the raw materials to make our new homes. Homes that would move with us, and carry us ever further away from the desolation of our former land. As we walked, we drank in the gentle beauty of the rolling plains, and our hearts were gladdened. Our legs grew strong, and our hearts too, at the new song the winds sang. The Un-Named One continued to provide, and in time we gathered new goats that walked with us. We walked many leagues and each land we passed through was different, unsettling, and none felt like home to us.

Shiqaba returned, and with him came a miraculous gift—the horse.

He gave us this good beast, and in return he asked us to resume the sacrifices we had made in our former lives. Many of the Kyan argued with him, saying we could not afford to lose our sons and daughters as we had before, because we were much fewer in number. The perils of the way, and the sickness of the lilies had claimed many. But still there were some who were willing, and with Shiqaba they went to the west.

We that were left taught the horses with gentle words and touch to serve us. Always we bred them for strength and for fire, until they were like to us the song of the wind made flesh. With these beasts we were able to travel ever greater distances to the west, and at last we came to the populated parts of Yrth.

### Kyan Rhodri speaks of the Time of Parting

At first we thought to make of these new peoples our brothers and sisters. Though they were not like us—their skin was as white as the belly of a fish, and their eyes were pale like cold lake water, we recognized that we were all part of the Un-Named One's grand design. But it soon became clear to us that the people we had found did not wish us to share their domain. We believed we had a right to settle in Yr, for the lands were vast and mostly empty. Yet everywhere we traveled we were met with unfriendly eyes, and bitter words. They shunned us, called us 'darky' and worse. In return we named them Gruagán, the white devils. In the end, there were battles, and many men from both sides were maimed and killed.

Shiqaba returned to us once more. He told us we must separate into small bands and travel lightly, like the birds of the air. We must tread the paths on which the Gruagán would fear to follow. So the time of the Great Parting came to pass. Some of our people could not endure this rootless existence, and many passed away to the west with Shiqaba when he left. Those that remained called themselves the Firaithi, which in our tongue means 'the surviving ones'. We had passed through sickness and death, war and hatred. What other name could we have?

Arkady Svalbarad appended the following note to the above accounts:

I heard many other tales on my travels. Some the Kyan did not permit me to transcribe. Others seemed to remain in my memory only fleetingly, as a dream does upon awakening from sleep. The above accounts form a rough chronological history, though the Firaithi sense of time is very different from my own.

No scholar has been able to verify the authenticity of the oral histories of the Firaithi, for their homelands to the east have never been identified. There is no mountain range called the "Sentinels" that I have ever heard of. It seems likely to me that the experience the early peoples had with the 'lilies of the field' was some form of addiction to papaver somiferum. Certainly the modern-day Firaithi are forbidden to indulge in any form of intoxicant, and this may well be a result of the accounts of the Dardisea.

# Appendix IV

## Glossary

**Abaryanite** – Holy soldier of Prime.

**Acorn** – Jacq and Katkin's stone cottage on the grounds of her late father's former estate, Tintaren. Burned down by the King's Guard after Jacq's arrest for spying, and rebuilt by Queen Arkafina during her reign.

**Aermaran** – The airship invented by Maggrai.

**Anafiremad** – Weapon for the destruction of anafireon.

**Anafireon** – The spirit of the living.

**Anametronicus** – Implement for measuring anafireon.

**Asparitus** – The Firaithi way of life. It means to take little and return much.

**Astarene** – The spirit body of the dead. Pl. astaren.

**Autochthones** – The Amaranthine name for the Firaithi.

**Aza'thuwlas** – An indeterminate time, neither future nor past. Also called Nowhen.

**Azimity** – The force which holds the whirling strands of time close to the Gyre.

**Beaumarais** – A small country in the continent of Yr. Bounded to the east by the Mistmere and Mardon to the west. The northern border is shared with Secuny and the southern with Spanja. The capital is Isle St. Valery, an important trading hub on the inland sea.

**Black Guard** – Tristan's secret army.

**Bryn Mirain** – The secret meeting grounds of the Firaithi.

**Catena** – The network of farmers who grow foodstuffs for the Kindreds.

**Citadel, The** – The five-sided fortress that overlooks the City of Isle St. Valery. The abode of the ruling monarch and the Guard.

**Chamber of Deputies** – The ruling body of Beaumarais, consisting of one hundred representatives elected biannually.

**Chymike** – The mystical arts of severance and recombination. Adj. chymerical.

**Corsfyre** – The power source created by smelting anafireon.

**Dai Irrakai** – Amaranthine, seeker of the paths between the stars.

**D'angwir** – Jacq Benet's sword. Means "justice for all" in the old tongue.

**Dinrhydan, The** – Jacq Benet's code name. Translates as "true heart" in the old tongue.

**Firaithi** – A wandering people, comprised of twenty Kindreds, who traverse Yr trading in horses and handcrafts.

**Felag** – The unbreakable fellowship between Fynäran raiders.

**Feringhall** – Eydis' house on the wild coast of Starruthe.

**Firemma** – Discipline of Hana that keeps body and soul together after death.

**Fyn** – A god of the Fynära, beloved of Lalluna.

**Fynära** – A marauding, sea faring race.

**Geya** – A Triple Goddess of the Amaranthine. Her sisters are Raven and Moonlight.

**Gruagá** – Firaithi name for the settled peoples of Yr. Means "white devil." Pl. Gruagán

**Gyre** – Everything that is or ever will be winds around the infinity of time in the Gyre.

**Ikor** – Uncle in Firai.

**Ikora** – Aunt in Firai.

**Juvenie** – A Unity apprentice.

**Juvenead** – An apprenticeship in the Unity.

**Keth'fell** – Gwenn Faircrow's sword. Means "death crow" in the old tongue.

**Keth Dirane** – The name that the Amaranthine Raven was given by the Firaithi when she came to Yrth. Lit. "Death's Shade."

**Kindreds, The** – Divisions of the Firaithi people. Normally a group of around thirty to forty adults and children.

**Khalama** – Home village of Arkady's old teacher, Dawa Tinley.

**Kymatre** – Grandmother in Firai. Grandfather is Kypatre.

**Kyan** – Elders.

**Lathie** – Child in Firai. Teenager is kylathie.

**Lutyond** – The Divine Mariner, god of the Fynära.

**Mardon** – A neighboring but unfriendly country to the west of Beaumarais. Several wars have been fought between Mardon and Beaumarais over disputed territories. Citizens from Mardon are called the Mardonne.

**Mebbain** – Passageway to the worlds between.

**Mistmere** – The large inland sea that brings trade and exchange to Beaumarais. Isle St. Valery is on a peninsula that extends into the Mere.

**Moera** – The Goddess of Fate.

**Moonlight** – Amaranthine. Sister of Geya. Also called Lalluna.

**Pellicle** – Part of the Amaranthine system of addressing points on the Continua. Pl. pellicula

**Raven** – Amaranthine. Sister of Geya. Also called Keth Dirane.

**Secuny** – The neighboring country to the northwest of Beaumarais.

**Tsmar'enth** – The moon gate. Firaithi expression for death.

**Skyre** – The heavenly reward of the Fynäran raiders, an eternity of feasting and fighting.

**St. Valery's Acre** – The vast forest that clothes the western shores of the Mistmere.

**Tane** – Leader of a particular Firaithi Kindred. An inherited position.

**Triske stones** – The divination method used by the Firaithi. Consists of three octahedral bone carvings—each face is incised with a different symbol.

**T'Shang** – Mountainous country to the east of Yr.

**Uri'el** – Keepers of the astaren.

**Wayfarers, The** – The four planets beloved of the Firaithi. Their names are Unda, Herd, Zephur and Ruber.

**Yr** – The continent on which Beaumarais is located.

# Author's Acknowledgements

Mike Goodwin helped, as always, to make this book better. Martyn Folkes, my publisher, is a fount of patience and wisdom. My family puts up with my obsession without complaint, and for that they deserve my deepest thanks.

I must also say thank you to my friends on WordPress who have given me wonderful encouragement and suggestions this past year. You can meet them all at www.suzannefrancis.com.

# About the author

Suzanne Francis believes the genesis for her inventive Song of the Arkafina series lies in her chronic travel sickness as a child and young adult. While growing up in England and on the Continent, she happily participated in many family and school trips, though riding in the back seat of a car often left her suffering from nausea for hours on end. To help pass the time, she began telling herself stories, serialized over many days and weeks, often featuring the landscapes through which she was traveling. These imaginary adventures, along with a life-long love of reading good books (but only when sitting still) sparked her interest in writing. Since then she has penned many fantasy short stories and sonnets, as well as two novels.

After earning her BA in Geography, Suzanne worked for several years as an urban planner in the USA, before retiring to have children. A series of part-time jobs followed, everything from migrant farm worker to dishwasher, retail manager to massage therapist. Her appetite for voyaging has taken her to such far-flung places as the Cook Islands, Mexico, across the deserts and Deep South of America and on many adventures through the capitals of Europe. She has drawn on these life experiences to amplify and embellish the unique characters and settings of her novels.

In addition to writing, her passions include neo-paganism and playing a perversely difficult musical instrument called the hurdy-gurdy.

She is a member of the Troth, and the Otago Writer's Guild.

Presently, Suzanne lives in rural Dunedin, New Zealand with her husband Michael and four children.